CUPIDITY

A Novel

Patricia Wood

This is a work of fiction. Names, characters, places, and incidents either are the product of the author's imagination or are used fictitiously, and any resemblance to actual persons, living or dead, business establishments, events, or locales is entirely coincidental. The author does not have any control over and does not assume any responsibility of third party websites or their content.

ISBN: 1502844311
ISBN 13: 9781502844316
Library of Congress Control Number: 2014918665
CreateSpace Independent Publishing Platform
North Charleston, South Carolina

To Doctor Barinas
A man who engenders hopes and dreams.

"There's a sucker born every minute."

David Hannum

CHAPTER ONE

I was arrested right after I tacked up my ad on the telephone pole outside Shop and Save. I was admiring how I stuffed all those words on a 3 by 5 index card. Hard to write between those itty-bitty lines.

TAKE CARE OF GOPHERS IN YOUR GARDEN ONCEANDFORALLWITHAWHIRLIGIGSPECIALLY MADE BY THE WORLD FAMOUS UNCLE E TYREE. HE'S GOT TWEEDY BIRDS, SYLVESTER CATS, ROADRUNNERS, AND CUPIDS. HE'LL PRETTY MUCH MAKE ANYTHING YOU WANT THAT HAS LEGS, WINGS, OR FINS. $15 APIECE OR 2 FOR $30. PLUS FRESH EGGS $3/DOZ FOR LARGE AND 3.50 FOR SMALL. ODD JOBS DONE THE ODDER THE BETTER BUT NOTHING ILLEGAL. CALL MISS

TAMMY TYREE 555-2656 IF MY BROTHER JAR PICKS UP KEEP CALLING UNTIL HE STOPS HE WON'T TAKE A MESSAGE SO DON'T EVEN TRY TO LEAVE ONE AND IF UNCLE E ANSWERS YOU CAN'T LEAVE A MESSAGE WITH HIM NEITHER AS HE'S DEAF IN ONE EAR AND HIS HANDWRITING SUCKS SO SAVE YOURSELF SOME GRIEF AND EMAIL ME TAMMYATTWOSPOONSDOTNET. HAVE A NICE DAY.

Officer Clarence Smithers scrunched my ad into a tight ball and tossed it on the ground. He clicked a handcuff on my left wrist. "You have the right to remain silent Tammy Louise Tyree," he said.

A normal person would be scared, but I had to bite my lip to keep from laughing. With his long jaw and big ears, Smithers looks exactly like a mule. His upper teeth even stick out.

"Wipe that smile off your face," he brays. "I'm serious this time, you'd best believe it."

"You ruined my ad and littered to boot. Now I'll have to make another one, and what am I arrested for anyway?" My tone is reasonable. "Is it against the law to put something on telephone poles without permission? And how could it be against the law if everybody in town does it?"

Smithers snaps his fingers in my face. "No back talk. Stealing is against the law, Tammy Louise. Annette Sutter's pressing charges. Said the check you wrote her at Gas And Go bounced." Smithers' chin is exactly like in eighth grade when he caught a bunch of us spraying shaving cream on his daddy's cop car on Halloween. He was a big fat nosy parker tattletale then, and he's a big fat nosy parker tattletale now. Perfect law enforcement material.

"I'm no thief," I say and firm up my own chin plus narrow my eyes like Uncle E taught me for tangling with bullies, teachers, and the IRS.

"The facts of the case demonstrate otherwise." Smithers grips my arm like a fat trout he doesn't want to let go of. "You Tyrees are all the same." He growls. "Between your cousin stealing cars and that uncle of yours being a public nuisance, I got my hands full."

He pats his back pocket. "Dang it all, I forgot my chits." He glares at me. "Now don't you run away."

I scowl as I watch Smithers' fat ass waddle back to his cop car. I can't be responsible for what my Uncle or cousin does. That crack about Tyrees was uncalled for. And where would I run to anyway? Smithers' cop car has got Dolly wedged in. Dolly is my tan and brown Ford. Uncle E christened her after Dolly Parton, as he was impressed with the heft of her front bumper. The truck's, not Dolly's. The name stuck.

Smithers returns with his clipboard. "Name and Occupation," he states.

"Oh, for pity's sake just two seconds ago you said my name." I roll my eyes. "And you sure as heck know one of my occupations as I serve you lunch at Two Spoons Café every single day." I give him my best waitress look for customers who can't make up their minds on what they want to order.

Smithers' eyes brighten. "What's today's special?" he asks.

"Salmon patty melt sandwich," I answer. "Same as all the other Wednesdays."

"What's the soup?" He licks his lips and adjusts his drooping pants.

"Tongue bisque." I say.

Smithers tilts his head like a dog hearing a strange noise.

"It's not bad if you pick out the pieces of skin," I tell him. "You know Leo. He doesn't waste a thing."

There's a cost-promise to eating Leo's food at Two Spoons Café. Soup and coffee are served with every meal, even breakfast. The coffee isn't bad, but Leo's soup inventions can make a starving man think twice.

Smithers presses his lips together as if his appetite has been pretty well nipped in the bud permanently. "Age?" he asks.

"Older than my teeth and not so old as my hair," I say smartly.

"Tammy," Smithers says warningly.

I sigh. "Twenty-three."

"Address?" His manner is businesslike.

"Wait a sec," I say. "I never told you about the rest of my occupations. Thursdays I work for Peggy at the Cut N Clean, every second Wednesday I help out at the

Bookmobile for Madeline, then there's me taking care of my brother, and me raising hens for eggs."

Smithers hits his own head with the palm of his hand. "Shoot! That reminds me. I was supposed pick some up for the Missus."

"I got two dozen left. They're in the back end of Dolly." I'm grateful for the change of subject and jiggle my hand.

"I'll take them both," Smithers says.

"Well, then, can you remove these cuffs so I can open my cooler?"

Smithers undoes the lock.

Once free, I hitch my uniform skirt up and hop onto Dolly's tailgate. It'd be a waste of time to escape, as I know deep inside Smithers won't do the paperwork it takes to make my run-in with the law official. It isn't polite to call him lazy to his face, but he is.

Uncle E says an indolent policeman is a gift straight from heaven. He also says it doesn't pay to be ornery with the judicial system. He's a judicial expert, having his name pretty much on a stamp at the county jail because of his drinking.

"Here you go." I hand over the eggs and slide back off the tailgate as gracious as I can.

"I guess I'll overlook it this time." Smithers says slowly. "But you'll have to make that check to Annette at the Gas And Go good," he warns. "Or I'll send you in front of Judge Donna and she'll throw you into jail. Or worse yet, make you do community service and give you a fine."

"If you send me to jail then I guess I'll just have to ship Jar over to your place for you and your Missus to watch when Uncle E goes on one of his benders." I say.

It's satisfying to see a worried frown appear on Smithers' face.

"And if you want to know the truth, it's that skinflint Walter Howard who needs community service. We'd have been all right and tight if he'd paid us for the whirligigs Uncle E made for his store. I wrote that check to Annette thinking it'd be good after Walter paid up."

"That's kiting checks and it's wrong." Smithers wags his finger in my face.

"It isn't kiting." I wag my own finger right back. "It's Walter not paying what he owes. He's a cheat! He pays us ten bucks wholesale and then sells them in his hardware store for twenty-five."

"He says your brother damaged his window. Wait. You sell whirligigs to him for ten? Can I buy one for eleven?"

"Nope, I told you that's wholesale," I say. "Fifteen is retail we charge at the flea market. And the window Jar broke was already cracked."

"Can I have one for twelve?" Smithers juggles a carton of eggs to fish around for his wallet. "And broke is broke. You still owe him for it."

"I can do thirteen fifty, but that's final." I say. "And Walter doesn't have a thing to complain about. I've been paying on it regular. What kind you need?"

"The Missus been wanting a cupid for the back yard ever since she drove by and saw the one in Josephine Munn's yard."

"I have everything in the back of Dolly, except a cupid," I say. "But I think there's one in the workshop that just needs to be painted. Sorry, cupids are real popular," I lie.

I don't tell Smithers the only reason a cupid was in Josephine's garden is because Uncle E stuck it there. When Josephine notices, she'll pull it out and throw it in the trash. Uncle E will retrieve it and put it back in a different place in her yard. My uncle considers that free advertising.

"Set one aside for me then," Smithers says.

"I will if you pay me for it now."

"I can do that. Of course, if it were up to me I'd get one of your uncle's Roadrunners. He does them real fine. Man, I love that cartoon! The coyote can't win for losing." Smithers hugs his eggs and beams.

"Uncle has a flair for it, he does," I agree. "Careful with those eggs or you'll be eating them scrambled." I make a show of looking at my watch. "You can buy them both if you want." I start tapping my foot. This discussion about Uncle E's whirligig talents is getting me going nowhere fast.

"I just might do that," Smithers says slowly. "Will you take an IOU?"

"How about you pay Annette what I owe on the no good check and give me three and a half bucks and we'll call it square. I'm due at the café."

"Can I give it to you in quarters?" Smithers digs in his pants.

"Sure, money's, money. Here's your Roadrunner. You can pick up your cupid soon as the paint's dried."

I have to sit cooling my heels for ten more minutes while Smithers methodically counts his coins. He loses track a couple times and has to start over. Math was never his strong suit. As I think on it, neither was English or history. Lucky for him he doesn't need any of that to be a police.

After he drives away, I pick my ad off the ground and stick it back up. When I get behind Dolly's wheel, she takes a notion not to start. I have to hop out, open her hood, and wiggle her battery terminals, getting grease smears down the front of my uniform. It's pastel pink with dark maroon writing across the chest that spells *Two Spoons Café* and a heart shaped nametag that reads *Tammy*. It's real pretty and would fit my shape like a second skin if I had curves.

I've gotten an occasional manly whistle of appreciation from behind, but when I turn around, the whistle gets sucked right back down the guy's throat and nearly out the other end of him. Plain girls get that kind of reaction. Actually, I'm not so much plain as unremarkable. The color of my hair falls between mud brown and dishwater blond like it can't make up its mind and I have a face that blends into whatever background I'm in front of. Customers have to study my nametag just to remember who I am.

Dolly shudders and shakes as she crawls down Main Street. I'd like to leave her in our driveway and just walk down the hill to the Café but she conks out again between the hardware store and Peggy's Cut N Clean. That's the combo hair salon and laundry here in town. Folks here think it's convenient to be able to do two things at once. I can see Peggy's bobbing head through the window. I give a wave, but she's busy doing a shampoo.

I step out of the truck and head for the café.

I live in Spring, Washington.

Spring wasn't named because of any pretty water pools or nothing. It was a guy called Myron Spring naming every single thing he saw after himself. We have a Spring Corners and Spring Bluff and a Spring Slough. We even had a Spring Creek until it dried up after they built the highway. Now it's just a ribbon of mud. Uncle E remembers fishing in it. At least he thinks he does.

"It was either that creek or another," he says. "We still got Spring Hill anyways or at least until they finish the bypass."

A rumble makes the ground vibrate under my feet. More of Spring Hill being blown to smithereens by the construction crew to make way for progress so people don't have to go through our town on their way to someplace else.

I take in a harsh breath. The air is full of the scent of pine needles coupled with the faint smell of burn barrel. It starts to rain and the drops hit me full in the face. As I mentioned before, it's real wet here in Spring. Uncle E says if you can see the mountains it's going to rain, and if you can't, it's already raining. I can't see the mountains so I run across the street like a turkey dodging an ax.

I have tougher things to deal with than our hill being blown to kingdom come, I have the reputation of being a Tyree, which is a severe trial on account of Tyrees generally being criminals like my cousin Lonnie or drinkers like my uncle, or not quite right like my brother, Jar. I'm the only who's average. Just the thought of that makes me satisfied. Aim high, that's what Uncle E always tells me.

Right when I think that, something whooshes past my head and a herd of construction workers blaze by like they're two-timers being chased by angry husbands. One is rubbing a reddened cheek and the other is holding his hard hat over his chest like a shield. "There's a midget over there throwing rocks. Somebody call the cops!"

Just the words midget and rock throwing tells me it's my brother Jar acting up again. Him taking pot shots is all I need to make by day complete. I put my hands on my hips and try to look stern. I march to where the rock originated from.

"Jar Tyree is that you behind the Dumpster?" I put my hands on my hips. "Get your butt out here. I mean it!"

I see Jar speed behind Leo's old VW van. He flattens himself against the drivers' side door and peeks at me around the corner.

It can be tricky dealing with my brother. I have to sound serious enough, so Jar knows it's not a game, and happy, so he thinks he won't get a licking, which I'm sorely tempted to deliver, even if it does make him buckets harder to catch the next time.

My brother has always been called Jar. Not because he tends to babble a load of nonsense, which is true, and not because his head is sort of shaped like a jar, which is also true. He's called Jar because it's short for Jarld. It was supposed to have been Gerald, but the way our family talks the visiting nurse who filled out Jar's birth forms had her work cut out for her. She did her best, but like Uncle E always says, sometimes your best just ain't good enough.

Jar peeks at me from behind Leo's bus. He's real fair, like an albino, and short and squat. No bigger than a minute. His pockets are bulging full of every kind of stone there is.

"No Skittles for you!" I threaten. "What did Uncle E tell you about throwing rocks at people and cars?"

"Apple wart," Jar says.

My brother talks like a sloppy echo. I'm pretty much the only one who understands him.

"That's right. He said never to do it," I say inching closer to him. "You're in deep trouble, Mister."

"Ack!" Jar goes. He hates to be called Mister.

Jar takes off and I take off after him.

Walter Howard is standing outside his hardware store holding a potted plant. "What's all the racket?" he calls out. Walter doesn't see Jar, but Jar sees Walter. My brother is hunched over doing a low crawl to where Dolly's parked. He reaches deep in his pocket. Before I can catch up to him, he's launched a handful.

The rocks soar up and spatter against the frame of Walter's front window. I'm thankful to see he's missed the glass, but both Walter and his plant hit the sidewalk.

Jar is poised to run. There's a blast of a horn as Madeline Moorehaven pulls up in the bookmobile van. At the sight of the van, Jar hesitates. He loves the bookmobile van. Plus Madeline always has cookies for him. Indecision flickers over his face.

The door of the van swings open and Madeline slides out. She turns around to flatten her mirror and Jar launches another rock. It bounces off the side of the van, hits Madeline in the rear end making her scoot, and then ricochets, hitting Walter in the noggin. Most of the rock's energy had to be spent by that time, but Walter bellows and clutches his forehead. *The big baby.*

Whoop! Whoop!

Officer Smithers pulls up alongside us with his siren going. He launches out of his car. Great, I think, just great, Tyrees having a run in with the law twice in one day.

"Whoop. Whoop." Jar mimics. "Whoop!" He lobs a rock at Smithers.

"Duck, Clarence!" I snatch my brother by the collar and shake him like a mop. "What's got into you?"

"ACK!" he goes. He hates to be shaken like a mop.

Two Spoons' parking lot is full to the brim with gawking construction workers.

"Jarld Tyree is that you being trouble again?" Officer Smithers roars.

My brother starts shrieking and I hug him tight. "Hush, Bug," I croon. "Don't make me smack you!" I whisper in his ear.

Madeline shakes her finger at Officer Smithers. "You know better than to be yelling at Jar. And excuse me for saying so, Clarence, but you're using the word *trouble* incorrectly. Someone can *be in* trouble or *cause* trouble, but they can't *be* trouble." She tilts her head and places a finger on her nose thoughtfully. "At least I don't think so. I'll have to look that up and double check."

Smithers glares at my brother, Madeline ticks her tongue at Smithers, and Walter glowers at me.

"I'm pressing charges!" Walter sticks his lower lip out. "That midget's a nuisance! I could have been killed right in front of my store and Madeline could have been mutilated!"

"Don't be silly. It was only a pebble. And it barely grazed us both. I broke its trajectory." Madeline says proudly. She pulls out a handkerchief and dabs at Walter's hairline. "It's only a flesh wound. You probably did it hitting the sidewalk. And you know very well Jar's not a midget. He's only a boy."

"For a boy he's a menace." Walter scowls harder.

Madeline tuts. "First of all he's too young to be a real midget, he's just short for his age, and second you're not supposed to use the word midget. It's Little People."

"He's a big fat pain!" Walter snarls.

"People in glass houses, Walter," Madeline warns. "You still owe $2.35 in library fines on those business texts you borrowed. Now that's a pain for our system. Causes a real back up." She glances at Smithers. "And you, too, Clarence. That book you checked out on surveillance last spring isn't back. It'll mean a lost book fee or your privileges will be revoked. I can do that, you know."

She turns and smiles at me like a Madonna. "Of course, Tammy Louise always returns her books on time. She frowns. "Not like most Tyrees. That Uncle E of yours has had that book on folk art design nearly forty years."

"Jarld Tyree you are a one man crime wave." Officer Smithers holds up his fingers and starts counting. "We got ourselves the broken gumball machine incident. The letting air out of tires along Main Street incident. The thievery of candy bars at Shop and Save incident. And now rocks through windows incident times four. Those are too many incidents for one year. I'm going to have to file a report." He frowns and turns to Walter "You hurt?"

"No," Madeline answers for him.

"I could have been." Walter sticks his lower lip out.

"But are you hurt?" Smithers pulls out his clipboard.

"I might be! I told you. I'm pressing charges. Attempted assassin." Walter slowly moves until he's well hid behind his pansy display. "Clarence do your duty!"

"Officer Smithers to you," he says.

Madeline clears her throat. "Actually what you mean to say is attempted *assassination.* Attempted *assassin* would be incorrect usage."

"Anyway, no such thing. You weren't killed." Smithers scratches his head. "But we can call it vandalizing. How about that?" he says brightly.

I can tell vandalizing is less paperwork than attempted assassin.

"But Jar didn't damage anything this time," I protest.

"Terroristic threatening!" Walter's voice is shrill. "He's a juvenile delinquent! I want a restraining order!"

By the look on Smithers' face, restraining orders must mean mounds of paperwork to fill out. I cheer up.

"Jar's no terrorist. Don't be a booby," Madeline chides. "Come on over here, Sweetie." She waves to Jar and then quickly adds. "Empty your pockets first."

Walter edges closer to his front door. Jar demonstrates his pockets are empty and scuttles over to Madeline.

Officer Smithers scowls at me. "That brother of yours is going to get himself hurt. He's assaulted an officer of the law by aiming at me. You and your Uncle need to keep a better eye on him. I'm thinking this time, there needs to be a fine."

"He's barely fifteen," I say. "And we can't afford a fine."

"Fifteen will get him slapped into juvey," Smithers glowers.

I consider. Juvey would be like a free Jar-sitting service. But then there'd probably be bars on the windows. Jar would hate that. "How about another warning?" I suggest. "Warnings are free," I say. "And Uncle E and I will watch him better. I promise." I hold up two fingers. "Scout's honor."

Smithers scribbles out a warning and hands it to me. "And if you see that cousin of yours tell him I need to talk to him about a gold Cutlass."

"I don't see that cousin of mine if I can help it," I mutter. "Thank you Clarence," I add sweetly.

Smithers tips his hat and drives away.

I turn to my brother. "Jar Tyree what am I going to do with you?" I wave the pink copy of the form at him. Jar bats it away. "I have to be at the café." I look at my watch. "Ten minutes ago."

"Let him spend some time with me," Madeline suggests. "He'll be okay."

"I'd consider it a favor." I say gratefully. "Just until I get a hold of Uncle E."

"Well, I appreciate the break," Madeline says. She likes Jar to visit the bookmobile. It gives her some down time as when people come in and see my brother in there reading books and flapping his hands like portable fan, they leave right away.

I carefully tuck Jar's pink warning slip in my coat pocket and walk back over to Two Spoons.

It's important to keep track of all our misfortunes. I add Smithers nearly putting me in the jail to my mental pile. I add Walter not paying us. I add Dolly not starting and me getting my uniform dirty. I add Jar's warning. That makes one thousand nine hundred and sixty eight bad things that have happened to our family. And that's just over the last four years. Of course, those are only the major misfortunes. The little things like the electricity being turned off or our refrigerator going on the fritz are filed under minor catastrophes.

It's something called Karma.

Uncle E was the one who told me about it.

"You see Sissy, Karma is the way the world works," he explained. "The more bad things that happen to a family the more they're due for something good. Misfortunes are just nature's way of saying that a spectacular bonanza is coming in the near future."

He told me that a long time ago when we couldn't make a trip to Disneyland because he'd gotten laid off at the mill. Jar and I always wanted to go to Disneyland.

"Can't afford it," Uncle E had said.

"How about anywhere, then?" I'd asked. I'd never been out of Spring.

"Maybe next year. Or the year after."

Time to me then seemed endless. I'd kicked the dirt in disappointment.

"Don't worry." Uncle E had said. "We'll make a trip somewhere else just as good another time. You got to be an optometrist like me." Uncle E said.

"What?" I'd tilted my head.

"It's a person who looks at the world through rose colored spectacles," he explained.

I liked the sound of the word so much I started using it every chance I got. When Madeline Moorehaven from the bookmobile heard me, she said I was wrong, but I told her it was Uncle E's word.

She'd clicked her tongue and shook her head. "Your uncle's always using the wrong word. An optometrist is a person who prescribes glasses. They make sure you have twenty-twenty vision," Madeline said. "Your Uncle E means optimist."

"No he doesn't," I'd insisted. "It's to do with his rose spectacles."

She'd just pressed her lips together.

When I'd gone back home and told Uncle E what Madeline had said, he got a funny look on his face. "That woman never did think out of the box." And he shook his head sadly.

I'd still like to go to Disneyland or somewhere else just as good. Maybe even to Canada and see Harrison Hot Springs. It'll happen. I know it. Being an optometrist and looking on the bright side of things makes perfect sense to me. Not only is it more cheerful that way, it's a whole lot easier to see.

I pat the warning slip in my pocket and smile.

CHAPTER TWO

I whoosh into the entry of Two Spoons Café and jerk off my coat. There's nobody around to notice my tardiness. Of course, the moment I think that, Curtis the manager emerges from the pass-through.

"You're late." His frown makes his face look like a dried apple.

"Tell me something I don't know," I say.

Curtis studies me as I tie on my apron.

"Your uniform is dirty. I'll have to dock you," he taps a pen against his chit tablet. "Plus there's the talking back." He pauses. "Again," he emphasizes.

I sniff. "Why is it you always point out when I'm late, but never say nothing when I'm early?"

"Early is meets expectations, that's why," Curtis says airily. "And for your information nothing is wrong. It's anything. Never say nothing."

"That's what I said. Never say nothing."

"No. Never say ANYTHING. Otherwise, it's hick-speak. Makes you look stupid." Curtis is an authority on being stupid.

"Never say anything," I whisper under my breath. "Never say anything." I don't want to be considered stupid.

Leo the owner strolls into the room. Even though they're cousins, he and Curtis aren't a bit alike. Leo is a heavyset biker with a salt and pepper ponytail and a handlebar mustache. He rides a '62 Harley Panhead he rebuilt himself. One of his hobbies, besides cooking, smoking dope, and playing the guitar, is fixing things, so there's always old car and bike parts piled up in Two Spoons' graveled lot so customers always have to park on the side of the road. He also drives a 65 VW van wildly painted with flowers and peace signs.

Curtis has a blond crew cut and hates living in Spring. He has no hobbies and drives a Toyota.

"It's not hickspeak. It should be Springlish," Leo says without missing a beat. He hangs up the specials sign. "Spring? English? Springlish? Get it?"

"Of course, I get it." Curtis scowls at Leo. "Don't encourage her."

"Springlish," I try it on for size. "I like that."

"Figures, as it's even stupider," Curtis says.

"Whether a person's stupid or not, ought to be earned by what they do and not determined by the way they talk," I mutter. "And besides it's not like you came from California. You were born and raised two skips and a hop away in Quincy, so don't act so high and mighty."

"I work on using proper English and may I remind you that being early and not talking back is *employee meets expectations,* which you would know if you paid attention during your evaluations. Talking back is a very big *not meets,*" Curtis puts his hands on his hips.

"Oh, take a flying leap," I say. I don't need any reminder that I get evaluated by him. Curtis totals everything I do. If I get an *exceeds expectations,* then I'll get a raise. I only get *barely meets* and *not meets.*

"Temper, temper," Curtis wags a finger. "And I don't plan on being here forever," he says. "I'll be in LA this time next year. Guaranteed!"

"I heard that before." And toss my head. My braid flips like an angry cat's tail.

"Are you two going to stand there arguing or get to work?" Leo heads into the kitchen.

"Tammy's turn to do the side work." Curtis says this to Leo's back. "Ketchups and salts need filling."

I wave my hand in the air. "Right after I check my email. Just got through putting up all my ads," I say. "And I signed up for a message board on being an entrepreneur. That's a person who does a bunch of jobs. It ought to give me more business." Which I neglect to say I need real bad. Curtis doesn't need to know my personal beeswax. Email and Internet access is a Two Spoons employee benefit instigated by Curtis and, according to him, worth some money. I'd rather have had a raise.

"Nothing doing." Curtis shakes his head firmly. "You need to get busy before you take breaks. We'll have hungry customers that want their food and it's not my job to do your side work."

I roll my eyes while he talks. Curtis doesn't own Two Spoons, Leo does. I pretend to start on the salt and pepper shakers, but as soon as Curtis disappears into the kitchen, I hightail it over to the computer. My heart leaps when I see I have three messages.

I click on the first one. It's an ad for weight loss pills. I don't need to lose weight. Fact is, I need to gain it, plus grow a few inches of height. If I did that people wouldn't always be looking down on me and I'd fit into my uniform better. Peggy at the Cut N Clean is always searching for ways to trim off pounds. I'll print it out and give it to her, as she doesn't believe in computers. She'll thank me later, I'm sure.

The next one is for vitamins. Everybody knows if you eat right, you don't need vitamins. Madeline is a big one for vitamins. She does the whole alphabet and then some. I forward that one to the library marking it ATTEN: Madeline: Bookmobile. She's got her own email. She's real modern for a librarian.

The last one is a giant picture of a guy's willywagger. Holy Smoke! I cover my eyes and then peek between my fingers. It's a guarantee of increased size using some super grow drug. My face gets all hot and I know I'm probably red as a beet. I quick make sure there's no one looking over my shoulder and then I read it two more times. After that, I delete it.

I fan myself with a menu and frown. There isn't a single garage-cleaning job. No trash-hauling query. No egg order. I chew my bottom lip. I have to have business on my part time deals. This will mean penny pinching this month, not to mention a ton of over-due notices.

The pass-through door slams making me hop to it. I pretend I've been wiping the counter.

"Tammy?" Curtis says warningly. "Not following orders is a *not meets*."

He's a wet blanket that Curtis. I get right to work moving from table to table filling the salts and ketchup containers. I go into the kitchen to pick up a clean tray of coffee cups to distribute. "How's it going Leo?" I say and flash him a peace sign. Leo's chopping onions so he doesn't flash one back. Instead, he swipes his eyes with his wrist in a sort of teary wave. "It's going," he says.

I like Leo so much it hurts. His full name is Leonard Johnson Skinner, but nobody calls him that. He has a hand carved sign in the entry that says, *One cannot have two much music, two much dope, two much soup, or two much coffee in one's lifetime.* Leo says it's his credo, which is sort of a religion. The intentional misspellings are examples of him being a self-described anti-establishment libertarian. So is him smoking weed. Rumor has it that he grows it out back in the woods somewhere. But that's just what people say. He has an old smelly Wonderbread bag that he's real careful of that I find in unusual places. I close my eyes to that. Nobody's perfect.

Curtis complains about Leo's café sign all the time. "It's hokey and makes us all look like hicks," he says.

You can't move to California if people think you're a hick.

I'm still hovering by Leo when Curtis comes through. "Get back to the front," he snaps.

"I'm getting," I say and scoot. The front of the house is restaurant-speak for dining area. That's where I'm supposed to stay. The kitchen where Leo cooks is called the back of the house. I'm never where I'm supposed to be according to Curtis.

When a group of construction workers tromp in for the early-bird-gets-the-noon-worm special, I don't have time to think on Curtis or fronts or even hicks. My legs are fairly run off to nubs.

Being a good waitress is an art. You have to act interested in what folks want to eat even if you're not, but not too interested as if to be a nosy parker. And then there's protocol such as suggesting hefty people order the cottage cheese plate or urging skinny people to go on and order a couple extra desserts.

At a brief lull, I grab a cup of coffee but barely get a sip before Sue Ann Nedermyer strolls in with her mother in-law Audrey. The women have on matching yellow pantsuits with scarves. The color looks good on Audrey, but mustard on Sue Ann makes her look jaundiced.

The two of them sit in a big booth meant for six. I went to school with Sue Ann.

"Hey, Tammy." Sue Ann's honeyed voice holds a touch of vinegar. "How's that brother of yours doing? I hear he had a run in with Smithers. Or was that your uncle, again?" She purses her lips as if she wouldn't be surprised to hear my uncle was in the slammer.

"We're all good," I say wondering for the umpteenth time how she knows anything about our beeswax. Smithers must talk to his wife who must talk to Sue Ann.

I don't know what I ever did to Sue Ann, but she never liked me, not even in school. Uncle E says it's like our chickens in the hen house. Somebody is always picking on somebody else to make themselves feel better. Thinking of Sue Ann as a chicken helps. She's even got a pointy nose. I smile.

"Can I interest you in the luncheon special?" I say.

Sue Ann taps her nails on the table. "You still haul trash? I got a load that needs going to the dump."

"Yes ma'am," I say. "I have next Thursday free."

"Put me down for Saturday," she says.

"I can do that," I say. "Noon works best for me."

"Make it two-thirty," she says.

"I'll pencil you in," I say. "So have you made up your minds?

They study the menu like it's printed in Chinese. I smother a yawn.

A customer at the counter waves his chit in the air and whistles at me.

Audrey heaves a sigh. "I just don't know."

It's not rocket science, I think. "Why don't I give you a few more minutes? I'll get your waters." I quickly take care of my other tables and then make a detour into the kitchen with a tray of dirty dishes. A good waitress never goes anywhere empty handed.

Leo finishes ladling soup into bowls then slides over a tray full. "Here you go, Kiddo."

I grab it up. "Sue Ann's here with her mother-in-law Audrey," I say. "Must be nice being able to do lunch at a café any old time you want."

"Don't waste your time being envious of Sue Ann," Leo says. "She's got to be Sue Ann her whole life, and think of working at the Shop and Save and having the last name of Nedermyer? That's got to be a bummer." He shrugs.

That cheers me right up. I snort a laugh and skip out the pass-through, drop off the contents of my tray, and then swing by the big booth hoping Sue Ann and Audrey will have settled on something.

"You decided?" I poise my pencil thinking of what Sue Ann had to feel going from a perfectly good last name of Clark all the way to Nedermyer.

"What's the soup?" Audrey asks.

"Tongue bisque," I say.

"Tongue?" she says weakly.

"Yeah, tongue," I narrow my eyes. "Something wrong?"

"No," Audrey says quickly.

"The special, I guess." Sue Ann says.

"That's what I'll have too." Audrey clears her throat. "But. Er. No bisque for me. Doctor says I have to watch my cholesterol."

"Well, watch it someplace else," I say. "You know the drill. Soup comes with. No substitutions."

I stomp back into the kitchen.

"Audrey's fixing to give trouble about the soup," I say.

"Soup's not negotiable." Leo scowls. "You tell her she better not make me come out there. I'm too busy."

Curtis pushes open the pass through and hangs his chits up. "Four more specials," he says to Leo and then he stares at me pointedly. "Another break?"

"No," I say airily. "I'm talking business with Leo.

When I come back out to the front I nearly run into Uncle E.

"Can a body get any service around here?" Uncle E hoots. Him hooting means he's been on the sauce.

"You're in the dog house," I hiss. "You were supposed to watch Jar. He got loose and did his rock throwing at Walter's."

Uncle E shrugs. "It ain't my fault. Lonnie came by and we were gonna get lunch and Jar just disappeared."

"He's with Madeline, now. You need to get on over to the book mobile and get him."

He frowns and shifts his feet. "I don't favor going over there."

"Too bad. Just rap on the door of the van," I say. "Jar will come out when he hears that. Bring him here for a bite of lunch," I suggest. "And then you can take him on home."

My Uncle reluctantly sways out and returns a few minutes later with Jar trailing behind. My brother's hands are flapping and he's peering around suspiciously. He doesn't like it when Two Spoons is full up.

"You have fun with Madeline?" I ask.

"Otter," Jar says.

"Well, you should have told me you were hungry." I motion to the only empty table. It's in the middle of a group of construction workers. "You can sit over there."

I give my brother a tight hug as he passes by. He squirms.

"Hog wit," he says. Jar doesn't like to be touched.

The two of them track chips of mud across the floor as they go to the table. It gets real quiet in the place. One of the construction guys motions toward Jar and nudges his neighbor.

"What's with the hands? You planning on flying away?" The man says.

Jar's face pinches.

I bite my lower lip. A good waitress controls her temper.

"What's wrong with him, anyway?" Another guy asks.

Uncle E turns to the man. "If you want to know Jar's a fifteen year old alien. Yes siree, Bob. We got ourselves an honest to gosh outer space resident here in Spring," he chortles. "Fact is, we ought to be charging money when people stare at him. You thinking of contributing?" Uncle E winks.

"What kind of name is Jar?" The man lifts his eyebrows.

"A good one," I finally snap.

Uncle E leans back in his chair. "What are you called?" he asks the man casually.

"Tom," the man answers.

"You sure you're not Dick?" Uncle E gives a broad wink.

The rest of the construction guys burst out laughing and the man reddens.

I tend to get riled, defending my brother, but Uncle E knows just how to defuse a situation. I give Jar a Dutch rub on his head and notice his jacket pocket has a bulge.

"If that's another rock in there hand it over. No weapons in the dining room," I warn.

"Okey dokey," Jar says, but he doesn't make a move.

I reach inside to grab the rock but my brother hunkers down.

"Lap unit!" he growls.

"No way, Jose!" I growl back at him.

"ACK!" Jar says. He hates to be called Jose.

"Stop bickering you two," Uncle cautions. "No need to be bossy."

I scowl. Uncle E always accuses me of being bossy.

"Give it up!" I snap. "I'm the one who's still paying on the last broke window. And we're not bickering."

Jar covers his ears. "Lalalala," he goes.

"That's it then!" I fold my arms over my chest. "Don't come crying to me when Curtis kicks you out and bans you from Two Spoons," I warn.

Jar sticks his tongue out and I stick out my own back.

"Being banned would be a favor," Uncle E snickers.

"It isn't funny!" I say. "I hold you directly responsible for encouraging that smarty pants attitude of his!"

"It's no big deal." Uncle E protests. "He don't aim that good. Give him a break. He's only fifteen."

"Fifteen or no, a person could get real injured if he did. And he aims good enough for windows."

"You worry too much," Uncle E says. "He'll be okay."

"You worry too little," I say. "And of course, he'll be okay. He doesn't make a practice of hitting himself. Only other people and windows."

Jar swings his head back and forth from me to Uncle E like he's watching a Ping-Pong match.

Uncle E rubs his hands together. "Now how about that lunch." My uncle is real good at changing the subject whenever he wants. I head to the kitchen, annoyed.

When I come back with one PB&J and one special, Uncle E is jiggling his keys and being shifty. I know that posture real well.

"What's up?" I ask.

"Nothing," he says quickly.

"Spill it!" I fold my arms tight.

"Well, I got a deal going. Something special. You might say it's an investment for you and Jar's future." He fondles the tabletop like the head of a dog.

I narrow my eyes. "What kind of investment?" I ask.

Uncle E lowers his voice and places a hand by the side of his mouth. "I'm not at liberty to say. Not here anyway. Eavesdroppers," he jerks a thumb over at a vacant booth. "Spies."

"Can I at least have a hint? I want to know what to be prepared for."

Uncle E frowns and shakes his head. He tucks into his patty melt special.

"What's the surprise?" I whisper to Jar. "Is it like last time?"

"Okey dokey." Jar nods his head. His mouth is full of peanut butter and jam.

Both Jar's okey dokey's and Uncle E's surprises aren't always what they're cracked up to be. I head back to the kitchen. There's a pile of dishes in the sink and I quickly do them. When I finally come out, the table is empty. Just crumbs under Jar's chair and a four dollar tip from Uncle E. That isn't as good as it sounds. Uncle E never pays his lunch tab so it ends up being deducted from my paycheck.

After a few more back and forth trips, I notice Sue Ann and Audrey's booth is empty as well. I make a detour to bus it. Seventy-nine cents sits on the table and Audrey stuffed a fistful of napkins in her soup bowl to sop up the contents.

"Like that will fool Leo," I mutter to myself. I pocket the coins. Every Nedermyer's so tight they squeak when they walk, but seventy-nine cents is seventy-nine cents more than I had a few minutes ago. There's the gap between lunch and dinner when Two Spoons slows, then it gets starts to get busy again. Closing time takes forever to roll around. By the time the café is empty of customers I have a blister on my heel, writers' cramp, and a headache in the back of my eyes.

I stack the chairs while Curtis tallies the register. After I finish that, I go into the kitchen for the broom to sweep the floor. Leo's got his Wonderbread bag on his cutting board and is sorting out leaves from seeds.

"Drug fiend," I say as I slowly sweep.

He lifts one eyebrow. "It was a good day," he says.

"Good enough for a raise?" I ask.

"Not that good." He closes up his Wonderbread bag and sticks it into a drawer. He motions to a foil wrapped package on the counter.

"Leftovers," he says. "Take them home. You need to eat more." His eyes crinkle.

"You're mixing up short with scrawny again, Leo," I say. "How is eating more going to help my height?" I poke him with the end of the broom in the ribs a touch too hard and he winces.

When Leo wanders out to the front, I follow close behind sweeping.

"I know what else you are besides short," Curtis pokes his head up from doing the receipts. "A smart-mouthed table-waiting, garage-cleaning junk hauling chicken raiser. How about adding taxi driver to your resume?" And he snickers. "Or maybe house painter."

"Eavesdropping is rude, Curtis." I point the broom at him like a gun. "Don't be making fun of my careers. And for your information, you look in the mirror recently? Your own appearance won't win you any prizes." And I stare fixedly at him.

Curtis pats his receding hairline and scowls.

"What's the matter?" I say. "You think I need only one full time job? Like what? A nurse? You got to have some college. Or a teacher? You have to like kids *and* have some college. Or a meter reader. That's even harder. You have to know somebody in the police department and take a test. It's not that easy. Plus Jar would have a fit about me wearing a police uniform and Uncle E would get me into trouble by making me excuse all his tickets."

"I wouldn't be listening to any advice about jobs from that Uncle E of yours," Curtis snickers through his nose.

"What exactly do you mean by that?" I raise the broom again.

"You know what I mean." He steps back. "The exotic-hairless-cats-he-was-going-to-raise-that-were-only-shaved deal. The vitamin-supplement-diet-pills-that-were-laxatives deal. The investment-in-a-uranium-mine-right-here-in-Spring-that-turned-out-to-be-an-abandoned-septic-tank deal. Do I have to go on?"

"That turned out to be a cesspool," I scowl. "Anybody could make that mistake. And the cats were real friendly and perfectly good mousers."

"Yeah until their hair grew back. You're gullible," Curtis says.

"I'm not gullible, I'm an optometrist." I say back.

"What. That another job you thinking of doing?" Curtis says.

Leo gives a time out sign like a referee. "Can't you two be civil? Live and let live, that's what I say. Tammy's uncle is merely looking for opportunity. You never know what will pan out. Folks thought Edison and Einstein were nuts and look at them now." He gives Curtis a little push towards the register and gestures for me to go the other way.

"They're dead that's where they are, now," Curtis mutters. "Dead and buried." He sniffs.

After sticking out my tongue at Curtis behind Leo's back, I make a detour the long way around to the computer. At least I can check my email.

I hunch over the keyboard and cross my fingers, hoping I have a job offer, an egg request, or a big fat whirligig order. As soon as I sign in, three more willywagger ads pop up. Hells bells where are they all coming from? I press delete.

I sigh real big and move the cursor to sign out. Right then a new message pops up.

IMPORTANT! It says.

I straighten up.

ATTENTION: MISS T TYREE

My own name! I put myself to attending. My heart starts thumping.

STRICTLY CONFIDENTIAL!!!!!

I glance to the side. Curtis is making a phone call and I hear Leo rattling pans back in the kitchen.

I cover the computer screen with my arm, lean closer, and start to read.

CHAPTER THREE

UNION BANK
BOTSWANA
DEAR MISS T. **TYREE,**
HOW ARE YOU TODAY? I HOPE YOU ARE DOING WONDERFULLY WELL? PLEASE BE INFORMED THAT YOU HAVE AN EXCITING OPPORTUNITY OF FORTUNE AS A POSSIBLE ESTABLISHED HEIR OF THE MOST ESTEEMED AMERICAN RELATION **TYREE** WHO HAS BEEN RESIDING IN OUR COUNTRY FOR SO MANY DECADES AND THEN DEATH. AFTER MUCH DILIGENCE, YOUR CONTACT INFORMATION CONSTRUCTED FROM HER AFFAIRS WAS YET ESTABLISHED.

I INTEND TO CARRY OUT WITH YOU THE NECESSARY BUSINESS SO PLEASE ENDEAVOUR TO SEND THE REQUESTED INFOS SO THAT I CAN FILE IN A FORMAL APPLICATION FOR THE RELEASE AND ONWARD REMITTANCE OF THE MONEY FROM YOUR RELATIVE'S ESTATE **FIVE MILLIONS AMERICAN DOLLARS** TO YOUR ACCOUNT VIA TELEGRAPHIC TRANSFER (T.T.)
WE REQUEST YOUR TAX ID / SOCIAL SECURITY NUMBER. PROVSIONAL EVIDENCE OF RELATIONSHIP TO DECEASED ACCOMPANIED WITH YOUR BANK ACCOUNT AND ROUTING NUMBERS AND **FIVE HUNDRED DOLLARS** FOR INITIAL SOLICITOR'S FEES. THIS IS TO FUND THE RESEARCH NECESSARY TO PROVE BEYOND A DOUBTING THAT YOU ARE THE PERSONAGE WHO YOU POTENTIALLY CLAIM TO BE. TIME AND CONFIDENTIALITY IS OF PRIME ESSENCE IN THIS NEGOTIATION.
AWAITING YOUR IMMEDIATE RESPONSE.
BEST REGARDS,
DR. BARINAS
EXECUTOR AND MINISTER
FAITH BASED CHARITY GOVERNMENTAL DEPARTMENT
GABORONE, BOTSWANA

The wording is hard to understand so I know it's official. I read it again more slowly this time. My mouth goes dry. Money coming to me? I read the letter a third time. It must be a mistake. It has to be. But maybe it's not. But maybe it is. Maybe they mean another Tyree. But then there aren't that many around here. And how could someone from Botswana get my address? But maybe it's because I have email now. Computers can do everything can't they? Even track a person down?

I study the email line by line. It says I'll get five million dollars if I send five hundred, and there's a solicitor and minister plus an executor involved. That's to do with estates. I've heard about searches for lost heirs. Maybe I'm a lost heiress.

I think about our family. I seem to remember someone sometime mentioning Tyrees had some sort of evangelical relations. Shirttail relatives who moved to Spokane. Did any of them go to Africa? Uncle E would know. I could ask him.

Five hundred dollars to get five million. That's a good deal. A real good deal. If it's true, that is.

The pass-through door bangs. I quickly print out the email and tuck it into my pocket. I sit there for a few more minutes biting the end of my braid and cogitating. I have to figure out what to do. Confidential means to keep quiet. I can't spill the beans about any of this. But I should talk to my Uncle. Get his take on the matter. Does confidential mean I can't tell him?

Five hundred dollars to get five million. A great deal.

It's worth a chance. And then I get to thinking. All those hard times we've had? Maybe this is the turn-around. Karma finally paying us back with a windfall. I just need to come up with five hundred bucks. But five hundred bucks might as well be five thousand. I frown when I think about what Curtis said. He was wrong. My uncle gives decent advice. I tick the best ones off.

The more a guy tells you he ain't drunk, he is. Fat people know the best restaurants. Don't get caught behind a car with a smoking tailpipe or a person walking a big dog that's sniffing the ground.

I never take kindly to anybody bad-mouthing my uncle. After Momma and Daddy died? He was the only one who came through for Jar and me. My brother and I were orphans and not the good kind with money. We were the kind social services wanted to split up.

"A facility would be the best thing for Jar," our minister told me. "You're too young to take charge of your brother. The county can place you with a temporary foster family until you're 18."

"I'm not leaving Jar," I said.

A social worker called Eunice told me I didn't have a choice.

"It's your chance to make something of yourself," she had said. "Focus on what you want," Eunice had urged

"But I am something," I remember telling her. "And I want to be something more for Jar. What kind of a chance would it be, for me, if it meant turning my back on my brother? I have to take care of him."

"You have to think of your future," Eunice had said. "He'll hold you back."

I can't stand the name Eunice to this very day because of that.

Thank goodness for Uncle E. He swooped in and took us to live in his trailer. He even gave up having his own bedroom so Jar and I could each have our own.

"But where will you sleep?" I'd asked. I knew it wasn't polite to take someone else's bed.

Uncle E just waved my worries aside. "Out here in the living room. I purely luxuriate sleeping on a couch," he'd told me. And he threw himself backwards on it to prove his point.

"Makes it easier to watch TV," he said. "And I got me a cot out in my work shed so I can make whirligigs day and night. Hammer to my heart's content. Yep this whole arrangement is going to work out to my complete satisfaction. I got a smart young niece to do my housework and a youngster I can train to help with the chores. So don't think I'm making sacrifices for you. Besides, the county can't pull us apart. We're family." And Uncle E grabbed both of us real tight in a bear hug.

I'm thinking on that when a heavy hand falls on my shoulder. It makes me jump like a bunny. It's Leo.

"Hey, there, Kiddo," he says. "You spending the night here?"

"Nope." I leap to my feet. "Nope, I'm done." I fumble for my foil package of food. My hands are trembling.

Five hundred for five million.

"You okay?" Leo studies me closely.

I turn from his gaze. "Yeah," I say and hear my voice shake. *I'm rich. I'm going to be rich,* I think.

"Coming? I'm ready to lock up," Curtis calls out.

"In a minute." Leo chucks me under the chin. "Tammy?"

"I'm fine," I say and grab my coat off the hook.

"*Sweet dreams,*" I hear Curtis hiss softly as I pass by. He has that look on his face like he's caught me mooning over Leo.

I go out the door. It's dark and the wet wind chills me. I wrench the collar of my coat up around my neck and run all the way up my driveway thinking the whole while about the email burning a hole in my pocket. I need to speak with Uncle E.

But Dolly is gone when I arrive back at the trailer. There's only empty ruts filled with muddy water where her tires stood. Uncle E must have gone off on one of his benders. I barely get to the door when it flings open. Jar runs out.

"Hag wit!" he says. Jar's wide eyes and flapping hands make him look like one of the moths flitting around the porch light.

"Get back in. it's cold," I say. "And where's Uncle E? You shouldn't be by yourself."

"Doo bucket," Jar says.

"I don't care if it's only been five minutes. He shouldn't leave you alone."

Even though he's fifteen, my brother requires extraordinary looking after. When he was only a year old,

Momma took him from one doctor to another. She had shaken her head in disgust. "Brain damaged? His head looks okay to me. And what do you mean developmentally delayed? And I don't need to pay good money to learn my boy's puny," Momma said.

"He could be autistic," the last doctor told her. "But it's too soon to tell."

Momma got all puffed up. She thought he said artistic and started giving Jar crayons to draw with, which he immediately ate. It made his poop real pretty. Just chock full of color. It was only later that Madeline Moorehaven brought Momma up to speed.

"Luella, the doctor means he's probably *autistic.* Means his perception is altered. He probably won't ever be like the rest of us. But being little like that, well, he's cute as a bug's ear isn't he?"

"Bug's ear or no! That's it for those quacks!" Momma had said. "Each time I bring that boy in, they tell me he's got something else. It don't hardly seem fair." She said this last part staring straight at me.

I felt guilty. Like I'd had something to do with the way my brother was. Maybe I dropped him accidental? Or I gave him something bad to eat?

I look at him now. Whether Jar's artistic, autistic, arthritic, or athletic, it doesn't make any difference. Jar's, Jar. I ruffle his hair. "Hey, there, Bug!" I say. Jar likes being thought of as a bug. He's partial to insects.

He shirks under my hand. "Can lit," he says, which means he hopes I'm not too tired from working a double shift at the café. Jar's thoughtful that way.

I straighten the whirligigs that are mounted all along our porch rail. Uncle E likes to show off our merchandise. Jar gives the wings of a Tweedy Bird a spin.

The two of us go inside. Every light in the place is on. "So where'd Uncle E go off to, anyway?" I ask. "I got leftovers from Two Spoons. Corn and bean lasagna."

I know full well Jar will pick out all the corn and bean bits. Jar isn't fond of vegetables unless they're in sugarcoated cereal. I stick the foil package into the oven and follow Jar back into the living room.

He flops on the sofa. "Runny tap," he says.

"A bar?" I narrow my eyes. "You sure he said he was going to a bar?" This information isn't pleasing. It'll mean a delay unloading my news.

"Lop," Jar adds.

"He's with Cousin Lonnie?" I frown. My cousin isn't a good influence on Uncle E.

"Stop pail!" Jar fiddles with the TV dial. When he hits a commercial, he pauses. Jar enjoys commercials, especially ones with talking babies or drums.

"Don't give me your baloney," I say. "You could have thrown one of your fits. That would have slowed him down."

"Okey dokey," Jar turns his head away.

"Aw, Bug, I'm sorry."

Even though I'd like to, it isn't fair blaming Jar. There's no stopping Uncle E from a liquor temptation. And cousin Lonnie is real good at tempting. Plus he'll try to bum a few dollars off Uncle E as well. That always leaves us deeper in the hole. But then we won't have that problem soon. I smile real big.

"Sop sart?" Jar asks.

"Nothing," I say and quickly go straight faced.

My brother looks at me suspiciously. He's hard to fool. I head into my bedroom.

I stuff my tip money in my rainy day coffee can that I keep under my mattress and then change into sweats. After hand washing my uniform in the sink, I hang it up. I'm pleased to see the grease stains from Dolly mostly came out. As I unbraid my hair, I stare at the framed photograph of my folks hanging on the wall.

Luella and Raymond Tyree is scrawled across the bottom. I'm the one who chose that picture for their obituary in the Tribune. The two of them are standing together, arm in arm, Momma with a smile on her face, holding a purse to her chest and Daddy with a grin, wearing the belt buckle he won from the hot dog eating contest. A real handsome couple. Not like Jar and me. Of course, Uncle E never sees a thing wrong with our appearances.

"A fine gal, Tammy Louise is," he tells people. "Could stand to gain a few pounds. That girl's so skinny she has to run around in the shower just to get wet." He'll chuckle as he rubs his whiskers. "And that Jar is really something. Got his own entire language. And there's not a buzzer or bell invented he can't imitate. You can take that to the bank," Uncle E says. "I have a real talent for recognizing a person's potentialities."

I agree I have positive attributes. Like my long hair. It's nearly to my butt. Of course, growing hair can't really be considered a talent, as it just happens. Momma liked my hair long.

"It's your saving grace, Honeybee," she'd said. She always called me Honeybee because I constantly buzzed around helping out and taking care of Jar. I touch the edge of the photo with my finger. Nobody calls me Honeybee now.

The smell of burning food rouses me. "Holy heck! The lasagna!" I rush into the kitchen and use a dishtowel to jerk the hot foil packet out of the oven.

Jar trots in hard on my heels. "Unlit book." he says.

"Yeah, well, when you start doing most of the cooking, you can complain," I say. "Get your rear in the chair." I point. He sits obediently. I feel bad for being bossy. "Please?" I add.

The lasagna is black on the outside, but the inside is still good. I set out our plates and serve it up. Sure enough, Jar proceeds to pick out the corn. The beans are hard to identify so he eats those. I gobble every bit of mine up burned bits and all.

"There's nothing left for Uncle E. Serves him right for taking off," I say.

"Topper tap," Jar agrees.

"Don't talk with your mouth full. It's impolite."

Jar helps me do dishes. I wash and dry, and Jar puts away because it doesn't matter where anything goes. Well, almost doesn't matter.

"Jar don't be putting the plates in the garbage. We need those for the next meal." Jar is good at accepting constructive criticism.

While my brother watches TV, I settle at my desk, dig out the checkbook, and start in on our accounts. I start humming. *I'm going to be rich. I'm going to be rich.* Is there a way to come up with five-hundred dollars somehow?

After adding my paycheck from Two Spoons, I get a positive balance. It's fine but fleeting feeling. I open up the bills one at a time.

The first one is for the electricity. It's sky-high, but I'm not surprised. Our lights are always on as Jar won't sleep in the dark. Heck, he barely tolerates cloudy days. I put that payment into the envelope for the phone and put the check for the phone in with the electricity bill. That will keep both utilities busy.

Next is the statement from the ER for when Jar received two black eyes and a nosebleed from stepping on the end of a hoe. I accidentally on purpose don't sign that check. They'll figure I'm still discombobulated from worrying about my brother.

I leave the stamp off the envelope for our insurance. That trick can get a bill going back and forth for weeks.

Sometimes I tear an old stamp in quarters like I was in a real hurry but had good intentions.

Of course, I pay the whole amount to Mike the plumber for when our pipes burst in January. Can't fool with Mike. I have to keep on his good side for when I need him next.

I put a bit aside for our property tax bill in the fall.

It's possible when Uncle E's social security gets deposited that I might be able to swing the five hundred bucks. And getting a windfall? Well, we'd be set for life. I stretch my arms high into the air. Rich!

A glare of headlights bounces against the wall accompanied by the sound of crunching gravel. I go to the window and pull the curtains aside. My uncle staggers out of a strange car along with another person.

"Hells bells just as I figured. He's got Lonnie with him." I frown.

"Drop pea." Jar says.

"You're right. It's better than him being in a ditch somewhere."

There's foot stomping on the porch and Uncle E bustles through the door. From the smell, he's tied one on good. Cousin Lonnie traipses in after him. They plop themselves on the sofa next to Jar. They're both grinning like a couple of well fed hounds.

"Where you been?" I scowl at Uncle E. His fuzzy grey hair makes him look freshly electrocuted.

"What's he doing here?" I point to Lonnie's greasy form reclining on the couch. "And whose gold Cutlass is that? Where's Dolly?"

"Questions. Questions. Your truck is safe as houses at the Silver King. I thought you'd appreciate me not letting Uncle E drive in the condition he's in. We was both celebrating." Lonnie says. "And the Cutlass is a friend's. I borrowed it." He folds his hands behind his head and settles back like he's planning to stay.

"Don't get too comfortable," I warn him. "And celebrating what?" I look from Uncle E to Lonnie suspiciously.

"A business venture," Uncle E says. He sways on the couch and belches. "Lonnie show her the box." And then to me. "It's the surprise I was talking about."

"Shoop!" Jar wrinkles his nose.

"That's right," Uncle E beams. "Surprise."

What Jar actually said was the two of them smell like stale beer.

"It's still in the car," Lonnie says.

Uncle E doesn't meet my eyes, but Lonnie stares openly.

"Bring it on in." Uncle E orders grandly.

Lonnie clumps out and returns hugging a large box. He kicks our door shut with his heel.

"It was your job to Jar-sit," I hiss to Uncle E. "Not go off gallivanting with Lonnie."

"Pshaw! It don't hurt Jar none to be on his own. He's a teenager. He needs to learn responsibility. Besides, he's smarter than you give him credit for."

"Not hardly," I say.

Jar sticks his tongue out at me. It's from habit I stick my own right back.

Uncle E pats the top of the box fondly. "This here is a deal Lonnie and I got going," he croons. "A top of the line weather machine. Guaranteed by a guy from Darrington. Lonnie was the one who introduced the two of us."

"What guy?" I ask. "And what do you mean weather machine? There isn't any such thing."

"Yes there is. You heard of them planes flying through clouds and making it rain? Well, this here gadget is just the opposite. It takes moisture out of the air. I mean to have a chat with Josephine at the B&B. She's planning on doing weddings and putting up honeymooners. I can charge her brides, grooms, and newlyweds for a guaranteed sunny day. Not to mention any folks that want to hold outdoor parties and celebrations." Uncle E leans against the sofa. "You see it's science. You just plug it in and TA DA! Sunshine! This contraption will make all our fortunes."

I lift the lid and examine the inside.

"Read the fine print on the brochure," Lonnie says. "It says it takes moisture out of the air. Right there in black and white. And the guy's the real deal. Some sort of mechanic inventor."

"How much did you pay for this?" I stare at Uncle E. "It looks to me like a dehumidifier. Same as the one Leo uses in the pantry."

"Just a small deposit." Uncle E tries to give himself a high five but misses.

"How'd you get money for a deposit? Who is this guy?"

"Bob," Lonnie says. " Or Rob. Or maybe Larry."

"I post dated a check," Uncle E says pushing out his lower lip. "It'll be good when my social security is deposited."

"But we need it for bills," I protest. My heart sinks at not having five hundred dollars for my own deal.

Uncle E waves me away. "This sucker will take care of all our finances when we start getting weather clients. I just have to pick up the rest of them and make a final payment."

"Final payment? For how much?"

Uncle doesn't look me in the eye. "It's a lucrative investment," he says. "You'll see. And it ain't that much. Less than a thousand. Or maybe more."

"A thousand?" I hear the screech in my voice. "A THOUSAND? You have to call that guy and get your money back." I urge. "If it's such a good deal there'll be plenty to pick up where you left off. You said there's a guarantee."

"Yep." He pulls the brochure out of the box. Says here it's all guaranteed to take water out of the air. But why would I want to take it back? I may not remember the guys name but I got his number." Uncle E digs in his pockets. "Somewhere." He searches his in his wallet. "Anyway Lonnie knows him real well."

"Lonnie knows him real well, but can't seem to come up with his whole name? And that doesn't worry you?" My voice is way past shrill. "Dehumidifiers take water out of the air. That's what they do. But they can't change the weather," I shout.

Lonnie sweeps his hand in the air. "It's complicated. You get a bunch of these boxes plugged in and surround the event. It can be raining all over but will stay dry in the middle," he shakes his head. "You don't have a brain for science but I do," he brags. "It's like them Amish heaters that don't use no electricity."

"What do you get out of the deal?" I stick out my lower lip.

Lonnie smirks. "A commission," he says.

"This is all one giant rip off," I say.

"It's not a rip off and the Amish is honest," Uncle E says stubbornly. "Jimmy over at the Silver King swears by his heater." Uncle E folds his arms over his chest. "It works!"

"Dammitall!" I holler. "This has nothing to do with the Amish!"

"Aw, don't get like that," Uncle E glowers. "I did it for the both of you. I weren't good about putting something by when I worked at the mill. I want you taken care of after I'm gone."

Jar throws himself on the floor. He rolls over on his stomach and kicks his legs.

Uncle points. "Lookee here. That tone is giving your brother one of his fits."

"EEERRR," Jar goes.

"He's just mad we're not paying attention to him. Stop it right now Jar or I'll give some attention to your butt with the flat of my hand," I say. "You're too old for fits."

Jar quiets right down. I turn to Uncle E. "And as for you? You're not dead yet. And we've been taking care of things just fine," I yell.

Uncle E yells back. "I thought you'd be pleased!"

"Pleased?" I throw a sofa cushion at him. "Hells bells, I don't have time for your nonsense! I worked at the café all day today and have to work all day tomorrow, and then I have to go over to Cut N Clean and help Peggy. I don't have the luxury to gad about bar hopping like you."

"I told you I was celebrating." Uncle E belches again. "It was a deal."

"Deal shmeal." I turn and to Lonnie. "And you!"

My cousin slowly unfolds off the couch. He hovers like a thin vulture. "What about me, cuz?" His smile doesn't reach his eyes. They're glittery. Like ice.

I lift my left knee just a smidge and Lonnie backs up.

"Once removed or gonna be," I say. Lonnie has a notion what that left knee of mine can do.

My cousin sidles out the door like a crab. "This has nothing to do with you, Tammy Louise. Last I heard Uncle E was old enough to make his own decisions," he says. "His social security check is his to spend as he wants. You can't control everything everybody does." And with that, Lonnie leaves.

The engine of the Cutlass roars to life and soon the only thing I hear is Uncle E's snores echoing. I stomp over and shake his shoulder. "Hey, there! Wake up! Tell me more about this deal. We have to talk," I insist. But Uncle E is passed out cold. I drag him next to the sofa so he isn't in the path to the bathroom.

"Upper dapper," Jar suggests.

"Nothing doing!" I snap. "He doesn't deserve a blanket!" I grab a hold of Jar's ear. "And speaking of blankets, it's time for you to go to bed."

"Otter slip," Jar whines.

"It isn't either too early," I drag him all the way into his room.

"Letter plod," Jar says under his breath, but he pulls on his pajamas.

I smooth the tape over my brother's light switch. "It's on. See? You got your flashlight?"

Jar fumbles under his covers. I have to stand there until he finds that and his headlamp and then help him adjust the strap around his head. When he's done, he looks like a coal miner.

"Now sleep tight," I say sternly.

Besides hating the dark and police uniforms, Jar doesn't much care for thunder and lightning, big dogs, and cowboy hats. But he likes leather coats with zippers and rocks and Skittles. That much is true. And he purely loves nightlights. We got them stuck all over our place so Jar can make it to the bathroom to pee at night or into the kitchen for a snack of cereal when he gets peckish.

I march into the living room and pace back and forth stepping over Uncle E's left leg each way. It's hard to believe my uncle is stupid enough to think a weather machine is something you can buy in a bar. But then again it isn't really. When he's drunk, he believes he can fly just like one of his whirligigs. Him thinking he's bought a weather machine is not so far off the mark, I guess.

I stare at the pile of bills on my desk. If I thought we were on the edge before, well, I guess that means we're falling off the cliff. That certainly doesn't help me think any better. I sit down and lay my head on the smooth surface of the desk to collect my thoughts. They're tumbling around in my head like shoes in a dryer. *Life's a Bitch Bitch Bitch.* That turns into *Rich. Rich. Rich.*

But first, I need to come up with five hundred bucks.

I think back on Curtis's look as I left Two Spoons. Sweet dreams indeed. And I wasn't mooning over Leo. No siree. There's a lesson I learned from a very young age. It doesn't do any good to be dreaming of things you can't have.

But then that's just what I end up doing. I fall asleep imagining money falling from trees and romantic impossibilities.

CHAPTER FOUR

ER ER ER ER ERRRR! Our rooster Benny wakes me up at the crack of dawn with his caterwauling. I pull myself erect, drag myself into the bathroom, and look in the mirror. My skin's so creased I look like a map of the Andes. After splashing water on my face, it doesn't get much better.

My uniform is still damp, but I put it on anyway. I take a quick peek into Jar's bedroom. My brother is snoring under his covers. I wish I could sleep that sound. I grab a glass of water and head into the living room. Uncle E is spread-eagled on the floor. I dribble water on his face. He makes a feeble attempt to open his eyes and then covers them with his hand. He groans.

"Shhh." I place a finger on my lips. "Jar's asleep." I spill more water on him.

Uncle E rolls over and props himself up on his knees.

"What happened, Sissy?" His voice is gravely. "Was I in an accident?"

"Yep. You had a head on collision with cousin Lonnie," I tell him. "Get into the kitchen. You and I need to have a serious chat."

Uncle E stumbles after me. His hair looks like it went through a blender and his eyes are bloodshot. He slumps into a chair.

"Coffee would hit the spot," he hints.

"So would a kick in the rear," I say but I shove a steaming cup across the table anyway. Uncle E huddles over it gratefully.

I press my fingers around my own cup and take a deep breath.

"That weather deal you think you have? Both of us know it's a losing proposition," I start out.

"We don't know that," Uncle says stubbornly.

"You have to return that machine and get your money back," I insist. "We need that money for other things."

"What other things?" Uncle E shuts his eyes and takes a sip of coffee.

"Like something I might have going." And I reach into my pocket for my email. I come up with a soppy clump. My confidential missive has turned into paper mache.

"Hells bells!" I blurt out. "It was still in my uniform pocket when I washed it." I study the gooey mass in my hand.

"What was?" Uncle E lifts his head.

"An important email, but it's ruined now. I'll have to print it out all over again." And then I think long and hard. Karma works in funny ways. Not ha ha funny but the other kind. This may be a sign that I need to keep mum for a bit. I stare at Uncle E. The email said confidential. Can Uncle E keep quiet?

"You don't look so hot," I say slowly. "We can talk later."

"What about an email?" Uncle E narrows his eyes. "You keeping something from me Sissy?"

I switch gears.

"You have a string of chores to take care of this morning." I count on my fingers. "First off, you need to hitch a ride over to the Silver King and pick up Dolly before she gets towed again. We don't have a hundred bucks to spring her."

Uncle E places his fingers to his temples.

"Next pick up more feed for the hens at the hardware store. And the coop is knee deep in chicken manure. It needs to be raked into the pile. Jar can do that part. He's great at raking crap. Josephine Munn needs a load for her garden and don't you dare leave another cupid in her yard. It's pissing her off."

Uncle E looks a bit green, but I keep going.

"And then get your butt into that workshop of yours and start back in on making whirligigs. We need more cupids. Smithers ordered one yesterday. And mow the lawn out front. It's so high, it looks like we're making hay." I hesitate. "You know if we baled it, we could sell it for goat feed." I stare out the window consideringly.

"Don't talk so loud." Uncle E holds his palms over his ears.

"I wouldn't have to talk so loud if you'd listen harder." I get to my feet and jerk on my coat. "It's nearly eight. I have to get to work. Some of us bring in a regular paycheck, you know."

I make sure I slam the screen door extra loud so Jar wakes up. That'll get Uncle's rear in gear. Of course, afterwards I feel guilty for the disrespectful way I talked, but somebody has to be the responsible party, don't they?

I tromp down the driveway. It's important to act normal. I can't let slip that a windfall is due me. *Five hundred to get five million.*

I'm able to sneak into Two Spoons without Curtis seeing, but I don't have time to get on the computer to reprint my email. The place is packed with hungry customers standing in line waiting to be seated. I hardly have time to tie on my apron.

There's a group of construction guys loudly complaining at table three.

"The food here sucks," one of them says. "Just like the atmosphere. Can't lay a hammer down at the site without it walking off."

"Don't be calling people in Spring thieves," I mutter. "And you're doing way worse stealing our hill."

The construction guys give me dirty looks and mumble to themselves.

A bearded man seated at the center table flags me down with a menu. "Tammy! Yoo hoo! Over here!"

I'm relieved to desert the construction workers.

"Hey, Kev. How you doing?" I wave my hand. Kev used to be a marine and now runs his own survival skills school. He's a regular and comes in with his clients every few days. He's got a table of them now. They're candy-assed rich urban businessmen who we refer to as crubs.

"We're on a tight schedule," Kev says. "Eggs, potatoes, toast, bacon, sausage, and pancakes all around." He orders for everyone. "What's the soup today?"

"Hold on, let me check the placard." I lean to the side. "Hearty flapjack and onion chowder," I read. That's how Leo uses up all his left-over pancakes. "Now that'll really stick to your ribs." Not to mention the roof of their mouths.

Kev beams. "Flapjack chowder! My favorite!" He smacks his lips.

"So what are you going to do with these guys today?" I ask.

"Today's orienteering. You know. Using a compass. No GPS. Nada. We're doing it the old fashioned way. Going to see if these crubs can distinguish their own candy-asses from a hole in the ground."

"You be safe out there," I say.

"I'm always safe." Kev jerks with his thumb. "It's them I have to worry about."

"You ever find those two you lost last season?" I ask casually.

"Nah," Kev says. "But I'm sure they'll turn up."

The current crubs exchange nervous looks.

"No soup for me, pretty lady." The crub shakes his head.

"It comes with," I say firmly.

"You have to have soup, Harold," Kev warns.

"I don't eat soup for breakfast," the man complains.

"You can take it up with the cook." I head into the kitchen with the order.

"Trouble on table two," I call out to Leo. "A crub name of Harold won't take the soup." I clip the chit on the rail.

Leo wipes his hands on his apron, loads up a tray, and shoves through the double doors. He slams the bowls down one at a time and his eyes glitter with displeasure. He rears up like a grizzly. "Which one of you is Harold?" Leo snaps.

A man slowly raises his hand. "I am," he says.

"The soup comes with." Leo glares. "You have a problem with that?"

The man shifts uncomfortably and slowly shakes his head.

"Anything else?" Leo says.

“Nope.” Kev says. “We’re all good here.” And he digs into his chowder.

“Good,” Leo softens. He forms his fingers into a V. “Peace,” he says and tromps back to the kitchen.

When I clear their table later, all the soup bowls are empty and I get five decent tips. I grab the coffee pot and head for the window booth. I like doing window booths because people think they have my full and undivided attention when I’m really looking outdoors.

Today, I’m watching Walter Howard setting out fancy begonia baskets on the sidewalk in front of his hardware store. Walter wears a hat even when it’s dry, and uses both suspenders and a belt.

“An overly cautious man,” is how Uncle E describes him. “I can’t trust a man who don’t trust his pants. And he’s got two first names. Walter and Howard. That fact alone makes me leery,” he proclaims.

Walter isn’t one to take insults sitting down.

“And I don’t trust a sneaky low-down scam artist whose brother married his first cousin and who runs a tab that he don’t ever pay,” Walter snaps back.

“Luella was my brother’s second cousin! Firsts is illegal!” Uncle E will retort.

“Libertarian!” Walter will mutter, as Uncle E strolls past his store.

“Republican!” Uncle E will sneer.

As for myself, I hold a soft spot for Walter. He came to Momma and Daddy’s funeral in a suit and brought a real nice wreath of lilies tied with black ribbons and everything. I was still touched, even though I know he gets them on discount, being in the business and all.

Walter's got a new display in his front window. I noticed it the other day. A rock tumbler. Now that's a stupid thing to have. Who'd go into a hardware store in the middle of nowhere for a rock tumbler? Walter is arranging his baskets into a pyramid. A goodly amount of throat clearing gets my attention. There's a couple in front of me seated in the booth.

I poise my pencil on my pad. "Welcome to Two Spoons," I say to a middle-aged couple. "Coffee and soup comes with and the special is blueberry pancakes and ham."

The man starts to order the special but his wife interrupts.

"We'll both have a mushroom, tomato, basil, egg white omelet," the wife interrupts. "No hash browns. We'll have fruit. But only if it's fresh. And tea, but only if it's herbal. Do you have bottled Evian? Oh, and no butter. Not a smidge. Use a clean pan. And dry wheat toast. With honey, but only if it's organic. What kind of juice do you serve?" She looks right through me.

"We have tomato, orange, pineapple, apricot, cranapple, grapefruit, prune, mixed berry, and Hawaiian punch," I rattle off.

"Oh." She nibbles on her lip. "No juice then."

"Suit yourself," I say. I don't tell her that the eggs, yolks and all, are going on the same grill as the others.

There's no special skillet. The fruit will be fresh out of a can and the herbal tea will be coffee, like everybody else gets. I don't say anything about the soup. Leo himself can take care of that when she tries to send it back.

I work straight through to the end of lunch. At two fifty-five, the café is empty. Dinner starts in an hour and thirty minutes. I mosey on over to the computer, but Curtis has beat me to it.

"Just looking over LA rentals," he tells me. "Keeping my finger on the pulse. Isn't this your afternoon at Peggy's?"

"It is," I say reluctantly. "But I have a few minutes to kill." Week day dinner can be slow so Curtis lets me off to work across the street at the Cut N Clean. Sometimes if it gets busy, he'll call me back.

Before I head over to Peggy's, I want to reprint out my email and then head home to check on Jar and verify Uncle E has retrieved Dolly, returned that weather machine, and gotten his money back. I sit down at the counter dawdling over coffee, sneaking peeks at Curtis, and wishing him gone. I'm afraid he'll hang over my shoulder and confidential is confidential.

Five hundred to get five million.

I study the pictures on the wall.

There's a one of Leo riding a jet-black custom chopper. It was taken years ago when he was young and lean. He sure isn't young and lean now. Leo has no helmet on and his hair is wild. I never rode a motorbike, but I'd sure like to. It'd be right up there with seeing Disneyland and Harrison Hot Springs.

When Curtis disappears into the kitchen. I quick like a bunny log into my email. Maybe it's gone. Maybe it was my imaginings. Maybe I misunderstood it.

But no. There it all is. IMPORTANT is still extra big and bold at the top and CONFIDENTIAL has four exclamation points. I study it again. *Dr. Barinas.* He's a doctor not a mister. It certainly is impressive.

I print it out and put it inside my shoe in case I forget again and launder my uniform without checking my pockets. While I sometimes make the same mistake twice, I rarely make it three times. I'm happy to see that I also have a query about a combo garage cleaning and trash haul along with another weight loss ad.

The slamming sound of the kitchen pass-through makes me jump. Curtis comes up behind me.

"So," he says. "You make a practice to be late for all your jobs?"

I frown. Curtis is a thorn in my side and a pebble in my shoe all in one. A twofer.

I think about our bills and needing five hundred dollars for Dr. Barinas. For a split second, I consider asking him if I can get an advance on my paycheck, but then I nearly snort out loud. Curtis giving an advance? That'd be the day. He'd give me *not meets* for eternity just for asking. And then what would I do next month? I'd be short even more.

"I'm not late and I'm getting gone now," I say and head across the street to Peggy's Cut N Clean.

I feel the email lump in my shoe and it makes my step lighter. I'm bursting to tell someone, anyone, my good news. But then I remind myself. *Confidential means confidential.* I go into the Cut N Clean bouncing on my toes.

Peggy's place is top-notch. She has two washers and a couple big dryers along the back wall. Along one side, she has her shampoo station and hair dryer and opposite that, she has three chairs, and a low coffee table set out nice as you please. There's always a fresh stack of magazines that people like to read, but won't buy for themselves like *Enquirer* and *Star* and *Celebrity News.* Mounted across is a giant TV hooked up to cable. Peggy can't miss her soaps. Next to that, she has an under counter refrigerator filled with diet Coke. Peggy's always on some sort of a diet, but it doesn't stick. She's fond of puffy sleeves and dirndl skirts that makes her look an upside down light bulb. That reminds me. I pull out the weight loss ad I printed for her and slide it under a stack of magazines so it won't blow away.

Peggy is teasing her blond hair into a beehive do and examining her teeth in the mirror. She doesn't say howdy. I fold my coat over the back of a chair, pick up a broom, and get to work. Peggy went to beauty school, which is as hard as being a lawyer. At least that's what she says. A Beautician diploma is posted on the wall between her Advanced Permanent and Hair Extension Certificates. Her cheerleading photo hangs above that.

In it, she holds pompoms and wears a ponytail on the top of her head. If she fixed her hair like that now, she'd be mistaken for a spouting whale.

Peggy studies me under her thick Tammy Faye lashes.

"Front windows need scrubbing and the outer dryer vents need the lint picked out. Oh, and the bathroom sink is clogged." She goes back to her teasing.

"Yes ma'am," I say. When I work for Peggy, I'm polite and do any job she needs doing like sweeping the floor, cleaning her sinks out with Draino and a snake. Hair clogs pipes something awful. A couple times, she's even paid me to walk back and forth in front of her store carrying a large cardboard comb advertising two haircuts for the price of one. I also do shampoos when she's busy and can bring Jar to work whenever I need to. Jar folds hair towels for her. He's a dandy folder, so it's a win-win for all of us.

"Only need you part of the time today," she says. "My four thirty cancelled, so I made a late appointment with my dentist." Peggy smiles wide at me. "I think I'll get my teeth whitened. What do you think?"

"They look okay to me," I say cautiously. I know from experience it's not wise to agree whole-heartedly when Peggy talks about changing her appearance. As I finish pouring Draino down all the sinks, the bell on the door tinkles. A middle-aged lady enters.

"Finally," she says. "My three pm head," Peggy puts down her teasing comb. "You're late Lucille," she says sternly.

Heads are what clients are called in beauty-school-speak. I've learned a lot of the lingo since I started helping Peggy. Like *Do's* and *Highlights* and *Rat's Nest.*

Lucille takes off her coat and murmurs something about explosions delaying her.

Peggy waves her hand. "That's nothing. They're just blowing up Spring Hill. It's for the bypass," she says. Lucille does not look reassured.

"So Sue Ann and Audrey were at Two Spoons the other day," I move the broom back and forth being careful not to raise dust. "She and Audrey wore twin outfits."

"I saw. Makes them look like a couple bookends don't it." Peggy cocks a well-plucked eyebrow as she pushes her client into the chair and pumps it up higher with her foot.

I stay silent; Sue Ann and Peggy have their spats so it's hard to know if they're currently speaking. I can't find Peggy's dustpan so I sweep everything out the door.

"Okay Lucille, you want your rinse more pink or maybe do a bit of blue this time?" Peggy asks. Lucille mumbles something that sounds like *neither.* Peggy moves to the sink to mix her colors.

"Anyway, I have to earn more money," I tell Peggy, thinking on my bills. "You know anyone who needs help?"

"Don't you have enough to do with waitressing and working for me and watching that brother of yours?" Peggy says.

"Can always do more," I say and press my lips together. Confidential means not blabbing and any bills I owe are my own beeswax. What would Peggy think if I ended up rich? I give her a side long glance. She's chewing gum like a sewing machine on high.

"Well, Josephine Munn was saying she needed somebody to clean at her Bed and Breakfast," Peggy says. She takes her comb and wrenches Lucille's head to the side. Lucille yips.

"Oh, you're fine, honey," Peggy chides.

"Always can use a few more bucks," I say instead and wonder why Josephine never mentioned anything directly to me about needing help.

"Don't we all." Peggy glances over. "She'll be in tomorrow for a shampoo and style. I'll tell her you're interested."

"I'd appreciate that," I say. "Cleaning Josephine's big old house would be a full time job."

"You're telling, me," Peggy agrees. "Only thing is rooms don't get dirty when nobody stays in them."

"Too true," I say. "But there's always dusting. Dust happens whether there's guests or not."

"No guests no money to pay workers," Peggy says. She's a real businesswoman.

I trek out the door and get to work spraying Windex and running a rag over the front windows. I wonder what it'd be like to have no financial worries. Probably peaceful. Not like being-dead peaceful, but like the world is right and tight peaceful. I'm grinning when I start in on the dryer vents. As I scrape and pull the gray fluff out of the filter I'm humming one of Uncle E's old songs, *Happy Days Are Here Again.*

A sharp wind comes up. I look over at the mountains and see angry steel-grey clouds moving in. In no time, the ridges are obscured. A sudden flash of lightening and roll of thunder cause me to jump nearly out of my skin. Seconds later, the rain comes down, drenching me like I've been dunked in a bucket of water.

I hope Uncle E did what he was supposed to. And I hope Jar is sitting there in front of the TV. But Jar hates thunder, almost as much as he hates the dark. And then I start in on my worrying. What if the electricity goes out? What if trailer gets hit by lightening? It's metal after all. And what if Jar takes it in his head to be frightened? And what if Uncle E took it in his head to take off again?

Dang it all! I curse that worrying nature of mine as I quickly trot back inside. Lucille is now under the dryer and Peggy is sitting next to her flipping through a magazine while puffing on a cigarette.

"It's storming and I got to make sure Jar's all right. I'll finish up on Saturday when I come in to do my laundry," I say.

They stare like a couple of cows.

"Suit yourself," Peggy shrugs. She stubs her cigarette out on top of her Coke can.

"Like I said, I got to be going. If there's nothing else." I wait expectantly. Shifting my feet from side to side. Peggy still owes me from last week. There's only the sound of turning pages. "Guess I'll take off," I finally say.

"I heard you the first time." Peggy sets down her magazine and pops open another diet Coke. She doesn't look like she's heading for the cash drawer any time soon, so I reluctantly leave.

Rain pelts me. It streams down my face. By the time I reach my porch, I look like a drowned rat.

"Uncle E!" I yell. "Jar?" I go from room to room dripping water the whole way.

The trailer is empty and Dolly isn't back. Now that's just what I was afraid of. I peel off my sopping uniform, and empty my shoe. After carefully tucking my email into the top drawer of my desk, I change into a pair of jeans and a flannel shirt.

I walk into the kitchen and find a chicken scratched note from Uncle E on the table. Best I can interpret is that he's hitched a ride to go to the *follies* or to maybe *pick up Dolly* and getting Jar to promise something that looks like *lay and hide*. The last line of the note has something to do with maybe a *wheelbarrow* or maybe *mashed potato*. I squint my eyes studying the scrawl.

"On top of the refrigerator!" I say triumphantly. "Jar's Skittles are on top of the refrigerator!" That's when I notice a chair pushed next to it and the back door hanging open. Muddy Jar-tracks lead down the stairs. An empty Skittles bag is crumpled on the steps.

Hells bells.

I didn't get my money from Peggy. I got drenched in the rain. And Dolly, my uncle, and Jar have all vamoosed.

I hate when that happens.

CHAPTER FIVE

First things first.

I check the coop on the chance my brother snuck in with the chickens. They're huddled inside all damp. The skylight on their roof is leaky. Well, it's a hole covered with clear plastic tarp, but I call it a skylight. I've been meaning to fix it. Rain patters hard on the plastic.

"Hey, gals? Jar been around?" I rub a few heads. They cluck their denials of seeing hide nor hair of my brother and complain about the weather. But then hens are always complainers.

I dart across the yard and peek inside Uncle E's workshop. Sometimes Jar fiddles with Uncle's tools. He's mortal fond of fiddling. There's no sign of him there either. Not even a scattering of lime skittles. Jar isn't partial to eating green so sometimes I can follow that trail to find my brother.

Not in the trailer. Not in the coop. Not in Uncle's work shed. Triple dang.

It's into the woods I have to go. Uncle E's hunting coat is hanging by the back steps. It's too big for me, but it's warmer than mine. I put it on. When I slide under the barbwire fence, my braid gets hooked and I have to yank it free losing a few hairs. Water trickles from my cheek to my neck. Under the trees, the downpour lessens to a drizzle. I don't favor a hike through the forest in the rain and particularly not with approaching dark.

A flash of lightening makes me cautious. I'd sure hate to be struck and burned to a crisp. That would slow me down. I feel for my brother's current predicament. Jar isn't foolhardy. He'd have never taken off in the middle of a storm. It probably caught him by surprise. No telling where he's hunkered down.

"Jar!" I call again. Thunder rolls so loud it makes my ears ring. Either that or the construction guys decided to take down the rest of Spring Hill all at one whack.

I crisscross the woods. Back and forth. Recognizing my own muddy tracks as I walk in circles. Brambles catch at my knees and hinder my movement. It's dark now. I'm kicking myself that I didn't grab a flashlight.

I cup my hands around my mouth and yell. "Jar, I'm giving you a wallop if you don't answer me!" I threaten. "I MEAN IT!" I add.

I hear a faint sound and still myself. At first, I think it's maybe some critter in the bushes or a bird, but I hear it again more distinct this time so I head in the direction I think it came from. There's no trail to speak of. I have to push through wet draping branches.

A movement catches my eye and I spy a huddled form under a thick blackberry bush. It's Jar. He'll be chock full of stickers and soaking wet. It's a miracle to find him the way he's hid. I'm so relieved, I'm annoyed.

"What in the world has gotten into your head?" I pull the thorny vines apart. "I'll be surprised if you don't catch your death of cold. Now get your butt on out of there. I'm getting all scratched up."

Jar just lay there shivering.

"I mean it. I'm not joking," I say. "You're too big to carry. You hungry?" I ask. I dig in my pocket and find an old cough drop. I offer it to him. It's yellow so he might be fooled into thinking it's a Skittle. Jar only shakes his head. This is surprising as that color of Skittles is his favorite.

"Why are you still sitting on your rump? Look here!" I spread my arms. "I'm wet and muddy to boot. You think I enjoy doing this? I don't! Not one bit!" It's then I notice spatters of blood on Jar's pant leg. The steely teeth of a mountain beaver trap have got him pinned squarely by the toes.

"Oh, lord! What in the world have you got yourself into?" I drop to my knees and snatch at the trap to try to pry it open.

"ACK!" Jar cries.

Mud streaks smear his cheeks and scratches stipple his forehead. I pull hard on the trap but its links hold fast to the stake.

"End go," Jar whimpers.

"I'm working on it, Bug." I say. "We'll head on out of here soon as I get you free." I jerk and jerk on the chain, but to no avail.

"Uncle EEE!" I cry out. But I know for a fact there's utterly no use calling for him. He is nowhere near.

Just about when I think I'll have to leave my brother to get help, I spy the side lever mechanism on the trap. Well, right then I kick myself hard in the mental behind. I know how traps work.

"You'll be okay, Bug," I croon. "Just as soon as I pop the release." I work on the lever. It's stiff and rusted. My fingers shake as I push and prod. When I jiggle it back and forth, the trap loosens and I'm able to pry the jaws open.

"We got to get you to the doctor." I wipe mud off my brother's face with the edge of my sleeve.

The two of us struggle home with me supporting Jar under his armpits. I give Jar courage by pulling on his ear and giving him a Dutch rub or two or three on the head.

When we get back to the trailer, I settle Jar on the sofa and run to get Dolly's keys, but there's only an empty hook where they're supposed to be hanging. Uncle E still hasn't returned.

I step out on the porch to check the driveway hoping against hope to see Dolly sitting there, but there's no sign of our truck.

"UNCLE E!" I scream. "YOU SON OF A BEESWAX!" I hit the side of the trailer with the flat of my hand, which only makes my palm sting. I go back inside and grab the phone.

First number I dial is Peggy's, but it just rings and rings and then her voice mail comes on. It's then I remember she's probably still sitting in her dentist's chair.

I could start calling taverns trying to find Uncle E, but that would take all night plus he'd probably be too soused to drive home to us. Lonnie's out of the question. Who else? How about Smithers! It's dinner hour. He'll most likely be at Two Spoons. Law enforcement gets free eats and, in exchange, they got to do their duty and give people rides gratis when they're in a pinch, not like an ambulance that charges. It won't do any good for me to call directly to Sally at dispatch, as she knows me too well. After all the tricks Uncle E's pulled, she figures no Tyree ever has any real emergency.

I decide to call the café. Five. Six. Seven rings. And then someone picks up. I'm so worried I'm babbling.

"Jar's gotten himself hurt and Uncle E has taken Dolly. I'm stuck and I need a ride to the hospital. It's an emergency," I add. "Not life or death, but it's still an emergency. Is Smithers there?"

"Nope," the voice says and hangs up.

I stare at the receiver.

"Peep," Jar tells me. "Hab trig."

"You said it, Jar. We certainly are in a fix."

But in two shakes of a lamb's tail, there's the sound of a motor revving outside. Quick like a bunny I snatch Jar up and run outside thinking it's Uncle E returning.

It's Leo in his van.

"Thought I'd better come myself," he says.

My heart gets to thumping. "I wasn't angling for a ride from you." I say as I help my brother into the front seat. "But I'm real grateful." I fasten the seatbelt over the both of us.

"Where to?" Leo still has his chef hat on. He backs all the way down the driveway without looking.

"ER. He'll need stitches," I say.

"EEEE!" Jar wails when he hears me say the word stitches. Leo winces.

"Sound bother you?" I say. "Those bikes of yours are louder."

"It's the pitch, not the volume," Leo replies.

"Sorry," I say. "Who's at the Café, anyway? Or did you close early?"

Leo shakes his head. "Nope. I left Curtis holding down the fort.

"Hells bells. That will get me a *not meets* for sure, Curtis being stuck all by himself."

Jar starts to whimper again.

"Shhh, Bug." I kiss the top of his head. "I know you hurt."

"Why do you call him Bug?"

"Because he used to be cute as a Bug's ear plus he hunts for them."

"You hang in there, Bug," Leo says.

"ACK!" Jar protests.

"It's my own personal name for him," I say. "He takes exception to anybody else calling him Bug."

"Sorry," Leo says.

Trees whip by as we fly down the highway. The rain hits the windshield and Leo's wipers bang out a hard rhythm. He taps his fingers on the wheel and hums.

"You know this is all due to you running off," I whisper into Jar's ear knowing full well how mean I'm being to place blame after the fact. "I won't be a bit surprised if you don't get a shot out of the deal."

Jar gives a sharp wail at the word, shot.

"So what happened to him?" Leo asks.

"Mountain beaver trap," I say. "And I have to admit I'm surprised. Jar knows to watch out where he's going in the woods. You're smarter than that," I chide my brother. "You're lucky you weren't stuck out there all night in the dark. That would really put you into a prime tizzy."

"Organ wallop," Jar snuffles.

"You're right," I say half-mollified. "It really is Uncle E's fault."

Leo has a habit of speeding, so we get to the hospital lickety split. The van pulls up in front of the ER entrance.

"You don't have to wait," I say as we slide out. "It'll take forever. And I can get a hold of Uncle E later. He's most likely over at Silver King or maybe the Buzz Bar."

Leo's face is expressionless. "I'm going to park." And he drives into the side lot.

The ER is crowded. I sign in and we sit down on a long bench against the wall.

"Best settle yourself," I tell Jar. "We're in for a real wait."

"Caboose." Jar kicks his good foot against the seat.

"Don't you dare act like that," I say. "Those who traipse in the woods and get into trouble by being stupid have to pay the piper."

A few minutes later Leo walks through the door. I'm cheered.

"Over here, Leo!" I wave him down.

He's carrying his guitar. I scoot over on the bench to make room. A large woman on the other side of me starts hacking. I turn away, shifting Jar. He yelps like a puppy.

"Shush," I say and snap him on the ear. He yelps again, this time softer. "And sit up straight. No playing possum," I warn. "Or throwing yourself on the floor. You're getting too old for that."

Leo starts strumming a song about a blackbird singing. My brother immediately quiets. He reaches out a finger and Leo lets him pluck a string.

I hear low-voiced comments behind us.

"What's wrong with that kid?" I hear people whisper.

But Jar and I are used to being whispered about. Leo plays something else about two muskrats that sound like a lullaby. Jar closes his eyes.

"Okey dokey," he murmurs. There's a smile on his face.

An hour and forty-five minutes later, a nurse walks out with a chart in her hand. "Jarld Tyree?" She looks around.

We pop up for our turn and leave Leo sitting. I help Jar walk.

"You can go on home, now, Leo," I call back. "We'll be a good long while."

But Leo keeps on singing like he doesn't hear.

The nurse leads us into a curtain-partitioned cubicle and I help Jar up on the bed. He lays out stiff, like a wooden puppet. I sit beside him in a folding chair. Nearly an hour later the doctor walks in. His white coat is rumpled and his hair is askew. Even with all that, he smiles nice at us and I'm heartened. There's something that feels good when people in charge smile at you.

He's reading Jar's chart.

I notice his name tag says Doctor Harms, which I think is an awful name for a physician.

"Who's going to go to a Doctor Harms?" I try to whisper to Jar without the doctor overhearing. "He ought to change it."

"Heb cap," Jar murmurs.

"Well, Doctor Healer is nice but a little obvious," I say to Jar. "How about Doctor Comfort?" I say.

"Lobo drip," Jar says.

"Yeah I guess it does sounds like a liquor," I say. "But it might be an advantage. Uncle E says whiskey is real healthy. It's got vitamins. Plus it relaxes you. He should know, him being a drinker and all."

"What's that?" Doctor Harms looks up. He's got black rimmed glasses that make him look smart.

"This is my brother, Jar and he got himself tangled with a mountain beaver trap," I say quickly hoping the doctor didn't overhear our previous conversation.

"Mountain beaver?" The way the doctor says this I know he's not from around here.

"Boomer? Ground bear?" I say. I'm thinking maybe he knows it by another name. "Giant mole? It's a sort of rodent that lives in the woods and digs holes. It has fur, but it's kind of a pest."

Pest gets a flicker of recognition so I leave it at that.

The doctor looks from the chart to Jar and back again. "How old is your brother? His file here says fifteen."

"That's right. He's short for his age," I say.

Doctor Harms bends over Jar's foot. I want to warn him about the way my brother is, but the doctor seems to know already. Jar flaps one hand and hums under his breath. But the doctor talks real quiet and kind of sing songy. Lickety split Doctor Harms has Jar's shoe off, his foot numbed and cleaned up, and is hard at work stitching. I'm surprised Jar is letting him off the hook so easy, and tell him so.

He smiles.

"My sister has Asperger's," the doctor says by way of explanation. "Singing soothes her."

"Well, that's real nice for her," I say hoping Asperger's is a good thing.

The doctor stares at me. "It's a form of autism. Like your brother has," he says.

"Well, color me red. You got a sister like Jar?" I say. "I don't worry what anything's called. It doesn't seem to help much to know what Jar's got, if you want to know the honest truth."

It's then I notice Jar's sneaker. I hold it up. "Oh, man! It's in tatters. He'll need a whole new pair. Can't buy just one," I say with disgust. "Although you'd think you'd be able to. I mean, what do people do without a leg? Maybe they pair up with a buddy that's missing the other limb," I say.

The doctor's eyes crinkle so I know he'd like to laugh, but he's a professional, so he doesn't. Professionals can't have a sense of humor.

"It could have been worse," he cautions. "Your brother could have lost his foot."

"That'd be good. It'd slow him down some. My Uncle E says never tempt worse because worse is always right around the corner just itching for an engraved invitation."

"Your Uncle E sounds like a wise man. Has your brother had a tetanus shot within five years?"

"I don't know. Probably. Doesn't it say in his file?"

"No it doesn't."

"Let me think." Shots cost money. Doctor Harms stares hard like it'll help me think better, but it doesn't.

I look up at the ceiling trying to remember. "A couple months ago he fell off the roof of the coop and then before that it was a spill down our driveway and before that he fell out of a cedar tree. He might have had one then. Oh, fudge!" I sigh. "You might as well give him one."

When the nurse lowers Jar's pants, Skittles or no, Jar knows that can't be good. Our ears ring with high-pitched Jar-shrieks. It takes two orderlies, a nurse, and me, plus the doctor to hold him down. Afterwards, the nurse hands Jar a sucker. It's green so Jar throws it on the floor. I help the nurse search in a drawer for a yellow and two reds. I stick them in my pocket to give to him later.

"He's has a couple deep scratches on his face," she says. "You'll probably need an antibiotic salve so they don't get infected."

Jar starts rocking back and forth so I pop a few more Skittles in his mouth. He takes them like a baby bird.

"That's just from being tangled in a trap in the woods." I say and cuff my brother on the ear. "You should be paying me for telling you what's wrong with him."

The nurse, bless her heart, laughs. She gives Jar a gentle pat on the shoulder and he shrieks. It makes her jump. "You have somebody watching him while you work?" she asks.

"Oh, yeah, I got a full time nanny," I say, thinking I don't have time for this.

She gives me discharge papers to sign.

"You have insurance?" she asks and I give her my eye-rolling look.

"Doesn't your brother qualify for aid? DDA? Or SSI?" The nurse pauses her pen over the clipboard.

"N-N-No," I stammer on purpose. "Tyrees take care of their own," I say. "Anyway have you tried filling out those forms? I don't have that kind of time to waste."

The nurse presses her lips together and turns away. At first, I think she's mad, but then I see she's searching around in a cupboard. She comes up with antibiotic salve samples, a couple extra bandages, and some pain pill samples. She puts it all in a bag and hands it over. "Here you go," she says.

I look at her nametag. "Thanks Nurse Caldwell. We surely do appreciate it." I say with a smile. It's important to use people's names when you want to thank them.

The nurse's face softens. "You take care of him." And she ruffles Jar's hair.

Well, then, Jar lets out another blood-curdling siren-like holler that makes her leap right out of her skin.

"Shhh, Bug!" I say to Jar. The nurse looks stricken. "Don't worry," I say. "He hates his hair being touched by anybody but me."

When the two of us hobble out to the waiting room, Leo's still sitting there strumming his guitar. He's got quite a captive audience. I look at my watch.

"Three hours and forty-six minutes," I say proudly. "That's a record for us."

"Yeah, it was a long time," Leo says sliding his instrument into its case.

"What do you mean long?" I say. "This here is a record for being short," I brag.

Leo has such a surprised expression on his face that I burst out laughing. "Haven't you ever had to go to the ER?" I stare.

Leo shakes his head. "Nope," he says.

"Well, I guess some people are just plain lucky." And I give him a wink.

On our way back to town, I get to thinking about this new hospital bill to add to the others. I sigh so deep I'm surprised those lungs of mine stay in my body. I'm going backwards getting that five-hundred bucks.

"What's wrong?" Leo asks.

"Nothing," I say quickly. The lie comes easy. I give Jar a handful of Skittles. I sigh again. Well, heck, it's Leo, I think.

"It just seems the closer I get to being even, the more charges Jar drums up. I may have to dip into my rainy day fund," I say. "That's a coffee can in my bedroom," I explain. "I put all my tip money into it. It's for full-blown emergencies."

"Good thinking," Leo says. "So you use it for when Jar gets hurt?"

"Oh, no. It's got to be a real emergency. Maybe a typhoon or hurricane. Or an earthquake. We're real lucky we never had one of those. My fund has never had to be tapped into."

I'm proud of that. And I get to thinking. Maybe it's time to borrow from my fund to get my inheritance. I could pay it right back when the money comes. It takes money to make money.

I wonder how much I got in my can, now. Six hundred? Eight hundred? I'm suddenly antsy to count it.

Leo pulls into our driveway and brakes to a stop. I slide out supporting Jar.

"You need help?" he asks.

"Nope. I got it. Thanks for the ride," I say quickly. "I owe you."

"You owe Curtis," Leo shrugs. "He's the one who got stuck alone at the Café." And he gives a laugh like he doesn't feel sorry for Curtis one bit. And then he drives off.

Dolly is still not back, but I don't care about that now. I get Jar situated on the sofa with a pillow under his foot and a couple under his head. He lies there rubbing his eyes while I flip on the TV. It's too late for any of his programs, just old movie reruns.

"How about something to eat?" I ask, itching to get into my bedroom and check out my fund.

"Okey dokey," Jar says.

Good things come to those who wait. I stir up some leftovers. Cream of Brussels sprouts soup, from Two Spoons. I think on how we're poorer because of an abandoned mountain beaver trap. But then, as I pour the soup into bowls, I consider that we're lucky. We get as much soup from Two Spoons as we want. We got Uncle

E's trailer to live in free and clear thanks to Momma and Daddy's death benefit from the logging company. My brother didn't get anything hurt but a couple no account toes. And best of all we're going to be rich.

Yep, we're lucky all right.

When I get Jar settled for the night I march into my bedroom and pull the coffee can out from under my bed. It's heavy. When I pour it out, I discover there's hardly any money in it. Only rocks. Someone must have discovered my stash and I know exactly who did.

Uncle E.

No wonder he had enough for that danged weather machine. I'm so mad I toss the can across the room. It ricochets off the wall and strikes my mirror breaking it into a gazillion pieces. I sweep them up in my dust pan, throw them in the garbage, and then hunt for a new place to hide my rainy day fund. Great, I'm thinking, seven year's bad luck. Just exactly what I need.

CHAPTER SIX

I was grateful to note that no more bad luck happened to me over the next three days.

Saturday dawned cloudy, but the good part is, it wasn't wet and Jar woke up and ate breakfast all by himself. Maybe Uncle E is right. Maybe my brother is ready for responsibility.

This evening is chicken fried steak potpie special so Two Spoons will be packed. Not only that, it's laundry day and I have chicken chores to do, plus I have to figure out where my rainy day fund money vamoosed off to in order to have enough to pay the five hundred bucks to get five million.

I poke my head out the back door. "Jar?" I sing. "Where are you?" He pops out of Uncle E's workshop.

"Somebody needs to help me out today and you are elected," I say.

Jar likes to be elected and grins a toothy smile. "Okey dokey," he says and hop-limps over.

"Aren't those toes of yours getting better?" I give Jar an especially vigorous Dutch rub as he goes past.

"Ort!" he squawks.

"Man up!" I tell him. "It's the Tyree way of expressing affection. You need to learn how to do it."

I grab my purse and our laundry.

"Come with me to Peggy's. You'll like that won't you?"

Jar flaps his hands meaning he's agreeable and the two of us make our way down the hill to Cut N Clean with our bags of dirty clothes.

When we come through the door, Peggy is staring in her mirror applying mascara. She gives us a wave with the wand. "Hey, there," she says. "Sorry to hear about Jar. Curtis said he lost a foot."

"Hey, there, back," I say. "Don't know how Curtis would know, being as he wasn't at the ER. Leo was. And Jar's still got both feet, if you notice."

I put Jar to work sorting clothes on the floor and drag out the broom. I'm thinking that it won't be long before I won't have to have all these part time jobs. I can hire somebody else to do my laundry. Jar and me could even start going on vacations. Disneyland. Harrison Hot Springs. That Seven Flags place. Or is it Six Flags? *Rich, I'm gonna be rich.* I sing to myself as I sweep. *Five hundred for five million.*

"My, you're cheerful," Peggy says.

I suck the song deep into my throat. "I'm not," I say. "But thanks."

"Notice anything?" Peggy clenches her teeth together and grimaces.

"What?" I look up. "Oh, your teeth look pearly white," I say. "Just like a movie star's." Peggy's partial to celebrities.

She frowns. "No, I ended up not getting my teeth done. It was going to cost four hundred bucks. I'm showing you my new lipstick. Classic Ruby Red. Marilyn Monroe's favorite." She grimaces again.

"Oh, yeah, it's real pretty," I say. It makes Peggy's lips look like they're gushing blood.

Peggy frowns. "And I'd sure like to know the smart ass who left a weight loss ad on my table," she complains. "I'm curvy. Always been big-boned. You think I need to lose a few pounds?" Peggy sucks in her cheeks.

"Not at all," I say quickly.

"What's he doing upright, anyway?" Peggy points to Jar. "Isn't he supposed to be in bed convalescing?"

"Nope, the doctor said he's got to get exercise," I tell her. "Besides I need him to help me sort clothes." Soon we can pay someone else to sort our clothes.

"He's sure tubby around his middle," Peggy says. "Short people always got to watch their weight."

"Just baby fat," I say.

"Isn't he a little old to have baby fat?"

"Poop," Jar says and he gives Peggy a dirty look. He hates being called tubby.

"Hold on, Jar," she chides. "You got to separate whites from darks. They'll run otherwise." She pops in a gum and starts chewing.

Peggy picks up a magazine and sniffs. "Telling his colors was something he should have learned by now. Makes him look like a dodo head."

"Jar's no dodo head. He's just got a different idea of sorting is all," I tell her. "Over here is inside clothes. That's outside clothes. Soft things there, rough things here. Fuzzy things. Smooth things. Denim things." I give Jar an approving pat on the rump with my broom. "There's more to sorting than color," I say.

Peggy rolls her eyes. "If he plans on doing it for hire he's gotta do color. Folks don't like dingy underwear."

"Gut butt you." Jar shoots a dark look in Peggy's direction.

"What's he saying?" Peggy frowns.

"Just that he likes working here," I lie. "By the by, I was wondering if you want one of our whirligigs out front," I say hurriedly. "A cupid would be real cheerful and you could always let people know where you got it from. It'd be good advertising for us."

"No way." Peggy shakes her head. "I like my name on my sign. And I have to consider what my customers think. Whirligigs are low class."

"I don't think they're low class," I protest.

"That's because you live in a trailer. You can't be the judge." Peggy shakes her head sadly and clicks her tongue. "It's well nigh impossible to quell trailer trash roots. You can't change your nature, Tammy Louise. It's what you're born with. That's why you hanker after potato chip and ketchup sandwiches, love anything sparkly, and consider mayonnaise the fourth major food group." Peggy goes back to reading her magazine. "Trust me. Whirligigs are low class."

"Mayonnaise is not the fourth major food group," I grumble. "Lard is. Everyone knows that."

"Whee!" Jar imitates the washer alarm.

"Machine's unbalanced," Peggy says without looking up.

Later, while our laundry dries, we sit around watching Peggy's soaps. It's real nice, almost like we're friends, instead of employer and employee. Peggy even pays me five bucks. She still owes me twenty-two, but people owing me money won't bother me soon.

"Don't you have any shampoos and sets today?" I ask. "It'd be nice to earn a few more bucks."

"Just Audrey, but she's always late. But Josephine told me she's interested in you doing some cleaning when she gets some guests. Why do you need more bucks for, anyway?"

"I always need more bucks," I say carefully. "And I sure do appreciate you speaking with Josephine. When did she say I could start?" I have to watch what I say.

Peggy may get suspicious that my circumstances are about to change.

"No idea," Peggy says. "She's certain to get some tourists next week. Or the week after."

Well, that leaves me right back where I started. In order to be rich I need some money and in order to get money I need the jobs. I frown.

"Program." Jar wipes his nose with the back of his hand.

"You coming down with a cold? Use a Kleenex." I say and hand him one out of my pocket.

The door tinkles and Peggy grinds out her cigarette. "Here comes my head," she says. "Hey, Audrey. Have a seat."

Sue Ann's mother-in-law, Audrey, gives Jar a wide berth as she walks past. I notice she's got her mustard pant suit on again. When we're rich, people won't give us a wide berth. I smile.

Peggy sees me smile and narrows her eyes. I turn away but keep my smile.

When our laundry is dry, we fold it and stick it in our bag. Jar carries it all the way home without dropping it in a puddle.

"That's a record, that is!" I say and swat him on the butt. "It's important to keep track of records."

"Yard court," Jar ducks. Compliments embarrass him.

Dolly is back in her place when we get home, which relieves my mind. I make a plate of sandwiches and call for Uncle E out the kitchen window.

"Uncle E? You want lunch? It's Peanut Butter and Jam!"

A loud banging comes from the workshop. "Innaminute!" Uncle E calls out.

I'm glad to hear he's back to work. I hope that means he isn't after chasing rainbows and has decided to settle down and earn money by doing real work for a change. Summer and Christmas are our best times of year for Whirligigs and we need to build up stock. I need to convince him that he needs to send a few bucks my way. I know Barinas said to keep it confidential, but Uncle is kin.

I wander into the workshop carrying a plate of sandwiches with Jar following close behind.

Uncle E lays his screwdriver down and smiles. "Well, how about that?" He helps himself to a half sandwich.

"You don't happen to know how my rainy day fund went missing, do you?" I say this real sweet.

Uncle E furrows his brows. "Didn't know you had one."

"That's a big fat fib," I scowl at my uncle.

"Well," Uncle E drawls. "Maybe I knew you had one, but I didn't know where you kept it," he says. There's no shifting of his eyes.

I hesitate. Uncle E eats his sandwich. I have to re-think.

"Agg warpal," Jar says. He grabs a sandwich.

I stare at my brother. "How do you know it was under my mattress?"

Jar gets shifty eyes. "Prat."

"Did you take it?" I stare at my brother. Jar's incapable of lying to me.

"Otter." He crams the sandwich in his mouth.

"It isn't yours. Stealers go straight to hell."

"ACK!" Jar doesn't want to go to hell.

"I better get every cent back," I say. "That money's mine." And then I shrug. "Well, no matter," I say airily. That's to put Jar off the track. Now that I know he took my money, I can find it easy. It's probably in his room. I change the subject so Jar doesn't get suspicious.

"How about let's all go for a walk in the woods, Uncle E? Jar needs to use that foot of his. And we haven't hiked together in a dog's age. I got a while before I have to be at the Café."

It's also an opportunity for my heart to heart conversation with Uncle E. Bring him in on my inheritance deal.

"Zip!" Jar says eagerly. "Okey dokey!"

Uncle E munches on his sandwich and tilts his head. "I got things to do. Maybe tomorrow."

"You been AWOL for days. Time to stick around home," I say. And away from Lonnie, I want to add.

"Okey dokey?" Jar pulls on Uncle E's arm. "Okey dokey?" My brother is hard to resist when he's begging.

"Aw heck," Uncle E says and he stuffs the last of his sandwich in his mouth. "A short one then."

"EEE ya!" Jar takes off like a shot to open up the coop.

"Now you've done it. He wants to bring the chickens," I say.

"Let him," Uncle E shrugs.

We head into the woods.

Hiking is Jar's favorite and bringing the chickens along is the high point. He turns over rocks and helps them find bugs. This is good because it saves on chicken feed and makes our eggs taste better. Whenever Jar sees a perfect sized stone, he scoops it up and puts it in his pocket.

He kneels in the middle of the muddy path and opens his arms. Annie, the barred Plymouth Rock, comes close. He nuzzles her and she nuzzles him back. I guess he's telling her his secrets. Annie gives a couple low vibrating *brocks* as if to answer.

"I'm grateful Jar has somebody to talk to besides me," I say.

"True, that," Uncle E says. He dodges our white leghorn Cauliflower's sharp beak. "That hen likes going after ankles nearly as much as she likes going after bugs."

I purely love the woods out back of our trailer even though Tyrees don't own them, a developer somewhere in Oregon does. Tree sprigs branching like skeleton hands. Moss thick and fuzzy. Like mold on bread. The smell of new growth. Of wet.

"Jar's cheating on his walking," Uncle E points out. "Use your whole weight. You need to be working that foot or it won't ever heal."

Jar makes a face and keeps on his track of limping.

"He was doing better earlier," I say. "Maybe he's tired."

"Tired smired!" Uncle E says sternly. "Walk normal or you'll be a limper your whole life like that hunchback fellow in the movies. You already got a strike against you on account of you got a square head. You want to be a limper too?" Uncle E asks.

"Okey dokey." Jar gets to flapping. That means, no he doesn't, and he's sorry for giving Uncle E grief.

I start to think on my email letter. I give Uncle E a sideways glance. This may be the time to bring Uncle E in on the deal.

"You know anything about any Tyree missionaries," I say casually.

"Missionaries?" Uncle E looks puzzled. "What makes you ask that?"

"Evangelicals in Spokane," I say. "Weren't they do-gooders?"

Uncle E snorts out a laugh. "That was Walla Walla, not Spokane," he says. "And I think they were granddaddy's cousins. They stuck around there because so many of them were in the federal penitentiary."

"But I thought they were church people!" I protest.

"That don't mean they weren't criminals."

"Did any of them go to Africa?" I ask.

"Africa?" Uncle E stops in the path and stares at me. "Stop beating around the bush, Sissy. You got something to say, say it."

"I got a letter that says we might be heirs." I pull out the email and give it to Uncle E.

He reads with his lips moving. When he finishes, he lets out a long whistle. "Well, how about that. I guess a few of those Spokane missionaries did go to Africa. Halleluiah." Uncle E slaps his hand on his thigh.

"But how could missionaries save five million?" Religious people are poor." I worried about that fact.

"Well," Uncle cocks his head. "Maybe the Africans were grateful. Missionaries don't spend much. And churches don't pay taxes. And they get to collect money from people every Sunday week after week with no accounting. It's sort of a scam, but there you have it."

Uncle E has a point.

"So you think this is real?"

"I'm thinking this is a potential opportunity for us," he says. "Boy will people sit up and take notice when we show up in our Cadillac. I can't wait to tell the guys over at Silver King."

"NO!" I snatch the email back. "We can't say a word. See here? It says confidential. And don't you dare say a thing to Lonnie. We'll never hear the end of it if you do."

"I know about confidential," Uncle E sniffs. "It means to keep quiet." Then he stops and stares at me hard. "Maybe we shouldn't be talking."

"But we're family!" I protest.

"So's Lonnie," Uncle E says.

"He's only a cousin," I say. "Once removed. Don't tell him."

"I think we should bring him in on it," Uncle E says. "It says here you got to come up with five hundred bucks."

"I can read," I say.

"How you going to do that?"

"I was thinking you could help."

"All my cash is tied up in this Darrington deal." Uncle E is scratching his chin. "But let me think on it." Uncle E brightens. "Hey, I got an idea. How well do you know this Barinas fellow?"

I roll my eyes. "How well do you think? I only got the one email."

"You mean you didn't answer it right away?"

"Not yet," I say.

"Well, you better," Uncle E warns. "Or he might send the money to somebody else."

I hadn't thought about that. Now I'm worried

"Answer him as soon as you can," Uncle E urges. "Tonight when you go into the café. You might see if he'll take part of the payment at a time. Like layaway. Half or even thirds would work real well for us. Asking don't hurt nothing. And it'd be like a test, to boot. Check out his amiability quotient. If he said no, we'd be no worse off," Uncle E says.

I consider. "That's not a bad idea." I hesitate. "So you're convinced it's possible I'm an heiress. That we had relatives in Africa who left money?" I say slowly. "That it isn't other Tyrees they mean?"

"It's more than possible," Uncle E says. "And possible should be good enough for us."

He sounds so certain.

"How do we prove it? It asks for something called provisional evidence of relationship," I say.

Uncle E rolls his eyes. "That's easy. I got ID that says I'm a Tyree and so do you. That's evidence of us being Tyrees. And us being Tyrees means we're related. There ain't that many around." Uncle E makes serious sense.

Suddenly I'm in a real hurry to get to the café and answer that email. I hope I haven't missed any deadline.

"Come on! Hike's over." I turn my brother around. Jar whines at the prospect of it being over. He drags his bad foot. When we reach the trailer, I push him towards the coop.

"Put the girls back, feed them and latch up the door real good for the night," I tell Jar. "We don't want foxes or raccoons to get in." The impatience in my voice is sharp as a stick.

Uncle E goes into his workshop.

"Cluck! Cluck!" Jar calls from inside the coop yard. All the chickens run straight for Jar through the gate, squawking and carrying on. My brother plops down in the dirt and all of them surround him, even Cauliflower. It makes me smile.

"Jar is really something." Uncle E beams as he comes out of his workshop.

"Yeah he's a real chicken lover," I say.

"Not that," Uncle E shakes his head and holds up his toolbox. "I wanted to show you what I found." He shakes his tool box and it jingles. He holds up a hand full of coins and bills.

"That's my money!" I sputter.

"It's exactly two-hundred and fifty dollars. That's half what you need to send to that African fellow. It's a sign for what we need to do," Uncle E says. "And you know where signs come from."

"Karma," I breathe. "Signs are from karma." And then. "Only two- hundred and fifty?" I'm perplexed. "That can't be all there is." Uncle doesn't meet my eyes.

"ACK!" Jar grabs at the tool box. "Panfry!"

"It is not yours," I hold my brother away with a hand on his head. "Earn your own if you want a rock tumbler and I don't care if Walter has one in his window. Where's the rest of it?"

"Otter," Jar howls.

"You did too take it. You just said you did."

"ACK!" Jar goes. He hates being caught in a fib.

"It's all of ours," Uncle E says. "Finders keepers. Share and share alike."

"Fut." Jar mutters.

"Share and share alike nothing," I say and snatch the toolbox. I stalk into the house and empty the cash into my can. The rest of my rainy day fund has got to be in Jar's room.

I close my bedroom door and look around for a new hiding place. Under my mattress is too obvious. I decide to use the bottom drawer of my dresser. When I return the tool box to the workshop, neither Uncle E nor Jar will speak to me. Uncle E mutters, "Stingy," under his breath.

That's just great. I head into work.

Later, after my shift is over and Curtis and Leo have left for the night, I sit in the empty dining room of Two Spoons. It's dark and spooky. The building creaks and groans, like it's settling down for the night. The computer screen glows in front of me.

I finish my reply to the email and read it over.

Dear Dr. Barinas,

I am purely sorry that I have taken so long to answer your email. I hope you are well.

First of all thank you for letting me know about my dead relations. I guess I can tell you the Tyrees have an evangelical or two or three in our background (according to my Uncle E) so it's very possible one or the other of them ended up dead in Africa that is to say, Botswana. I wonder. What's it like there? Do you have to be on the lookout for lions? We only got an occasional cougar, but I never actually seen one. We got deer, though, and a ton of squirrels.

I know you're a busy man but I have to say our family is short of cash being as my brother got hurt and we had to go to the hospital and my Uncle has some deals going and I'm waiting for my wages from the café (did I tell you I'm a waitress? Well, I am.) And we're owed money for whirligigs (those are wooden things with legs that rotate in the wind and are real popular in America).

And I let Uncle E in on it even though it said confidential but will keep mum and not tell anybody else.

This money would come in real handy for us. I don't want you to think I'm greedy for myself. It's my Uncle and brother who need taking care of.

So I need to know is it okay to send the money half at a time? And where do I send it? You didn't really explain this well (I don't mean to be critical or anything). How about cash in an envelope? There are people who say you can't trust anybody to do that, but you're a solicitor (I looked it up and it said it meant lawyer). Did you go to school a real long time to be that? Curtis (that's the manager at Two Spoons) said I'd be a good lawyer because I'm always arguing.

Anyhow, you have yourself a mighty fine day. How do you say that in your language? We say have a mighty fine day.

Sincerely, Tammy Louise Tyree

I hit send. There's a tap at the door. It's Uncle E.

"Did you answer the email yet?" he whispers.

"Right here." I bring it up on the screen.

Uncle E reads it. "You didn't give them your Social Security number," he reminds me. "Or proof you are who you are."

"They say it's not a good idea to send that number anywhere," I say.

"But it's to an executor person."

"Maybe we should wait."

"I got our bank info right here." Uncle E digs in his pocket and pulls out our checkbook. "I think we better send our address don't you think? And my own Social Security, too as being older I'm probably the nearest heir. Fact is, if I had my own email account they would have sent this to me instead of you. They probably think I'm dead."

"You're going too fast," I say to Uncle E.

"I know you're overwhelmed. It's not every day you find out you're an heiress," Uncle E says. "But you got to strike when the iron's hot. I wonder how long it will take to get our money. Why don't you send another email and find out?"

Before I can do that, a new message pops up. It's from Barinas.

We look at each other. My mouth drops open. Maybe this is on the up and up.

"Well, that was fast." Uncle E sounds gratified.

I read it out loud.

IMPORTANT

CONFIDENTIAL

BOTSWANA UNION BANK

MS **TYREE**

MULTIPLE SUBMITTED MONETARY REMUNERATIONS HALF OR A THIRD AT A TIME WILL BE MORE THAN SATISFACTORY. PLEASE SEND AMERICAN DOLLARS TO THE POSTAL SERVICE ADDRESS GIVEN MARKED ATTEN: DR BARINAS AND CASH IS ACCEPTABLE INITIALLY UNTIL WE ESTABLISH A CONGENIAL RELATIONSHIP.

YOUR CONFIDENTIAL CRITERIA INCLUDES MR **E. TYREE** BUT REMAIN DUTIFUL OF AFOREMENTIONED CONFIDENTIALITY AGREEMENT. WE WILL ENDEAVOR TO ACCESS PROBATE IN ALL DUE HASTE WHEN WE RECEIVE ALL IDENTIFYING INFORMATION

MUCH WELCOME TO OUR BUSINESS DUTIES TO COME

DR. BARINAS

EXECUTOR AND MINISTER

FAITH BASED CHARITY GOVERNMENTAL DEPARTMENT

PO BOX 2145 GABARONE, BOTSWANA

GABARONE, BOTSWANA

“How about that!” he breathes. “I knew he was a reasonable man. You got to reply right away and show him we’re serious. Get the ball rolling.”

I hit reply and then stop. I have to think. Uncle E is pacing behind my back.

“Don’t do that,” I say. “It makes me nervous.”

“Tell him we appreciate his amenability in his desire to get us our inheritance faster. And tell him I do remember my Tyree missionary relations with fondness and I doubly appreciate them thinking of us when it comes to leaving their wealth,” he recites.

I type it out.

How’s that look?” he asks.

"Real nice, Uncle E. But maybe—"

There's the sound of squeaking.

"Someone's walking in the kitchen," Uncle E whispers.

Both of us listen hard.

"Spies," Uncle E hisses. "After our inheritance. We'll need body guards."

"It's not spies," I hiss back. "And we won't need any bodyguards if you watch your loose mouth. Most likely, it's only Curtis forgetting something. I'll check it out."

I leave the shining screen of the computer and push open the pass through door. I walk into the kitchen and look around carefully. It's empty. All the lights are off. There's no one there. I hang up a stray dishtowel and go back out to the dining room.

Uncle E is sitting at the computer typing with one finger.

"What are you doing?" I march over not caring how much noise I'm making.

"Just what you should have. Taking the bully by the horns." Uncle E says waving his check book. And before I can stop him, he hits send. I read his answer. Uncle E gave them all our bank numbers, our birthdates, and both social security numbers.

There's no going back, now.

CHAPTER SEVEN

It took me a couple days to actually mail the money to Barinas.

First stop was the bank. I deposited my weekly check from Two Spoons and turned all my tip money into larger paper bills. I would have needed a box if I'd sent Barinas the coins that had been in my coffee can.

"Are two hundreds and a fifty all right?" The teller asked me. Her nametag said Nancy. I was torn. Twenties would have been impressive. Made it look like I was sending more, but it would be too fat for my envelope. I had to think about the postage. I dithered.

"All fifties," I finally told her. That seemed to me to be a good compromise.

The post office was crowded. I had to stand in line.

"How much to send this letter to Africa?" I asked the clerk.

"Africa? You know somebody there?" she said.

"My relatives," I said. "They're missionaries."

"Interesting," she said.

Nobody ever said something that had to do with me was interesting. I stood a bit taller and pulled my shoulders back. I paid for the stamps and let her put the envelope in the bin.

"How long will it take to get there?" I asked.

"A week or maybe more," she said.

A week. That's when it hit me.

If I'd been able to send all five hundred at once, I'd be counting down the days until my inheritance arrived. It's just like Uncle E says. You got to spend money to make money. I decided then and there to send the rest using my Two Spoons paycheck. I run back to the bank and make a big withdrawal even though I've written checks on what was deposited.

By the time my inheritance comes, I can make those checks good. I go straight back to the Post Office and mail it off. There was a different clerk who didn't care where my letter went.

All the way back to Spring, I daydream about driving down Main Street in a brand new truck tossing handfuls of hundred dollar bills out the window.

When I get back home, I tell Uncle E what I did.

"Good thinking Tammy," he says approvingly.

"But what about our bills for this month?" I ask.

"They'll keep," Uncle E replies.

I make a mark on the calendar. "Two weeks, tops" I say. "And the money should be here."

"They going to mail it?" Uncle E asks.

I hesitate. It was something I'd forgotten to ask Barinas. "I don't know."

"Five million bucks would be a mighty big box."

"Maybe it'll be a check," I say.

"That makes more sense," Uncle E rubs his chin. "But then we'd have to wait for it to clear. Maybe they'll make payments to us."

We settle at the kitchen table and plan what we'll do with the money. We make a list.

"Number one, new truck," I say. "And then fix the trailer roof or even build a real house."

"Repair the chicken coop."

"Go on a trip somewhere."

"Harrison Hot Springs!" I suggest.

"Las Vegas!" Uncle E beams.

"Gag wallop!" Jar calls out from the sofa where he's watching TV.

"Don't interrupt! We're having an important discussion." I say. "And going to the Greyhound Bus Station in Everett is free. We can go any darn time you want."

The next day I hear Uncle E get up at the crack of dawn and leave. I don't have early shift at the café so I stay in bed and dream about being rich. Having new clothes. Buying a new sofa. One that pulls out into a bed. Heck getting a new twin bed. Maybe even a double.

By the time I roust myself and get dressed, it's nearly noon and Uncle E is back in the living room scrutinizing himself in the mirror over my desk.

"You look real good. What's up?" I ask.

"Nothing's up," he says. "I just got back from Peggy's. She gave me a haircut. You being an heiress and all plus the other investments I got going. It's important to keep up appearances."

"Appearances costs money," I say. "I got to thinking with me using my paycheck to pay the inheritance fee, we'll be doubly short this month. You could have gone to Shop and Save and picked up a few things instead of giving Peggy our hard earned cash. You didn't let anything slip did you?"

Uncle E pantomimes zipping his lip. "Nope. You woke up worrying about bills? Don't need to do that," Uncle E says. "We'll soon be on easy street, USA when our money comes. Anyway, I got a deal to help with that. I'll need Dolly later."

"Money tomorrow doesn't pay bills we got today," I say. "And before you go to any appointment you need make more whirligigs. We're down in inventory. I'm calculating that Walter owes fifty for his batch and Allison owes another hundred. If you make a few more, we can catch up with our bills and be A-okay when the money comes."

"But that's what I'm saying. This deal of mine will bring in more than a paltry load of whirligigs. We'll have plenty for our bills and then some."

"That's iffy money. Whirligigs are a sure thing." I protest.

"I can always get a loan to tide us over," Uncle says. "I'll explain about our inheritance."

"We can't. My inheritance is confidential. Besides you're not a good risk."

"I'm a good risk. And it's OUR inheritance."

"You need collateral for a loan. And the email was sent to me."

"I got collateral." Uncle E says. "Our inheritance."

"And I told you it's supposed to be confidential," I warn. "Uncle E? Don't you screw this up for me," I add. "For us."

But Uncle E walks out of the room.

I kick the wall with my bare foot and then hop around until it stops hurting. I've been told people coming into money have confrontations and arguments, but I never thought it would happen to us.

The back door slams shut and I peek out just in time to see Uncle E disappear into the workshop. That's his tactic for when he has no reasonable argument against me and doesn't want to give in, but I'm hoping it also means he's taken what I said to heart and will make more whirligigs. He knows as well as I do they're our real bread and butter if we want cash under the table quick.

"Jar you dressed yet?" I call out. My brother wanders in from the kitchen wearing an inside out hooded sweatshirt and unzipped jeans. He's eating a hand full of Lucky Charms straight out of the box.

"Put that away and come help me with the chickens, Bug." I zip him up. "Now put your sweat shirt on right side up."

"Garbage clown," Jar frowns.

"Too bad if I'm bossy! Somebody around here's got to be."

We go outside.

I fill the feeder and do the water while Jar searches for eggs. The hens feel my ornery mood. The Reds huddle in a group. The Banties are spread out looking for bugs. Cauliflower strolls up to Annie and starts pecking at her. No sign of Benny, but roosters come and go as they please.

"Don't make trouble" I shoo Cauliflower. The minute my back is turned she starts going after the Banties. "You behave!" I grumble. "I got enough characters around here who are in the mood for fighting."

Jar shuts the gate.

"Good job," I say. It's important to tell Jar when he does a good job.

"I'm going over to Allison's and pick up the money she owes us at least," I raise my voice and rap on the workshop door. "You hear me, Uncle E?"

Loud hammering is going on inside but by the rhythm of it I know it's fake. Uncle E's just doing it to make noise. I know he'll be annoyed to hear me taking the truck when he told me he wants it.

"For all the time he spends in there he doesn't get crap done," I say this loudly to Jar hoping to offend Uncle E.

"Carp!" Jar says loudly and giggles.

"I don't hear you!" Uncle E sings out. "And don't be using that language around Jar!"

"I don't hear you more!" I sing back. "And I can say what I want!"

"Carp! Carp! Carp!" Jar claps his hands and hops around in a circle full on laughing now.

"Stop that right now or I'll wash your mouth out with Naphtha!" I pull Jar by the ear around front. The whirligigs on our porch are spinning in the wind.

I get an idea. "Hey, Jar," I say. "We can have a reason to go to Allison's besides just begging for our money. We can take these demo ones from our porch to give her to sell, plus it will double annoy Uncle E," I say. "She might even give us an advance. Kill two birds. Pay on our bills and irk uncle."

Jar claps his hands. Annoying anybody is good fun to him. "Come on Bug," I say.

In two shakes of a lamb's tail, we have the porch stripped and the back end of Dolly full. It makes our place look normal and sort of barren. But it's not like our trailer has ever been in contention to be on the cover of Home and Garden.

Dolly starts right up and we head out. It takes forty-five minutes to get to Allison's as there's road construction, but it doesn't dim my good mood. The whole way I'm calculating. I turn it into a song.

"Walter's fifty plus Allison's hundred she owes, plus what we got here with us in Dolly and we're in like flint this month. EEE I EEE I OOH!" I chortle. "And then when my inheritance comes I am made in the shade."

"Egg way," Jar says.

"Okay then our inheritance," I say. "And we are made in the shade."

When we pull up in front of Allison's her place is dark and the parking lot is empty. There's a sign on her door. *Back In An Hour Or So.*

I pace in front of the truck. "Did she stick that up there a while ago or just now, I wonder." Dolly sits there idling. Well, coughing and sputtering actually.

"Lab mark," Jar says. He's rolling the window up and down.

"But I don't have time to wait around," I tell him. "I got my shift to do. Dang it anyway." I get back into Dolly and smack the steering wheel with my hand. This is purely annoying.

"Carp!" Jar rocks back and forth in the front seat. "No booby."

"You got that right," I say not bothering about his language or warning him about soap. "I should have called first."

I slowly turn Dolly around and head for home. "We'll keep these suckers in the back and deliver them later, I guess."

"Okey dokey!" Jar says happily.

I'm biting my lip all the way back home. I hate wasting gas for no reason. And I hate even more that Uncle

E will be smug at all my work for nothing. I don't want to depend on one of his deals for our bills or sending any money to Dr. Barinas.

I wonder what Barinas is like? I imagine a tall portly man with wire framed glasses wearing a black suit. No a grey suit. With pin stripes. And he has a neatly trimmed beard. But then is it too hot to wear a suit in Africa? I wonder about that for a minute.

When we get back home, I stick rocks under Dolly's wheels and pull my brother along by the shoulder.

"Now you go let Uncle know I'm leaving and remind him again about making more whirligigs. He'll listen to you," I say. "And don't tell him we didn't get the money from Allison."

"Inch wing nut," Jar wags his finger at me.

"It's not childish." I wag mine right back. "We're having an altercation," I say. "Kids bicker and adults have altercations."

I hang by the corner of the trailer and watch as Jar limps over to the workshop. He pokes his head in and then looks back at me. He flaps his hands.

"Organ," he says.

I raise my brows. "He can't be gone. I have the truck. Shoot. He was supposed to keep an eye on you while I'm at work. He must have called Lonnie." I frown.

"Oop swallow," Jar says.

"No way, Jose."

"ACK!" Jar sticks his tongue out at me.

I sigh. "You know very well why. You get into trouble when you're left alone," I say. "But I guess I have to trust you some time. You stay put until Uncle comes back."

"Okey dokey." Jar flicks his fingers at me.

"Well, I guess you'll get walloped if you don't," I warn. "Just so you know, I got a brand new bag of Skittles with your name on it if you're good."

Jar beams and immediately makes an about face and trots into the house. The sound of the TV blaring follows me all the way down the driveway.

Two Spoons is packed when I walk in the door. This will mean decent tips. I cheer up at the thought of being closer to my inheritance. I'm humming as I hang up my coat and tie on my apron.

"Nice of you to join us," Curtis says as he walks by carrying a handful of plates. "Did I forget to issue you an invitation?"

"Invitation?" I'm mystified.

"Yeah invitation." Curtis points at the clock on the wall. "You're two hours late."

I widen my eyes, speechless.

"Being two hours late is a very big *Not Meets,*" Curtis continues. "It's going on your permanent record."

I shake my watch and hold it up to my ear. "It's stopped running. That has to be considered an accident," I say. "It must have broke."

Now I know why I had all the time in the world to go to Allison's, fight with Uncle E, and do chicken chores.

"I'll stay late. I promise! And I'll do the coffee refills, and make the new pots, even the decaf, and do all the side work."

Side work is a job everyone hates. The customers always complain about the coffee and whoever does side work is blamed.

Curtis sets down his plates and comes back. "Being responsible is an important employee quality. The basis for all raises and promotions," he chides.

I start to swallow my back talk and then I remember that I'm going to be rich.

"I am responsible." I stick out my tongue and march into the kitchen. Curtis trots after me.

"Hey!" Curtis says. "HEY! It's impolite to walk out of the room and stick out your tongue when somebody's talking. I'm making a point of sharing my managerial views with you," he says.

"What do managerial views have to do with being late?" I ask. "And who cares what you think anyway?" I toss my braid around.

"Talking back to your employer is a *not meets expectations*," he says. "A very BIG *not meets expectations*."

"Stuff it!" I feel powerful. When my inheritance comes, I won't need to listen to Curtis.

"Well!" Curtis says and stalks out of the kitchen.

I stare after him and smile. I guess Curtis doesn't know how to handle someone standing up to him.

Leo walks up to me with a tray of soup.

"He's sure in a snit," I say and take the tray.

"Don't mind him. He's just worried about the new bypass. But you know Curtis." Leo shrugs. "He's always in a snit about something. These go to table seven."

After I deliver the soups, I notice Curtis' furrowed brow.

"Business is real good," I say and wave my hand airily. "We're packed to the gills with customers."

"We won't be when they finish that bypass," Curtis says darkly. "An article in the Tribune says they're adding a second shift to finish faster."

"Nothing the government does gets finished faster, you know that."

Curtis frowns. "The bypass will be an exception. The Tribune said it'll be completed in three months."

"Then we ought to raise a little hell! Tell the state it isn't right," I say. "Anyway you're set. People always have to eat. This place stands out. And aren't you moving to LA anyway?"

"I'm not there yet." Curtis scowls. "And it's not good for Leo. Cars won't have an opportunity to stop at his place. No exit near enough and they won't double back."

It's when he turns to go back to the kitchen that I see the slump in his shoulders. But then Curtis is a sad sack from the get go.

I smile. That stupid old bypass won't affect me. *I'm going to be rich.*

Soon I'm running my legs off. Squeezing between tables and daydreaming as I take orders. Handing out waters here and menus there. The whole while, I'm floating on air. *I'm going to be rich any day now.* Kev is back with another group of crubs.

"Well, you look happy tonight," Kev says to me. "What's the scoop?"

"No scoop." I try to look serious. "Soup is Egg drop-grits gruel," I say. "Leo says it's that new fusion cooking. Asia running smack into Alabama."

I grab the coffee pot and make the circuit topping off cups with fancy ideas of what I can buy with my inheritance in my head. I feel a big grin on my face. I don't look where I'm going and run smack into a customer. And it isn't any customer. It's my cousin Lonnie.

The grin slides off my face. "Well, just exactly what I don't need," I say. Part of me is annoyed but a small part of me is glad. If Lonnie is here, he can't be with Uncle E.

"Well, hello. Cousin Tammy." Lonnie's voice is as oily as his hair. "How's the little moron? I hear he got lost." Lonnie staggers over to a table and slides in tipping over the salt and pepper shakers with a clatter. A waft of alcohol drifts up. Construction workers at the next table look over.

"What are you idiots staring at?" Lonnie glares at them.

They look away.

"What'll you have?" I say to Lonnie. "And you better have the money to pay."

I keep my tone even. Lonnie drunk is likely to cause a scene and I won't put Leo and Curtis through that. Not today.

"Coffee and the special," Lonnie slurs.

I fill his upturned cup and the coffee sloshes. It spills down his shirt.

"Hey!" Lonnie cries. "No need to get pissy!" He dabs at his front.

A shadow looms. It's Kev. "You need a hand, Tammy Louise?" Kev's beard and fuzzy hat makes him look Russian. He stares fixedly at Lonnie who's still rubbing coffee stains off his shirt.

"Nope," I say. "Just a little friendly cousin back and forth. No harm, no foul."

"Well, okay then," Kev says. "We'll all have the pot pies. And extra ketchup." He goes back to his seat.

Later when I deliver Kev's food, he takes me aside. "You let me know if that cousin of yours gives you any more guff. I'll take care of him," he says. "I've beaten up men smaller than me before. I don't mind taking advantage."

I smile at him. "I don't need any help with my cousin. But thanks," I say and head into the kitchen.

It makes me sad to think back to how it used to be. After our folks died? Lonnie was like an older brother. He showed me and Jar how to sneak through the bushes and make forts in the woods. Which trees were the best to climb. Where the berries grew best. He thought Jar was real cute. But that all changed when Lonnie got older. He made new friends and didn't need us. I swallow hard.

Another herd of construction guys bustles through the door. I seat them in the middle of the room. "Hey, there, Sweetie," one of them says. The others laugh. They order the specials.

"Some crook stole a truck off the site today."

"Last week my toolbox was taken."

"This town is full of crooks."

I close my ears to their conversation and focus on one thing. I'm coming into money. A lot of money.

I see Curtis stop at Lonnie's table. The two of them are talking. This is surprising. Usually Curtis won't give Lonnie the time of day.

Next thing I know Lonnie is gone and Curtis is standing there holding Lonnie's chit. "He told me you were good for it," Curtis says.

"I never said that." My good mood and daydreams vanish. "It's not fair that Lonnie's meals comes out of my paycheck," I protest.

"Your cousin," Curtis says.

"Once removed," I remind him.

Curtis studies me and says slowly. "Maybe I can let it go this time. Coffees need refills. Do you want me to do it or do you have time?"

Now I'm thinking Curtis is developing a brain tumor. Letting Lonnie's chit go and offering help.

"I have time." I say and straighten the hem of my skirt. "I'm sorry for talking back and I'm sorry I was late this morning. I guess that gives me a gazillion *not meets*." I take the pot from him.

"Something like," Curtis says.

I watch him disappear into the kitchen, then I leave the pot on the counter and quickly sign into my email account. Another garage cleaning offer. I use the café phone to schedule it for next Saturday morning. I'm just about to sign out when I'm distracted by a soft chime that tells me I have a new email. I quickly hunch over the screen.

IMPORTANT
CONFIDENTIAL
BOTSWANA UNION BANK
MS **TYREE**

THANKYOU FOR THE NOTICE OF YOUR FINANCIAL REMITTANCE. WE ARE ARRANGING SUITABLE CONVEINIENCE TO TRANSMIT CURENCY INTO AND AWAY FROM YOUR ACCOUNT ELECTRONICALLY AT YOUR AFOREMENTIONED FINANCIAL INSTITUTION FOR REMITTANCE OF YOUR INHERITANCE MONETARY SETTLEMENT. THE DEPARTMENT OF TAXATION REQUIRES AUTHORITY TO AUTHORIZE PAYMENT. AN MINOR ADDITIONAL PROCESSING FEE IN THE AMOUNT OF 150 AMERICAN DOLLARS IS NECESSARY TO ENSURE DOCUMENTS.

DR. BARINAS
EXECUTOR AND MINISTER
FAITH BASED CHARITY GOVERNMENTAL DEPARTMENT
PO BOX 2145 GABARONE, BOTSWANA
GABARONE, BOTSWANA

A hundred and fifty dollars more? It isn't minor to me. My heart sinks. I print it out and stuff it into my pocket. It's then I remember Jar's all by himself. I have to get home. Curtis stands between me and the front door.

"I need to get my jacket," I say.

Curtis is staring at me. "Is it true?" he says. "What I heard from that cousin of yours?"

My heart starts thudding. "Lonnie lies like a snake," I say. And then. "What did you hear?"

"That you and that uncle of yours are coming into money. That you've been left an inheritance from relatives."

"No. No. And double no," I tell him. That dang Uncle E. He had to let something slip to Lonnie and loose-lipped Lonnie said something to Curtis.

I dodge to the side and snatch my jacket.

"That's just what happens when people get rich. They get close mouthed and tight fisted," Curtis says.

"Tightfisted? You are hallucinating," I say. "I'm not rich." Yet, I think.

My face must have given me away.

"You can't fool me, Tammy Louise," Curtis says. "You denying it doesn't make any difference."

"I said no and I mean no," I say.

"So you can swear on the bible you're not getting money from a relative?"

I hesitate.

"Ah HA!" Curtis says. "I knew it. Your cousin Lonnie told me you'd be coy about it."

I brush past him and charge out the door. Confidential, shmonfidential. I got a bone to pick with Uncle E.

CHAPTER EIGHT

Uncle E knows I want to give him an earful and makes a point of avoiding me all weekend. But uncle's shenanigans are pushed right out of my mind when bright and early Monday morning I get a phone call our electricity is being turned off. They have to warn you so you'll know you'll be cold. The heat is no big deal as it's nearly summer, but cooking and seeing is important.

I call right away. Begging and pleading. "Didn't you get my check?" I say to the lady who answers the phone. "It's in the mail. Must have gotten lost. I'll send another one." My fingers are crossed. She gives me an extra week.

Lying is a sin. I vow to put money in the church collection plate as soon as my inheritance comes and just as soon as I pick a church to go to.

That afternoon I shame Walter into paying what he owes, add it to my tips, write a check for cash at the bank using the last bit in our account and mail the one fifty off to Africa. There. Now there's nothing to do but wait for my money to come.

I leave a note for Uncle E in the workshop. *We need to talk,* is what it says. I'm excited about the future. About being rich. But I have today to worry about. Uncle E's disappearing acts aren't making it any easier.

Tuesday dawns sunny for a change but I know that means it'll rain real good later. Breakfast shift at Two Spoons is busy. Curtis is wrong about us losing business. I pass by the mirror and glance at my reflection. I have a goofy smile on my face. I'm so startled, I drop the plate of eggs I'm carrying. I bend over to clean it up and flip over a tray of pastries setting there on the counter.

"Coffee's overflowing!" Curtis yells. "Someone forgot to put the filter in!"

That was me. I forgot to put the filter in. I rush over to clean it up and then take my pad over to Peggy Rutledge who's taken over the corner booth. I'm surprised, as she doesn't usually favor frequenting Two Spoons. She calls the café low class.

"Hey, there, Peggy what will you have?" I ask

"Oh, the special, I guess." She flutters her lashes at the table of construction workers across the room. "But I probably can't eat it all. I have such a delicate appetite."

I bite my tongue. Peggy's as delicate as a heavyweight boxer.

I come back with her soup and set it down in front of her. She stares at it and back to me.

"What's that?" Her eyes are big.

"Cold Gazpacho of orange juice and leftover sausage."

She blanches. "No thanks. Orange juice gives me gas," she says. "And cold sausage is only good on leftover pizza."

"You know Leo and his soups," I warn.

"Well, then, be a friend and get rid of it for me."

"Throwing food away is a waste," I say. "There's starving kids in Ethiopia."

"Fine," she says. "You're perfectly welcome to send it on over to them."

I can't help but smile imagining Leo's soup stuffed in an envelope and mailed to Ethiopia. And then thinking of that, makes me think of Botswana. My heart starts thudding.

Peggy studies me closely. "You coming by the shop later? I got some work for you."

"Yeah, sure," I say. Usually I have to ask her if I should come in, not the other way around.

"What are you looking so cat's-got-a-mouse for? You got secrets?" Her tone is casual.

"Nope," I say. "No secrets."

"By the by that uncle of yours came in for a haircut. He looked just like you do. Said something about a ship coming in."

"He did?" I squeak.

"Anything you want to tell me?"

"Nope," I say. "Not a thing. Nada. Nothing." I'm blabbering. "I'll get your eggs and muffin," I say. "I mean the special."

When I come back, Peggy has scooted her chair over and joined the construction workers' table. I notice her soup bowl is empty.

I slide her plate of food in front of her and top off the coffees.

"Did you hear that, Tammy? Foreman said they're waiting on police to come. Got someone stealing materials," Peggy says.

"Probably one of their own men," I say. "And they'll be waiting forever if it's Clarence they've called for," I snicker.

The workers mutter amongst themselves.

Peggy widens her eyes. "I get nervous at just the thought of criminal elements lurking around."

A dark haired construction worker leans across the table. "I can walk you home if you like, Ma'am."

I stare. Peggy has men clustered around her like flies on a sticky trap.

I head back in the kitchen to collect my last couple of orders. Curtis is standing there talking with Leo. They stop when I come through the door.

"I just have these and then I'm through. Did you need me to stay for lunch? I can go to Peggy's after," I say.

"No go on," Curtis waves. "It'll be slow."

That means I'll have time to go on up to the trailer and check on Jar. I smile. Any other time I'd be disappointed as I'd want the hours, but with me coming into money, I'm cheerful.

When I catch Curtis staring at me, I quickly turn away. I grab my coat and run out the door. I don't even say goodbye to Peggy.

I trot all the way up the hill to the trailer. When I get to the porch, I'm breathless.

"Hey, there, Bug," I say as I come through the door.

Jar is sitting on the couch watching Price Is Right.

"Bye per! Bye per!" Jar sticks his finger in the air. That means higher. Either that or it means he has to go number two. His arms are decorated with black and red pen marks. "Okey dokey," he says as soon as he sees me.

"Good job for staying out of trouble." I give his head a rub. "Those are mighty fine tattoos." I lick my finger and rub dirt off his nose. "You're just like Leo. All you need is a bad attitude and a motorcycle."

"Syco," Jar agrees.

I take a deep breath. "Now listen up. I don't have time for any of your hi-jinks today," I warn him. "I'm going over to Peggy's. I can't have you chucking rocks, breaking store windows, and having Walter or anybody else press charges, forcing Officer Smithers to arrest you, so you have to go to juvey, or worse I end up with a fine I can't pay."

I squeeze my brother's cheeks together and make him look me straight in the eye. "You want to go to juvey like cousin Lonnie?" I ask.

Jar gulps like a fish and shakes his head.

"I thought not." I let him go and give him a gentle cuff on his ear. "You hang out with Uncle E in his workshop or keep watching TV, okay? We'll make an inside fort later on with blankets and chairs and we can have a living room camp out tonight with Skittles and everything. How about that?"

His expression brightens. "Forp," he sings happily. Jar loves making forts above nearly all things.

"Stay or no more Skittles!" I warn. I head out the door.

Before I head down the driveway, I take a peep around back and see Uncle E's workshop door is closed, but the light is on. It means he's in there. I'd sure like to have a face to face about paying those bills we got hanging above our heads. And we need to discuss how we're going to handle finances when my inheritance. Our inheritance arrives.

I frown.

But then, maybe Uncle E is right. Maybe I'm worrying too much. We're coming into money, after all. I think about this all the way back down the hill and over to Peggy's. It turns into another *Rich, Rich I'm gonna be Rich,* song.

When I come through the door Peggy gives me a wide smile.

"How you been, Tammy?" she says.

I stop. "No different than when you saw me at breakfast," I say cautiously.

Peggy's chair is empty and I get an idea. I feel the bulge in my pockets from my tip money.

"Actually I'm real good, Peggy. I think today, instead of working, I'll be a paying customer. Going to get a trim."

Her mouth drops open. I smile broadly. This is worth any amount of money. I settle myself into Peggy's empty chair.

"Just like your uncle the other day," Peggy muses. She shakes out a cloth and lays it over my chest.

"That so?" I say. It's best to play a little dumb.

Peggy undoes my braid and holds it up. "Hair's awful thick. How about I thin it and then give you a perm?"

"I don't think so." I shake my head.

"How about wave?" she wheedles. "Just an itty bitty one?" She combs me out.

"No way. I saw what you did to Sue Ann. She looks like a dandelion gone to seed."

Peggy sniffs. "You don't have to be nasty about it. Fine hair doesn't take real good to chemicals." She starts snipping aggressively. I'm hoping she won't slice me with her scissors.

"So anything new?" she asks.

"No," I say quickly. "Nothing at all.

"Nothing?" she lifts one eyebrow.

And suddenly, I don't know, I just can't help it. "Can you keep a secret?" I ask.

Peggy stops mid-snip. "What kind of a secret?"

"Any kind," I say.

"What do you mean by any kind? Like I wouldn't, if it was illegal, or maybe something I think somebody else ought to know, like if a husband was messing around. That's a secret I wouldn't keep or maybe—"

"Oh, for pity's sake, listen!" I say. "A normal secret. Can you keep it under wraps?"

But it isn't a normal secret. I smile.

Peggy crosses her fingers. "Hope to die. Absolutely." Peggy isn't looking me in the eye.

And then suddenly I know. "Did Uncle E tell you about my inheritance?"

"No. Not really. Only a little. Like he might have said you had a missionary relation who died and left you money."

"I knew it! He told! He wasn't supposed to." I nearly hop out of the chair.

"It doesn't matter. I won't say a word. How much is it?" Peggy asks.

"It was confidential," I say. "Highly confidential. And it's a lot."

"I get it. It's confidential," Peggy waves her hand. "How much is a lot and when will you get it?"

"I got an email bout it. It's complicated. All these fees to pay and important questions to answer to claim it. You know probation or protraction or something. And it's five million dollars."

"Five million?" Peggy's lips form a pout. "Some people have all the luck. What are you going to do when you get the money? Buy a fancy house and move away? Travel? What?"

"Well," I hesitate. "I hadn't given it much thought," I lie. "I expect I'll have to give a bunch to charity being as it came from an evangelical and all."

"That's a waste." Peggy frowns. "You know what they say. Charity begins at home. You should spread it around Spring."

"Well, I guess—"

Peggy interrupts. "I know what I'd do. First, I'd get liposuction and then buy a ton of new clothes and, let me see." Peggy closes her eyes and wrinkles her brow. "And replace the washers and dryers. And get a new outfit. Heck, I'd get ten! A hundred! That's what stimulates the economy you know. Spending."

"I guess that I'd—"

"Shush!" Peggy says. "I'm not finished. And maybe hire a girl to help out. That's the providing jobs part of the economy."

"You got a girl," I say. "Me."

"I mean a real girl. One with training. Maybe a manicurist. What will you do?"

I think hard. "Pay off all our bills. And Uncle E and I discussed getting a new truck and I might even buy a car for myself."

"What kind?" Peggy's eyes are bright like a bird searching for seed.

"Something sporty. Maybe like your Mustang," I say. "But gold or green, not red. You get pulled over by the cops if you drive a red car."

"They got some new ones in at the dealership. We could go by," Peggy says eagerly.

I shake my head. "Not so fast. It's complicated like I told you. I need to actually get the money. And I know there'll be plenty of papers to sign." I give a finger wave like I know what I'm talking about. I catch sight of my reflection and pause. "Maybe even get myself some serious plastic surgery." That last one is a new idea I just thought of.

She studies me. "What would you have done?"

"I don't know," I admit.

She swivels me over to the mirror and stand behind. "Forehead? Nope it's fine. Eyebrows? They just need a pluck." She reaches for the tweezers.

"Ouch!" I yelp.

"Oh, hush," Peggy says. "There that's more like it."

She stares at me. "Highlights," she says with finality. "Now you just hang tight."

Peggy paints chunks of my hair and wraps it in foil. She puts me under a dryer and goes back to looking at my face. "Nose job? Chin augmentation? Nope," she shakes her head.

After she rinses the color out, she shampoos me and gets busy with her scissors.

"I won't take no for an answer," she says.

I end up looking like I been reborn. My hair is still long but the ends are slightly curled. She's layered it around my face. The highlights brighten my eyes. I look more than passable. Almost good.

"Thank you Peggy," I say slowly. "What do I owe you?"

Peggy nibbles on her lip as she pulls the plastic cover off my shoulders. She looks dissatisfied. Like she's jealous. I'm not used to having people being jealous of me and it feels good. I stand up. I'm a bit worried. This makeover will be more than my tips, I'm certain. I pull out my check book. "How much?" I ask again.

Peggy waves her hand. "Nothing. It's on the house," she says.

"You're kidding," I say.

"Now, why in the world would I be kidding? Consider it a present. To make sure you don't forget us little folk when you get all high and mighty and rich." Peggy says.

"Thank you, then, " I say carefully and slide my checkbook back in my pocket.

I walk home slowly. Peggy finds out I'm coming into money and she gives me a free make over? Hells bells. And then I start feeling guilty. I let the cat out of the bag. I didn't keep things confidential. I pass our mailbox and stop. Maybe there's a check in there already. My inheritance might have already arrived. I run back to the box and grab everything out. There's a thick buff envelope from the bank. It's addressed to Uncle E, but I open it anyway as I head up to the trailer. A coupon book drops to the ground. I bend over and pick it up. LOAN PAYMENT BOOK $345 DUE ON THE 15th. $375 Due after the 25th. What in the world?

My mouth runs dry as I read the enclosed papers. I see the word mortgage and the words fifteen thousand dollars. Uncle E went and used our property as collateral. It was the one thing we owned free and clear and he pledged it for a measly fifteen thousand dollars. I'm so steamed my hands are shaking. He did all this without consulting me.

"Uncle E!" I charge the rest of the way up the driveway.

Jar meets me halfway. "Forp?" he sings.

I march past him. "I don't have time for no forps! I got words for Uncle E. Now scoot inside."

He stands in front of me barring my way. "Forp," he says again. There's a stubborn gleam in his eye. When my brother gets an idea, he hangs on tighter than a burr on a dog's butt.

"No forps!" My tone is sharp. "Now git!"

Jar skulks away, sending me dark looks.

I march to the workshop and kick uncle's door open. A haze of dust wafts up.

"Uncle E?" The bare light bulb swings above me. "You and me got to have a talk."

My uncle is in his chair leaning forward on the worktable. His head is resting on his hammer. "That's got to be uncomfortable," I say.

Uncle E doesn't answer. I swing the door back and forth letting in some air and then wave my hand in front of my face.

"Pee-ew!" I tell him. "It stinks in here! No offence, but have you been eating beans?"

Uncle E still doesn't answer.

"Don't go all silent on me. It's not like we're having a real fight," I say. "But I do have a bone to pick with you. This mortgage deal? What's up with that?" And I shake the papers in front of him. I step closer. Uncle's eyes are closed.

"You asleep?" I give him a push. "Wake up," I say. But my uncle doesn't wake up. Fact is, he tips right over and hits the floor, chair, and all. When I grab his arm, it's stiff and cold. Uncle E is dead.

I sink to my knees. "Uncle E you lousy son of a bitch!" I cry. "You two bit no account piece of shit!" I beat the floor with my hands. "What in the world are we going to do now," I moan. "What in the world?"

And that's all there is to say about that.

CHAPTER NINE

It doesn't seem possible Uncle E is gone. Fact is, I know everybody's got to die at some point, but I really had a feeling Uncle E would be the exception. I'm sure he did, too.

Jar and I sit on our porch with the urn of ashes between us. Blue Oyster Cult's *Don't Fear the Reaper* is blasting on an old cassette tape. It was Uncle E's favorite song. Well, that, and Johnny Cash singing *A Boy Named Sue*. I give the urn a good tip back and forth. Uncle E's surprisingly heavy.

"This is what's left of Uncle E," I tell Jar. "He's gone."

"Okey dokey." Jar shrugs.

"No he won't be back," I say. "He's not at Silver King and he's not taken Dolly. See? She's sitting plain as day in our driveway."

Jar frowns. He slides down off the porch and trots over to our truck. First, he checks her front seat and then the bed. He even opens the egg cooler and peers in.

"Uncle E isn't hiding. Besides he can't fit in there." I shake my head. "Use some common sense."

Jar crawls down the steps and looks under the porch like he's thinking Uncle E's playing a game of hide and seek with us.

"Hopper great?" Jar calls.

"He can't fit there either," I say.

Jar gets to his feet and his forehead wrinkles. Next thing I know he's jumping up and down and pointing. "Lop poop!" he yells and flaps his hands.

A gold Cutlass is making its way up our driveway.

"I know it's cousin Lonnie," I tell Jar. "But Uncle E isn't with him." My flags of caution are flying high and I reach over and give my uncle's urn a hug for courage.

There's a soft squeak and clunk as Lonnie sets the brake. He gets out. His tall thin frame looks bent.

"Looks like you been rode hard and put away hot," I say.

He gives a grim smile. "Not far from the truth," he says.

"Guess you heard the news about Uncle E."

Lonnie clears his throat. "You guess right."

"We would have called if we knew where you were." I cross my fingers. That was only a tiny white lie.

Jar blows a big raspberry at Lonnie. "Fu you!" he says and darts off.

"Don't you dare say that!" I snatch Jar's pant leg as he goes by. "I'll wash your mouth out with Naphtha!" I threaten. Jar skedaddles around back.

"He alright?" Lonnie asks.

"He's looking for Uncle E. Probably checking inside the coop now." I raise my voice so Jar can hear. "And he better not be saying that F word anymore! Or I'll give somebody I know a blistered bottom."

"Didn't you tell him?" Lonnie asks.

"Of course, but he doesn't understand," I say. "Or doesn't want to. He's fooling himself. Maybe it's better that way."

Lonnie plucks a strand of grass and gets to chewing on it. "You sure got him figured."

"You did pretty good yourself back in the day," I admit. "Teaching him fort building was your idea."

"That was a long, long time ago," Lonnie says.

"That and running off into the woods getting out of chores. Lucky for me Jar's afraid of the dark or else he'd never come out."

Lonnie looks away. "Yeah, well," he says.

I kick the porch with my heel. "We're gonna spread Uncle E's ashes now," I say. "You're welcome to join us."

Lonnie shrugs. "Maybe I will. Good you're doing it that way. Uncle E wouldn't like being cooped up in a casket."

"Plus it's cheaper," I say. "Coffins cost nearly a thousand and then there's the grave. These cardboard urns come with the cremation and we can spread him for free." I lift the urn up. "Come on, then."

We go around to the back yard. Jar is standing in the middle of the yard surrounded by chickens. His brow is furrowed. "EEE?" he calls.

"Uncle E's going in the woods," I put the urn under my arm. "Come on with us."

"Clucker!" Jar says. "Okey dokey."

"Sure the chickens can come," I say. "But leave Cauliflower in the coop. We don't want our ankles bit."

But of course, Jar ignores that. Cauliflower and him have a relationship I guess.

The three of us tromp into the woods following the old logging road up the hill. The chickens are tangled in our feet. A doe leaps across the path making us all jump.

I press my hand against my chest. "Uncle E's ghost," I say.

"No," Lonnie shakes his head. "Uncle E would be a bear or a mountain lion."

"More like a raccoon," I smile. "A rascal always getting into mischief."

The three of us crisscross through the forest looking for likely places Uncle would want to be. When we find one, we sprinkle some ashes. The breeze is makes it cheerful even though it's a cloudy day.

Jar provides sound effects. "WEEEE!" he cries tossing ashes in the air.

"Jar, stop throwing Uncle E around like chicken feed," I say.

"Maybe he don't understand how you got to be solemn when dealing with death," Lonnie says.

I study my brother. "He sure is having fun." Jar's hands are smudged with grey. "Don't be licking your fingers!" I warn. "Or Uncle E will go right through you."

"The hens are the same," says Lonnie. "Half of Uncle E is going down their gullets."

Sure enough, I see them race to the spot where Jar is flinging handfuls. Pecking away.

"Shoo!" I wave my hands.

When the urn is empty, we walk back. My steps get shorter and slower. I want to stretch this out. This person here is the old Lonnie. The one I used to know. The one I looked up to. I want it to stay like this between us. I give him a sideways glance and he catches my eye and smiles for real. There's a lump in my throat.

Back at the trailer, I take my time banging the last of Uncle E out along our fence line. I hold up the container. "This is a nice shape and size. A shame to throw it away," I say. "It could come in useful."

I'm thinking maybe I'll invite cousin Lonnie for supper. I open my mouth to issue an invitation, but then I stop. Lonnie is looking at our trailer appraisingly. Hands in his pockets. Head tilted back.

"I need to know where Uncle E kept his cash. We had a deal going," Lonnie says smoothly. "How much life insurance did he have?"

"None," I say.

"What about this inheritance I'm hearing about. Who'd Uncle E leave his share to?"

"There is no inheritance," I say real quick. "And there is no shares."

Lonnie stares at me appraisingly. "I heard different," he says.

"You heard wrong," I say.

Lonnie shrugs. He takes out a cigarette and lights up. "When are you going to sell this place and get out of Spring?" he asks

"We're not," I say carefully. "And Uncle E put everything he had into that stupid weather machine deal that you talked him into. Every dime." I say this firmly. "There's nothing left."

Lonnie stares at me, and then gives a long low laugh. "You never could lie to save your life," he says. "But we can talk about that later."

"There'll be no talking," I say and follow him to the Cutlass. When he opens the door, I notice the back seat is piled high with construction tools and orange highway cones.

Lonnie sees me looking. His face turns hard. He pulls a tarp over to cover it.

I'm suddenly tired. Tired and far sadder than I was. That fort building Lonnie, that fun loving Lonnie, that kind and considerate Lonnie, is as dead and gone as Uncle E. I turn tail and march back to the trailer without saying goodbye. I hear the crackle of gravel as Lonnie drives off.

Later that night, I sit Jar down at the kitchen table and grab both his hands. He tries to wriggle away, but I hold on tight.

"Listen up!" I say. "You and me need to have a little chat," I tell him. "Things are going to be different now without Uncle E around."

"Okey dokey," Jar says.

"No, he's not coming back," I say. "That's not the way it works. You got to trust me on that one."

"Gum boot," he says.

"Well, for one thing whirligig making will be up to me," I tell him. "And the chicken chores and all the yard work are your job, at least until my inheritance comes. And I have to figure out how to keep you in line when I'm off at work."

"Clip." Jar says.

"You know darn well what I'm talking about. You running off and getting lost," I say. "Not to mention the stone throwing and the window breaking. You're fifteen. You got to start acting like it."

"Okey dokey," Jar starts rocking back and forth. I feel bad.

The stone throwing had been Uncle E's idea. It was not long after our parents were killed.

He'd led us out into the back yard and scooped up a rock.

"Let me tell you something. A body's life is like this here pebble," Uncle E had said. And he leaned back and hefted it up toward the sky. He really let her fly. It went high up in the air, hesitated briefly, and then it fell back down to earth.

"You have the beginning, which is you being born. Nobody has control over that," Uncle E explained. "Watch close." And he tossed another.

"Keep your eyes peeled. Notice how it slows before it gets to the top?" He tossed another and another. "Lookee now. It's starting on down. It's like life. The steeper it falls, the worse it is for a body. That highest point is called a peak. Everybody's got some kind of peak to their lives, but often times they don't recognize it until they're on the way down. Unfortunate that is."

And Uncle E dusted off his hands.

"You can think of them rocks as messages to heaven. It lets your folks know you're thinking of them. That you need their council," he said. "Now you try." And he handed a pebble to each of us. As I tossed pebbles into the air, it felt good inside to think I was letting Momma and Daddy know they weren't forgotten. And I held on to the hope my life would only get better from there.

That inheritance money from Dr. Barinas will be the start of good things for both of us. I can dream on that.

My brother reaches into his pocket and pulls out a rock. He offers it to me and I take it. It's a pretty one. All flecked with mica. It glitters.

"Jar," I say. "I know that you miss Uncle E. If throwing stones will make you feel better and let Uncle E know we miss him, I guess you can do that. But not here in the kitchen. Only outside in our yard. And not at any living creature. Or at a window or nothing. Understand?" I stare at my brother.

"Okey dokey," Jar murmurs. He gets back to rocking from side to side. I know that means he's having worries. That things aren't going the way he'd anticipated. Well, that makes two of us.

I leave him there in the kitchen and walk outside, the rock Jar gave me in my hand.

The lowering sun puts me up on stilts. The chickens are spread over the back yard. I watch them hunt for bugs.

"Lucky for you there isn't a fox lurking." I settle down on the back steps. The chickens cluster around and I pet their backs when they come close. "How you doing? I don't have any scratch for you. Or no ashes either."

My chest is tight and achy. When I catch sight of Uncle E's darkened workshop, my throat chokes up. Uncle was a ton of trouble. He never picked up after himself. He was loud mouthed. He bought anything from any salesman who wandered through town.

"Got to give them encouragement, Sissy," he'd tell me. "Otherwise they'd give up."

Encouragement. He gave that to me when I'd come home from school crying because a group of boys had roughed me up at the bus stop.

"Stop that blubbering, wipe those tears up, and listen to me." He sat me down on the porch and gave me what for. "People are going to underestimate you, Tammy, because of your size and being a girl and, well, because you're a Tyree and all. That will be to your advantage. You remember that."

"Advantage? How?" I'd wiped my snotty nose on my sleeve.

"You need to learn to defend yourself," he'd said. "And I'm gonna teach you." And he led me out to the back yard.

"First of all make certain you can finish what you start," he said. "If you get a swarm of bees riled up, it's difficult to put them all back into the hive. You got to know your limitations. Now pay attention."

And Uncle E proceeded to demonstrate five of what he called upper thuds to the jawbone, and seven lower thomps to the neck, and then showed me twenty-six different ways to put a man on his knees, if you catch my drift. I have to say I was a quick learner.

Uncle E admired my skill. "Another talent you got!" he'd said. "It's quite an advantage."

I stare at my fingers now and curl them tightly into a fist. *Advantage.* It always seemed something other people had.

The chickens are crooning. Clucking amongst themselves. Assuring me that, unlike my own set of circumstances, they've all been fine and dandy. That life overall is good for them. That there's no cause for any poor spirits in their vicinity. Annie struts up to me. I tickle her soft downy breast and pull her close. She brocks low and soft.

"Uncle E's gone," I whisper to the side of her head. "He died doing what he liked best. Drinking and making whirligigs. I won't be able to talk with him anymore. None of his stupid jokes. Won't be able to ask him about what he knows about our family or things that happened in the past. It will all stay a mystery," I say. "Everything's a mystery."

Annie nibbles at my cheek as if she agrees.

It begins to drizzle. And then it starts to come down hard. Drops spatter on the roof like drum beats. Uncle E liked rain.

"Freshens things up, Sissy," he used to say. "Washes away the dirt. Gives us all a brand new start."

A brand new start. I swallow hard. Uncle E was a real pain, as I think on it. Yes sir, he got us into a lot of trouble. Tickets for parking Dolly in the wrong places. Forgetting to fill her up with gas. His drunken sprees.

I rub my face across Annie's feathers.

"You and the rest of the girls haven't any worries, now," I whisper. "No more Uncle E stepping on your babies, or pulling your tail feathers, or scaring you silly with singing at the wee hours of the morning. It's all good for you, now I guess. You be sure and pass it on to Benny when he comes around," I whisper to her. "I'm sure he'd appreciate knowing."

I set Annie down and sit there until it turns dark, until I can take in air without my breath catching, until I can see without a blur of water in my eyes. Then I clear my throat of its frogs, wipe off my face with the edge of my shirt, and toss the rock that Jar gave me high into the air. Then I scoop another rock up off the ground and pitch it, too, upwards into the night sky. And then I scoop up another. I toss rock after rock upwards.

"I love you Uncle E," I call up to the stars. "And I'm thinking on you."

My eyes are dry. There's no use crying.

I learned that lesson real good when Momma and Daddy died. There was never any use to crying then, and there's no use in crying now.

CHAPTER TEN

Things are different without Uncle E.

"You have to stay inside while I'm at work," I say to Jar. It's important to keep my tone serious so Jar knows I'm not kidding but not so serious as he gets mutant. "Watch TV. Don't be messing around, or traipsing off, and no rock throwing," I tell him.

"Pompom?" Jar tips his head sideways.

"I told you already. I have to be at work in twenty minutes." I'm still in my robe.

I take a shower, but when my hair is all lathered, the steamy hot turns frigid. Water heater is on the fritz again. Shivering, I quickly reach out for the soap. It's only a sliver. I need to buy more. A chill gives me goose bumps all over my body. No clean dry towels in sight and the laundry is piled high in the corner. My uniform sits on top in a crumpled ball. There's a gravy stain on the skirt. I try to scrub it out, but it stubbornly stays. That's a lack of employee cleanliness, which in Curtis's book is a very big *not meets.* I look at my watch. I'm already late. My phone rings and I quickly pick up before Jar can grab it.

"Tammy speaking."

"Hey, there. It's Allison. That Uncle of yours gonna bring me by some more whirligigs?" I guess the Flea Market Emporium is another place that didn't get the news.

"Hey, there, Allison. I'm afraid not," I say. "Uncle E's passed on."

"Gosh that's a shame," Allison says. "Was it sudden?"

I hesitate. No good repeating what the coroner said. Between the unseasonably cold weather along with a habit of alcohol consumption, Uncle E was probably dead for three or four days near as he could tell. The persistent garbage burn barrel smell and chicken coop odor meant I couldn't come up with a better time line.

"I guess you might say he lingered," I tell Allison and cross my fingers. It's close enough to the truth.

"Well, then," Allison says slowly. "I don't want to bother you in your bereavement, but I did give your uncle an advance for the next batch as he said he was short. It was 50 bucks. You either need to pay me back, or give me the merchandise."

So, instead of Allison owing us, we owe Allison? I frown.

"But I'll need another load before the end of the month," she continues brightly. "Can you do that or should I find another supplier?"

"We can do it," I say with all the confidence I don't feel. "I got a batch ready to go." Another white lie.

"You sure?" Allison says.

"Sure I'm sure."

"I'd like to help you out then. Can you up the count to thirty-five? I got the Farmers' Market coming up."

I gulp. Thirty-five? I never made a single whirligig. Well, maybe sanding and painting. But none of the putting together. "No problem," I say. When I hang up, I'm sweating.

I'm thankful it's a busy morning at Two Spoons, but I still spend half the time peeking out the window to make sure Jar's not running loose. The worry of it gives me a bellyache. On my break, I check my email. I'm cheered to get a missive from Barinas.

Finally.

The good news is he received all of my payments. The bad news is he made a mistake and left out a zero. It wasn't 150 I needed to pay. It was 1500. I owe 1350 more. But the good news is it's all set up so it can be deducted right out of my checking account as soon as I give him the word. Deducted that is if I had it in there. I frown.

After work, I don't stay to make small talk with Leo or Curtis. I go straight home to check on Jar and agonize over needing to come up with more money. I'm afraid if I don't, they'll send my inheritance on to someone else.

On my way up the driveway, I grab the mail out of the box. Even more bills, plus there are invoices from the beer joints Uncle E favored. One for thirty-five fifty from the Silver King, another for fifty-two from Dot's Tavern, and still another for twenty-six bucks from the Buzz Bar. Uncle E was charging his booze even with the cash I gave him. There's also a reminder notice from the bank. The loan payment is past due.

When I walk inside the TV is blaring, but Jar is nowhere in sight. I drop the mail on the table, switch off the TV, and head outside.

I start with the coop. "Jar?" I yell. "Where are you?" The chickens scatter as I fling open the gate to their pen. It rattles on its hinges.

"I do NOT want to hunt for you in the woods," I yell.

"Jar? Answer me!" I holler. The door to the workshop is cracked open and the lights are on even though it's broad daylight. I hesitate, not wanting to go in, but then I push the door the rest of the way. Jar's sitting in the middle of a mess on the floor and has one of Uncle's cupids in pieces like it exploded. I'm relieved to see he isn't bleeding.

"What are you doing?" I pull on his arm. "It's a mess in here and I don't need you getting hurt or ruining any whirligigs."

"Okey dokey," Jar says stubbornly.

"I know, Bug, but I can't afford to have you mess it up."

Jar frowns. "Org wallop," he says.

"Now, none of that! I'll chain up this door good and tight if you don't promise to stay out," I warn. I yank my brother by the ear and he whimpers. "Tell you what," I wheedle. "You can come into Peggy's and fold towels with me. That'll be fun and you can watch her big screen TV. I can have her put on cartoons. Would you like that?"

"Gag poop," Jar mutters.

"Now don't be calling Peggy names. She's good to us. And you didn't used to be too old for cartoons!" I glare at him and he glares back. "You behave or. Or. Or else!" I threaten.

We march into the Cut N Clean later looking like a couple of mules.

"What's with the stormy faces?" Peggy puts down her teasing comb.

"Jar's being a ornery teenager and I got bills," I say without thinking. Then I clam up. I don't need everybody knowing my beeswax. "You have some towels for him to fold?"

"Everybody's got bills," Peggy shrugs. "You at least got a windfall coming. Towels are fluffing in the dryer."

"Teek! Teek! Teek!" Jar goes.

"That's the timer. They must be done," she says.

I give Jar a scowl. After clearing off the coffee table, I get him set him up folding towels. Soon his expression is somewhat mollified. I watch him work. I wish I could get cheered up after a bad mood folding towels. I frown so hard my forehead feels shrunk.

"Why so gloomy? Jar looks like he's doing fine without Uncle E," Peggy says. "And you're getting an inheritance."

"True that, but I got Uncle E's mess to clean up, now."

"You don't need to clean up after him," Peggy says. "It's his mess, not yours."

"I'm no shirker," I say.

"It's not shirking," Peggy says.

I heave a sigh. "Jar and I owe Uncle E. He took us in when nobody else would. I can't have his reputation sullied not paying. It's a matter of principle. And besides, I'll be good for it soon. It's only a matter of time," I say.

"I wish I was coming into money," Peggy mutters. And then she brightens. "I told Josephine you were all set with a windfall. She was real disappointed and said she'd have to hire a high school girl to clean on weekends as you're not available now."

"What do you mean I'm not available? What'd you do that for?" I say. "I was all ready to start whenever she had any guests," I stare at Peggy. "Why'd you tell her anything, anyway? I told you it was a secret!"

Peggy looks puzzled. "I'm sorry," she says. "I thought you'd be cutting back now that you won't need the extra money. And I thought it was only a secret for a few days."

"It's a secret until I get my money and not before!" I can feel a headache coming on. "I'm in a fix. If I can't come up with the cash to pay that mortgage loan Uncle E took out, I'll lose the trailer. Then there's the cremation fee. I should have just tossed a match to his workshop as much good as that's doing us," I say. "Plus I got more taxes for my inheritance."

"I could lend you some," Peggy says. "Just to tide you over."

"No," I shout. "Absolutely not." I'm pretty well peeved. I could have used that cleaning money. I grab Jar by the shoulder and march on home. I don't even wave goodbye.

"With friends like that, who needs acquaintances?" I say to my brother.

"Can tray," Jar agrees.

I give a deep sigh. "Look," I say. "I guess we can at least go into Uncle's workshop and straighten it up. Maybe I can see about me trying to put one whirligig together." It's hard to keep the worry out of my tone. And then I cheer up. Maybe Uncle E stashed some money in there.

Jar beams. "Hog way! Blip!" he says and gives me a high five.

When we reach the workshop, I unbar the door and prop it open with a shovel. I unlatch the tiny upper windows letting air in and turn on the dangling light bulb.

"No need to work in a dismal cave. What a mess!" I dust off my hands. The floor is thick with scraps of wood and sawdust. Boxes are heaped to the ceiling on the rest of the walls.

Jar plops down in the middle of a pile of body parts and picks up a cat paw. He twirls it above his head.

"Wheee!" he goes.

"That's not helping," I say. "We need to clean this up."

"Okey dokey," Jar says cheerfully.

"Let's start over here." Uncle's workbench is cluttered with tools. "It's a miracle he could find anything."

I sweep, straightening as I go, sticking the screwdrivers together in a can, pounding nails in the wall, and hanging up saws. I pick up trash and dodge the mice running for cover. Soon the garbage can outside is filled to the brim. I start going through shoeboxes lining the shelves.

"Uncle E kept everything," I say. "Look, here's the Valentine's Day card you made. And my progress report from school. *Tammy Louise Tyree has a lot of potential.*" I look over at Jar. "Now that's a real laugh," I say. "Me having potential."

My brother's head is bent over a pile of whirligig pieces.

"I guess it's time to figure this out," I say.

There's a heap of wood parts in a jumble. Some are cut out others are traced on boards. I get down to sorting. Uncut parts in one pile. Dowels in another pile, cut parts in yet another pile. Half put together bodies in another stack.

"How did Uncle E find anything?" I say. Where to begin? A completed Sylvester leans against a wall. It just needs to be painted. I study it carefully. Taking my finger and twirling the paws around. Jar takes a screw and starts to push it through a hole.

I grab his hand away. "Now put that down before you lose it."

"Wind tar!" Jar reaches past me.

"I don't see how," I mutter and turn the piece this way and that trying to fit it together. "I can't figure out how to make the legs turn."

"Gate pig." Jar picks up a dowel.

"I told you! Set that down. Don't be messing things up." Using a screwdriver, I undo the wings on a completed cupid.

"Org whallop," Jar warns.

"Fine then!" I shout at him. "I'd like to see you do it!" And I slam down the tools. "You're either for me or against me. Which is it?" I glare.

"Okey dokey," Jar says in a tiny voice.

"Okey dokey, then," I say. "Now I'll give you a job. Here's a put together Tweedy body and a rack of paint. Use yellow. Be real careful. Got that?"

An hour later, I'm no closer than I was. I can fit the wings on, but nothing I do makes them spin. Jar on the other hand has painted the Tweedy body and has even done the black feather lines on the wings.

Jar points to the box. "Egg. Too. Great. Bar pit."

"You know your colors. Aren't you smart," I say and ruffle his head. This makes his brush spatter my uniform.

"Dang it all! I should have changed." I sputter. "This will mean another twenty bucks for a new one if I can't get it clean." I stand up. "Serves me right. Look. It's getting late. I need to put on dinner. You close up the paint cans and come in when you're done."

I head inside to change. After putting my uniform to soak in soapy water, I set a pot of beanie weenies on the stove. When it's heated through, I remove the pan and turn off the burner.

Jar hasn't come back. It can't take that long to put away paint. I go out to the shed. He's still in there but instead of putting stuff away, Jar's sitting under the worktable with even more wood pieces strewn around him.

"Holy darn cow! Didn't I warn you about making a mess?" I'm just itching to grab a hold of one or the other of his ears.

"Grape pork apple," Jar says and holds up a put together whirligig. It's a hummingbird.

"You find it like that or did you do it?" I say.

"Fact tattle." Jar says.

My mouth drops open. "What do you mean it's easy?"

He shrugs. "Hack tarp."

"Did uncle teach you?" I ask.

"Poke gut," Jar sticks his tongue out at me.

I pinch his ear and he yelps. "No, I'm not calling you a liar!"

There are two finished whirligigs leaning against the wall. They've all been painted. My brother works fast.

"That one's pretty creative being purple and all, but people expect a skin-colored cupid. You got to make what they expect," I say.

"Okey dokey," Jar says. He has a dab of red paint on his nose.

"These need to dry. You're getting into all the colors. I told you cupids have to be flesh colored. You can do brown and tan but nobody will want a rainbow Cupid."

Or will they? I consider this while watching Jar dexterously fit legs to bodies.

"What you got there?" I ask. "It looks like cat paws."

Jar holds up a body. "Hopper boob."

"That's not right," I say. "You got a bird body. Folks expect wings on a bird. I told you. You have to make what folks expect."

"Rare cattle." Jar smirks. "Dodo head."

"Don't get wise! The only reason I got paint on my uniform was because you put it there!"

"Okey dokey," Jar shrugs.

"Apology accepted," I say. "And I guess you got a point. We might as well keep working."

The both of us get busy. I cut out using the jigsaw and sand the pieces smooth. Jar screws them together and paints. By midnight, we got ourselves a passel of finished whirligigs.

"At this rate we can have another load for Allison in no time!" I say. "Good job, Bug!" And then I remember our beanie weenies sitting in the kitchen getting cold.

"Hells bells, I forgot about our dinner," I say. "We can do more tomorrow." But Jar doesn't want to quit. I have to drag him out by his ear. We eat frigid beanie weenies while planning the next step.

"We got all the stuff for Allison's orders," I say. "But we'll need more supplies before we can make another batch," I add. "We need wood, dowels, and hardware."

"Nag huddle." Jar says.

"Don't talk with your mouth full. It's impolite," I say. "And I know we can get it all at the hardware store. I just don't know how to pay for it. We have bills. And other things." I stare at a rusted place in the ceiling.

"Cat poop," Jar says.

"Don't be bad mouthing Walter. And it's my problem not yours. Let me think on it," I say and give him a brisk Dutch rub to the head. Jar's still never learned how to do a proper Dutch rub so that's one point for me.

The next morning the two of us head out to Allison's with her whirligig order in the back of Dolly. Most of them are normal, but Jar threw in a few extra of his own creation. Sylvesters with Tweedy wings. Cat paws on hummingbirds. Cupids the color of the rainbow.

"That's okay Bug," I tell him. "They twirl real good. I will say your whirligigs are unique. Unique is almost as good as normal."

When we pull behind the Flea Market Emporium, Allison comes out. "Just in the nick of time," she says. "I got a big crowd expected this afternoon. Let me help you unload." She sees Jar's special whirligigs first off. "I don't know about these," she frowns. "They're not the usual."

"Put them with the others," I raise my voice for Jar's benefit. "Yeah, I agree. They are the best ones. Those should sell fast. Like hotcakes!" Then I whisper to Allison, "I'll take them back later."

"Job people," Jar announces. "By pear!"

"What's he saying?" Allison asks.

"That his should cost more," I say. "Mark the strange colored ones at eighteen and the mangled body part ones at twenty."

"Twenty?" Allison sounds dubious.

"Twenty-five then. Call them Limited Edition Alien Whirligigs," I tell her.

Jar beams and claps his hands. "At way! Gopher head!"

"What?" Allison says.

"He's glad we did the deal," I lie. I stand around waiting expectantly for Allison to go to her cash drawer, but she doesn't. Instead, she walks me back to the driver's side of Dolly.

"I'll need to sell all these before I can pay you," she says. "I got a liquidity problem this month. Besides," she smiles at me. "I hear you have a fortune coming your way."

I shake my head. "No," I say firmly. "Don't know who told you that. It was a mistake. Whatever you heard was a mistake. It must have been about somebody else. I'm not going to be rich. I don't have expectations."

Allison gives me a knowing smirk. "If that's the way you want to play it," she says.

"I'm not playing anything," I say, but even to my ears, I sound shifty.

I head back home.

The thrum of the wheels on the pavement sounds like a tune. *Rich. Rich she's gonna be rich.*

I find myself whispering along. *Rich. Rich. I'm gonna be Rich.* We make the turn to Spring and roll past the hardware store. I slide Dolly close to the curb and set the brake.

"Come on, Bug." I grab Jar's hand and walk inside like we belong.

Jar immediately slips out of my grasp and runs over to the rock tumbler. He plays with the buttons and gets to flapping like he's been wound up.

Walter's head jerks like a yoyo on a string. "What's he doing in here?" He stabs a finger at Jar.

I snatch my brother's hand and drag him away from the machine. "We're here on business if you don't mind. I got a proposition for you."

"Attle," Jar reminds me.

"*We* have a proposition," I say.

Walter folds his arms over his chest. "What kind of proposition?"

"We need help for our whirligig business. Fact is, we're expanding. Jar's doing the building and I'm doing the dealing." I take a deep breath and decide to play the sympathy card. "With Uncle passing on to the hereafter," I sniff. "We need to charge materials until we get paid."

"I don't do charges. Never have and never will," Walter says firmly.

"Nettle poop," Jar says.

I give my brother a poke.

"What'd he say?" Walter's brows shoot down.

"That we're good for it," I lie.

"But your Uncle E wasn't." Walter ruffles through a drawer next to the register. "I was meaning to send you these when you got over his demise."

He pulls out a fistful of checks and waves them in the air. From where I stand, I can plainly see the words INSUFFICIENT FUNDS. It's stamped across the front of each check in red ink.

"These are all from that no-good uncle of yours. He was supposed to pay me and he never made good on them."

"Don't you dare call Uncle E no-good." I say. My heart sinks right down to my toes. "How much?"

"Three-hundred and twenty dollars all together," Walter says. "And that's not even counting my returned check fees. That adds another hundred, I guess. I got it all right here on this invoice. Plus you never fully made good on that gumball machine your brother broke."

"That was ages ago. And we paid you for it."

"Not the gumballs inside," Walter says.

"You shouldn't have put the machine by the mallets," I say. "And those gumballs were still good. They just needed to be brushed off."

"They needed to be replaced," Walter snaps.

I grit my teeth and swallow my pride. "I'm sorry for the misunderstanding. I'm sure it was merely an oversight," I say stiffly.

"It's no oversight. Just your Uncle not paying what he owes. You Tyrees are all alike." Walter juts his chin out making him look like a totem.

"Gog," Jar whines. He's always been scared of totems.

"Don't you mind him, Jar," I say and stuff Walter's invoice into my purse. "We'll take our business elsewhere."

I stride out the door with my head held high. "Uncle E is not going down in Spring history as a welcher. Not if I can help it," I whisper. "Nobody deserves that."

I walk past the Cut N Clean to Dolly. Jar follows. I glance over at a movement through Peggy's window. She's waving us inside. I look around to see if she was meaning to wave someone behind me, but there's no one there.

The two of us enter. I push Jar in front of the TV.

"What do you want?" I ask. "Has Josephine changed her mind about having me work at her place?"

"How are you doing?" Peggy asks.

This is the first time Peggy has ever been interested in how I am.

I count on my fingers. "I need more work. My bills are piling up. Uncle E got us into a mortgage and Walter Howard just told me I owe him on whirligig materials and those gumballs of Jar's. And everything is partly your fault. If you hadn't told Josephine I didn't need the work I'd have had that job at least." I'm flapping my hands in the air just like Jar.

"But you're getting an inheritance," she says.

"I know but it isn't here yet," I say. "And I'm afraid if I don't come up with the fees they'll give my money to somebody else."

"How much do you need?" Peggy says suddenly.

"I'm not begging for charity," I say.

Peggy opens her purse and takes out her checkbook. "I'm not talking charity," she says. "I'm talking about an investment," she says. "It's like this. I'll give you what you need right now, and you pay me back with interest, and invest in my shop when you get your money. How about that?"

I shake my head. "No," I say. "It wouldn't feel right."

"I'm saying it's right," Peggy says. "You don't want your money given to somebody else. Somebody who doesn't deserve it."

"Saying it's right doesn't make it right."

Peggy starts writing out a check. "It's an investment," she says. Her tone is business-like. "I'm putting it down on paper. See? A contract. Sign right here." She points.

"Well, if it's a contract," I say. "Are you sure about this?"

"As sure as you're getting money from an inheritance," she says with satisfaction.

"Okay then," I say reluctantly.

After I sign, she hands me a check for two thousand eight hundred and fifty dollars.

"Now you let me know when you need more," she says and waves me off.

With that check in my hand, I feel lighter than air. The very next day I go to the bank and deposit it and the day after that, I let Barinas know he can deduct the rest of the money from my account. I hold my breath and check my balance every other day. I start to breathe when $1350 is gone from my account. Poof.

Ten days later, I get a new email from Barinas:

MADAME TYREE,

SPRING APPEARS TO BE A MOST HEAVENLY ABODE.

SINCERE THANKS FOR YOUR REMITTANCE OF THIRTEEN FIFTY AMERICAN DOLLARS. WE ARE PLEASED TO REPORT MATTERS ARE PROGRESSING TOWARDS THE CONCLUSION OF OUR SUCCESSFUL FINANCIAL ENDEAVOR. THE MINISTRY OF INHERITANCE REQUIRES NOW A DEATH PAYMENT OF GOOD FAITH OF ONE THOUSAND AMERICAN DOLLARS WIRED TO THIS ACCOUNT AS RAPIDLY AS YOU CAN MANAGE WILL BE OF PRIME NECESSITY. AND WE WERE NOT INSULTED BY YOUR COMMUNICATION LANGUAGE OF HOW YOU SAY SPRINGLISH? IS THAT A DIALECT OF YOURS?

HAVE A GOOD DAY,

BEST REGARDS,

DR. BARINAS, EXECUTOR

I smile about Springlish, and frown about the *one thousand American dollars* and the *prime necessity*. Where the heck am I going to come up with another thousand bucks anyway?

And then it's like a miracle. The very next day the government deposits Uncle E's social security check into our bank account. I thought it would stop when he died but there it is. It's not the whole amount but it's close.

And close for me now is good enough.

CHAPTER ELEVEN

It takes money to make money. That's a prime investment rule. But should I put the extra money remaining from Peggy's initial investment into whirligig materials or pay some on my bills? It's a dilemma Uncle E used to call having a caterpillar.

Madeline Moorehaven set me straight when I used the word in her presence.

"I have a problem that's turned into a real caterpillar," I'd said to Madeline one day.

"You mean conundrum, Tammy." Madeline had shaken her head. "Those are unsolvable quandaries. Confusing issues. A caterpillar is a bug."

"Conundrum," I'd repeated. "Conundrum." I'd gone back to Uncle E to let him know he'd gotten it wrong, but he'd just shrugged.

"I said caterpillar I meant caterpillar," Uncle E told me. "Caterpillars is confused. They can't decide whether they should take wing or crawl around. Butterfly or worm. They have an identity problem. It's the same thing."

"It isn't at all the same thing," I said uncertainly. "Madeline said—"

Uncle had held up his hand to stop me. "Madeline said? I tell you what. You say conundrum and I'll say caterpillar," Uncle E told me. "Tell Madeline I appreciate her opinion."

I went and told Madeline what Uncle E had said.

She'd frowned. "If he appreciated it, he'd do what I suggest."

Even though they never talked face to face, Uncle E always spoke admiringly of Madeline.

"A real fine woman, plus she's got a quick mind. Could argue the socks off a parakeet."

Arguing the socks off a parakeet was high praise from Uncle E.

Working at the café takes my mind off any caterpillars or conundrums or socks arguing. It's full to the brim with highway workers, but also a carload of tourists who've lost their way, along with a table full of professors from the university studying slugs. They come by the droves to Spring, as there're plenty of slugs for them to study here. I frown. Professors are always lousy tippers. Probably because they're absent-minded.

I move from table to table daydreaming. Not really paying attention. *Money in the bank.* What will I do when I have money in the bank? I look down. Definitely new shoes. I touch at my temple. Fancy barrettes would be nice. As I scribble the order for table five on my pad, I examine my fingers. Maybe nail polish. I could even go with Peggy to get a manicure. I've never had one of those. It could go with my makeover. I can feel a smile forming on my face.

"Why are you so cheerful?" That drawl is unmistakable. I turn around and it's my cousin Lonnie. His flannel shirt has oil stains and his boots are covered with mud.

"None of your beeswax," I snap.

"Those that don't have pretty faces need to have a sweet disposition. Didn't anybody tell you that?" Lonnie rolls a toothpick around his mouth and studies me carefully. "I'll have some breakfast," he says.

"You don't get breakfast unless you have money to pay for it," I say. "And my disposition is just fine thank you very much."

"And why you still working here? Thought you'd be flush with cash by now. How's about staking me a meal or two," Lonnie says. "For old times' sake."

"There's no cash and no stake." I flounce away leaving him sitting there. Lonnie thinking I have money is not a good thing.

Two seconds later there's a crash. One of the scientists has dumped a whole pot of coffee over the table, the booth seats, and themselves. I grab a rag and race over. After cleaning it all up, I deliver a fresh pot to them and pause to straighten my skirt.

A throat clears. "I wouldn't mind coffee." Another voice I recognize. Walter Howard. He's sitting there nice as you please at the table next to Lonnie. I frown.

Walter is wearing a crisp tan-striped shirt with a carnation stuffed in his lapel. As opposite of Lonnie without being a completely different species.

Lonnie stares at me. "And I'd like some too. I get grumpy when I haven't had my coffee." There's a threat under those words that I take serious. Leo doesn't need trouble in the café.

It takes steely resolve to remember I'm a professional. Waitresses take care of everybody exactly the same, even if we do happen to hate the customer's guts or suspect they won't pay their bills. I pour both men a cup and then poise my pencil on my pad.

"What'll you have?" I say through clenched teeth. "And the soup today is breakfast meat gumbo."

"Two eggs over easy with hash browns and pancakes," says Lonnie. The smile on his face doesn't reach his eyes. As I head toward the pass-through, I see Smithers stroll in. I glance over at Lonnie. *My lucky day.*

"Come on over here, Clarence!" I wave extra cheery.

Lonnie immediately slumps down in his chair hiding his face behind the menu. Smithers ambles over, holding his hat in his hands.

I motion to Lonnie's table. "I was just now telling my cousin Lonnie that you were looking for him a while back. You mentioned something about a Gold Cutlass? Sorry, it slipped my mind. The two of you might like to share a table."

I beam at them like they ought to be pleased as punch. Lonnie slides down further in his seat and Smithers squashes his hat back on and frowns. He hikes up his pants. Next thing I know he's got Lonnie by the elbow and is escorting him out front door. I'm grinning broadly as I tear my cousin's chit up in teeny tiny pieces.

I turn to Walter. "Sorry for the interruption," I apologize. "Now what will you have?"

"Let me see. I think eggs over medium." Walter says. "And what's in the breakfast meat gumbo may I ask?"

"Everything but the kitchen sink," I say and then scowl. "And by the way it's not a good morning because you're being a tightwad about me charging whirligig supplies." I sniff. "Ham or bacon?"

"Now, don't get all huffy. Ham please," Walter says. "And you have to understand about collateral. I can't afford to give things away."

"I'm not talking about giving. The sausage is better today. Ham's kind of dry. And nobody can afford to do nothing. And I have collateral. I have eggs," I growl. "You want orange juice?"

"Eggs aren't collateral in a hardware store, and orange juice gives me gas. Anyways I happened to be talking to Peggy and she said something about you getting left some money. Sausage is fine."

"Peggy's a blabber mouth." I snip. "Don't listen to a thing she says. How about cranapple then. And my financial position isn't any of your concern. White or wheat toast?" I ask.

"But that's what I'm trying to say. It changes things, between us. White toast I guess," he says.

"How does that change things? Wheat's more healthy or I can give you an English muffin if you'd prefer."

"Muffin sounds good, thanks," he says. "And you coming into money means you've got collateral. I can set you up with materials if you like. If you want you can come by my store, later"

"Don't thank me, it's my job," I say, slightly mollified. "And what's Peggy doing telling you my beeswax anyway? You want jam on that?"

"She was only trying to do you a good turn," Walter says. "You have strawberry?"

"Sure do. And you really mean that? Jar and I can pick up the wood and any other stuff we need?"

"You can bring your truck over this very afternoon," Walter says.

"Well, I'll do that. Thanks," I say.

After eating his breakfast, Walter salutes his hat to me as he walks out the door. He even leaves a tip for the first time. It's only fifty cents, but it's the thought that counts. I walk past the register and Curtis's eyes burrow into mine.

"Why are you so cozy with Walter all of a sudden?" he asks. "And where did Smithers go with your cousin?"

"None of your beeswax times two," I say, not caring how much of a *not meets* that is. When I deliver my orders to the kitchen I'm fairly kicking up my heels. Even Leo notices the difference in me.

"You look chipper," he says. "Think you can pull an extra shift? With the construction back on I want to take advantage while I can."

I have to waffle on that one. Peggy doesn't care when I show up to do my chores, but I shouldn't leave Jar unattended that long. On the other hand, even with my inheritance coming I can't turn down work.

"Sure." I say reluctantly. "I guess Jar will be okay. He's getting used to being alone."

Leo studies me carefully. "Maybe it isn't good to leave your brother by himself without your uncle around."

"What choice do I have?" I can't help speaking sharp. It's always easy for other people to say what I need to do with Jar.

"Tell you what," he says. "I can use someone on pans. Why don't you bring him in on trial?"

"You mean it?" I say. "For money?"

"I can afford to pay him ten bucks a shift if he works out," Leo says easily.

I consider. Having Jar with me would be a blessing. Pans can't be that much harder than whirligigs, I think.

Has Leo heard about me getting money? Is that why he's being nice? I stare at him but his expression is bland. He's back to rolling out dough. I run out of the kitchen.

"Curtis! Cover for me," I order and speed off, not even removing my apron. I don't wait to hear Curtis' answer. It takes me five minutes to run up my driveway and grab Jar.

"I got a surprise. A job offer. Pans at the café for ten bucks!" I tell him. "How about that? You can do your part to earn money for Barinas."

Jar frowns. "Otter pony," he says.

"I don't care if you'd rather build whirligigs." I say. "Jobs for money don't grow on trees!" I offer my hand.

"Flop stone," Jar says. "Okey dokey."

"A rock tumbler is not on our list of things we need," I say. "But groceries are. Let's go."

We head back to Two Spoons. I empty Jar's pockets of rocks before going inside. We saunter past Curtis.

"What's he doing here?" Curtis points at Jar.

"He's our new employee," I say. Jar and I go through to the kitchen.

"What do you mean employee?" Curtis follows us. "I didn't hire anybody."

"He's our new pan man," I say. "Isn't he Leo?"

Leo and Curtis exchange looks.

"Okey dokey?" Jar asks.

"Leo will tell you what to do," I say. "And you mind him."

I get Jar set up on a chair front of the sink.

"Bye per," Jar says.

"Yeah, I guess you do need to be higher," I say and I get a box of napkins from the storeroom. "Don't you look fine," I say to Jar. "Like a king on his throne!" I slide plastic gloves on my brother's hands. He immediately gets to flapping.

Curtis stands akimbo. "This will be a disaster," he predicts. But Curtis is the kind of person who sees a half full glass as one that needs to be washed, dried, and put away.

I stick a dirty pan in the sink and fill it with detergent. "Here you go."

"Egg fart." Jar mutters, sending Curtis dark looks.

"What's he saying?" Curtis says.

"That he can do the job," I lie. And I get back to work. Every few minutes I pop into the kitchen checking on my brother.

Lunch special is Reuben sandwich potpie and the soup is cream of sauerkraut. I get extra tips for not making a big deal out of people not finishing their soup. I dump it in the sink Jar's working at so Leo doesn't see.

"Another clean bowl," I say cheerfully.

Leo smiles. "The best recipe yet. I'll have to make sure I add it twice in the rotation," he says.

"Oh, no," I shake my head. "That's too much of a good thing," I say. "Keep the rotation as it is."

At one forty-five, the workers come in as a herd. They yell back and forth. Their hands are filthy and their boots are covered with concrete dust. I take turns sweeping and filling coffee and explaining for the millionth time why they have to take soup with their order. Even Curtis looks like he's getting annoyed as he works the register. I check on Jar. He's still happily washing pans.

"Weep! Weep! Weep!" Jar sings, dead on imitating the oven timer.

When I go out front a customer flags me down. "Hey! My pot pie's raw in the middle," he complains.

Too late, I remember I forgot to warn Leo about Jar's buzzing. I have to take back all the pot pies I just served so they can finish cooking. I bring them in on a tray and set them down in front of Leo.

"Jar does buzzers real good," I explain to Leo. "And car alarms. And chimes."

Leo looks at Jar with new respect. "That so?" he says and puts his pies back in to cook.

"Weep. Weep. Weep," Jar goes.

"Shush, Jar!" I say.

"Rattle boob." Jar tosses his wet towel to the floor.

"Well, then, get a dry one," I say.

He slides off his box and opens the linen drawer. He pulls out a Wonderbread bag.

"Weep," he says holding it up.

"I got that Jar," Leo says quickly. He swipes the bag out of my brother's hands and gives him a dry towel.

"You need to keep that crap somewhere else." I frown at Leo as I help Jar clamber back up on his boxes.

"Fuzz counter," Jar whispers. "Carp!"

"I don't know, I'll ask him," I say to Jar. "And watch that mouth of yours. Hey, Leo, Jar wants to know if he's working out."

Leo nods. "He's doing great."

"At way!" Jar slaps the water with his sponge getting me wet. "Org pat?"

"I'll ask Leo about your ten bucks later," I whisper. "And it isn't your money by the way. It's ours."

My brother scowls and I scowl back.

"Carp!" Jar says. "Ding!" He does the chit bell.

"Get that, Tammy," Curtis calls out.

Leo stuffs his Wonderbread bag high in the upper cupboard. "I wonder if Jar can do guitar chords?" he muses.

"Don't think he's ever tried," I say. "But he does the doorbell at Shop and Save."

Leo puts all the potpies that have finished cooking for the second time along with bowls of soup on a large tray. It's too heavy for me so Leo himself heads into the dining room. I follow behind.

"Were you here a couple months ago?" A voice booms out. "Some weird kid was out there chucking rocks. Did you see him?" It's a fat bellied flagger running off at the mouth.

"Probably the little thief that's vandalizing our site."

Another hoots. "This town full of freaks, or what?" There's a trickle of laughter.

"Spring. Perfect name for this town. Full of drips." More snickers.

My face burns. Leo slams his tray down. The soup sloshes in the bowls. He gives a room-sized glare.

"Enough!" he announces. His voice echoes. "That kid who was out there?" Leo says. "Happens to be a world champion discus thrower. He's practicing for a movie that's being filmed here. It's been in all the papers. Don't you Neanderthals read?"

"Movie?" A worker widens his eyes.

"Yeah, a documentary." Leo says.

"What kind of documentary?" The worker looks dubious.

"A wide angle one," Leo scowls. "So, we can fit every single one of your fat asses on the screen."

He whips a potpie across the table and the man catches it just before it slides off. "Steam punk re-imagined documentary film making," Leo says. He sends three more bowls of soup across the table like he's dealing cards. Not spilling a drop. "Yep, we're all actors, in this place."

I stand there with my mouth open.

"What's the movie called?" someone asks.

"The Vanishing of Spring." Leo says. "Everybody has a role," Leo continues. "This pretty lady here?" Leo places a hand on my shoulder. The heat of his fingers burns through to my skin.

"She's the star. The construction company is the villain." He glares. "And the Café? And Howard's Hardware. And the Shop and Save? It's all pretend. Fake. Every bit. In fact, the whole damn town is just a set."

Leo suddenly looks bleak. "Come back next year and we'll all be gone."

He turns his back and disappears into the kitchen.

CHAPTER TWELVE

A week later Josephine Munn and Peggy Rutledge come into the café arm in arm. I watch them go from table to table before they settle into a booth. Peggy waves me over.

"Come sit with us for a second," she says patting the seat next to her. I look over at Curtis. I can tell he's trying to eavesdrop.

I slide in and start right off apologizing. "It's quitting time for me. Lunch is over," I say. "No mackerel-noodle-cheeto-casserole left."

Peggy flutters her hand. "We didn't come to eat."

"That's kind of the point of being in a café," I say.

They are both bright eyed and leaning forward. Josephine is tearing a napkin into tiny pieces. If Peggy resembles a whale, then Josephine's got to be a stork. All neck and legs. She's wearing a flowery skirt and loopy earrings that swing back and forth. Just like a gypsy except for her hair is a short grey helmet instead of long dark curls. Plus Josephine's on the way shady side of sixty. She's looking from me to Peggy. And then I get it.

"You told her!" I feel those brows of mine shoot down. "And you told Walter as well!" I hiss. "He came in last Tuesday."

Peggy gets all huffy. "I had to. You were in a fix."

"I am not in any fix."

"Of course, not. You're an heiress," she soothes. "I got to thinking. Five million dollars is a lot of money. You can't spend it all on yourself. Seems to me you should sprinkle it around Spring. Otherwise people will think you're a skinflint like those Nedermyers!" Curtis walks by and she lowers her voice, "You need to take in more investors," she says.

"I don't need investors!" I shout.

"Shhhh," Peggy holds her finger to her mouth.

"If it was an heiress," I back track. "Which I'm not."

Josephine clears her throat. "I'm perfectly willing to contribute, but I don't suppose you have proof about this deal."

"Proof?" Peggy looks shocked. "Why Josephine Munn that's the meanest thing I ever did hear. That's practically calling Tammy, here, a liar."

"Proof is good business!" Josephine protests.

Proof. I think on this. I don't want people calling me either a skinflint or a liar, but I also don't want them knowing my business. A real caterpillar as Uncle E would have said. I lean back and stick my hands in my uniform pocket. Right off, I feel my last email folded up. "Fair enough," I say and pull it out. "Is this what you'd call proof?" I hand it over. The two of them bump heads in their eagerness to make themselves privy to the contents.

"How about that!" Peggy says. "It's an official correspondence."

"Botswana," Josephine says. "That's where those lady detectives come from." She knits her brows. "What's a solicitor?" she asks. "Is that like a salesman?"

"Nope," I say proudly. "It's a foreign lawyer. I looked it up."

"It says here you need a thousand dollars for the taxes. You sent that off yet?" Josephine asks.

"Not yet. Things are..." I hesitate. I was going to say tight, but I don't. "I'm getting my affairs in order." Now that sounds like I'm dying. "I'm settling things up." That sounds worse. I frown.

"You better not dawdle sending it off," Peggy warns. "I know a gal who was on Price is Right and she couldn't come up with the taxes. She had to give up a perfectly beautiful dining room set with a credenza and everything because she couldn't pay. She even lost out on a vacation to Mexico."

"Isn't a credenza a desk? What do you need a desk in a dining room for?" Josephine asks.

"Well, maybe it was a living room, or maybe a den. It's not important. What's important is we have to help Tammy figure out how to come up with a thousand bucks."

"I don't need help," I say.

"Oh, yes you do," Peggy snaps. "I'm being your manger here."

"I don't need a manager."

"I have some money put away," Josephine says. "I can come up with half."

"I can put up the other half. How about that, Tammy?" Peggy says.

"I don't need help," I say stubbornly. "Allison owes me plenty and I get my check from Two Spoons tomorrow." I look at my watch.

"And I don't have time to chat. Jar and I need to high tail it over to Walter's"

"Walter?" Peggy squeaks. "Why do you need to see Walter?"

"He's been letting us charge the materials for our whirligigs. We're ready for the next batch." I head into the kitchen.

Today Leo has Jar putting napkins in the dispensers. With those small hands of his, he's doing a good job.

"Way to go, Bug," I say. "But our shift is over. We got to go."

Jar frowns. "Egg poor."

"I know you like working here but don't you want to do your whirligigs?"

Jar flaps his hands enthusiastically and rips off his apron. It's hard for Jar to switch gears from one thing to another. When he's at the café that's all he wants to do and when he's in the workshop he doesn't want to come out and when he folds towels, he wants to do it forever.

Curtis walks in with his apron in his hand, frowning. "What's going on? You ladies look like you're planning something."

Curtis has never referred to me as a lady. "We're not," I say. "Come on Jar. We have to grab Dolly and get over to Walter's."

I feel Curtis staring at our backs as we walk out. When I get to the hardware store, I make Jar stay in Dolly.

"Walter doesn't need to be reminded of any stone throwing and I don't need you mooning over that dang rock tumbler," I say. "Here's some skittles."

"Carp," Jar mutters.

I give him a warning Dutch rub on the noggin. Peggy and Josephine are standing at Walter's counter when I walk in.

Walter is bellied up to his register. He's making eyes at Peggy and she's fluttering hers back. They look like a couple of pigeons.

"What can I do for you?" Walter oozes.

"Just here with Tammy while she gets her whirligig stuff," Peggy says. She's twirling a loose strand of her hair extension.

"Me too," Josephine interjects. "Just here with Tammy." She glances over at Peggy and winks broadly.

"I don't know that you've heard, Walter, but we're in business together," Peggy says. "There's three of us. Tammy's going to help me expand my store and do the same with Josephine's B & B."

Walter's forehead furrows. "That true?" he says looking from me to Peggy.

"No," I say.

"Yes," Josephine and Peggy say together.

"Okay, well, it's one or two of my potential investments," I say reluctantly.

I hand Walter my list of whirligig materials. Too late, I realize I gave him Barinas' email instead. I try to snatch it back, but he holds firm.

"Dr. Barinas," he reads. "A solicitor? Five million?" he looks up his eyes wide. "It's true then. You are an heiress."

"No!" I say.

"Yes she is. Don't you dare lie Tammy Louise," Peggy says. "That's a sin!"

"A solicitor is a lawyer," interjects Josephine proudly. "And I'm helping Tammy out lending her money for the taxes."

Walter frowns. "I had no idea it was this large."

"And they have Tammy's account numbers so they can wire the money to her all legal, now. It's business," Peggy says.

"How do you know that?" I say.

"Your Uncle E asked my advice about banking. He was always asking my advice. He knew I was a bona fide businesswoman," Peggy sniffs.

"So you're all set then?" Walter says. "You just pay this amount and they send you the money?"

"Yep," Peggy says. "And Tammy doesn't need any more partners. Don't want to get too complicated. Just waiting for our millions to come."

"So, it's just you women?" Walter asks.

Peggy narrows her eyes. "What of it?"

Walter rubs his chin. "It's only you might get taken advantage of, being women and all. Other countries are different. It might be best to have a man involved in the process."

"We got a man," I say. "Barinas." I imagine him now clean shaven. A fatherly figure. With kind brown eyes. And a cane. He has a limp from an injury received probably saving a small child from a lion.

"Tammy? You listening?" Josephine gives me a shake.

"I don't think we need any, but thanks for offering," Peggy says sweetly. "Us women can take care of ourselves."

"Seems to me Tammy is already in business with me on the whirligigs. I can put up a stake. How's eighteen hundred dollars sound?" Walter pulls out his checkbook.

I hesitate.

"How about twenty-eight? You want me to make it out to cash?" Walter doesn't miss a beat.

Peggy cocks her head and taps her nails on the counter. "Hmmm," she says consideringly. "Walter has a point. Having a man involved." She looks over at me.

"No," I say. "I told you I don't need any more fingers in my pie."

"Thirty five hundred?" Walter's pen is poised.

"Think about it Tammy," Peggy says. "The whole town will benefit. Walter and me can go together on a parking lot."

Without waiting for me to answer, Walter writes out the check and hands it to me. "Four thousand. It's a deal now," he says firmly. "You got my money. No fair to back out." And he loads my supplies in the back of Dolly.

Later, when I'm heading for the bank, I consider. It's like being run over by a snowball. One minute I owe money and the next I got three checks in my pocket to deposit into my account. It's more than enough to pay the fees for Barinas, settle the rest of my bills and then some.

That evening Jar and I eat an early dinner of toasted cheese sandwiches and then head into the workshop.

"Fat tap," Jar says.

"Yep we are definitely in fat city," I say. "Whirligig supplies up the kazoo."

Jar pulls the electric jigsaw out from the toolbox. "Pump teeter."

"Oh, all right," I say. "But be careful."

Watching Jar work the saw gives me the heebie jeebies, but he does real well.

"Here." I put a pair of goggles on his face. "Uncle E used these for welding. I don't want you getting sawdust in your eyes." I adjust them. "How's that?"

"Okey dokey." Jar's head wobbles from the weight.

"You look like a mosquito," I say. "Now get back to work." I must say it's relaxing watching someone else toiling for a change."

"Tuck nit," Jar says.

"Well, yeah, I guess you're a Jack of all trades just like me," I agree.

Jar is able to get a goodly number of whirligigs cut out. I notice he's really gone to town with mixing up all the parts. Looks like a regular cartoon demolition derby.

"Now build some of them correct," I warn. "We really need to sell these."

"Wallet yap," Jar holds up a cupid body attached to a flamingo head.

"Hells bells Jar! I told you. People like normal things. Different makes them antsy."

"Get woop," he says right back. He's got that lower lip of his stuck out so far he looks like a toad. It's a sign he won't back down.

"I'm not gonna waste time arguing with you. I'll make you a deal. If Allison still has your other ones left unsold then you got to re-do these right."

I know it isn't fair to take advantage of Jar, but I will if I have to.

"At way!" Jar laughs at me at the same time he picks up the jigsaw. It slips out of his hand and flips sideways cutting his other arm. Blood wells up.

"ACK!" Jar yells and starts to rock.

"Holy smoke!" I grab a rag and tie it tight. "It figures," I say. "We haven't had a trip to the ER in a dog's age."

I have the routine down pat. Bundle Jar up, grab the keys to Dolly, pray she starts and hit the gas when she does. Soon we're rolling down the road heading for the hospital.

"Keep that bandage tight," I say. "I don't want blood on the seat."

The ER isn't crowded and we walk through the door straight into the treatment room.

"A world record, Jar. How about them apples?" I say.

We get the same doctor and nurse as before when Jar was stuck in the trap.

"Well, hello there, Doctor Harms," I say. "I hope you don't. Harm us that is." And I slap my knee.

We get Nurse Caldwell again. "Hello, Jar," she says. "Let's see what we have here." She tugs at Jar's bandage. Blood has soaked the rag.

"How'd it happen?" Doctor Harms asks.

"A jig saw got loose," I say. "He's got butterfingers."

The doctor frowns. "He uses power tools?" He shakes his head. "He probably shouldn't be doing that. What if something happens?"

"Something did happen. We're here aren't we?"

"You have a point," Doctor Harms smiles. "But there's a danger of infection with a saw. He'll need antibiotics to be on the safe side." The doctor writes on a pad. "You need to keep him from doing things he's not capable of."

Jar scowls at the doctor.

"Pills. Great." I roll my eyes "Hope they look like skittles. And he's more than capable."

"Hog butt," Jar says. He doesn't like his capabilities doubted. "Okey dokey," he adds.

"What's he saying?" Doctor Harms asks.

"He wants to know if he gets stitches this time," I lie. The doctor doesn't need to know any of the names Jar used on him.

"No, it's not that deep. Nurse Caldwell can bandage him up." Doctor Harms takes a moment to give me a pat on the back. "You do a good job with him. He's lucky."

"He won't be so lucky when I pop him up the side of the head for being so clumsy," I say. But I'm pleased all the same.

And just like that, we're on our way home.

"On a scale of one to ten of ER visits this was a three," I tell Jar. "And Doctor Harms says you're lucky."

"Upper ferret," Jar says.

"Okay two then," I say. "And I guess I'm lucky too."

We pull up to the trailer and go inside.

"Okey dokey," Jar says. He's got a stubborn look in his eye.

I watch him march out of the living room, through the kitchen, and down the back steps. The light goes on in the workshop. It's late and Jar should be in bed but I let him go.

What the doctor said hurt Jar's feelings. I could see it in his eyes. Being doubted about your abilities makes a body want to do something extra hard.

I stare at the kitchen clock and then look through the window at the workshop. Ten minutes. Twenty minutes. No blood curdling screams. I pace. When I can stand it no longer, I stroll out to the workshop real casual. Like I was just ambling through the neighborhood.

I poke my head through the door. Jar's putting together a cat-bird and cupid-cartoon whirligig. It has wings on its head. He's got another that looks like a dragonfly with double wings spinning on its back.

"Nice," I tell him. "Real creative."

"Winter canter," Jar says.

"You said it, Jar." And I give him a high five.

Yes siree, my brother's hit the nail right on the head with that one. You can't have too many wings. Especially if you got a job of making whirligigs.

With Jar otherwise occupied, I sneak over to Two Spoons, let myself in through the door, and settle behind the computer. I have to let Barinas know the money is in my account.

Dear Dr. Barinas,

Hey, there, how you doing? I'm the Tammy from Spring.

Just to let you know I got the rest of the money in the bank. In five days, the checks will clear and you can pay the rest that I'm owing by deducting it like last time. So when will I get my inheritance? Don't think I don't appreciate your efforts on my behalf, but I got obligations here. And our summer's half done, not that we can tell as it's always raining. Is it summer where you are or

are you backwards from us? I don't have a globe. Just a flat map so I don't know if you're underneath us or not.

Anyways you got yourself a wife or any kids? Like I said before or maybe I didn't I have a brother. He's out of the ordinary and takes a lot of watching but I guess brothers are like that. You have brothers or sisters?

Yours truly,
Tammy Louise Tyree
By the way, my phone number is 360- 555-2436.
Call anytime. I mean it.

Sending this makes me feel pretty good. It even gets me to thinking that maybe I should be expecting a call from Africa. I did tell Barinas he could phone anytime. And being as they have computers in Botswana, they for sure have phones. In fact, Barinas could be calling me right now this very second. I rush right home.

The very second I walk through the door my phone does ring. It's like I'm psychic, or a magician, even.

My hand hovers over the receiver. I hesitate. *How should I answer anyway?* Four rings. Five rings. Six rings. *What should I say?*

If it's Dr. Barinas, I probably should answer with Madame Tyree. But will that confuse people calling for a garage cleaning? Maybe I should say Miss Tyree or Tammy Tyree or even Tammy Louise Tyree. But what if it's Leo calling about pulling an extra shift at the café? He'd be expecting me to say just plain Tammy or nothing at all. And why would he call rather than just tell me to my face what he needed? I stand there like a fool waffling and finally pick up on the ninth ring.

"Hey, there. This is Tammy Tyree," I say hurriedly and cross my fingers.

"Tammy? It's Allison. I hope I'm not calling too late."

"Allison." My voice falls flat. "No it's not late. Thanks for the payment you sent."

Allison is always good as her word about mailing out a check. Not like me. When I say a check is in the mail you can be guaranteed it isn't.

"I need you to bring in more whirligigs. A bunch of them," she urges. "As many as you can make. And not just the regular ones." she adds. "I especially want the ones your brother made up special. Painted all different colors? And with extra wings? And different bodies and legs? People are going hog wild for them."

"Hog wild?" I think maybe Allison spent too much time in the sun. Or maybe she drinks. I don't know her real personal. "You sure about that?" I ask.

"Of course, I'm sure. Fact is, I ran out of them so fast it'd make your head spin. Folks are streaming into my place saying they want one or two or three. Putting in their orders. Especially those rainbow colored cupids. Rainbows are real popular. That's why I thought I'd better call you right away."

"Okay then," I say slowly. "Jar will be pleased as punch when I tell him."

"And we can sell them for thirty-five. How soon can you deliver?"

"Soon," I say. "Real soon." Like all Tyrees, I'm a pleaser. If Allison wants whirligigs, she'll get whirligigs.

I replace the receiver and stroll out to the workshop. Jar looks up as I enter.

"Map super," he says.

"Glad to hear it," I say. "I knew you weren't hurt real bad."

I shift my feet, hemming and hawing. "By the by," I finally say. "You'll be glad to know that Allison was finally able to sell your special whirligigs." I pause. "Fact is, she said they've sold out."

"Tarp lumen." Jar turns off his jig saw and sets it down.

"That's what I'm telling you. She wants more. And I suppose you can go to town on the spots and stripes and mangled bodies," I say grudgingly. "Don't be saying I told you so. I'm already fixing to eat my words. Although that eight winged cupid with a cattail looks mighty like a centipede in my opinion. I guess I'm lucky slugs don't have legs or you'd make them too," I sniff. "But I guess people are wild about bugs."

Jar laughs. "At way!"

"Don't gloat," I growl. "It's impolite."

My brother is cutting out whirligig shapes like an expert. Following the lines and everything. He shouldn't be able to do that, but he does. It's like he's learning new things. Maybe he was bored before, or maybe none of us gave him a chance to do new stuff.

Or just maybe Momma was right about him all along.

He is artistic.

CHAPTER THIRTEEN

Days pass by and no reply comes from Barinas.
A week passes by.

Two weeks pass by and no word.

It's been nearly three weeks and still there's not a peep from Barinas. I make up a little song for luck. *Botswana and Barinas and Bucks. Botswana Barinas and Bucks.* I sing it each time I pass by the computer at Two Spoons. Every break and then some I check my email. Each time there's nothing.

Maybe Barinas is sick. I imagine him in the hospital. Maybe he's had a heart attack? Such a kind hearted man probably has stress in his life giving money to heiresses.

Week four.

The money in my account is shrinking fast. I had to make good on the mortgage payment. I got carried away spending too much money on groceries. Buying fancy stuff like ground round and brand name cereal instead of generic. I'm getting a little nervous. Maybe I did something wrong. Didn't follow directions. I'm worried there's a snafu.

I go over to Peggy's.

"I'm kind of concerned," I tell her. "I haven't heard anything from Barinas yet."

Peggy snorts. "Why are you waiting for him to email you? Take the bully by the horns yourself." She tosses her hair back. "I was real popular back in high school. If a boy I liked didn't ask me out then I'd walk right up to him and do the deed myself. Invite him to take me to a movie or get a hamburger. Nobody ever turned me down."

She takes me by the shoulders and pushes me out the door. "Go on. You email first. And keep on emailing until he answers."

So, that's just what I do. At the gap between breakfast and lunch when I know it won't be busy, I settle in front of the computer and send an email all on my own. It's just to make sure Barinas knows I'm depending on him. To keep the connection going. Niggle his memory a little. Offer condolences if he's ill. When I hit send, I feel instantly better.

Curtis comes in as I finish. "You making a practice of coming in when you aren't scheduled?"

"You complain when I'm late. You complain when I'm early. And now you're complaining just for the sake of complaining," I say. "Make up your mind."

"You can have a half-shift for lunch if you want," Curtis sounds like it's being pulled out of him under duress.

I'd like to say no thanks, but I better not. "I can do that," I say. "As a favor to Leo."

"See you in two hours," Curtis says.

I buzz back home and peek in on Jar.

He's got a pile of whirligig parts cut out.

"Pork rabbit," he says.

"Yeah I guess I can help you for a bit. And then I have to go to the café. Leo offered me an extra shift. And we have to get these whirligigs done for Allison."

"Rod torp." Jar hands me a stack of bodies to sand.

I grab the sandpaper block and get busy. I don't even stop to think that it's Jar calling the shots now.

"Are you fooling me, Jar?" I ask. "Is there more than what meets the eye with you?"

But my brother is intent on attaching a twirling leg to a body with a screw and doesn't answer. We work together for an hour straight.

EEEEEEEE! There's the sound of a siren coming up the driveway.

I sigh. "Now what?" I say. "You been up to no good that I'm about to find out about?"

"WHEEEE!" Jar drops his half finished whirligig and runs into the yard. I take off after him.

EEEEEEE! Goes the siren.

"Eeee! Eeeee!" goes Jar trotting around in circles. He pulls his mask off and throws it on the ground.

"Knock it off! You got work to do." I yell at Jar.

Smithers steers his vehicle in front of the coop. His tires sink in the grass. All the chickens scatter except for Cauliflower. She lowers her head and advances toward Smithers' car.

"What now," I say. Wishing Smithers parked his car in the front of my trailer like a normal person. The grass back here is ripped up from him driving on it.

"Poop head," Jar says, but he hides behind me as he says it. Smithers' uniform gives him the willies.

"Don't let Clarence catch you saying that," I hiss and try to push him out in front of me.

"Hey, there, Tammy Louise." Smithers leans out his window.

"Hey, there, Clarence," I say cautiously. Smithers doesn't have his handcuffs out so it's probably all right.

He slowly unfolds out of his car. "Well?" he finally says.

"Well?" I say back.

Cauliflower gives a long threatening cluck. "Watch out for her," I say.

"You doing all right?" Smithers asks. "It's only a hen," he adds.

"Why wouldn't I be? And Cauliflower is not your normal run of the mill hen," I say. "She's a white leghorn. They're ornery."

Cauliflower lunges for Smithers' pant leg. He tries to kick her and misses. She struts away imperiously.

"That hen will have it in for you now," I tell him.

"Egg worm," Jar says. He snatches up his goggles and throws them at Smithers, who catches them with one hand.

"Good aim. And that's a pretty decent siren sound you make," Smithers says.

I don't bother to tell him it's no use making up to Jar.

"Plththt!" Jar goes.

"Stop doing farts and throwing things! It's not nice." I turn from Jar to Smithers. "You here just for a visit or you need more eggs?" I say.

"EEEEE!" Jar goes. "Plththt!" He pulls off his gloves and sends them one at a time flying toward Smithers who dodges one and catches the other.

"Stop!" I flap at Jar and he flaps back.

"Don't need any eggs," Smithers says and hands me a glove back.

"Jar! Quit! Smithers is gonna arrest you!" I threaten.

"ACK!" My brother runs and hides behind the coop.

"I'm not going to arrest him," Smithers drawls. He studies me like I'm a bunch of words he has to memorize. "So. What's new with you?"

Now this is getting weird. "Nothing," I drawl back.

"Nothing?" Smithers slowly shakes his head. "It's just I hear tell you're about to come into a pile of money from a relation. That one of your evangelical Tyrees came through for you. That true?" he folds his arms and leans back against his car.

"No," I say.

"Tammy lying is a sin."

"Is everybody here an expert on sinning?" I fold my own arms back at him. "Who told you that, anyway?" I ask. "Was it old blabbermouth Peggy?"

"No."

"Josephine?"

"Nope."

"Who then?"

"I heard it first from that cousin of yours and then at the hardware store."

"Lonnie AND Walter? Is there anybody who's not blabbing about my beeswax?"

"People are interested when stuff like that happens, that's all." Smithers says. "You know. Good things to one of their own."

"I guess." My tone is grudging. Spring folks never considered a Tyree one of their own before, but then maybe it's another sign the circumstances of my life are changing.

Smithers stands there opening closing his mouth like a cod.

"Look," he finally says. "Walter was saying how you're looking for investments and I got sort of an idea. I'm studying for my PI license. I'm gonna be like Mike Connors in Mannix. Or Jim Rockford."

"I don't know either of those guys."

"Like Perry Mason? You know, people in trouble call me and I can investigate things for them. If it goes good,

I can expand and hire five or six guys. Real specialized. Former law enforcement and all. Anyway, you interested in being a backer?"

"Backer? But I don't have the money." I say. "Yet," I add quickly. "I got all the solicitor stuff to do before I get it," I say. "And I got my own bills to take care of in the meantime. It's that liquid problem like they talk about in the paper. It's like that."

Smithers bites his bottom lip. "Now see here. That's just what happens when people's circumstances change and everybody else's around them doesn't. It seems you'd be a mite more charitable."

"Charitable! How can I be charitable when I don't have a pot to piss in?"

"But you will have a pot. You got expectations. That makes all the difference, Tammy." And reaches out to chuck Jar under the chin. Of course, that makes Jar scream like a girl and hightail it to the porch.

"EEEEEEE!" Jar goes.

I stand there like a dummy. *Expectations.*

Before I can respond to Clarence, his radio squawks. He hops into his car and answers it.

"This is important. I got to go. They're missing a crate of dynamite over at the construction site," he calls out to me. "You think on it Tammy." And he reverses all the way down the driveway nearly taking out our mailbox.

Later that night I'm pacing back and forth in the living room unable to sleep. I'm excited. Nervous. Christmas and dentist all rolled up into one.

I'm just aching to get my money and have this whole deal done with and behind me. Jar's snoring away but I can't seem to close my eyes. I peek between the blinds. It's dark. No moon. But I notice the lights are still on in the workshop.

"Hells bells, there's no one around here responsible, but me." I mutter as I slip on my boots to go out and turn it off.

It's quiet and peaceful in the yard. I open the workshop door walk inside. The spirit of my Uncle is strong here. I sense he's with me and suddenly my belly settles and my mind calms like I stepped into a warm bath. There's a whole pile of whirligigs stacked against the wall. I touch one and smile. That brother of mine has been busy. I hold another one up and examine it. A green and yellow striped cat with bird wings. It's real pretty. Seems my brother is on a roll of capability.

I carry armfuls of whirligigs out to Dolly until her bed's full. I notice wood scraps and sawdust littering the floor so I grab a broom and sweep them up. I brush it into the dustpan and dump it in the trash. As I push the broom under the worktable, I notice for the first time a small shelf underneath. I get down on my hands and knees to investigate. There's a box tucked between two studs. An oversized shoebox. It's thickly covered with dust. When I wipe it off I see the words, *Steel-toed work boots size ten.* And over that in large felt pen letters, *To Madeline Moorehaven* in Uncle E's scrawl.

Well, the whole thing is mystifying. I dither for a bit trying to decide whether to open it up or leave it be, but then Uncle E is dead and I'm real curious. Too curious to wait and certainly too curious to give the box to Madeline without looking inside.

I open it up. There's something square wrapped in yellowed tissue. I pull it off. *Americana Folk Art. Spring Valley Public Library* is stamped on the inside cover.

"Holy moly!" I exclaim. "It's Uncle E's overdue library book!"

There's something else underneath wrapped in tissue paper. It's a miniature cupid whirligig. Moreover, it's not just any whirligig; it's real tiny and wonderfully carved. All with fancy curlicues and doodads. The wood looks like cherry. It's varnished to a high sheen. I'm thinking it's too tiny to be a real functioning whirligig, maybe it's meant to be a Christmas ornament as it's on a string. It dangles from my fingers and slowly spins on a cord attached to a gold ring screwed in the little guy's head. I study him for a bit and then wrap him back up carefully.

The book is still in good condition thank heavens. It doesn't look like it's been man handled, but I'm thinking the fine's got to be a thousand bucks at least. I sit there for a while thinking. Considering what to do.

These things should be taken to Madeline. That much I know. And the thought of that gets me to a recollection.

"The best person for advice is Madeline Moorehaven," Uncle E always used to say. "If you ever get yourself in a sticky wicket, you go straight to her."

It's like a sign, I think. Being in a pickle and then finding the box labeled with Madeline's name. I get chicken skin up and down my arms. I close my eyes and feel Uncle E's hand on my shoulder.

"Sissy, you know what to do," his voice is there in my head.

The timing couldn't be better. Tomorrow being bookmobile Wednesday. It's perfect. I can return the library book and whirligig to Madeline and at the same time, I can bend her ear about what's going on in my life. Verifying whether I'm on the right track and what to do about all the people who want to give me money.

Yes sir, this surely is a sign. It's Karma leading the way. I settle into Uncle's chair and place my head on my forearms.

And just like that, I fall asleep.

CHAPTER FOURTEEN

The next day it's raining. Jar and I sit in Dolly between the hardware store and Peggy's Cut N Clean waiting for the bookmobile. Our windows are rolled down so they don't steam up. I'm getting wet drops all over me.

At ten minutes to two, Walter marches out of his store wearing a garbage bag. It's his cheapskate way of saving on a raincoat. Madeline drives up in her van twenty minutes later and parks in front of his store. She slides out of the front seat wearing a yellow raincoat buttoned up to her chin. The glasses on her nose are quickly splattered with raindrops. A plastic flowered bonnet covers her sensible bun. She waves to us cheerfully when she sees us in Dolly.

"You have to back up!" Walter calls out to her. "You're blocking my entrance."

"The side of the road isn't owned by anyone. Besides I'm a public service vehicle." Madeline says. She walks around placing a chock behind each van tire.

Walter trails after her. "My customers won't be able to find my door," he complains.

"It's not my problem you have stupid customers." Madeline turns her back on him and opens the side door of her bookmobile van. There's the throb of a generator starting up.

During the next lull in the rain, I slip out of the truck and pull Jar after me.

Walter forces a smile when we walk by. "Hey, there Tammy," he says.

"Duck butt," Jar mutters.

I elbow my brother in the side.

"What's he say?" Walter furrows his brow.

"Nothing," I say to Walter. "Naphtha in your future," I whisper to Jar.

Walter shakes the drops off his garbage bag and disappears inside his hardware store.

"Why are you so ornery, anyway? You like the bookmobile," I say to Jar. But I've been ornery ever since I was made an heiress. I wonder if money will turn us both crabby permanently. I hold the shoebox and my purse tighter to my chest and make my way to the doorway of the van. I shudder the water off my back like a dog and step inside. Madeline is straightening books on a shelf.

"Hello, Tammy, Jar." Madeline smiles. "What can I do for you?"

I push my brother into a kiddy chair and hand him a book. "Look at this," I order.

Jar tosses the book aside and kicks the legs of the chair.

"Suit yourself," I say. When I turn my back, Jar picks the book off the floor.

"I found something of yours in uncle's workshop," I say and set the shoebox on the short shelf in front of us. "It had your name on it."

I lift the lid and offer her the miniature cupid whirligig and overdue library book.

Madeline ignores the book and picks up the cupid by its string. She doesn't say a word.

"Is it yours?" I ask.

The cupid hangs there slowly spinning. Around and around and around.

"Madeline?"

"Yes," she breathes. "It's mine." I can barely hear her.

"Good then," I say. "And sorry about the book on folk art." I push the book over. "I'm sure Uncle E would have returned it sooner or later. Is there a fine? Or is that erased when a person dies?" I ask.

Madeline's eyes are unnaturally bright. She stares at the spinning cupid. "Sometimes your life doesn't turn out the way you think," she says.

"You sure got that right," I agree.

"He made this for me as a Christmas ornament. On my eighteenth birthday." She cups the cupid in both hands.

"He? You mean Uncle E?"

"The very same. He called it his cupidity. A miniature cupid. I told him he was wrong. That cupidity meant greed, but he said that words didn't have to mean what the dictionary says they do. That if something sounds like it fits, it does."

Madeline slowly shakes her head.

"I was a know-it-all even then," she says. Her tone is flat.

"You're not a know-it-all." I protest. "You just know it all," I say. "That's two entirely different things."

Madeline gives a tight smile.

"And Uncle E was always talking about you," I say hurriedly. "He told me there wasn't anybody else he'd rather have in his corner. That you were one in a million."

She gives a cry like a bird hitting glass.

"Did I say something wrong?" I ask.

Madeline tenderly caresses the cupid. Stroking the wood with a finger like it was alive. "Your uncle asked me to marry him. Did he tell you that?"

She says this in a way that makes me want to lie real bad, but I don't. I shake my head wordlessly.

"It was a lifetime ago," she whispers.

It's then that Madeline starts to cry. Soundlessly. Tears rolling down her face.

I'm embarrassed and look away. "How'd you answer?" I ask.

"Yes." Madeline whispers. "I told him yes. I was crazy in love. We both were. He made me laugh. The two of us were always laughing"

I see that eighteen-year-old girl in the curve of Madeline's cheek. In the set of her jaw. She takes a deep breath.

"My parents didn't approve. They were worried what people would think. Him being a Tyree. *Criminals or religious wackos*, my father told me. *You'll rue the day.* And he made me give back the ring and every one of his gifts. Mother made me destroy all his letters." She touches the whirligig with a finger. "Not a Tyree. Never any Tyree," she whispers.

"I know how it goes being one, myself," I say thickly and then add. "Don't think it bothers me being painted with that particular brush. But hey, think on the bright side. If you'd gotten married to my Uncle you'd have been stuck taking care of Jar and me and had a drunk to deal with."

I say this thinking to cheer her up, but there's an ocean of regret in her expression. Like a giant wave rolling over the top of her head. Vast and inescapable. I've had that same feeling.

Madeline starts talking. She tells me about an Uncle E I never knew. One I never thought existed. A young Uncle E. A hopeful one. One who liked to dance and wear a Fedora hat. One who loved baseball and fried chicken and movies. One who enjoyed long drives and walks on the beach and could play *Let Me Call You Sweetheart* on the piano straight through like a pro.

"Edward. I called him Edward," Madeline says. "And he called me Maddy. He was good looking. Dark curly hair and kind eyes. My, he had plans. Talked of joining the Army. Said we could see the world together. Maybe even be stationed in California. My folks wanted me to go to college. Marry a teacher. Someone solid. Dependable. And I had no courage. None at all." She stares at me. "Tyrants are made not born," she says. "And I let my parents be tyrants."

I say nothing.

"Sometimes." She takes a tentative breath. "Sometimes I think I made him a drunk by leaving him. That I forced him to be the way he was. My parents told me I was smart. That I did the right thing. But I don't think so, Tammy. Being married to a drunk you love is better than being seventy years old and alone."

I stand there next to Madeline wondering why Uncle E never said a word. Never even hinted. I start to wonder if there was more he kept from me.

"After we broke apart is when he started calling himself E." The words tumble out of Madeline's mouth. "He said the Edward I knew was gone. He said if I ever changed my mind all I had to do was ask for the miniature whirligig back and he'd be right there for me. I never did ask. I thought about it, but I never did. I think Edward kept that library book so I was forced to send him a notice each month to return it," she whispers. "So I was forced to remember."

"I would have liked to have you for an aunt," I whisper. "There were times I surely could have used one." I swallow the ache in my throat and think about the man I knew as Uncle E.

What a shame to lose your name. What a shame to go through life never being who you really wanted to be. A patter of rain rattles the metal roof of the van.

I look at my watch and realize I'm due at the café.

Before I go out the doorway, I pause. "You know it's not too late Madeline. It's never too late for cupidity," I say and smile at her.

When I get a smile in return, it gladdens my heart.

I leave Dolly sitting there in front of the hardware store and Jar and I walk across the street to Two Spoons. My whole idea of who and what my Uncle E was, has gone topsy-turvy. E wanting to be in the Army? I know for a fact E had kind eyes, but good looking?

"You go in the kitchen and do your pans," I tell Jar.

I hang my coat on the hook and tie on my apron. Jar heads into the kitchen, but Curtis spreads his arms blocking Jar's way. "Nothing doing!" he says. "Rocks need to be left by the door." He points. "NOW."

It's then I notice my brother's bulging pockets. "Sorry, Curtis," I say weakly. I'm all worn out from thinking on Madeline and Uncle E.

"Fut rag," Jar mutters. "Pffft!" He digs deep in his pocket and pulls out the rocks.

"What'd he say? You tell me what he said!" Curtis glares at me.

"He was saying, hello," I lie.

"It sounded like farts. And don't drop those rocks there," Curtis says. "Leave them on the porch."

"Poop foot," Jar says, but he does what Curtis asks.

When we walk into the kitchen Leo stops chopping onions and waves with his knife.

"Hey, Jar. I'm glad you're here." Leo says. "Oven's on the fritz. Pans all have burnt Lasagna on the bottom."

I drag the step stool over to the sink

"Carp head," Jar says. He climbs up. I help him put on his plastic gloves.

"You watch your language and do what Leo says. Is that clear? You can't be sitting in that workshop day and night doing whirligigs. It isn't healthy. And hardly anybody is lucky enough just to have just one job. Everybody has a bunch of things they've got to do."

"Coot otter." Jar makes one of his faces.

"I'm tired too." I make a face back. "Sick and tired."

As I leave, I hear Leo warn Jar. "Now, no buzzer sounds tonight. I'm not in the mood."

"*Weep*!" Jar sings. "*Weep. Weep*."

I get busy on my side work, placing silverware on tables and setting out water glasses and coffee cups. I can't stop thinking of Madeline and Uncle E.

"What's up with you?" Curtis pokes me in the arm with a menu. "Cat got your tongue?"

That's Curtis all over. He'll point out bird poop on a brand new car. I grit my teeth and say nothing. The salad dressing bottles need cleaning and ketchups need filling. When I'm done, I make the coffee. And when I'm done with that, I go out into the garden and pick basil for Leo. When I bring the basket into the kitchen, Curtis trails behind me.

"I said what's up with you?" he says.

"Nothing's up with me." I say. "And it's none of your beeswax."

"It doesn't seem like nothing." Curtis studies me.

"Well, it is!" I say tiredly. "You complain when I talk and complain when I'm quiet."

Leo bangs the counter with a ladle. "Can it! You two bicker like an old married couple."

Curtis blanches and I widen my eyes. Leo out of sorts?

"You put away that stack of clean plates, and you? You can write tonight's soup on the board. It's Goose Grease Bisque. Now go," Leo growls

When we open for dinner, there's no rush of customers. The two of us twiddle our thumbs. I start wiping down tables and dusting the register. It's important, at least, to look busy. At six thirty, Kev walks through the door with his girlfriend, Helen. I smile with relief. "Hey, there, Kev."

I don't see Curtis so I grab a couple menus and seat them by the window booth. They each order the lasagna special.

I go back into the kitchen and hand Leo the chit. "Where's Curtis?" I ask.

"He took the rest of the night off," Leo says. "If nobody else comes in, we'll close early."

I take the plates out to Kev and Helen. When I come back in the kitchen, my brother's not by the sink.

"Where's Jar?" I ask.

Leo puts his finger to his lips and motions over at the bench by the back door. Jar is stretched out snoring loudly. "He ate dinner, finished with all the pans, and was pooped," Leo whispers. "He did a good job too. Here's his ten bucks."

I stuff it in my pocket. "I need to put him to bed."

Leo pulls his leather coat off the hook. "Just let him sleep." And he covers Jar up with his coat. Jar doesn't even crack an eye. "We can close up."

"I guess it'd be okay," I say. "I don't want to give Curtis cause to toss another *not meets* my way."

"I never listen to him." Leo shrugs.

I go out to the front, bus the lone dirty table, and change the white dinner tablecloths for the red checked breakfast ones. Leo comes out of the kitchen with two plates of food.

"Hungry?" he asks. "There's plenty of lasagna. Guess we know what tomorrow's lunch special is. Good thing it's even better the next day." He fingers his mustache thoughtfully. "I might try my hand at curried lasagna mulligatawny soup." He looks over at me. "What do you think?" he asks.

"I think you might aim for something simple for once like tomato or chicken noodle," I say. My stomach grumbles loudly. "I guess I could eat."

We sit at the counter together.

I take a big bite of lasagna and swallow. "I never asked, but what's the deal about your soups?"

"What do you mean what's the deal about my soups?" Leo pours himself a glass of water.

I stare. "Oh, come on, Leo. That dog won't hunt. Your soups are weird."

Leo cocks an eyebrow. He almost looks amused.

"I mean that's what some people say," I add quickly. "Why don't you do vegetable beef or split pea? I mean I'm not never seen any Campbell flavors that you serve."

"If I tell you, I'd have to kill you," Leo says.

I widen my eyes.

"Kidding," he says. "Why do you think I do it?"

"Well, let me see." I have to think. "To make people try new things? Shove them out of the ruts they're in?"

"That's as good a reason as any," Leo says.

"How do you choose the flavors?" I ask.

"Ah," he wags his finger. "That's a proprietary secret." He lurches to his feet and carries his plate into the kitchen.

I follow him in. "Sorry, it wasn't busy for you, Leo. But it will get better."

"No matter." Leo shrugs. He sets his dish in the sink.

"Really it will," I say firmly. I make a vow that the very first thing I do when I get my money will be to invest in Leo's restaurant.

That reminds me that I need to check my email. I'm a tad bit anxious, but I want privacy. I don't want the chance of Leo hanging over my shoulder.

"Let me do the dishes," I offer. "I'll load them in and start it. You can go on upstairs." I don't wait for him to answer and move to the sink.

Leo stares at me for a bit and then walks out the door.

Jar snores softly. He's still asleep. I quickly do the few dishes and wipe down the counters. After flicking off the kitchen lights, I go back into the dining room. It takes forever to boot up the computer. Like Uncle E always said, a watched pot never heats up unless you turn on the stove.

I log in and my heart leaps into my throat. *There's something from Dr. Barinas.* I quickly print the email out and stuff it into my pocket to read later.

When I grab my jacket and go back into the kitchen, I'm intending on carrying Jar back to the trailer, but I hear music coming from behind the Café.

Jar is snug under Leo's jacket. I stroke the hair off his forehead and then slide out the back door. I tiptoe around the corner of the building to Leo's garden. There's a faint scent of weed mixed with incense. My eyes adjust to the dark. It's stopped raining and the night is warm.

Leo is sitting on a bench by the trellis strumming his guitar and singing. I sneak closer. A couple of frogs throb somewhere in a ditch. I stand there listening. Leo's voice is strong and deep. I don't recognize the song, but I like it.

I slip over to a large rock in the garden and settle myself down. I hug my knees and hunch over. Making myself smaller than I already am.

When Leo finishes, I clap softly.

He doesn't appear surprised to see me.

"What was that?" I ask.

He takes a slow drag off his joint and then carefully sets it down.

"*Cowgirl In The Sand*," he breathes out. "By Neil Young. Sheesh, I forget how young you are."

"I'm almost twenty-four," I say hotly. 'And it's not like it's God Bless America, you know." My tone is kind of snotty.

"No, you're right. It's not," Leo laughs.

"I liked it," I say. "Play another." I add. "Please?"

And he does. I ask him the name each time. And each time he shakes his head and laughs.

"You take requests like on the radio?" I ask.

Leo shrugs. "I probably don't know any of your songs but I'll give it a try."

"The one you played at the ER for Jar. Play that one again. It was pretty."

He furrows his brows. "Do you remember how it went?"

I close my eyes. "About a blackbird singing."

"Ah. The Beatles." He salutes with his hand. "You got it."

When he finishes that one, he plays another, and another. As he strums, I listen to each of the words. I think about the person who wrote the song and what they were trying to say.

Did I see you walking…so much pain. One goes.

"What's the name of that song?" I ask.

"Harvest," Leo says.

"Play it again."

Leo does. I can't help but start to hum the melody. *Did she wake you up…only a change of plans.* I try to sing along.

When he finishes he slowly nods. "A couple more times and you'll get it." He smiles. "You have a good voice."

I feel myself color up and I'm suddenly glad it's dark. "Well, how about that?" I say. "Something about me is good."

"A lot about you is good," Leo says. He keeps strumming as I pluck stalks of grass out of the ground. "You got a new hairdo."

"I didn't think you noticed. Nobody else did."

"I noticed," Leo says.

My email is burning a hole in my pocket. The feeling is prickly. Like a hedgehog in my belly turning around, finding a place to get comfortable.

"Did you know Uncle E and Madeline were an item back in the day?" I say.

"That so?" Leo keeps on strumming.

"I got to get back to Jar soon," I say. "He might wake up all alone in the kitchen." Knowing he won't.

Leo keeps picking at the strings. The music echoes and the crickets chime in.

"Leo," I say suddenly. "If you came into a pile of money, what would you do with it?"

Leo raises his eyebrows. "I don't spend much time thinking about things like that."

"But if you did" I persist. "What would you do?"

Leo doesn't answer. He picks his guitar and sings. *"Dream up. Dream up,"* he goes.

I lock my fingers together and wait until he finishes. "Well?" I ask again.

"Nothing different," he shrugs. "Why do you ask?"

"As a matter of fact, I'm coming into some," I say. "An inheritance from a relative I didn't know I had."

Something flickers across Leo's face. "Good for you," he says carefully. And he goes right into a another song. Something about a man needing a maid. The loneliness of it takes my breath away and makes my heart real sad and heavy. It reminds me of Uncle E and Madeline. I stare at Leo.

To get a love you got to give a love…be a part of…When will I see you again… And his word fly up to the sky and beyond. Over the hills and into the night.

When the last note dies, I stand up.

"Anyway," I say. "I just wanted you to know. I mean I'm not quitting Two Spoons or nothing. I just…" My voice trails off. "I just wanted you to know," I say weakly.

Leo says nothing in reply to this.

I walk home in the dark carrying Jar over my shoulder. When I get to the trailer, I put my brother to bed. He doesn't make a peep. I go to my room, pull out the email, and read it.

UNION BANK
BOTSWANA.

DEAR MADAME TYREE,
THIS IS TO INFORM YOU THAT YOUR TRUST WORTHINESS HAS IMPRESSED MOST ABSOLUTELY THE MINISTER OF EXTERNAL AFFAIRS.
THE REQUEST FOR FORMAL APPLICATION FOR THE RELEASE AND ONWARD REMITTANCE OF THE MONEY FROM YOUR RELATIVE'S ESTATE FIVE MILLIONS ENGLISH DOLLARS TO YOUR ACCOUNT VIA TELEGRAPHIC TRANSFER (T.T.)
IS CONTINUINGLY MOST SATISFACTORILY.
AGAIN, SECRECY IS OF THE ESSENCE.
WE HAVE NEED OF ANOTHER TWO THOUSAND DOLLARS TO FINALIZE THE TAX REMITTANCE AND SETTLE FEES FOR THE SOLICITORS AND BANKING OFFICIALS THAT WILL BE SENDING THE MONETARY ACCOUNTING WITH ALL DUE DISPATCH.
YOU WILL NOTICE AN ADDITIONAL MODERATE SUM AUTOMATICALLY DEDUCTED FROM YOUR BANK ACCOUNT. THIS IS AN INTERNAL TESTING MATTER AND SHOULD NOT CONCERN YOU.

WE ARE DOING SUMMER NOW. I HAVE A WIFE BUT ALAS NO CHILDREN AND ONE SISTER. I ENJOY WATCHING FOOTBALL.
BEST REGARDS,
DR. BARINAS
EXECUTOR AND MINISTER
FAITH BASED CHARITY GOVERNMENTAL DEPARTMENT
GABORONE, BOTSWANA

I'm so disappointed I practically cry. Barinas wants even more money. How could he possibly need any more? How much of my money does he have, now? How much of other people's money. Like Peggy's and Josephine's and Walter's? And doubt creeps in like a sneaky burglar. Maybe it's all a mistake. Maybe I'll never get my inheritance.

I press my fingers to my temple. My head throbs. I pull my jacket back on. The café is now silent and dark. Leo is no longer in the garden.

My email reply is short and sweet.

Dear DR. Barinas,
I'm all tapped out.
You'll have to make do with what you got.
Sorry about that, Tammy Louise Tyree

And I march back home and go straight to bed.

CHAPTER FIFTEEN

I'm not the brightest donkey in the barn.

That's the first thing floating around in my brain the next morning. My middle is aching like I was kicked in the stomach. There's sand in my eyes and my face is creased from being pressed against the couch cushion. I smell like grease from sleeping in my uniform so I stand in the shower with water streaming over me until the temperature cools. As I pull on my jeans and tee shirt, I do some mental kicking of butt.

Why did I answer that email so fast? Why didn't I stop and think. Uncle E always warned me against being impulsive. Of course, that was because he was lazy, but it was still good advice. Hells bells! It seems I'm always jumping the gun and leaping before I look.

And what about Barinas? He's probably going to be pissed off after all the time he's spent on my behalf. If he let me come up with half the money at a time once, what's to say he wouldn't have done the same thing again? I should have waited to respond. Slept on it. Double dang it all anyway.

I sit down at my desk and try to total what I owe.

There's Peggy. She's given me $2800, $500, and I think another $250. Or was it $350? And should I count all the free trims? Then Josephine's two contributions of $500 each. And she bought me lunch a few times. And then Walter. Well, there's his first $4000 and then another $500 and three or four loads of supplies for the whirligigs. I tried to pay him when I got the money from Allison, but he waved it away. I did drop off twenty whirligigs to his store, but I can't think that makes it even close. Fact is, I'm losing track. I would have written it all down but I didn't think everybody in Spring was going to give me cash each time I turned around. And that's not even including me saying I'd invest in their businesses. I don't even know what that entails.

I'm in deep. Real deep. I have to go the distance. That's certain now. But it's like a marathon race and in order to finish I have to come up with another two thousand bucks and how am I going to do that? Do these Botswana folk think I'm made of other people's money?

And speaking of money why isn't my own here, anyway?

There's a knock at my door. I shove everything back in my desk and peek out the curtain.

Curtis and Smithers are standing on my front porch. Holy darn Moses! An unlikely duo to be sure. What are they doing here this early?

It's then I notice Dolly's gone. Did I forget to stuff rocks under her wheels? Maybe she's flown the coop and hightailed it backwards into Two Spoons. But then I remember. She's still sitting in front of the hardware store. I never brought her back home.

I'd forget my head if it wasn't tied on.

I check behind me. The trailer is a mess. Clothes on the floor. I haven't done laundry for ages. Dishes are piled on the coffee table. There's the crust of a jam sandwich on the floor. I scoot it to the side with my foot.

I slowly open the door. "What can I do for you?" I say cautiously.

"We have something we want to discuss confidential-like," Smithers says. Curtis and him both take a step forward like they're joined at the hip.

I don't invite them in. Instead, I slide out onto the porch.

"I need to be someplace. Can you make it quick?" That sounds rude.

"Please," I add.

Smithers elbows Curtis in the side. "You first," he says.

"No, you can go," Curtis offers.

"That's okay," Smithers says. "You can start."

"No, you," Curtis says.

"Well, I can't stand here all day while you two decide," I snort.

Curtis clears his throat. "Uh, I was talking with Smithers here over at the café and Walter was there and he let slip something about there being a delay about your inheritance and needing a hand and then Peggy—" Curtis is stammering like a kid in front of the principal.

Smithers breaks in. "Anyway, we know for a fact you got some big deals going on with those other folk in town and we discussed it and the both of us want in."

Curtis straightens up. "Yeah, we want in," he chimes.

"Why is my beeswax everybody's concern?" I put my hands on my hips.

"Because it concerns us all, that's why," Smithers says.

"How do you figure?" I say.

"It's to do with our town. Peggy was telling me—us—."

"And just what was Peggy telling?" I look from Smithers to Curtis and back again.

The two of them shrivel like an ice cube on hot pavement. "That you need help with the details. That it's up to us to help out," Smithers trails off. "Look. I have three thousand in my savings but can withdraw more out of my retirement account if need be. Curtis here has all his LA money he can invest."

"What's that got to do with me?"

"The two of us talked and we figure you need additional funds. I mean you can have your place fixed up and get organized. You'll need to be having meetings and talking with lawyers. Heck, you'll probably have guys coming for miles around asking you out," Smithers says. "You might even need a body guard." Smithers straightens and sucks his gut in.

"I don't really see as I need any more partners," I say slowly.

"You do," Curtis says desperately. "Come on, Tammy."

It occurs to me that the more reluctant I am to take money the more people want to give it to me. Maybe this will solve my current fiscal problem. I'm thinking hard.

"The more the merrier." Smithers gives his hat a whop on his thigh. "Isn't that good business sense?"

"How does it work?" Curtis asks. He pulls out his checkbook. Clarence is writing his own check using the porch rail to write on.

"I put them in my account and then wire it on to Dr. Barinas in Africa. He's the solicitor," I say. "It's all professional. Real fancy. High class."

Curtis frowns. "A solicitor in Africa?" He looks at me sharply. "Not here in this country?"

Smithers grins and pokes Curtis with his elbow. "See? High class. How about that? A solicitor! Didn't I tell you? This is how big time investments work," he says confidently. "I read *Money* magazine," he assures me as he hands over his check.

"Yeah a solicitor," I say and trot over to my desk. I grab up the last email.

"If I let you read this you better keep my beeswax under your hat," I say. "Don't be a couple of loud mouths like Peggy and Walter."

Curtis takes the email and starts to read. He hands it back to me and scowls.

"This is nothing but a scam." Curtis puts his checkbook back in his pocket.

"Well, if you think that I don't need your money," I say. I start to hand Smithers' check back.

"No! No! Tammy," Smithers says. He glares at Curtis, "See what you did?"

"What?" Curtis says. "It's like one of those Nigerian scam letters. Anybody with one brain cell can see that."

I get hot under the collar. "For your information it's from Botswana. And it's no scam. It's from our Tyree missionary relatives."

Curtis stares from me to Clarence. "I don't know who's more gullible. You or her." And he stomps off.

I tear up Clarence's check. "See? I never asked for this. And I don't appreciate being called a liar."

"No! Tammy!" Clarence flutters his hands. He pulls out his check book and writes out another. "I can give you two thousand." He hands it to me and I rip that one up too.

"Three then?"

"I'm not begging," I say. "And I didn't come to you. You came to me."

"Tammy, Curtis is wrong. He's missing the boat and I'm going to tell him so."

"Don't you tell him nothing," I say, but I accept his fourth check for thirty-five hundred.

After he leaves, I quickly dial Peggy's number.

"You got to keep your big old trap shut and stop gabbing about our deal," I say. "Curtis and Smithers came by today, no thanks to you." I don't tell her what Curtis said. She'll find out soon enough.

"They did? I just let them know we had something going on. That isn't gabbing."

It doesn't do any good to get in a tangle with Peggy. She can argue in an empty house.

"I'm gonna be a tad late for you today. I have to run to the bank," I tell her instead.

"Is something new going on?" she asks all excited. "Did you get some of the money?"

"Don't know yet," I say.

I rap loudly on the desk with my knuckles.

"Someone's at the door I got to go!" I slam the receiver down.

I feel bad about telling a fib, so I check my door to make it sort of true.

Peggy doesn't know when to shut up. I could have been on the phone with her all day. I go into my brother's room. He's a bundle in the bed. Eyes squeezed shut.

"Hey, there!" I clap my hands. "You need to get up, now. We have to go to the bank!"

Nothing.

"Hey, there?" I say again. Louder this time. I shake his shoulder.

Still nothing.

"I'm getting a cup of cold water," I threaten.

"Okey dokey!" Jar tosses his blanket aside and leaps up fully dressed.

"Why you need to play possum like that I'll never know."

"Otter shoe." Jar flaps his hands.

"Yeah, well, it's getting old. Plus it's a game that will get your butt paddled. Now find your jacket and let's get going."

"Okey dokey" Jar makes a beeline to the kitchen.

"There's no time for sitting down to breakfast. You can eat out of the cereal box on the way. It'll be like going out to a restaurant. How about that? We're killing two birds with one stone."

"ACK!" Jar hates the idea of killing birds.

He heads out the door with a container of Fruit Loops under his arms. I snatch Dolly's keys and head out after him. It takes a good fifteen minutes to get to Dolly in front of the hardware store as Jar stops every so often to scoop up a likely looking rock. I'm in too good of a mood to quibble with his rock collecting.

On the way to the bank, I think about what Curtis said. I frown. My inheritance isn't a scam. It couldn't be. Not if Walter and Peggy and Josephine and Clarence believe it isn't.

I look over at my brother. He's nibbling on red and yellow Fruit Loops.

"No tossing the green ones on the floor," I say. "Hand them over and I'll eat them. I haven't had breakfast, either."

I think about the money.

Having it will change our lives. I consider. Like I told Leo, I'll still do my waitressing. Got to have something to do with my days. Jar will still do whirligigs as he enjoys it. But what then? It's a puzzle. What do people do when they're rich? I glance over at Jar. He's picking out the red loops. The two of us can only eat so much. Some new clothes, maybe. Jar could use a few more pair of jeans. Have to get a dresser for his bedroom if we do that. Jar keeps his clothes in a cardboard box, which makes it easier for him to dress himself. Things so low like that. I could pay somebody to make a custom miniature one. Jar would like that. And custom lamps real low to the ground. That would be real fancy.

I pull into the bank just when it opens. "You stay!" I order Jar.

"Okey dokey!" He's kicking the seat with his feet and eating his Fruit Loops so I know he's good for maybe ten minutes. I lock Dolly's door and run in.

"I need to deposit this," I wave the check in front of the teller. "How fast will it be good?"

"You have to wait five business days for it to clear," the teller says.

"Hells bells, it's written on funds in this very bank! Can't you make an exception?"

"No exceptions." The teller shakes her head.

"Okay then," I say. At least Barinas deducts it automatically. I don't have to send a wire any more with all the special overseas routing numbers. It's complex like all business deals.

When I walk out, I feel a mite dissatisfied that it'll take four more days. All those ads about sending money quick are a bunch of bull.

I pull out my email and read it again. It came yesterday. Then I frown remembering I emailed Dr. Barinas saying I couldn't come up to scratch. I better quick like a bunny email him again and let him know my prospects have changed. That ought to make it good.

When I get back to Dolly, Jar's in the driver's seat. "Move over," I say.

"Egg wrapper?" Jar likes McDonalds.

"No dice until those checks clear," I tell him. When I turn the ignition, my wipers, lights, and radio, all go on at once. Jar laughs and bounces in the seat.

"Poop carp!" he says.

"Why'd you do that for? Messing with all my knobs!" I smack my brother up the side of his head.

"ACK!" he goes.

"Jose!" I call him.

"ACK!" Jar goes.

"Jose! Jose! Jose!" I yell.

"ACK! ACK!" Jar hides his head from me.

Fighting with my brother is not going to get the money here sooner. I glance at the gas gauge. Dolly's tank is near empty. Time to swing by the Gas & Go and I hit the accelerator. Dolly shudders.

I pull into the self-service lane and roll down my window. "We're getting a near fill-up, Annette!" I yell.

Annette hangs out the open window of her kiosk and frowns. "You'd best have cash," she shouts back at me.

I wave a fistful of ones from my tip money. "I have it right here." I slide out and grab the nozzle.

Annette's surprised face is worth any price. I can hardly hide my smile. As the pump ticks away, I pretend not to notice Annette's puzzled look and whistle one of Leo's songs.

When the pump shuts off, I go over to pay Annette. She makes me stand there while she licks her fingers and counts my money one dollar at a time. She examines each bill carefully holding it up to the light. "I guess it's all right." She sounds disappointed.

I no sooner get back behind Dolly's wheel then I hear a whistle.

"Hold up there, Tammy!" My cousin Lonnie leans through Jar's open window. "Hey, there, little moron," he chucks Jar's under his chin.

"Otter!" Jar tries to bite the end of Lonnie's finger.

My cousin jerks it back. "Hey!"

"Don't call him that," I say.

Lonnie bops Jar on the head with one hand and taps his cheek with the other. "Moron. Moron."

"Ack!" Jar spits at him and Lonnie ducks.

"Teach him some manners why don't you." Lonnie wipes his cheek.

"Learn some yourself," I say.

I turn the key and pump the accelerator, but Dolly takes a notion not to start.

"You flooded her," Lonnie observes.

"No, I didn't," I say and keep pumping the gas and turning the ignition. Of course, then I do flood her. Dang it all.

"How about you give me a ride into town?"

Lonnie opens Jar's door without a by your leave and attempts to slide in, but Jar hunkers down and starts to pinch and slap him. Jar's a great pincher and slapper. Lonnie moves away to avoid Jar's fingers and Jar slams the door on him quick and locks it. He rolls the window up.

"Ear wipe!" Jar says.

"You tell him, Jar!" I say approvingly. "By the way, how'd it go with Smithers?" I yell this through the closed window real sweet.

Lonnie scowls at as both.

"Gag pooper," Jar says.

"What's he saying?" Lonnie asks.

"That you're wearing out your welcome." I warn.

"Fit! Fit!" Jar points at Lonnie. "Asswipe."

"Jar," I warn and try to start Dolly. The engine just grinds. Dang it all.

Lonnie walks over to my side and wiggles Dolly's side mirror.

"I hear you're days from getting that inheritance. And it's a whack of cash," he says through the closed window.

"You ought not to believe everything you hear."

"Do I need to remind you that I'm a Tyree too? That any money coming to you ought to come to me as well."

"You don't need to remind me of anything," I snap.

"Looks like I'll need to get a lawyer." Lonnie threatens.

"You don't scare me. Why don't you crawl back into that hole you came out of," I say.

"Don't be crazy. That's just what I'm going to say to my lawyer. You're crazy. In fact..." He gives me an appraising look. "Maybe you need to see a head doctor or something." Lonnie says. "Maybe you aren't responsible enough to be in charge of Jar or that much money."

He gives a laugh that doesn't sound like he thinks anything's funny.

I lean all the way forward, turn the key, and press the gas. Dolly starts and we peel out leaving Lonnie in our dust.

"You think about what I said, cousin Tammy!" I hear him shout.

"Ant pie." Jar's brows are pushed down.

"You worried? Aw, Bug, don't be worried." And I give Jar a twitch on his ear. "Remember what Uncle E used to say. Cousin Lonnie is all swagger and no stride."

"Okey dokey," Jar says.

"That Lonnie may be street smart, but there's only one road in Spring, so it isn't saying much," I chuckle. Saying that may have reassured Jar, but I get to worrying. Will Lonnie really go to a lawyer or is he bluffing? Could my cousin really get me into trouble? I'm Jar's sister. Why would Lonnie make a threat about me being crazy?

Jeeze Louise. I shake my head. I'll be glad enough when this money gets into my account. If I throw a few dollars his way, Lonnie will most likely skedaddle.

I wonder how much he'll want. That makes me frown all over again. Why should I give that user anything at all? Double darn. No. TRIPLE darn.

I pound on Dolly's wheel. It isn't fair with Lonnie snooping around, like a bear after garbage. If being rich means I got to fight moochers off every damn day it might not even be worth the trouble.

CHAPTER SIXTEEN

One thing leads to another like beads on a string and if it doesn't, then you're under the ground, dead and buried. At least that's what Uncle E used to say. The news of my inheritance predeceases me.

Somebody put an article in the Tribune. The fat's in the fire, now.

HEIRESS WORKS AS WAITRESS is the front-page headline. It discusses my beeswax in detail. It talks about Jar and lists the things we want to buy when the money comes. There are even a few lines about Uncle E and our Tyree missionary relatives who went to Africa.

I'm madder than a wet hen. I go straight to the Cut N Clean.

"Peggy!" I burst through the door. "Did you do this?" I holler, knowing full well she did.

"I may have," Peggy bites her lip.

"For your information I was born at home, not Everett General." I shake the paper in Peggy's face. "And Momma's name was Luella. Louise is MY middle name."

Peggy pats me on the shoulder. "Calm down. You'll drop of a stroke like your Uncle E," she says. "And it wasn't supposed to go in yet. That reporter promised to wait until you got the money," Peggy frowns. "He lied to me."

"He's a reporter," I say. "Lying is what they do."

My mood is stormy as I walk out her door. I'm on my way back home when three construction workers wave me down

"Is it true what was in the paper?" the first one asks. "You're one of them *airesses*?" He looks at his buddy and winks.

"Maybe I'll propose," the other one says.

"And maybe I'll give you a knuckle sandwich," I fold my fingers into a nice sized fist and shake it in his face.

He backs off. "Just kidding," the third one says.

I dodge between them and march up my driveway kicking rocks as I go. Everybody knows my beeswax, now, thanks to that article. My tail's in a knot for sure. I pace back and forth in the kitchen and fuss at Jar.

"My inheritance deal was supposed to be confidential. What if Dr. Barinas finds out about the article and thinks I'm not trustworthy? Will he decide my money ought to be left to someone else? See there? I'm already thinking of it as my money." I look at Jar. "Our money," I correct myself.

"Hard not," Jar says.

"Isn't that the truth," I say. "Greed is a negative trait, for sure."

I hustle around trying to think of something to fix for lunch. "How about toast and eggs?" I ask. "You want scrambled?" I feel around in the drawer. The breadbox is empty. "Okay so no toast."

Jar sticks his tongue out.

"You do that often enough it'll stay that way," I scold. "You're getting too old for that crap."

"Okey dokey," Jar says and helps me by hunting under the sink. "No go," he says.

"That's right. Our cupboard's empty like Mother Hubbard," I say. "We need bread and milk. I guess we'd best get provisions."

"Foot booty!" Jar claps his hands. He likes to go grocery shopping.

"Yeah, Fruit Loops, too. Come on, then," I say. I make a quick check to make sure he doesn't have any rocks in his pockets and then we pile into Dolly instead of doing the walk. Neither of us likes carrying grocery bags all the way up our steep driveway.

"You got to stick by me and keep your act together," I warn. "Sue Ann won't stand for any of your shenanigans," I warn as we pull into the parking lot.

The Nedermyers frown on Jar being at Shop and Save. My brother has a habit of checking things out before we buy them. Makes sense to me, but the Nedermyer's take exception to it. We usually buy what he opens, so it shouldn't make any difference. Well, except the squished grapes. Jar likes to pinch them until they pop. Like that plastic bubble stuff. The bell chimes as we walk in.

"*Inckel. Inckel. Inckel,*" Jar goes. He's spot on.

I grip my brother hard by the shoulder.

"You behave," I whisper.

The store is empty except for Sue Ann Nedermyer at the register. She's doing her nails pastel pink. I'm all ready to defend my brother's right to be in the Shop and Save, but to my surprise, Sue Ann gives us both a cheery smile. Fake or no, it feels special.

"Hey, there Tammy." She leans across the counter to Jar. "How you doing, buddy?"

"ACK!" Jar hates to be called buddy.

He eludes my grasp and snatches a pack of gum off the counter.

"Put it back," I say. "Or no skittles."

He grudgingly puts it back. It's only a little squished.

"Go on. Let him have it," Sue Ann says.

"Gum is not a good idea," I say to her and wonder if she's had a personality transplant.

"You give my brother an inch and he'll take a handful of candy."

Jar hangs monkey-like on the side of the cart as I push.

"Don't Jar! You'll make it tippy!" I thwack his ear.

"Oh, leave him be," Sue Ann says. She picks at her nail.

Now, I know she's either on drugs or been drinking. Sue Ann never says more than a couple words to Jar and it always includes *stop* or *don't.*

I peek at her sideways as we go up one aisle and down the other, but she's not paying any attention to me. There's only a little left in my checking account so I have to be careful even though the money should be here soon. I buy a day old loaf of bread and a box of powdered milk. Cans of beets are on sale. Probably because nobody eats them. If I got a can, it would be a waste no matter how cheap it was. Jar uses the juice to paint his face and won't stick them in his mouth. Dented pork and bean cans are two for a dollar so I get four. Jar puts a box of Fruit Loops and a box of Sugar Smacks in the cart.

"Only one," I say. "Not both." I put the Sugar Smacks back.

Jar's face gets stormy and he grabs it back off the shelf. "Dude hole," he says.

I know that tone and it isn't good. "Too much sugar turns you wild," I say. "And it's not nutritious. I promised you Fruit Loops, not the whole dang cereal aisle." I dangle a small bag of skittles in front of him. "None of these if you act up and that's a promise. I'm gonna put it back." I warn.

"Poop head! Carper!" Jar hugs the cereal to his chest and scowls

"Watch that mouth!" I scowl right back. "Just for that no hotdogs for the beanie weenies."

Jar brows furrow.

"You decide," I say, tapping my foot.

"Butt wipe," he mutters.

"Sticks and stones!" I mutter back.

Sue Ann is peeling lipstick off a front tooth with her thumbnail.

I set my stuff on the counter. As she rings me up, she nibbles on her lower lip like she hasn't had lunch. "You sure you don't want eight of these?" she points to the beans. "We got a special going on."

"Special or no, I'm on a budget," I say shortly. Being poor has never bothered me except in the grocery store. But then it won't be long before we can buy anything we want.

The Tribune is spread out on the counter.

"I read the article." Sue Ann taps the newspaper with a sparkly nail and takes a deep breath. "And if you want to know I also talked to Josephine Munn." Sue Ann's voice is hard "I know the deal you got going with Peggy and Walter and the rest and I just want to tell you it's not fair."

"What do you mean not fair?" I ask.

"That thing you got going with them." Sue Ann lifts her chin. "It isn't fair to leave me out."

"There is no deal and that article was all wrong. Peggy's a blabbermouth. And I didn't leave you out." I don't say I never thought about her being in one way or the other.

Sue Ann has a pout on her face.

"I'm telling you I want in. I don't have money to give you, but I can let you run a tab here at the store. Buy anything you want. I can make it all work out so you don't need to worry. Glenn and his daddy don't need to know a thing about it."

Her husband Glenn is a stickler against credit. "But I don't know when my money will get here," I say. "There are still taxes and fees and important paper stuff. It may take a while. Like even another month or more," I tell her.

Sue Ann expression turns into one just like in high school when she wasn't able to be first to use the mirror in the girl's bathroom. "I think you're being mean and spiteful and stingy, Tammy Louise Tyree. You're paying me back for being a cheerleader and popular."

"I'm not being mean and spiteful and stingy. And you haven't been popular or a cheerleader for years."

Sue Ann's eyes widen in shock.

I wrest a package of hotdogs out of Jar's fingers. "I told you either hot dogs or cereal. Not both!" I say. "These gotta be put back."

Sue Ann's face darkens. I can tell all the signs of a tantrum. Jar has them often enough.

"Well!" Sue Ann blusters.

"Add train," Jar whines. He starts trying to tear off a corner of the hotdog package knowing full well we'll have to buy them.

"You better not open those!" I warn. "If you do then no Skittles." I snatch the bag of candy off the counter.

"ACK." Jar says. "Whirp do."

"Hells bells," I say. "Hells bells. I guess you made your point. You do work hard on the whirligigs."

I turn to Sue Ann. "Okay. I guess it's a deal."

Her face clears and she smiles.

"Go on out there and fill up your cart," Sue Ann flutters her hands at us.

And that's what we do. I get hamburger and lettuce and both Sugar Smacks and Fruit Loops and two giant bags of Skittles. Then I pile on tomatoes and some Nestles chocolate and real milk instead of powdered and apple juice along with eight frozen Banquet fried chicken dinners. For dessert, we get hostess Ding Dongs and ice cream and potato chips. The total comes to $138.25. I never spent that much in one place before. We can barely fit the bags between the two of us in Dolly.

I turn the ignition and Dolly's engine struggles to turn over.

"*Er. Er. Er,*" Jar mimics.

"Yeah, I know. We probably need a new starter. And we need more gas."

It's been several weeks since Lonnie caught me off guard at Annette's, and I been avoiding going there, but Dolly needs gas and I got my tip money left that I didn't have to spend on groceries.

I heave a sigh. "Let's get this over with." I head over to the Gas & Go.

When I pull up to the pump, I grab Jar by the ear. "You keep an eye out for Lonnie. You hear?" I tell him.

"Poop dot," Jar says. "Okey dokey."

"You got that right, but he snuck up real good on us last time, smell or no smell. You stay here." I grab my purse and head over to Annette's kiosk.

"One, two, three plus a five. That makes eight bucks worth." I lay my tip money down in front of her.

Annette puts down her magazine and gives me her narrowed-eye stare. She counts my money three times. "Only eight?" she grumbles.

"That's what I said, Miss High and Mighty. Set it at eight. There isn't any law that says people have to fill their tanks up to the top."

"I know that," she sniffs. "But I figured you'd be filling her up now. Clarence Smithers told me you're on the hunt looking for investors for some money you're getting from an inheritance. I figured you were on easy street, now." Annette shakes her head. "Must just be talk."

I frown deeply. "Smithers told you that?"

"And he said he's quitting the department and going into business for himself. That he's got an investor backing him. I'd like to get me some tow trucks, but I don't have any investors dropping money into my lap." She jerks her thumb at her chest. "I'm saving. Doing it all myself." And Annette studies me. "Of course, I told Smithers I thought it sounded fishy. The world isn't like that. Tyrees getting a windfall just when they need it."

"Well, it's not," I snap. "And it's true. It's even in the Tribune. The world's working different, now," I say.

I go to pump my gas. The gauge stops at $8.50. I march back to Annette.

"I told you eight even!" I say hotly.

"I heard you say $8.50." Annette says firmly.

"Hells bells!" I head back to Dolly and dig in the bottom of my purse. I find a nickel and four dimes. "Can I come back later for the rest?"

"Nope," Annette shakes her head firmly.

Jar and I have to scrounge around on the floor of Dolly for pennies. We come up with three.

"Jar, check your pants pockets." I say.

"No go." Jar's eyebrows shoot down. That tells me he's holding out on me.

"If you got some money hand it over!"

A Chevy pulls up to the next pump. Two young girls stare at Jar through their window. I catch them pointing and hear their giggles. I feel myself redden as I hunt in my brother's pockets. I find a dollar that looks like it's been washed and dried a couple times. The two of us start in on a tug of war.

"Ack!" Jar cries. "Ack! Ack!"

"Give it up, Jar!" I growl. "It's your fair contribution to our financial effort."

"Org carp," Jar mutters.

"Pan money is not either yours. I'm telling you our funds got to be pooled."

"Poo?" Jar perks his ears up. He loosens his grip and I get the dollar.

"Ha!" I say. "And no we're not getting a pool."

"Ack!" Jar throws himself back against the seat.

I toss the rest of the money to Annette and she hands me my change.

I flee. Lucky for me Dolly starts.

It's been a long time since I was embarrassed about anything. High school was the last time. My face gets hot thinking about it. I was a senior.

"Uncle E can you not bring Jar when you take me to school?" I'd said casually. This was after I saw my classmates point and whisper behind hand-covered mouths when I walked past them after Uncle E picked me up or dropped me off. It wasn't just the whirligigs twirling in the back end of the truck. Uncle E stared at me so hard I had to drop my eyes.

"You shamed of your kin, Tammy Louise?" He'd said.

"No," I'd muttered.

Uncle E had snorted. "Blood is thicker than water, Tammy. You start being ashamed of your family next thing you know you're ashamed of everything in your life," he chastised. "And shame grows on you. It does," he cautioned. "Pretty soon it's the only thing you feel." And he gave me a swat on the bottom to emphasize his seriousness even though I was far too old for it.

I reach over now and tousle Jar's head.

No, I'm not ashamed of my brother. Might as well be ashamed of our trailer, or our chickens, or the fact we make whirligigs. Heck, might as well be ashamed of the weather in Spring. All gray and misty.

My brother's got his face pressed to the window watching the scenery pass. Every once in a while his pink tongue darts out to lick the condensation off the glass. He gives a smile like it tastes pretty good.

There are times I suspect Jar's smarter than I give him credit for. He gets taken care of, a place to stay, his meals fixed. He pretty much gets to do what he wants except for excess rock throwing and window breaking. It'd be nice to be taken care of like that, but then I see that worried expression in his eyes like he suspects there's something more everybody seems to know about life that he doesn't.

I reach over and ruffle his hair again. "I'm sorry, Bug. You can throw rocks all day and night, if you want to. I promise," I whisper.

My brother sends a flap in my direction. "Okey dokey," he says happily.

It's a tall, tall world my brother lives in. The thought of that breaks my heart.

CHAPTER SEVENTEEN

I'm living for Barinas-Botswana emails. I check my account twice an hour, sometimes more, when Two Spoons is slow. I get a few jam orders, couple of garage cleaning requests, plus more ads for weight loss pills and willywagger stretchers, but nothing from Barinas. And then, just when I start to lose hope, one comes. I read it over and over, squinting, not quite believing my eyes.

UNION BANK
BOTSWANA.
DEAR MADAME TYREE,
THE MINISTER OF EXTERNAL AFFAIRS HAS RELEASED THE REMITTANCE FROM YOUR RELATIVE'S ESTATE FIVE MILLIONS ENGLISH

DOLLARS TO YOUR ACCOUNT VIA TELEGRAPHIC TRANSFER (T.T.)
THE MONETARY ACCOUNTING WILL BE CONCLUDED WITH ALL DUE DISPATCH.
CONGRATULATIONS ON YOUR GOOD FORTUNE. YOU HAVE PROVED YOURSELF WORTHY OF OUR CONSIDERATION.
BEST REGARDS,
DR. BARINAS, EXECUTOR

Well, butter my butt and call me a biscuit! I'm worthy! And the money's on its way. I don't even have to send any more of my own. Maybe it's even in my account now. I rip my apron off and toss it in the air.

"Hot damn!" I holler. "Hot damn!" Then I dance back and forth across the kitchen of Two Spoons in a polka. I even give Leo a twirl.

"Was it something I said?" He goes back to dicing celery for his Velveeta and Cheese Whiz Brule.

"It's on its way!" I send a high five up to the ceiling.

"What's on its way?" he asks carefully.

"My money!" I sing.

Leo gets a shuttered look and goes back to his cutting board.

Curtis pushes open the pass-through. "Customers are saying somebody's going crazy back here," he complains.

When I blurt out the news, Curtis stands there with his mouth open.

"You mean it's in your account?" he says. I'm satisfied to see a look of amazement on his face.

"Not yet but it's going to be," I say.

Leo doesn't lift his head up. "You know the old saying of not counting your chickens?" He keeps on chopping celery.

I just laugh. "I have chickens to spare. Just look in my coop. Plus Camille had her new bunch of babies. Shoot!" I say. "Now I can redo their roof."

I waltz over to the phone and dial Wendell's Construction. A real person doesn't answer, so I leave a message on their machine.

"This is Tammy Tyree and I'd like to schedule a roof estimate for a chicken coop repair," I say. "I'm over in Spring. The driveway across from Two Spoons Café," I add then hang up.

Curtis rolls his eyes. "You're doing the coop before your trailer?" His tone is incredulous. "Of course, if it were me, I'd tear your place down and start all over."

"You aren't me," I say. Nobody can dim my good mood. "I'm taking the afternoon off," I say.

"Tammy," Leo holds up his hand. "Can you wait just a minute?"

I wave him off. "Not now. I got to go," And I high tail it out the door not even taking time to grab my coat. My first stop is Peggy's. I poke my head in.

"Don't have time to stop but it's got here!" I tell her. "The money! Or nearly. I'm celebrating," I say. "Jar and I are going to pizza and a movie. You want to come?"

"Halleluiah!" Peggy says, "Give me a rain check. If I put a down payment on my new washers and dryers today, I'll get a discount so I'd better head to the mall." She switches her open sign to closed.

I dart over to the Shop and Save. "Hey, there, Sue Ann. I got real good news," I say. "The money's on its way. Being wired as we speak. Guaranteed. Jar and me are going to party."

Sue Ann gives a little hop. "How about I give you a hundred cash to celebrate?"

"I wouldn't turn it down," I say, knowing I can pay it back when my money comes.

Sue Ann takes a handful of twenties out of the register not even counting it. I shove it all into my pocket. I hit Walter's on my way to the trailer.

"You'll be pleased to know the money's on its way," I tell him.

Walter beams. "Time to order more plants." He picks up his phone. "And I guess I'll go ahead and sign the contract for my garden addition out back."

My heart is pounding from the excitement so I take a short rest. Walter has a bin full of half price items. I rustle through it as I catch my breath. "Are these screwdrivers half price too?" I pick up a package. "Jar needs some good tools."

"Yep. And drills are on sale. This one's cordless. See?" Walter holds it up.

"Cordless, huh?" "That'd be a real good surprise for Jar.

"You charge it up on this stand," Walter explains. "And you just plug it into the wall."

"Can I put it on my tab?" I ask.

As an answer, Walter picks up a box and sticks it into my sack with the screwdrivers. As I walk out, I see the rock tumbler in the window. I stop and point.

"Walter how much is that?"

"The Rock Tumbler? It's a good one. Professionals use this it. It's an AR-12."

"Rock Tumbler," I muse. "And it polishes rocks real well?"

"It's top notch. Makes them look like gemstones. I can let you have it for $185."

I don't know why my brother wants it. Or if he really knows what it can do. Or if he can ever run it on his own, but none of that matters. He wants one. That's good enough for me.

"Set it aside for me, will you?"

As an answer, Walter tapes a SOLD sign on it.

My mood is a Christmas one as I trek home. I stop by my mailbox and grab out what's there. A circular ad and a pile of bills. Bills don't make any difference now no matter how many there are. I'll be like a queen dividing up her gold coins pretty soon. I dump the mail on the kitchen table and then change into my jeans and a good shirt.

I toss my uniform in the corner with the rest of the dirty clothes. Soon I'll be able to pay somebody else to do my laundry. Better yet, I can get a washer and dryer of my own. To be able to laundry any time I wanted would be like a rich person. Heck, I'll be a rich person.

The Sears' Catalogue advertises a machine that's all in one. Dryer on top and washer on the bottom. Eight hundred and ninety-five bucks. That will be the first thing I order. Maybe I can call tomorrow? I grab up Jar's presents and stroll out to the backyard. I won't tell him about the rock tumbler. That will come later.

Our grass is lush and green from the recent rains. The lilacs have finished their bloom. Bees are buzzing around. Sweater weather. The chickens start in on their chattering as soon as they spy me. I toss corn.

"You girls ready to get your digs all spruced?" I ask.

They assure me they are. I hear hammering coming from the workshop and I peek inside. Jar's got a stack of whirligigs in front of him.

"Hey, Bug. How about the two of us take a night off? I got a full tank of gas and money to burn." I hold up the twenties. "We can do a movie and get ourselves some pizza. It's not even half-price matinee. How about that? We're celebrating. Plus look! More Skittles!"

"Organ otter?" Jar tilts his head.

"Because our money's on its way, that's why! And I think you'd better empty your pockets," I answer. "They'll kick us out of the theatre if you do your rock thing.

"Hodder," Jar says.

"Yeah you can throw popcorn. But not at people's heads. And only in the dark."

Jar's brow wrinkles. "Noodle," he says and starts emptying his pockets. There's quite a pile of stones.

"Leave them there on the floor and you can choose the movie. As far as the pizza goes pineapple ham works for me if the other half is pepperoni olive."

"Doodle dee?" Jar asks.

"Sure the front row. Even if it makes us both blind as bats." My brother drives a hard bargain. "Look here. I got more presents." I lift the sack. "Check them out and then we can go for our night out."

But Jar isn't looking at his presents. He's looking past me.

"Okey dokey!" he says this like a warning.

A hand grabs my shoulder and I'm slammed against the wall. Jar's bag drops to the floor. Cousin Lonnie looms over me. He sways slightly so I know he's been drinking.

"What are you doing?" I sputter.

"A night out? What a fine idea! I haven't had a night out for a long while, but pizza and a movie sounds lame. Silver King Tavern is more my line." Lonnie says. He has his hand griping my chin. I turn to the side.

"But I think the little moron is gonna have to stay home. You and me have some serious talking to do."

I pull at his hands. "Stop." I croak. "You're hurting me."

Lonnie pushes harder. "Hurting you?" He raises me up until my feet are off the floor. "I'm sorry. Guess I don't know my own strength."

I try to kick with my feet and wrench myself loose, but Lonnie's got me pinned like a moth against a board.

"So," he says smoothly. "I heard the good news. Your inheritance has arrived. Oops, I meant to say my inheritance. And in the nick of time, I might say. Me having what you would call pressing obligatory necessities," he says. "Share and share alike. What's mine is mine and what's yours is mine too." He snickers under his breath.

"Yours?" I say hoarsely. "That money isn't yours," I protest.

"Oh, I think it will be," Lonnie says. "This is my suggestion. You give me half and I leave you and the little moron alone. How about that?" He squeezes my cheeks together like a vise. "Or maybe I'll take more. How does seventy-five percent sound?"

It hurts something awful, but I don't cry out. Instead, my squeeze my lips shut.

"What's the matter?" Lonnie asks. "Cat got your tongue? Where's that smart mouth of yours, now?" Lonnie presses his arm across my throat making it impossible to breathe.

"Help," I squeak out.

Jar throws himself at Lonnie's legs and Lonnie swings a boot and viciously kicks him.

"Ack!" Jar goes. He huddles there on the floor.

"You're both at a severe disadvantage." Lonnie smirks.

Disadvantage. My whole life has been full of disadvantages. I don't think I'm inclined to be disadvantaged any more. Lonnie's attention is still on Jar who's struggling upright. Lonnie's grip on me loosens. I make myself go limp and Lonnie's grip loosens even more.

"You want another boot in the behind, moron?" Lonnie says. At the same time, my arms come up sharply and I throw my cousin backwards. Then I start giving him some well placed kicks of my own.

The minute I'm free, my brother Jar grabs at his pile of rocks and lets fly. Stone after stone ricochets off Lonnie's head.

My cousin tries to shield his face with his hands. Jar keeps tossing rocks. Blood trickles from Lonnie's temple.

"Jar! Skedaddle outside, now!" I roar. And he does. His legs are churning.

Lonnie gets to his knees and makes a futile swipe at me. I haul back and kick his manly parts with everything I got. They nearly end up in his throat.

"I guess I don't like being thought of as disadvantaged anymore," I say. "It makes me cranky."

Another kick to Lonnie's chin snaps his head back and puts him in a heap. Down for the count you might say. My cousin lies there motionless.

I march outside. Jar follows, his eyes wide as saucers. He gives me a high five. "Paddle bummer?" he asks.

"It's only something Tyree women do when they're in a pinch," I say. "I'll teach you next year when you're sixteen." I give my brother a brisk Dutch rub to the head.

The two of us hop into Dolly and I get a real good thought.

"Gimme a sec, will you?" I say to Jar. I run back inside and dial Smithers' number.

"Hey, Clarence," I say. "Jar and me had to defuse a burglar in our workshop just now. Can you head over to our place and take care of it? We'll be out for the evening."

"No problem!" Smithers assures me. "I'm heading your way, now."

We zoom off in Dolly. I'm thinking he'll arrest Lonnie. Or maybe there's a warrant out on my cousin already. He's done enough mischief. I'm feeling on top of the world.

The pizza was hot and we ate every bit. No leftovers. Not a one. The movie Jar chose was full of car chasing and gun shooting. Jar hid his eyes the whole time, but I watched every second.

Three hours later when we get home, the workshop is empty. No sign of cousin Lonnie.

"Good riddance." I tell Jar. "Now hop like a bunny and get yourself into bed."

"Poop sweep." Jar says.

I like it when my brother speaks French. He sounds educated.

"Yeah quick as you can," I say.

"Odd pack." Jar looks thoughtful.

"You're right, Jar, it is important to defend yourself. It isn't a crime to fight back when someone's trying to take advantage of you. Remember that," I say.

"Okey dokey," Jar agrees.

"Yes siree, Bob," I say to Jar. "I don't feel one bit bad. Sometimes a woman's got to do what a woman's got to do."

"Okey dokey," Jar reminds me.

"And a teenager," I agree.

And we leave it at that.

CHAPTER EIGHTEEN

Big wire transfers, especially foreign ones, take time. That's what the teller at the bank said the next morning when I call to check on the money.

That afternoon Clarence Smithers ambles into Two Spoons and flags me down.

"Tammy, can I bend your ear for a sec?" he says. "It's kind of important." He's twiddling with the edge of his hat.

I'm chin to chest carrying plates. "Lunchtime rush," I say. "As soon as these construction guys are finished I'll be right with you. Have a seat at the counter," I tell him.

But Smithers doesn't sit. He waddles after me from table to table like a baby duck that's misremembered its mama.

I pour coffee at an elderly couple's table. Smithers starts to speak but I hold up my hand. "Just a moment," I say. "What can I get you?" I ask the couple.

"Is the patty melt good?" The gray haired woman asks.

"No, ma'am." I shake my head emphatically. "It's fairly greasy and Leo uses Limburger instead of cheddar, but the chicken pot pie is a heck of a deal. People been saying it really sticks to your ribs." Actually, people have been saying it sticks to the roof of their mouths, but it's the same thing.

"You serving normal chicken pot pie today?" Smithers interrupts. "If you are then maybe I'll have a pre lunch snack."

I take the couple's order then usher Smithers over to the counter on my way to the pass-through. He sets his hat down and slides onto a stool. It teeters precariously. I don't think a person ought to be sitting on something half the size of their butt, but then I guess Smithers must have better balance than I give him credit for.

"Soup's cock-a-leekie. It's Scottish," I say. "And Leo didn't make that one up. It's a real soup. Honest. Chicken and leeks." I hustle back to the kitchen. I don't mention Leo added squash bits, minced clams, and smoked oysters into the mix.

In forty minutes, the pace has slowed so I'm able to take a short break. Smithers is eating the last of his third pie. Some snack. I settle into the stool next to him with a cup of coffee.

"Isn't the pot pie good?" I say. "I think it's the tripe Leo adds. Or maybe it's the chicken's feet."

Smithers looks alarmed.

"Just kidding, Clarence," I say, but I'm not.

He pushes his plate away. "I thought you'd like to know. That cousin of yours is pressing charges," he says.

"On who?" I ask.

"On you," Smithers says.

"Me?" My mouth hangs open. "For what?"

"He says you attacked him," Smithers says.

"He attacked me first!" I slam my cup down so hard the coffee sloshes and spills. "That snake in the grass. Besides, he had it coming," I fume.

"You don't deny it?" Smithers widens his eyes. "I doubted what Lonnie was saying being as you're less than half his size. Couldn't see how you managed to send a grown man to his knees."

"I could to save my life," I say. "He had me by the neck. And he was on my property. He assaulted me first. And he was drunk."

"Did you file a report?" Smithers asked.

"Of course, not," I say. "It was taken care of by me."

"Well, your cousin did. You have any witnesses?"

"Jar," I say. "He saw it all."

"I mean a real person."

"Jar is a real person," I snap.

Smithers rolls his eyes upwards. "Yeah, well, we all know your brother. It'll be Lonnie's word against yours.

And another thing. He's been saying that you're unbalanced. Crazy even."

"Crazy like a fox maybe," I agree. "I have to be with what I got going in my life." And I chuckle, but Smithers doesn't laugh with me.

"He's serious, Tammy Louise. He's spreading it around."

"Nobody will believe that." I wave my hand.

"Maybe not but he told me he's thinking about taking you to court. Had the doctor photograph his bruises and everything."

"Court? That's a laugh. It'd sure be a tough one for Judge Donna. Tyree against Tyree," I snort. "Maybe she'd call it a draw."

"You need to take this all serious," Smithers says. "I'm bending the rules letting you know ahead of time that you got to have your ducks all in a row."

"My ducks are just fine," I say. "My ducks are sitting pretty as a matter of fact."

Smithers fiddles with his fork over the empty plate. "So anyway, about that money you got coming," he says.

I hold up my hand. "It'll be here any day now. The bank says it's not in my account yet. I mean to call again before they close, but I been running my legs off. You in a hurry or something?"

"Sort of." Smithers says. "It's just it'll put me in a pickle if it don't come by next Monday. My P.I. supplies should be arriving. I ordered them COD. The infrared surveillance scopes are expensive. I got me two of them," he says proudly and gets to his feet. The stool squeaks with relief.

I watch his ample ass saunter out the door and think, he's in a pickle if it doesn't come? What about me? My checking account is bone dry, Uncle E's loan is owing, and I believe my electricity is about to be shut off. Nobody's in a bigger pickle than me. Plus-sized dill, if you want to know the truth.

I check my email again real quick, but there's nothing. Just exactly like the last thirty times I checked. Leo's on the phone making a produce order so I can't make a call to the bank. In ten minutes, they'll close. I pace. When Leo finally hangs up, it's well after five. Dang it all anyway. I dry my sweaty palms on my apron.

Long after I've gone to bed that night, my phone rings. The digital clock flashes two in the morning. I quickly fumble for the receiver before it wakes Jar.

My heart starts to pound. It could be a call from Africa. I pinch my own arm to wake myself up better.

"Hello?" I answer. I envision Dr. Barinas behind his desk. Papers in front of him. Maybe he's tired. Working on a Saturday. Or is it Sunday there?

"Tammy?" a female voice whispers. "It's Sue Ann. We got to talk."

"This late?" I say.

"It's important. There's a hitch."

"A hitch? Can you speak up? I can barely hear you."

"I'm calling from downstairs. I don't want to wake Glenn up. And there's a problem," she says. "I need you to give me my share of the money real fast. Like tomorrow."

"Tomorrow?" My voice is stretched like a string.

"It's here now isn't it?"

"No," I say slowly. "But Monday for sure. Guaranteed."

"I thought you said by the end of the week?"

"Well, it had to come all the way from Botswana!" I hiss. "And it's the weekend there, now. They're ahead of us."

"If they're ahead then they should be faster," Sue Ann hisses back at me.

"They're not any faster than us," I yell.

"Tammy Louise don't you DARE raise your voice with me." She muffles the receiver. "Nothing, Pooh Bear. You go back to sleep," I hear her sing. She comes back on the line. "See what you did? You gone and WOKE Glenn up!"

"You woke Glenn up!" I say. "It was you hollering."

"Well, I get hollering when I'm anxious. And being anxious ruins my complexion. I'm breaking out in spots."

"I can't help you getting spots," I say. "It isn't my fault.

"Yes it is! Anyway the problem is Glenn's daddy's got a hotshot CPA coming in from the city because he took it in his mind to check out my books. I need to replace the money I gave you or my ass is grass."

"Can't you stall them?"

"Only a little," she says. "But you better have something for me on Monday or I'll...or I'll...or I'll," Sue

Ann's stuttering like Dolly in second going around a corner.

"Or you'll what?"

"I don't know," she says. "But I'll think of something."

"Come on, Sue Ann. You're the one who wanted in. Business is like this. Full of delays and legal stuff. And the money will be here on Monday. At the very least Tuesday. You can count on Wednesday. Guaranteed."

When I hang up, I suspect I've got Sue Ann feeling better, but I'm not. Fact is, I can't get back to sleep no matter what I try counting. Sheep. Ceiling tile rust stains. Pipe gurgles.

I oversleep my alarm, but even with that, I feel like I been crumpled up like paper and tossed in the bottom of a trash bin. There aren't any fresh uniforms in my closet so I leave Jar in his workshop doing whirligigs and head over to Cut N Clean dragging two pillowcases full of dirty clothes on my back.

"Where's your brother?" Peggy asks.

"He's full on into his whirligig making," I wave airily. "You can hardly pry him out of the workshop." I start stuffing the washer.

"Makes it easy for you then," she says.

Why do folks always think having Jar out of my hair is the easy thing? I bite my tongue. It's no good tossing pebbles at a bear.

"Fact is, I'm a teensy concerned." I try to sound exactly the opposite. "I don't know what's taking so long with the money."

I hope Peggy will have some practical advice, but she gives me one of her looks. "You're kidding me, right? Did you do everything that solicitor fellow asked?"

"Everything," I assure her. "I swear." But I drop my eyes.

I don't tell her there's one thing I didn't do. I didn't keep it confidential. I didn't zip my lip and keep it all to myself.

I don't how much Dr. Barinas can know about what goes on in Spring, but countries have security people everywhere. I think on whether I've seen a person wandering around who could be an African spy and can't think of anyone. Unless maybe Africa has started hiring blue-haired old ladies in track shoes to keep tabs on their business. Thinking on this fact, I don't pay real close attention to what Peggy is jabbering about.

"It's not just the washers and dryers I ordered," she's saying. "I also put a deposit on a new hair dryer for the shop because I thought I'd be getting something soon." She snaps her fingers in my face making me jump. "Are you listening to me?"

"I've got ears don't I?"

"I was just saying maybe it got put in this morning."

"On a Saturday?" I ask.

"Yeah. It happens. The bank stays open until noon."

Well, that cheers me up to no end. "I'll call right now," I assure her.

"Don't call. You know how snippy those tellers are. You need to go on down there in person." she pushes me towards the door. "They probably won't give you that kind of information on the phone, anyways." Peggy says. "And you'll want to get cash out for us investors. I'll stick your clothes in the dryer for you while you check on it."

"I'm much obliged to you!" I say and shoot out the door.

After grabbing my purse and checkbook, I get Dolly going. She starts right up. When it's important Dolly hardly ever lets me down.

Even though I hit traffic on the way to the bank, I'm able to pull in the parking lot at eleven thirty-eight. Plenty of time. There's a line in front of the one teller who's open. I stand there shifting my feet back and forth and get to thinking. Maybe I need to speak to the manager? I'll be a top client now. He'll probably be thrilled to chat about my plans.

I walk around back to his office.

The manager, Mr. Simon, and I, don't have much to do with each other. Only when I'm overdrawn. I'm thinking I'll be giving him good news soon. His door's closed. I rap on it, but there's no answer.

I wave to the teller. "You know where Simon is?"

"He's not in on Saturdays," she says with that snotty teller tone they have.

"Can you check my balance real quick?" I ask. "I'm expecting a deposit. Something real big, wired."

She points to the line. "You'll have to take your turn," she says. Three people arrive taking my old place in line.

"But it's important," I insist.

"It always is." And she keeps pointing. The new customers don't meet my eyes. They aren't offering to let me back where I was. Common courtesy is deader than a doornail it seems. *Double dang.* I scowl and decided there's no tip coming that particular teller's way when I finally do get my inheritance.

I stand there fuming. Packed between someone with body odor and another with bad breath. I take another sniff. The body odor is coming from me.

The line is creeping. Nothing's simple today. Everybody's got questions. One guy shouts about the bank making mistakes on his withdrawals. Somebody else starts in crying about how somebody else should have paid them and that's why they're overdrawn. Boy, do I know that song and dance.

It's eleven fifty-six and two people are ahead of me. Then one. I'm next. A bell rings. The teller shuts her window and sets up her closed placard.

"It's noon, we're closed," the security guard says. "Everybody out."

"Hey!" I yell. "Hey!" I rattle the sign. "I've been here since eleven thirty!"

"New policy. Computers down at noon," she says. "No exceptions."

"But I just need to know my balance!" I say.

The security guard motions to the door. "Listen to the teller. That's the rule." He pushes me out and slams the door behind me.

I shake the knob and glare through the window. They drop the shade. Triple darn. That's complete and utter unfair business practice.

I march out to Dolly. Boy, that teller is going to be real sorry when I get my money. Real sorry. To make matters worse Dolly struggles to start and when I finally do get her going, she lurches and slows every time I hit the gas. There's a smell coming from her back end that can't be good. Maybe I need oil. Dolly's gasket might be fixing to blow again. Nothing for it but I have to pull into the Gas & Go.

When Annette sees me, she presses her lips together.

I hop out, pop open Dolly's hood, and pull out her dipstick. "Hells bells, she's nearly bone dry. Can I get some 30 weight?" I ask.

Annette gives me a steady gaze. "Sure, if you can pay for it."

I hand her my last twenty reluctantly. "I'll take four."

"You need another five dollars." Annette says.

"Your oil is six bucks a quart? That's the cheapest?"

"6.25. And it's the only oil we got." Annette holds her hand out.

"I'll just take three then," I tell her.

The oil seems to rejuvenate Dolly. I roll right on past Peggy's even though my laundry is there drying. When I get to the trailer, I do have some good news. Jar's got a stack of whirligigs that just need to be painted.

"You're one fine producer, Jar," I say. "I know Uncle E would be bursting with pride at the sight if he knew. Fact is, he's probably up in heaven kicking himself that he didn't take advantage of your talents." I give Jar an abbreviated Dutch rub.

"Poppa gut." Jar says.

"Yeah, I guess he could very well be sweating down in that other place," I say.

My brother is standing there expectantly. Like he's waiting for a reward and I get an idea.

"There's no Skittles left, but tell you what, Bug. Why don't the two of us go for a walk? And hey, we can look for berries while we're at it. The fresh air will do us both good."

I turn away and smooth wrinkles off my forehead like I'm working clay.

"Okey dokey," Jar touches the small of my back with a finger.

I feel tears well up and I swallow hard. "And no, I'm not worried."

I lead the way up the hill. The trail is overgrown with dandelions. I know this early in the season the berries will be sour and the bushes sparse. When we reach the old logging road, salal bushes are thick on each side. Salal berries aren't ideal, but Jar likes them. He stuffs them in his mouth getting blue juice on his chin. I pick a few and put them in my pocket. For lack of Skittles, salal will do in a pinch to keep Jar in line.

"Let's go a little further," I suggest. "We can look for huckleberry bushes." I walk along the side searching for large cedar stumps that huckleberries like to grow on top of. My brother trots smack up the middle of the path.

I hear a rumble from below. "Something's coming," I say "Out of the road, Jar!" I warn. The sound gets louder and turns into a familiar motorbike.

"Free Lo!" Jar points.

"It sure is Leo," I say. "You got that right."

Leo swerves when he sees us and cuts his engine. He sits there straddling his bike.

"Picking berries, huh," he says.

"Nothing gets past you." I say and point to his head. "You'll lose what's left of your brains without a helmet." His ponytail hangs down his back. "Plus you're breaking the law."

Leo shrugs like breaking the law doesn't mean much to him one way or the other. He's looking at me.

"Want a berry?" I offer him a handful.

"Thanks," he says.

"When the blackberries are ripe I can bring some in for pies," I offer.

"Sounds good." Leo puts a salal berry in his mouth and makes a face.

"They're not full on ripe yet," I say. "Salal berries aren't really good for anything. Jar likes them though."

Leo doesn't respond to this. Just looks out to the trees. I don't know what's so interesting out among the trees, but I find myself standing there watching him. The sun is warmish on my back. I walk over to a fallen log and sit down.

"You come up here a lot?" I ask.

He nods.

"Harvesting, huh?" I say. I know his Wonderbread bag doesn't get full on its own. I don't say anything to anybody about Leo's weed growing.

"Tammy." Leo looks at me straight. "I suspect you're in some kind of trouble. And it has to do with money."

I frown. "You been talking to Curtis." I say. "He's wrong. I'm not in any trouble. I'm just waiting for when my inheritance comes, that's all," I say stubbornly.

"Ah, that inheritance of yours." Leo pulls a joint out of his front pocket and lights up.

He sucks on it for a bit and then offers it to me. I wave it away.

"None for me." The smell is pungent. "I don't do drugs."

"Good for you," Leo says.

"Luke dot," Jar says and reaches for Leo's joint.

"Don't you dare!" I warn.

Leo holds it up out of Jar's reach.

"Did Uncle E let you do that?" I grab at my brother's ear. "I'll blister your butt if he did!"

Jar squirms away.

Leo takes another deep drag. He holds it in. "Money's highly overrated. You have what you need don't you? Food. A place to live. People who care about you, right?" He breathes out.

I scowl at Leo. "People who say that crap about money's over rated have plenty of their own coming in. They just want to justify the fact that you have none and they have a pile."

"EEEEEE," Jar goes. He's answering a garbage truck that echoes far across the valley.

Leo is speaking soft like he's talking to himself. "Take a good hard look at what you got not what you don't have. That's my advice. You see, Tammy," Leo pauses. "You can't get something for nothing. It's kind of a rule of the universe. Energy is neither created nor destroyed. There's no free lunch."

"I know nothing comes free more than most," I say stubbornly. "I'm not stupid."

"I didn't say you were."

Leo squishes his joint out, stuffs the end in his shirt pocket, and starts his bike.

"Think on it," he shouts. And he motors away.

Part of me is annoyed because of Leo knowing about my beeswax and part of me is pleased as it seems Leo rode up the mountain specifically to see me.

Jar and I wander back home. Winding down the hill, I mull over what Leo said.

"Something for nothing," I mutter to myself. "You can, too. It's like lotteries or sweepstakes. And my cousin Lonnie's proof that if you hightail it out of Two Spoons without paying, you sure enough get a free lunch."

After I put Jar to bed that night, I stand watch over him. It's quiet and peaceful. Jar depends on me. I need that inheritance for him. We both deserve it. But what if it's like Leo says? That it's too good to be true? What will I do? I close my eyes and pray hard.

The money's got to come. It just has to.

CHAPTER NINETEEN

Business is slowing down at Two Spoons. Summer's end is usually full of people traveling up the mountain but I guess they don't want to fight the construction. Tips have all but dried up. My own personal finances are dire with a capital D. The phone rings off the hook with messages from collection agencies.

"Wrong number," I say. "They moved to Africa."

The money people have given me is all gone and I'm scared. Like being on a rollercoaster and flying straight down with your eyes closed.

I thought my inheritance would be here by now.

Walter told me repeatedly he wasn't in any hurry. Now it seems Walter has ants in his pants.

"I can't be carrying credit forever," Walter attempts to corner me between his begonias as I walk down the sidewalk on my way home.

"I have to be someplace else, Walter." And I dodge past him.

I fill Dolly up with whirligigs and make a dash up to Allison's. Whirligigs are keeping the wolf from our door. I look at them with pride. Jar's really outdone himself. Trotting birds and galloping cats. Multi winged bug-cupids. And the colors. I've never seen even half of the combinations my brother comes up with.

I'm betting Allison will be pleased and I breathe easier with the expectation of whirligig money coming in. When I pull up to Allison's place, I can't get close. There's a ditch dug up around her building. She's standing outside wearing overalls and holding a shovel.

"What's going on?" I ask. "You mining for gold or making a moat?"

"No," she laughs. "Septic tank overflowed. You can put the whirligigs over in the shed.

Allison helps me unload.

I hem and haw, hating to ask. "Could I maybe get an advance on these?" I finally spill out. Allison shakes her head.

"Sorry. Not until I open back up, but what's your hurry about getting paid? Josephine from the B & B said something about how you're an investor. How about investing in my flea market? It's a real moneymaker." Allison winks.

Hells bells. I travel on home the bed of my truck as empty as my wallet and my mood in a blue funk. When I walk into the trailer, my brother greets me enthusiastically.

"Yabba roller," he says.

"Nope," I say. "No making whirligigs for a bit. It seems Walter has temporarily cut off our credit supply. You'd best come in with me to the café. There's always a pile of pans to do."

"Hat pooh carp." Jar trudges slow as molasses. I'm turned into a collie herding a balky sheep.

"What's with you?" I brush his cheek with the back of my hand. "You turning into an unruly teenager, now?"

"Holy rat," Jar mutters. He's always leery when I rub his cheek.

"Your hair's getting long," I warn. "Time for a cut." I'll have to wait until my brother's asleep to do anything about it.

"Lard lope," Jar says like he's reading my mind.

"Oh, yeah," I roll my eyes. "That's just what you need." I say," A ponytail just like Leo. Anyway, we have to scoot or I'll be late. Come on!"

Jar follows me reluctantly down the driveway.

"You're quiet. You hatching something?" I ask him.

I look back when my brother doesn't answer. His pockets are bulging suspiciously. I grab him by the sleeve.

"Empty those pockets! Curtis is going to eat you up and spit you out when he sees what you got."

"Lone carp." Jar jerks away.

"Oh, yeah," I say, "And monkeys fly out my butt." I offer my palm. "Hand them over, pronto."

Jar shakes his head like a little mule and pulls his jacket tighter. He trots ahead of me down the driveway.

"Jar?" I warn.

"La la la la," Jar goes. He keeps himself just out of my reach.

When we get to the café Jar refuses to take off his jacket.

I tie on my apron. "I'm tired of fighting," I say to him. "You want to keep your jacket on, fine. But I'll look after those rocks if you want." I offer real sweet.

"Hose vandal." Jar keeps his hands deep in his pockets. He marches into the kitchen and I make a grab for him, but he's too quick.

"Ding! Ding!" Jar sings. "Otter fart."

"I'm rubber and you're glue," I retort. "Anything you say to me bounces right off."

Leo looks up and raises his brows when he sees me. "I thought you weren't coming in today?"

"Why wouldn't I be here? I'm on the schedule." I'm puzzled.

"The town's full of talk about your money plans, that's all," Leo shrugs.

"Well, I'm here." I say. "And I don't intend on quitting. And neither does Jar," I add.

There. Leo can put that in his weed pipe and smoke it. I don't have to explain myself to him.

Curtis walks in and stops dead when he sees Jar. "What's he doing here? And what's that in his hands? Rocks?" Curtis' voice tapers upwards.

I glare. "Stuff it, Curtis. He's good at pans. Even Leo says that." I brush past. "Unless you want to do them. And if you can get those rocks out of his sticky mitt, you're welcome to try."

"Not and get bit again." Curtis stomps off frowning.

Now this will certainly make for a pleasant afternoon, I think. Somehow, I'm busy even though there're not many tables filled. The customers are persnickety. Sending back things and asking for extras like tartar sauce, which we don't have as Leo doesn't serve fish unless it's canned.

"Tell Leo the spam chili is cold," I say to Curtis. "He's got to re-heat it. And here are my chits. Can you drop them off? I got a table to bus."

"Oh, and I'm your gopher, now? You're getting pretty full of yourself."

"I guess there's no asking you for favors," I snap and stomp into the kitchen with my chits.

"*Not meets,*" I hear him mutter to my back. "A very big *not meets.*"

I slam the pass through door hard behind me. Jar has finished doing the pans in the sink. He's doing the napkins.

"Cop fair," Jar says.

"I'm not having this discussion. Your income goes in the pot." I wet a finger to wipe ketchup off his chin. "Sure wish you'd stop wearing your food."

"Lard goober," Jar says. He reaches under the sink and holds up Leo's Wonderbread bag.

I snatch it out of Jar's hand and glare at Leo. "Look at what he's got. I told you to get that crap out of here."

Leos face looks like it does when somebody sends back his soup. He takes the bag from me. "I had that hid," he snaps. "And why are you so concerned about what Jar's got, now." Leo glares. "I thought as you're making a practice to ignore him you wouldn't care."

"Why would you say that? I'm always concerned about him." I feel my cheeks heat up. "It's obvious by his belly that he gets enough to eat and he's smiling isn't he?"

"You leave him on his own whenever you want." Leo has his hands on his hips exactly like Curtis. For the first time I see the family resemblance.

"Why are you so worried about my brother all of a sudden?"

My voice has made Jar's eyebrows furrow. I immediately plaster on a wide fake smile and make my tone cheery. I reach around and grab the Wonderbread bag from Leo. I might as well kill two crows with one slingshot.

"Throw this bag straight in the garbage, Jar," I say. "And while you're at it, empty the trash can bag into the Dumpster. You have your jacket on so you might as well do outside jobs. And Leo can keep his big fat nose out of our beeswax," I say pleasantly.

Leo pulls the Wonderbread bag back from me and stuffs it into a high cupboard. "I'm taking care of this one," his tone is snarly. "And don't touch that garbage, Jar. And by the way here's your wages." He holds a ten-dollar bill in his fingers.

"Don't listen to him. Take this out." I pull the heavy bag out of the trashcan. "And the ten bucks is mine thank you very much." I snatch it.

Leo snatches it back. "Here Jar," he says. "Probably not good for him to go out into the parking lot alone. Trucks have been cutting through there, today."

Jar grabs the ten and I swiftly grab it back.

"ACK!" he goes.

"Well, lucky you aren't the boss of Jar," I snap. "He knows about trucks."

Leo jerks the trash bag from Jar. "He can spend his time doing something safer. And you'd understand that if your head wasn't so full of money."

"Jar doesn't need safe." I hiss. "He does just fine. And what does money have to do with anything?"

I pull the trash bag back and hand it over to Jar. My brother laughs like it's a game. He hands the trash bag to Leo and I jerk it away. Leo snatches back the ten from my hand and hands it to Jar.

"Okey dokey!" Jar says. He takes the ten and quickly stuffs it in his pocket.

"Jar needs challenges," I say stubbornly.

"No, he doesn't." Leo says. "He's challenged enough."

"Yes, he does." I sing-song back. "And he isn't challenged enough. I'm his sister. I ought to know."

"Some sister you are. Sacrificing him for the almighty dollar."

"Sacrificing? Now, what's that supposed to mean?" I say.

"You know what it means."

"No I don't. Explain it real clear being as you think I'm so stupid." I stretch as tall as I'm able.

"I don't have to explain anything," Leo says. "And you were the one who brought up stupid."

As I think on it, I do concede Leo has a small point about trucks in the parking lot, but I feel too obstinate to alter my position. "Go on now, Jar," I urge. "You're promoted from pans to garbage detail. Be real careful," I warn for Leo's benefit.

My brother shuffles outside dragging the bag. Leo goes back to thumping onions with his knife and looking dissatisfied. I stomp out to the dining room.

My mood isn't improved when I see Sue Ann, Smithers, and Peggy all seated at the same table, heads together. They break apart when I approach.

" Hey, there. What'll you all have?" I try to sound like I haven't a care in the world. Peggy taps her scarlet nails on the table and purses her lips," Tea," she says, knowing full well we don't have any.

"I'm not all that hungry," Smithers says. "Just a couple hamburgers, potato salad, French fries, and a side of onion rings, I think. And maybe pie. Lemon or cherry if you got it."

"Only got strawberry-rhubarb," I say.

"That'll do!" Smithers nods. Peggy jabs him in the ribs. "And ice cream," he whispers to me.

I turn to Sue Ann and raise one eyebrow. She presses her lips together and looks away.

"Nothing for me," she says.

On my way to pick up soups for another table, I glance back. The three of them have their heads together again. Peggy looks up and catches me staring. Her face reddens.

Are folks talking behind my back? Is that what Leo was all fired up about besides his weed collection? And what do they know anyway? I dart into the kitchen. Leo's back is to the door. He says nothing to me and I say nothing to him. No chitchat today. I load my tray and go back out.

"Spam chili," I set a bowl in front of Smithers.

"Why is it green?" Smithers asks.

"Ask Leo." I don't look anyone in the eye.

Everyone will wise up as soon as my money comes and boy will they be sorry. I'll forgive them after a bit. It's the right thing to do. I imagine it in fine detail. Me in fancy clothes. Maybe driving a new car. A convertible like Peggy's. Waving with the top down as I pass on by.

The *beep, beep, beep* of a semi backing up in the parking lot echoes through the screen door. A sharp rumble of an engine, the spurt of tires in gravel, and excited shouts knock me out of my trance. The door of Two Spoons bangs open and shut and Walter rushes in. "Call 9-1-1!" he yells.

Madeline is right behind him waving her arms. "We need an ambulance!"

"For who?" I ask, but I know already.

I rip off my apron and race to the parking lot. Leo is two beats behind me and Curtis is well behind him. The rest of the customers spill out.

The driver of the truck swings down from his cab.

"I didn't know he was there, I swear." He paces in front of his vehicle. "I had no idea."

My brother is sprawled on the pavement like he's running sideways. I hit the gravel with my bare knees.

"You okay, Bug?" I stroke my brother's forehead. Trying to get him to open his eyes. Drool slides down the side of his mouth.

Leo hands me the fire blanket from the kitchen. "The ambulance is on its way," he says.

I lift Jar's shoulders to tuck the blanket around his body.

"Don't move him," Someone says.

"Is he dead?" Someone else asks.

I huddle there in the dirt.

The wail of a siren comes from far off. It gets louder and louder. I don't even see the emergency vehicle arrive. My eyes are on my brother. Paramedics load him onto a stretcher. He's stiff as a board. I crawl in and hold my brother's hand all the way to the hospital, but it's like I'm not even there.

At the emergency room, the nurse tries to push me away, but I grip my brother's fingers harder. People in white coats swarm like a herd of bees. *He's not responding. It may be a head injury. Call X-ray stat!* They're talking a language I don't understand.

"Get her out of here," a nurse says. That I understand.

"My brother needs me," I tell her.

"Let us do our job." She ushers me into the waiting area.

The plastic chair is hard. My shins are throbbing. They're scraped and bloody. The only words tumbling in my head are Leo's about me ignoring my brother. About me being focused on things that don't matter. I can see clearly that I've spent a whole lot of time worrying about something there's no point in worrying about. *Money*.

Leo was right. I've been setting my brother aside. Dumping him off on others or leaving him alone in the workshop making whirligigs while I waltz around like a woman with prospects. Like somebody important. It's all fake. I'm fake. Just like Leo said about our town.

I close my eyes and pray as hard as I can.

"Okay, God here's the deal. Do what you can to keep Jar alive. I admit I been a terrible sister. The worst. I been thoughtless and full of myself and prideful and—"

I have to think. No sense admitting to everything. God has a lot of other folks to worry about. Maybe he hasn't noticed every bad thing I've done. I don't want to turn him completely against me.

"You let Jar live and I'll be a better person. Now don't go expecting me to Bible thump. I'm not up for that, but I can do

other things, like stop lying and never steal or kill someone or kite checks again. That's got to count for something..."

I try to think of another thing God might want me to put on the table. I clasp my hands together and bow my head. *"Alright God, you got me. You let Jar live and I'll give up thinking about the money."*

After I say this, I get a feeling in my belly all warm and content. Like Uncle E, himself, is beside me giving me comfort. That he's telling me I have to take care of what's right in front of me and not be yearning for things I don't have.

A different nurse comes out. As many times as Jar and I have come in here, she's not one we've seen.

"We can't find anything wrong so far. But your brother's still not responding," she says. "We have to do more tests."

She hands me a pile of papers to sign.

"No matter how many times I fill stuff out for you people, you still need me to do more," I grumble.

"I've taken a look at his records," she says. "He's been here before." she stares at me. "Quite often, in fact."

"He's a regular," I say proudly. When she leaves I work on the papers. It's the least I can do for my brother.

Name. *Jarld Tyree.* My brother doesn't have a middle name. Momma and Daddy sort of gave up on him when they found out how he was. It's not fair Jar was shorted on his smarts, his height, and his name. I hesitate and then squeeze in *Edward* between *Jarld* and *Tyree.* There. Uncle E can have a namesake.

Childhood diseases. Other injuries. Previous surgeries.

They should know all of this. But I write it in anyway. Nosebleeds. Hurt foot. Chicken pox. Stuff that's easy. Fell out of tree. Off a roof. Cut with Jigsaw. Bumped head. Hurt finger. Scraped forehead. Two or three or four bellyaches from getting into Uncle E's chocolate flavored laxatives.

When I get to the part where it asks for the name of the insurance and the responsible party I just start blubbering. I'm so darn tired. My head sinks into my hands.

A rush of air blows in from an open door makes me look up. At first, I'm confused. I see people I know coming in. Kind of like that end of the tunnel thing when you're dying, only these folk are alive and hopefully I am too.

There's Leo. His leather jacket is over his apron. Madeline comes in next. And then Josephine. And Walter. There's no reason for any of them to be here. My throat gets full. "Hey," I say.

Josephine takes my hand and squeezes it. "Peggy is helping Curtis at the Café until Leo comes back and Jar's out of the woods."

Jar's in the woods again? Somehow, it helps to think my brother's run away in the forest. And then, I think, Peggy at the café? Well, that certainly can't be good. She'll chase away customers for sure. My lip is nearly bit off as I get back to chewing it.

Leo moves next to me. I watch a muscle in his jaw pulse. "You know I didn't mean any of what I said back there. You know that don't you? You're a good sister to Jar," he says. "The best." He reaches out to my face with his hand. Before it gets there, he drops it.

"I'm the only sister he's got, so it better be enough," I say and jab Leo in the stomach to lighten the mood.

An hour passes. I can't eat, but I suck down some coffee out of the vending machine. It's so hot it burns my mouth. I deserve that. Drinking it before it cools. Not waiting.

The doctor comes out. His brows are furrowed. "The tests are all negative, but your brother still isn't responding," he says.

"Can I see him?" I ask.

The doctor leads me into the room. My brother is hooked up with tubes and screens like a robot. Or maybe Frankenstein. I touch Jar's hand. It's cool and dry. I try to lift his arm to place my fingers in his hand, but he's like a piece of wood.

The nurse replaces a bag of clear fluid. "There doesn't seem to be any broken bones. No internal injuries that we can find," she says. "It's perplexing." She flips a switch. One of the machines starts blipping.

"Blip." My brother cracks an eye. *"Blip! Blip!"* he says.

The nurse jumps. Startled.

"Holy Moly!" I blurt out.

"Blip. Blip," Jar says again.

"Jarld Tyree! You playing possum again?" I kick the wheels of the bed so hard the nurse has to catch it before it hits the wall.

"Playing possum?" The nurse stares at Jar and then me. "What are you saying?"

"Answer me, right now!" I screech to my brother. "And playing possum is what Jar does when he thinks he's in a heap of trouble. Which he is, by the way!"

"Pip coot," Jar murmurs. He points to a bump on his forehead.

"No way Jose!" I snarl. "You got that yesterday from falling off the porch!"

"Ack!" My brother sits right up, frowning.

"Ack yourself, Jose!" I say right back. "And I'll do worse than call you Jose! Fact is, I'm thinking about having those doctors give you needles and shots and anything else they can cook up. The only reason I probably won't is it'll end up costing us more money," I howl. "You're lucky it's not free."

"Ack!" Jar cries and hides his head under the pillow.

"Calm down." The nurse inches towards the door.

"I am calm!" I holler. "And you can't hide from me, Jar. I know exactly where you are!"

"I better get the doctor." The nurse runs out of the room.

"And make that shot a big one!" I say this real loud. "The biggest!"

"ACK!" Jar screeches.

"And after you go I'm giving him a blistered bottom. And that's a promise." I turn on my heel and march out to the waiting room where everyone is huddled in a circle.

"Is he going to live?" Josephine asks.

"Not if I can help it," I say grimly. "He's nothing but a big fat faker. Doing his possum routine again." I hug myself and pace. "But it doesn't seem possible. He got run over by a truck. Jar's not superman. Madeline you were there. You were the one who saw him get hit."

Madeline shifts her feet. "Well, no. To be honest, I didn't exactly see it," she says.

"What?" I stop pacing and stare.

"He was lying on the ground. Walter said he was hurt," Madeline says. "He saw the whole thing.

"I didn't see the whole thing and I didn't actually say he was hurt. I said *somebody* was going to get hurt when I saw your brother creeping around lugging that bag of garbage," Walter offers. "I thought he was up to no good when I saw him fling a handful of rocks at the windshield of the truck."

"You either *creep* or *lug*. Not both," Madeline corrects Walter. "And a person *carries* a bag or *drags* a bag. You said you heard him being run over!" she says.

"I said I heard a sound," Walter says. He rubs his chin. "Now that I think about it, it must have been Jar's rocks hitting that truck." He points to Leo. "Anyway he said he saw it happen."

"I was in the kitchen. How could I see it happen?" Leo protests. "You told me what happened."

"I just said what I thought might have happened." Walter says to Leo. "You were the one who called the ambulance."

"You were the one who told me to call," Leo shoots back.

"I just said somebody probably ought to call for help," Walter says.

It seems I got me a bunch of loonies for friends. They all put two and two together and get seventeen.

I stalk back to Jar. The nurse is there standing by his bed.

"I hope you're satisfied," I say to Jar. "You've got everybody in town with their panties in a knot. You're going be spending a lot of time locked in that room of yours thinking about your behavior," I say. Of course, that's an empty threat. I don't ever lock him anywhere. But Jar knows I'm mad.

"You lock him up?" the nurse says.

"Otter peep," Jar says in a tiny voice.

"Or hang him by his thumbs," I say kidding. "No TV for you, mister, and it's bread and water for a month. I mean it." I turn to the nurse. "Can we go now?"

"We still need to wait for the test results," the nurse says cautiously. "A couple things we need to check on." She writes on a clipboard. "Then he'll be discharged." She doesn't look me in the eye.

When I return to the waiting room, it's empty except for Leo.

"Everybody went home," he says. "I was elected to give you two a ride back. How's your brother doing?" Leo asks.

"They said I have to wait for some more lab work and sign some more papers, and then after that I can get him dressed and take him home," I say. "You can come and wait with us if you want."

"Sure," Leo follows me into Jar's cubical.

The nurse walks in again. "We need a signature on this," she says.

I scribble my name without looking.

"Okey dokey," Jar says happily.

"Good for you," I say. "But it's no matter if you feel better." I lift up a shirt that's folded on the chair. "Come on let's get you dressed while we're waiting." The shirt comes apart in two pieces. I lift up his pants and they aren't any better.

"Hells bells! Everything's cut up! You going to replace these?" I frown at the nurse. "Those jeans of his were nearly new. You don't know how hard it is getting forty waists and lopping off twenty inches at the bottom. He'll have to go home in your hospital gown," I say to Jar. "And you better not charge us for it either," I say to the nurse. "Is Doctor Harms around? He's the one who usually sees us."

"Doctor Harms is on vacation. You really need to calm down. We always cut a patient's clothes off in an emergency." The nurse says. "And it shouldn't be much longer for those— tests." She walks out the door.

"Sounds like laziness to me," I mutter to her stiff back.

"Lone wrapper," Jar says. He's all hang-faced like he knows he's caused us a heap of trouble and he's sorry. He starts rubbing his temple.

"Lucky it's just a false alarm," says Leo. He puts his leather jacket over Jar's shoulders. "Now, I'm just lending you this," he tells Jar. "Don't be getting any ideas."

Jar gives him a big grin. He starts playing with all the zippers. "Totter twat!" he sings.

"Yeah, well, Leo may be nicer than me, but it'll be my hand in charge of your butt when we get home," I warn. "And no you can't learn to drive a motorcycle when you turn sixteen."

"Wipe spat," Jar sticks out his lower lip.

"That's right. And you'd better apologize," I say.

Another nurse walks in. Her face is familiar so I look at her nametag. It's Caldwell. She's the one we saw when Jar got his foot caught in the mountain beaver trap and was hurt on the jigsaw. "Hey, there," I say.

"There's a delay," she tells me.

"That's what the last nurse said."

"Has everything been alright at home?" She says slowly. "Have you both been under some sort of stress?"

"Stress is my middle name," I say. "But as for him, you can see he's all right and tight now," I say. "No stress in his life I tell you." I take my fingers and snap Jar a good one on his ear. He jumps guiltily.

The nurse frowns. "He's lucky he wasn't severely injured. And you shouldn't hurt his ear that way."

"Why not? It gets his attention. And he won't feel so lucky when I whale on his bottom for scaring the bejesus out of me," I say. "And I kept telling those doctors all the tests you do every time we come in are a waste of money."

I tap my brother in the chest. "I'm pretty well peeved. Least you could do was to be killed or have something important the matter with you," I growl. "That ambulance will cost some serious bucks."

"Coot rat," Jar grins.

"Sorry is, as sorry does," I say. "Can we go now?" I ask the nurse. "We're tired of waiting.

She clears her throat. "Um. No."

And that's when two uniformed policemen and three social workers walk into the room. I know they're social workers because they have clipboards and wear sweaters. Plus they have that busybody look.

"Miss Tammy Tyree? A charge of abuse and neglect has been filed against you," one policeman says. "We're here so there's no trouble."

"What?" My mouth drops open.

"Your brother is being removed from your care for his protection. He'll have to come with us," A social worker says.

"Good luck with that," I say. "He won't go and I won't leave him."

But they tell me the paper I signed without reading was saying it was okay to take Jar away and they tell me I need to get myself a lawyer.

A really good lawyer.

And the last thing I hear is my brother screeching as I'm led out the door.

CHAPTER TWENTY

"A lawyer? What do I need a lawyer for? I haven't done anything," I fume to Leo.

The two of us are waiting to speak with the social worker that's been assigned to my case. She works with patients at the hospital so her office is in the basement. We're outside her closed door sitting on a couple of hard chairs in the hall. It's over heated so I'm sweating like a pig. I wipe off the back of my neck.

"That's when you need one the most," Leo says patiently. "When you're innocent."

"How do you know anything about being innocent? You've never done anything wrong."

Leo gets a shuttered look on his face.

"It's a funny place to have an office," I confide to Leo. "All underground. And no windows to speak of." I look around. "Even those baby-puke-green walls. Makes it depressing."

"It's the situation you're in that makes it depressing," Leo points out.

"Situation nothing! You know as well as I do that I never abused my brother." I fold my arms tight and frown.

"I know it and you know it." Leo kneads my shoulder like he does bread dough. "But you have to admit it looks bad."

I shrug off his hand. "Then why didn't you say anything when we were in the ER? You just stood there." I glare.

"What did you expect me to do?"

"Defend me. Something more than nothing," I spit out. There's no time to say anything else. The office door creaks open and my name is called.

The two of us walk inside. There's the same baby-puke wall color along with a desk piled high with stacks of papers. A lady is seated there. Her nametag says Bernice.

There's only one chair. Leo pushes me into it and then stands behind me like a guard dog.

Bernice says nothing at first. She just opens up a folder with Jar's name written in big black letters across the front and starts perusing. I'm happy to see they added the middle name I gave him in ER. *Jarld Edward Tyree.*

That makes it official. I make a mental note to let Jar know his new name.

Bernice finally looks up from her reading. "We have some serious allegations here. Neglect. Physical abuse." She scribbles something on a paper with her pen.

"I wasn't abusing my brother," I say stubbornly. My voice echoes in the room making me sound guilty. "And there's no neglect. You talk to Doctor Harms. He'll tell you. He said Jar was lucky."

Bernice takes on a sour expression like she hears this particular song and dance all the time. She shakes her head slowly from side to side all the while clucking like Annie our hen.

"The nurses in ER mentioned you were physical with your brother. And you made threats."

"Physical? I don't get physical. I just do some ear pulling. Head thwaping. Butt smacking," I say. "And threats? Heck, the two of us were brought up on them. It's a demonstration of Tyrees' affectionate nature, along with Dutch rubs."

"There should be no rubs of any kind." Bernice looks serious. "None of that is appropriate reinforcement for those afflicted with a mental challenge." she says.

"He isn't afflicted! And you try and get Jar to toe the line without a challenge to his butt." I scowl. "He won't behave otherwise. Heck, he even gives me a good smack when I need one."

"Be that as it may we still can't release him into your care until we conclude our investigation. I notice you've taken your brother into the ER on a number of occasions."

"Well, doesn't that show I take care of him? ER visits are expensive."

Bernice holds up another folder. This one is real fat.

"His medical records document a number of concerning accidents," she says.

I roll my eyes. "Of course, they do! Jar's accident-prone. There isn't a door that Jar doesn't run into. Ever since he was real young. We had to turn his play pen upside down on top of him until he was nine just so he wouldn't run away."

"Are you saying you caged your brother in?" Bernice's eyes are wide.

"Yes. NO! No, I don't mean we put him in a bona fide cage. Hells bells you're twisting my words. Anyway, I'm not leaving here without my brother. Where is he?"

"The hospital won't release him until we can find a suitable temporary foster home the will take him."

"Foster home?" This sends me back in time. Just like when Momma and Daddy died. "FOSTER HOME?" I make a lunge across Bernice's desk but Leo grabs me by the shirt and jerks me back.

"Calm down, Tammy." Leo says. "We're done here," he says to Bernice. His tone is firm. "You'll be hearing from Miss Tyree's lawyer."

At the sound of lawyer, Bernice furrows her brows.

"Lawyer?" I say to Leo. "I don't have a lawyer."

Bernice looks relieved.

"You will," Leo says.

Bernice starts looking worried again.

Leo heads out the door pulling me along with him. Of course, I'm yelping the whole time about not leaving without my brother. Leo has to physically jam my ass into his VW and shut me in.

"Tammy! Quiet!" he hollers.

That gets me to pipe down. Leo's never yelled at me.

"You're not making your case any easier by losing your temper," Leo chastises. "You need to get your act together."

"I don't feel bad for yelling. They deserve it," I kick the floorboards of his van with my heels.

"Look Tammy," Leo says. "You have to control yourself or I guarantee you you'll lose Jar. Going wild will only make their case."

"But I'm not!" I protest. "If you were a real man you'd come to my rescue. Help me take Jar back," I mutter.

Leo hunches over the wheel. He doesn't say anything.

"You're a yellow-bellied coward," I say. "Content to let things happen the way they may. Not me," I say. "I'm a fighter. Not a bellyacher. Or usually a prayer. Fact is, I'm thinking praying got me into this mess in the first place. Crying and praying. I'm a wee bit pissed at God stabbing me in the back like this."

"Like I said before. You need a lawyer," Leo says doggedly.

And then suddenly I feel sorry. "I just called you a bunch of names, Leo," I say all contrite. "I apologize. And I don't need any lawyer. How can they do this, anyway?"

"There's a lot of latitude with abuse accusations. The county must think they have evidence," Leo says. "Don't be dense. Get yourself legal help. You can't do this on your own."

"I'm not dense. Legal help takes money. Everything comes down to that, anyway." I stare out the windshield. The white centerline whizzes by reflecting glints of silver from Leo's headlights. Rain splatters the window. The wipers go *woop woop* against the glass.

I need that inheritance to come ASAP.

When we get to the trailer, Leo pulls up close to my porch. "You'll be okay?" he asks.

"Do I have a choice? There're chickens to take care of. Livestock doesn't wait on any disasters."

"I got something for you." He reaches behind his seat and pulls out a nice sized rock. "I picked this up by where Jar was hurt."

"It's a nice one. You'll want to keep it for when your brother comes home."

Home. Well, that does it. Water fills my eyes and there's a tingle in my throat. I quick grab the rock and disappear through my door so Leo doesn't see me cry.

Once inside I start blubbering and bawling, holding the rock to my chest. Pacing back and forth. I go into the kitchen and grab a paper towel to blot my tears. It scratches.

When I go out to feed the hens even Cauliflower stands back. Not going after my ankles. The others huddle forlornly in a far corner. They sense my mood.

I give the girls a double portion of corn, and then look for eggs. There's only one. I stick it in the fridge and then go back outside. Annie stands at the gate looking at me. It's like she knows.

I scoop her up, and bring her inside. The two of us sit at the kitchen table. She looks around her with interest. I set the rock down.

"That's right," I say. "You never been in here. Pretty fancy, isn't it?"

She clucks her agreement and nestles in the crook of my arm. I stare sideways at the wall. That's where I spend the next six hours. Being sad and caressing Annie until the sun comes up.

Of course, later I figured out what a bad idea that was. I must have fallen asleep at some point, because Annie's crapped from one end of the kitchen to the other. Chickens produce a lot of crap. It takes me nearly a whole roll of paper towels to clean the linoleum.

By eight thirty, I'm showered, changed, have the place straightened and the chores done. Even weeded the garden.

I pack a pillowcase with things Jar needs. An extra shirt. His favorite hat and matching sweatshirt. I throw in some screws and screwdrivers and a piece of wood. I think about putting in his favorite rocks, but I decide maybe not. Rocks in a hospital may not be what the doctor ordered.

If those social workers are primed to send Jar to a foster situation, I better get going before they take him away. Dolly starts after three or four tries and I make a beeline back to the hospital. I march into ER and flag a nurse down. She's the same one who was there was Jar came in.

"I'm here to see my brother," I tell her firmly.

"He's not here." She avoids my eyes like she's feeling guilty about doing us a dirty turn.

My heart thuds. "You mean he's gone already?"

"No he's been transferred."

She checks a computer. "Fourth floor. Mental health unit," she lowers her voice. "Just between you and me they're having a bit of trouble finding suitable foster care."

"I get you," I say. "And my brother isn't crazy. Just so you know." And then I add. "Is Doctor Harms back?" I'm thinking he can put in a good word for me.

"Still on vacation," she says. "And your brother's visitors are restricted."

But I'm already heading for the elevator.

As I ride up to the fourth floor, I think about what Leo said. I set the pillowcase down and quickly tuck in my shirt and straighten my hair. The walls inside the elevator are shiny so I spit on my hand and clean up my face.

When the doors open, I waste no time. There's an orderly sitting at a desk. I notice a sign that says *all visitors must check in.* I have to be careful or I'll get my butt kicked out of this place. The orderly is reading a magazine. He looks up. I think fast and hold up my bag.

"Laundry," I say. "For Tyree. What room?" I try to look bored.

"406," he says and goes back to reading.

As soon as I'm out of sight, I run-walk down the hall. 406 is at the end. I slide through the door and close it behind me.

The room is dark. The shades are drawn. There's a huddled form on the bed buried under the covers.

"Bug?" I reach out to him. Jar looks sleepy like they've drugged him. His wrists are tied to the rails.

The pillowcase drops to the floor as I struggle to undo Jar's restraints. The buckles are stiff but I manage it.

"That's it! I'm springing you." I push my brother's shoulders to make him sit up but he slouches down. "Come on, Bug! You got to walk!"

"I got your blue sweatshirt. And your seed corn hat," I say. "I didn't bring any of your rocks although thinking on it now maybe I should have."

"Poop head," Jar whispers. His voice is raw and husky.

"Well, I feel like one too if it makes you feel any better," I say. "Get up now," I urge.

My brother flops back on the bed. He's lying on Leo's jacket. At least they didn't take that away.

The door opens and a nurse walks in. She stares when she sees me.

"What are you doing here?" She pushes a button on the wall. "Code green in 406!" she calls out. A bell starts ringing and I hear footsteps. Before I can make a move, two security guards in blue uniforms run in. They each grab an arm and pull me towards the door.

"I'm going. I'm going. I just brought some of his stuff. And my brother shouldn't be tied up," I shout.

"It's for his protection," she says in her hospital reasonable. "He was uncontrollable. We thought he'd hurt himself."

"He's only uncontrollable because you have him in the dark. It looks like you're the ones who are doing the abusing." I say. "You're going to hear from my lawyer," I shout. "Or a judge or somebody. I have friends in law enforcement, you know," I call out thinking of Smithers. But is he a friend? I'm not sure.

I'm taken out into the hall and meet up face to face with the social worker Bernice. And that's not all. My cousin Lonnie is with her. I notice his shirt is clean and he's freshly shaved.

"What are you doing here?" I growl.

Lonnie's smile doesn't reach his eyes. "I might ask the same of you?" He shakes his head sadly. "I had to speak out. I was afraid for that littlest cousin of mine."

"So you're the snake in the grass who started this," I spit. "Afraid? I'll make you afraid." I make a lunge for him.

"See?" Lonnie ducks behind the social worker. "Tammy's got a temper and she has a habit of assaulting. I'm mighty afraid of what she'll do."

Too late, I see his game. Leo was right. I kick myself in the mental behind and take a deep breath. "I'm just upset," I say.

"Has Miss Tyree always been this volatile?" The social worker is writing on a clipboard.

"She got it bad when Uncle E died." Lonnie says and crosses himself. "Rest his soul."

"I've never been any way. He's a lying sack of shit," I say.

"Language, Tammy." Lonnie sadly shakes his head. "Our pastor warned her about that around Jar."

"What pastor?" I spit out.

The social worker continues her writing. I take a deep breath. "When can Jar come home?" I ask real polite.

"Your brother is getting a full physical examination and then we'll need to do a home visit on your premises." She peers at me through thick glasses. "We are waiting for placement."

"Placement?" I ask. "What do you mean placement?"

"Put him somewhere while we investigate the charges. Make sure he'll be in a safe environment. Verify your brother will get proper care."

"And after that he can come home?"

"If everything checks out." Her tone makes it clear to me that she's certain it won't.

Lonnie stands there sucking his cheeks in.

"When can you come for this visit?" I might as well get this show on the road.

"We can set you up for Monday after next."

I think of Jar's room, my bare refrigerator, our workshop full to the brim of sharp objects, and lord knows what else in the yard not to mention the disaster of the chicken coop. I bite my lip. "How about the day after that," I say slowly.

Cousin Lonnie smirks.

Even though I want my brother home this instant, I see the wisdom of waiting. Making sure I can get things right.

"Fine," Bernice says and writes it down in her notebook.

Jar starts whimpering. I start to go to him, but the security guards grab my arms. I struggle and they lift me up and walk me out of Jar's room.

"You have to leave the lights on at night!" I yell. "You got to promise always leave the lights on twenty-four seven. He's scared of the dark. And if you use Skittles as a reward he'll behave near perfect." The guards relax their grip and I'm able to break away. I speed back into Jar's room. "Hang in there, Bug. It's only for a little while," I tell him. "Until I get this mess all straightened out."

Jar looks at me sleepily. "Okey dokey," he whispers.

The two guards drag me back out and are none too gentle about it this time. Lonnie stands there looking pious with Bernice.

"Keep the TV on," I shout hoping the nurse will hear. "He likes Jeopardy! EVERYTHING WILL BE OKEY DOKEY JAR!" I scream.

Hells bells, I'm tossed out of the hospital on my ear.

Maybe this is how Uncle E felt like being thrown out of the Silver King Tavern. It's not a comfortable feeling. Fact is, it's highly embarrassing with people looking on and figuring they know my beeswax. Like I'm an axe murderer or something.

I drive home in a dangerous mood.

Dolly conks out halfway up our driveway. Her emergency brake is on the fritz so I have a devil of a time shoving rocks under her tires. Have to wrench her wheel to the side.

"I don't have time for this!" I slam her door hard with my foot. "I have to clean the trailer, do the chickens, and get groceries to stock the fridge so it looks like I take care of Jar. Now I'll have to walk to the Shop and Save in the drizzle, no thanks to you."

I hunch my shoulders, and trek down the street. The Shop and Save bell tinkles when I enter. It sounds sad without Jar to imitate it.

I go down one aisle and up the other grabbing healthy things off the shelf. *Bisquick. Milk. Bread. Orange juice.* I pause by the meat and pick up a pound of ground round then I go to the produce and get a couple onions and a green pepper. I back track to the canned vegetable aisle and get four cans of kidney beans, stewed tomatoes and a can of Ro-tel.

I make a plan. *Chili.* Just like Uncle E used to make. That's sure as heck healthy. I also get all the stuff for cornbread. Chili and cornbread are one of Jar's favorites.

I'll make a pot tonight. He'll be home soon and it's good when it's aged a few days.

Sue Ann is tending the register. "Peggy said that Curtis told her Leo said that Jar got taken away from you," she says. "That true?"

My hands are trembling as I set things on the counter. I try to still them. "Yeah," I say.

"Why? What's he done?" She doesn't meet my eyes as she rings up my stuff. "Somebody said they're doing an investigation. Is he being put away?"

"Nothing and no," I say. "It's all a mistake."

"The county doesn't make mistakes." Sue Ann sniffs. She puts my groceries in the bag. "You know what they say. Where there's smoke." She tilts her head like a bird. "That'll be seventy-two twenty three."

"Put it on my tab," I say.

"No way," she says firmly. "I told you before. I'm in a bind. Glenn's already asking questions." She lowers her voice. "When is that money coming, anyway? For real this time."

"Soon," I hiss. "And I'm in a bind, too. I need to get this thing straightened out with Jar. And why is Glenn asking questions? You weren't supposed to tell."

"I didn't tell him anything!" Sue Ann protests. "Well, not much. He wasn't happy, I can tell you that." Her eyes slide away from mine.

"I need to put this on my tab just one last time," I say. "And you can't be in any more of a hurry than I am to get the money." I think about all my bills piling up. "Let me owe you," I say.

"No sir," Sue Ann says firmly. "No tab, no more."

"Sue Ann," I shake out my purse. "Here's ten fifty-seven. It's all I got. I can give you the rest tomorrow or the day after."

Sue Ann shakes her head.

"I'll bring by eggs," I say desperately.

"No. You got to put things back," she says.

So I do. I return the hamburger and the Bisquick. I'm doing math in reverse. I return the vegetables. The Ro-tel. I end up with a bag of cornmeal, milk, and two cans of kidney beans.

"It's a shame Jar being locked up," Sue Ann says as she takes my money and hands over a receipt. "But it's really for the best isn't it? Him being the way he is and all," she says this brightly. "In fact, it's a blessing in disguise for you, don't you think? Him going into one of them homes? That's what Curtis said might happen."

Thinking on it later, I shouldn't have thrown anything at Sue Ann let alone that head of lettuce I'd had to set aside.

There was no point to hanging around to find out if I'd injured her, or if she was really and truly knocked out. Romaine would have been no big deal, but iceberg is hefty.

When I get my one puny bag home, I'm regretting my actions even more when I stare at my near empty fridge with the pitcher of mixed powdered milk all by itself on the shelf. Manhandling Sue Ann was cutting off my nose to spite my face all right.

I stick a couple empty egg cartons on the middle shelf and then fold up lots of foil packages so it looks like we have leftovers. Next, I fill Tupperware bowls with colored water and set empty pots with covers on the bottom shelf. There. That will do in a pinch. I just hope nobody opens any of the containers to sample my cooking.

I head outside to do chicken chores. They all cluck their approval and the banties surround my feet. Cauliflower is missing. I look around the yard, but she's nowhere to be found. She could be anywhere. I make a search for eggs and find two. The one in the fridge makes three. Only enough for my supper.

I scold the hens. "You girls are falling down on your job. I can't fill even one box," I tell them. "You better get cracking or you'll end up in pies. Every one of you. Then I'll have plenty for the fridge," I threaten.

They look unconcerned. Annie comes over and pecks at my shoelace. I pick her up.

"Do some of your poultry praying, Annie. Jar and me are in real trouble," I say. When I set her down, she scoots off.

I leave the coop gate ajar and sprinkle a trail of feed outside, just in case Cauliflower is hanging around. White leghorns are good at fending for themselves, but any creature can use a little help. I stand there shifting my feet.

Hells bells.

I swallow hard and tramp off into the woods with a handful of corn and a flashlight, searching for that no good hen, Cauliflower.

I don't stop until I find her.

CHAPTER TWENTY-ONE

The next day I visit my brother and I'm told I can't be alone with him. I have to be supervised by Bernice. She stares at us. Her eyes bulge like she has a gland problem.

Jar seems to be getting used to being at the hospital. He doesn't do his buzzers. He just lies there playing possum and cracking one eye open to watch TV while I sit next to him.

I know he wants to go home and get back to tossing rocks and making whirligigs.

"Okey dokey," he whispers to me under his breath. I take that to mean he knows we're in a pickle and thinks he's done some crime and he's in hospital jail.

At least he's not tied up any more and his light is on. He's got a good nurse now. Caldwell from ER. She's one of the nice ones who smile with their eyes. She comes in and out straightening Jar's bed and checking that he has water.

Bernice the social worker is just the opposite of smiling eyes. Right now, hers are stone cold blue like a fish. She's a real nosy parker, plus she's gullible, as she swallows all the lies Lonnie spouts, hook, line, and sinker.

She stands there scrutinizing me.

"What are your long term plans for your brother?" she asks out of the blue.

"Long term plans? Let me see?" I place a finger at my temple. "Well, I'm fixing to send him to college next month. That what you mean by plans?" I roll my eyes.

"I'm serious." Bernice frowns. "I meant plans for if we release your brother to your care."

"Oh, those plans," I say. "Wait a moment! If? You hinting I might not get my brother back?" I sit up and take notice. "Who do you think has been doing everything for him his whole life? Fairies?"

"A report of abuse and neglect is not to be taken lightly." She clucks her tongue at me like a ticking bomb.

"I'm not taking it lightly. Where you getting your wrong info from?" I say.

"A concerned relative," she says.

"I don't have any concerned relatives, unless you're counting Uncle E, and he's dead. Oh, that's right," I snarl. "You're listening to that snake in the grass cousin Lonnie."

Bernice shakes her head. "He warned us you'd be uncooperative."

I get to my feet. There's no sense talking to her.

"Bye, Jar. We'll get out of this mess. Believe me," I say and give him a hug, I whisper in his ear. "I'm springing you Jar. Next time I come. Just you wait."

It's time to take charge of things. No more waiting. The only person who can save my brother is myself. I scowl. Those social worker experts don't know a thing. They only pretend they do. That's what smart is, I decide. Pretending you know, when you don't, and then making stuff up or believing liars.

I wake up well before dawn the next morning and head straight for the hospital. Instead of the elevator, I take the back stairs two at a time. I make it all the way down the hall and into Jar's room without anyone seeing me.

"Hey, there, Bug, ready to come home?" I whisper.

But his room is empty. I poke around. No hide nor hair of my brother. Not behind the lone chair. The bed is stripped bare to the mattress. I check the bathroom and behind the door. It's then I notice all Jar's personal stuff is gone. Even Leo's leather jacket.

A gray-haired lady comes in rolling a wash bucket and mop.

"My brother was in here. Where'd he go?" I ask her. My heart is pounding in my throat.

The lady shrugs. “Discharged or transferred. You’ll have to ask one of the nurses.” And she gets to work mopping.

I step into the hall grab the first nurse I see. It happens to be Caldwell.

“Where’s Jar?” I ask urgently.

She smiles at me. “I thought you knew. Your cousin Lonnie volunteered to take care of him as the social workers couldn’t find a placement. It seemed best to let him be with family.”

“You let Lonnie take him?” My voice comes from far away and everything turns black around the edges. Lonnie’s got Jar. These people don’t know what they’ve done.

I waste no time motoring as fast as I can back to Spring. Dolly belches a backfire and her engine knocks to beat the band.

“Calm down, Tammy Louise,” I tell myself real stern. “It’ll do Jar no good to panic.”

I take some deep breaths and consider as I drive. I can’t get past the fact that the snake in the grass Lonnie’s got Jar. I roll up our driveway and rush through the door of the trailer.

“Jar? Lonnie?” I call. Hoping against hope the two of them would be there. Hoping Lonnie would see the error of his ways. That he’s had second thoughts.

The trailer is empty with no sign of Lonnie, Skittle packages, or Jar-mess.

When I go out the back door the group of hens cackle to me from the coop explaining that they haven't been fed.

"I'll get right on it, girls, I promise."

Their bag of scratch is nearly gone. It only covers the bottom of the feed dish.

"You girls got to go on a diet or start foraging," I say. They all crow their opinion that they'd appreciate foraging. I prop open their gate so they can go in and out freely. Cauliflower's white ass is nowhere around. That hen's an escape artist, for sure. It's worrying having a missing hen. I add that to my main worry of Lonnie having Jar and my secondary worry that I haven't received an email from Barinas.

What's with that man anyway? Why haven't I heard anything? Maybe it's time to let him know of my current difficulties. I can't be beating around the bush any longer. Hearing my money woes may stop him dilly-dallying and force him to come up to scratch.

I look at my watch. Time to change into my uniform and go into Two Spoons for my shift. When I walk through the front door of Two Spoons, Curtis looks up from behind the register.

"You didn't have to come in early." He waves his arm. "No construction on the bypass today. No workers. Even Leo's taking some time off. Come back at twelve thirty," Curtis says.

"If you're hungry Leo's got leftover liver soup from yesterday with squaw bread croutons. It's on the back burner."

"No thanks," I say. My heart takes a nosedive at the thought of decreased hours and fewer tips. "And by the way I don't appreciate you talking about my beeswax to Sue Ann. It's none of her concern what's going on with Jar and me," I say. "Or yours."

Curtis presses his lips together. "You're my employee. If you've been doing something wrong, I'm affected. Tarred by the same brush so to speak. Your cousin Lonnie was saying—"

"Oh, now you're listening to that cousin of mine? That's rich." I push past Curtis and go to the computer. That belly of mine is twisting up tighter than a wrung mop. I need that money for sure now. I mean I needed it before, but I really need it now. What if something goes wrong? What if they decide I'm not a close enough relation? What if there are more taxes due? Or more fees to pay? Or they find out I been blabbing? Or they give it to Lonnie?

I hit *get mail.* There's nothing from Dr. Barinas. I hit it again, and again, and again until my finger is sore. *Nothing.* My mouth is cottony dry.

I walk out the door and stand there in the parking lot in a daze. I don't want to go back home and I don't want to stay.

Leo is standing next to his propped up bike. He nods when I approach.

"You okay?" he asks.

"Okay? How in the world can I be okay?" I snap. "With Jar taken away and those hospital goons handing him over to Lonnie and you don't have enough hours for me."

Leo is just wearing his Grateful Dead tee shirt.

That makes me remember. "Your leather coat is still with Jar. It's the only thing they let him keep to remind him of home," I say. "They said everything I brought for my brother was too dangerous."

Leo knocks the kickstand with his toe and throws a leg over. "It doesn't matter. It's warm out, even with the rain." He turns the throttle.

"Yeah, but that jacket's expensive!" I shout over the engine noise.

"Lots of things are expensive. It gives Jar pleasure. He can keep it as long as he needs it!" Leo says.

"I'll pay you for it if it gets ruined!"

"Not necessary!"

I shove a rock with my foot. It feels good. I shove another. Leo turns off his engine. The silence hurts my ears more than the motor did.

"Know what I do when things get too much?" Leo rocks back and forth on his Harley.

"No."

"What I'm doing now, I take my bike for a spin."

"I don't have a bike," I say.

"I'm offering you a ride." Leo says. "Come on." He reaches out.

"In this weather?" It's raining steadily. I look up the hill at my trailer. "And I have things to do. And I don't have a helmet." I glance at his bare head. "Folks like me need to keep all the brains they have."

Leo shrugs. "I can scrounge up a helmet if you want."

One minute I'm standing there getting wet in the rain thinking I don't have time to go for a ride, and the next minute my uniform is hitched up, I got a helmet jammed on my head, and I'm tight behind Leo, flying down the street.

"I've never been on one of these!" The wind swallows up my words.

"Time you were," Leo calls back.

The speed plasters my lips flat and tears stream down my face. The engine shatters my ears and the steady vibration flows up through my body and out my head. Holy moly! We're flying around curves, hurtling down the highway. Barely slowing to make the turn up the backside of Spring Bluff. Up. Up. Up. I shut my eyes tight and forget about everything.

We go high and higher. Dodging potholes and weaving around moguls in the asphalt. And then we slow. We pull over. And roll to a stop.

The engine throbs and then Leo cuts it. And it's quiet. My ears are buzzing with the silence. We're at the top of the bluff. Spring sits below like a miniature town. I can see from one end to the other. Tiny cars. Tiny people. The gash of the bypass through Spring Hill. I slide off.

"It's been years since I been up here," I say. I look over the ledge. It makes me nervous and I back up.

Most of the giant trees are gone from the logging, but smaller ones poke through the pine needles and branches littering the hillside. Leo lifts my helmet off. The cool wet breeze hits my ears and I rub them.

"Look here." Leo kneels. His hand brushes a miniature tree at his feet. The perfect branches lacey against his hand. "We're giants." And he looks at me real serious.

I stretch my arms and try to touch the gray puffy clouds. Leo is right. We're both larger than life. "I feel like an angel looking down!" I cup my hands around my mouth. "Hellloooooo!" I holler.

Nobody in Spring answers.

The bypass looks nearly complete. A pain pierces my gut. That will be the end of Spring, for sure. The end of everything I know. A hawk flies above. Wings folded to its body. Diving after something small and weak, a mouse maybe, or a baby bird.

I drop my arms. "What am I gonna do, Leo?" The sound of my voice is only a whisper.

"I don't know." He stares at me closely. "Sounds like you think there's a right answer and a wrong answer. A well-marked Y in the road of life. Sometimes there isn't an easy choice, Tammy. The world doesn't work that way."

"Well, the world needs to give me a hint, at least," I mutter.

Right at that exact moment, I want to confide in Leo in the worst way. I want to let him know what's happening about my inheritance. I want to let him know I'm having doubts about everything. I want to tell him I owe an impossible amount of money. That I'm scared for Jar, I'm scared for our town, and most of all I'm scared for me.

Leo squats on his haunches. Folding and unfolding his hands. Rain drips down my neck and trickles all the way under my shirt. I stare at Leo's craggy face.

"Tammy we need to talk," he says.

"Is this gonna be one of them Hallmark moments where you try to make me feel better and then we hug? " I ask. "If so, don't bother."

"Okay." Leo pulls a joint out of his pocket and lights up.

He offers me a toke, but I shake my head.

"You sure?" he asks.

"How do you think it'd work out for Jar if they catch me high?"

"You're probably right about that." He takes a deep drag.

I stare at him consideringly. "Aren't you too old to do that stuff anyway?"

He winces. "Ouch," he says and takes another drag.

"So what did you want to talk about?" I prop myself against Leo's Harley and play dumb.

"I don't know." Leo looks back down at the town.

"Now you can't do that. Not start and then stop. You made me curious."

Leo remains silent. Just takes an occasional puff of his joint.

"You'll get a disease doing that," I warn. "Like lung cancer or pneumonia."

"I'm thirty years older than you," he says suddenly. "Too old."

"How'd you figure that out?" I ask.

"Looked at your employee records and subtracted."

"And your point, besides you proving to me you can do math?"

Leo takes another long drag and holds his breath. "No point."

The wind ruffles my ears.

"What if they take Jar away from me?" I murmur. "What will I do?"

Leo shrugs. "You can get paralyzed thinking what you do matters in the scheme of things. That you have control. But none of us has any control. Life is just shit that happens."

"Now that's being real helpful," I say.

"Sorry." He shrugs his shoulders again.

"Sorry is as sorry does."

Leo clears his throat. "I didn't bring you up here to talk about that."

His gray eyes reflect the cloudy sky.

"You know the first time I noticed you?" Leo says. He doesn't wait for me to answer. "You were barely a teenager. Someone pointed you out. Maybe it was Madeline. She said you and your brother were orphans. That your folks had been killed in an accident. I felt sorry for you. I think I said something to Madeline, and you know how she replied?" Leo imitates Madeline's voice. "She said, don't waste your time feeling sorry for Tammy Louise.

That child's a survivor. A born optimist." Leo pauses. "Resilience is good. Optimism is good. Don't get me wrong. That's why I hired you if you want to know the truth. I'm a born pessimist. Been one my whole life. I thought having an optimist around would be refreshing. And I wasn't far wrong."

I straighten up. "You got something to say to me, then say it. Don't be pulling punches."

Leo blows air out his mouth like a balloon set loose. "I've been around. I know things. I've lived life. This deal you got going with the people in town? It's not right, I'm telling you." Leo studies me. "I told you before that you can't get something for nothing. I'm afraid you're headed for trouble and I'm afraid someone's going to get hurt. That you're going to get hurt." Leo says this softly. He pauses. "You have to let everyone know you made a mistake and make it right before shit hits the fan."

"I don't know that I made a mistake," I say stubbornly. I stop and swallow hard. It hurts to have Leo think less of me. "I don't know why you care," I say. "And it's not for nothing. I've been paying fees. And that Barinas fellow has been real understanding. He even took half at a time at first. And this last time he never asked for anything."

Leo shakes his head. "That may well be. But you know deep down inside something's not on the up and up. Don't you?"

"I don't know that," I say stubbornly. "I don't." The doubts I had are pushed aside. What is it in me that when a person tells me black, I say white?

Leo looks at me and sighs. "At least think on what I'm saying, Tammy. Promise?"

My shoulders straighten up. "I don't need to think. There's no need for any advice," I say. "And speaking of advice, you should talk with that Wonderbread bag at Two Spoons chock full of weed."

"Personal use," Leo says. He wets his fingers with his tongue and pinches his joint out. His face is expressionless. He lurches to his feet.

"I've been taking care of myself for a good long while," I say and then, I don't know why, but my eyes fill with tears. One spills over and dribbles down my cheek. Leo reaches over with a thumb and gently wipes it off.

He puts my helmet back on and buckles it under my chin. I stay so still I hardly breath.

"Let's go," he says. "That hair of yours is going to get all tangled up."

"I'm used to tangles," I say.

Leo motors his Harley down the backside of Spring Bluff a lot slower than he went up. When we reach Two Spoons, Leo lets me off by the back door.

He removes my helmet and chucks under my jaw with his finger. "Talk to me first if you don't know where to turn."

"I told you I'm not in any trouble." I say firmly.

"Whatever you say," he says.

My throat tightens. We walk through the door together. I stay in the front and Leo goes into the kitchen. Curtis is at the register.

"I told you it's slow," he says.

"They'll be customers," I say. "There's got to be." And like I can predict the future, just before two, people start coming through the door.

Tips can get me by, I think as I wipe tables and take orders. Tips will have to get me by, I think as I fill glasses of water and cups of coffee. They got to get me by I pray as I pour salt and pepper into empty shakers.

I make a vow to toe the line so Curtis can't fault my work. I make a vow to button my lip and just do my job, not even making small talk with anybody. Not arguing. More customers trickle in. It's not packed, but we have business.

Business. That reminds me of my own beeswax.

That brain of mine is really churning. So is my stomach. Time to make Dr. Barinas see how serious everything is getting for me now.

At three thirty, when Curtis steps into the kitchen, I take a quick break and sit down at Two Spoons' computer.

DEAR DR. BARINAS.

I use all caps for emphasis.

THINGS ARE COMING TO A HEAD HERE IN SPRING. I NEED TO KNOW WHEN TO EXPECT THE MONEY FOR REAL THIS TIME. I HAVE A SMALL MISUNDERSTANDING ABOUT MY CIRCUMSTANCES. MY BROTHER JAR IS IN TROUBLE. HE'S BEEN GIVEN TO MY SNAKE IN THE GRASS COUSIN AND I'M

GETTING INVESTIGATED AND ACCUSED OF BEATING HIM WHICH IS A LIE OUT OF THE MOUTH OF MY AFOREMENTIONED COUSIN LONNIE THE TWO BIT SNAKE IN THE GRASS WHO'S GOT HIM NOW (MY BROTHER I MEAN). YOU ALL DON'T REALLY NEED THE DETAILS BUT TO MAKE A LONG STORY SHORT THE COUNTY IS GIVING ME A REAL HASSLE. OF COURSE, THE LAW MAKES MISTAKES ALL THE TIME BUT WE THE PEOPLE STILL HAVE TO PAY FOR IT. I PROBABLY SHOULD HAVE COME CLEAN A WHILE AGO THAT I LET IN A COUPLE PEOPLE ON OUR BUSINESS DEALINGS. PEGGY RUTLEDGE AND THEN JOSEPHINE MUNN AND THEN A FEW OTHERS IN SPRING LIKE WALTER HOWARD FOUND OUT BECAUSE YOU CAN'T KEEP ANYTHING A SECRET IN THIS PLACE. FACT IS, PEGGY HAS THE BIGGEST AND LOUDEST MOUTH AROUND (SHE USED TO BE A CHEERLEADER). THEY BEEN HELPING ME OUT EVER SINCE UNCLE E DIED BUT I GUESS I FORGOT TO TELL YOU ABOUT UNCLE E DYING AND I NEVER TOLD YOU ABOUT THE BYPASS THE STATE IS BUILDING THAT'S GOING TO BE THE END OF US ALL. EVERYBODY IS DEPENDING ON THIS MONEY YOU'RE SENDING

There I am going off on one of my tangents. I have to stay focused. I have to stay on track. The door of the café slams. I look up.

Two uniformed officers walk in as if joined by their holsters. Even more customers. Good. I'm cheered. We don't usually get any law enforcement other than Smithers. Maybe it means Two Spoons' reputation is on the rise.

They sniff the air like dogs after a scent. One of the officer's nose wrinkles. He obviously hasn't heard of Leo's soups. I pull a couple menus from the pile, and shove them across the counter.

"Welcome to Two Spoons," I say. "The late lunch special is pork butt and cabbage pie and the soup's anchovy chowder. You won't want to add any salt to it. Not any pepper either. I'll be done here in a jiff and be with you to take your order," I say.

"We aren't here to eat," one of them says, just as Curtis walks out of the kitchen.

"Why you here then?" Curtis asks.

"Tammy Louise Tyree?" The other officer says loudly.

"That's my name right here." I point to the maroon writing on my chest.

"Ma'am, you're under arrest for theft." The one officer pulls out his cuffs.

The customers at the far table stop eating and stare. My heart starts thumping.

"If you take her away, you got to send a replacement. Friday nights can get busy." Curtis snorts like it's a joke.

I laugh weakly. "Good one, Curtis." I say.

The officers move closer. Bracketing me like a couple of bookends.

"Did Clarence Smithers put you up to this?" I ask them. "Boy, will I get that man when I see him," I say. "He's such a kidder."

The one officer takes my hand and pulls me to my feet. The other pats me down and I push his hand away. "Now, don't get fresh!" I say.

"Resisting arrest will only make things worse for you," the officer says.

"You have the right to remain silent," he continues.

It's right then I get that it's no gag.

I writhe out of his grasp, lean over the computer, and type out a last line to Dr. Barinas.

HOLY MOLY IT SEEMS AS I'M GETTING HAULED OFF TO JAIL AND ARRESTED. CAN YOU GIVE ME THE MONEY NOW????? PLEASE!!!!

I hit send and then I'm dragged across the floor.

"Hold on! I need my jacket and purse." I snatch them from the coat rack on my way out.

The officers walk me past Curtis. He does not look happy at the prospect of running Two Spoons single-handed on a Friday night, busy or no. He follows behind me scowling. Hells bells. This'll get me a *not meets* for sure. Getting arrested and hauled off to jail just before dinner.

"Tell Leo!" I say to Curtis. I drag my heels in the graveled parking lot to slow the officers down. "Hold on there. What did you say I'm being arrested for?"

"Theft, ma'am," the officer says. He opens the door to his squad car.

"Theft?" My voice comes out a squeak. "What am I supposed to have stolen? And from who?"

"The Shop and Save has filed charges," he says.

"Shop and Save? There's been a mistake. Have you talked to Sue Ann?"

As the officer pushes my head down to get me to fit in the back seat of the patrol car, Glenn and Sue Ann Nedermyer pull up in their king cab truck. Sue Ann rolls down the window.

"There she is. That's who stole all the money," she points at me. "I just turned my back on her and she took handfuls out of my register. And she's running a scam. Peggy and Josephine got taken in. And so did Walter Howard. And she's even been abusing that brother of hers who wouldn't hurt a fly." And then she starts to blubber. "It was supposed to be a surprise! I was gonna get my boobs done for you, Glenn!" she wails.

Glenn holds her in his arms. "Oh, Honey Bunny, don't cry. It's okay darlin'. Don't feel bad." He glowers at me. "See what you done to her? She's a wreck! We're suing for emotional damages."

"I got traumatic stressful disorder!" Sue Ann burbles. "It's given me SPOTS!"

There's no time to protest. The officer shuts the door on me. As we drive away, people in the parking lot stare. A crowd surrounds the Nedermyers. Jim stands with his arms folded across his chest and Sue Ann actively gestures. Her mouth is moving a mile a minute. I can't hear what she's saying, but I know it's about me, and I know it's bad. We come to the stop sign and I twist around to look out the rear window.

Leo is pacing in his apron. Curtis is standing with his hands on his hips. Walter peeks out the door of his store looking like thunder. I crane my neck to look for Peggy and instead spy my cousin Lonnie leaning against his gold Cutlass. There's another man in the passenger seat and a small figure huddled behind him in the back that could be Jar.

I watch my cousin cup his hands, and light up a cigarette like he hasn't a care in the world. He sees me staring out the back. Lonnie forms his hand into a gun and aims it at me. "Poof!" I read his lips.

All the way to the police station, I ponder this.

Cousin Lonnie hadn't looked one bit surprised at seeing me sitting in the back of a cop car. Nope. Fact is, he looked like a cat just about to gnaw on a bird.

Satisfied.

Real satisfied.

CHAPTER TWENTY-TWO

Jail is not an experience I envisioned for myself. They make me wear an orange jumpsuit and put my jacket, purse, and uniform in a paper bag.

One officer dabs my fingers in black ink to take my prints. Another gives me a wet handy wipe so I can clean my hands.

"Thanks," I tell them. At least I can be polite.

"You can have one call." The officer hands me a telephone. "You have three minutes."

One call. Whose number do I dial? Peggy, I think. She's the only one who didn't see me hauled away. I'm sure she must be worried. Heck, I'm worried.

She answers on the third ring.

"Peggy it's Tammy. Thank goodness, you answered. I need help real bad."

"Why, Tammy! I wondered how long it'd be before I'd hear from you. What kind of help do you need?"

"I need—" I stop. What do I need? "Well, somebody to get Jar away from Lonnie and somebody to take care of the chickens. And the police said something about coming up with bail money. And—" That's as far as I get.

"Bail money. Hmmm. Would you like that in cash, checks, or gold bullion?" Peggy asks. Her voice sounds funny. "Let me think," she says. "You got over $3000 from me already, not to mention what you wheedled out of Josephine and Walter and all the rest of us. Why don't you use those funds?" She acts all innocent.

"But that money went to Africa!" I wail. "You know what the deal was."

"One minute left," the policewoman says.

"Did I? Did I know what the deal was? Because if you ask me, I believe you've been pulling the wool over all our eyes. Well, too bad for you, we aren't fooled anymore! That cousin of yours has let the cat out of the bag. He even said you been beating up on poor little Jar."

"Lonnie's lying."

But Peggy talks over me.

"He's been telling us what you been saying behind our backs. That you cooked up a scam to suck us all dry. I should have known. Once a Tyree, always a Tyree," she says bitterly. "I can't believe I was your friend. I even felt sorry for you!"

"But I need money for real," I urge. "I'm in jail and I have to rescue Jar."

"Then, have those Africans send it on over!" There's a click and the sound of a dial tone drilling in my ear.

My legs are numb. I'm turned to stone. The policewoman has to remove the phone from my grasp.

"That one didn't work out. Can I get another? I got thirty seconds left," I hear my voice from far away.

"No, you only get one phone call," the policewoman says. "Most people use it to contact their lawyer."

"That isn't fair," I say. "It's like being disconnected. Peggy shouldn't have answered if she couldn't see through to helping me. And why would I call a lawyer anyway?"

"Didn't they explain it to you when you were questioned?" the policewoman asks. "They have to tell everybody. It's the law. You have the right to an attorney."

"Oh, that!" I wave my hand." They mentioned something about whether I wanted a lawyer, but I said no. Why should I? I haven't done anything wrong. I'm innocent. I thought they'd let me go hearing that."

"That's not the way it works," she says.

"Well, it should be," I say.

The policewoman shakes her head. "If you can't afford a lawyer, one will be appointed for you," she says. "I'm sure they told you that as well."

"I don't need one," I say stubbornly, but then stop. "If they appoint one, is it free? The lawyer?"

"Yes," she says.

"Free? For real? Then I better have one," I say reluctantly. "I might even need two."

"One to a customer, but you'll have to wait until Monday, anyway," she says. "Nothing goes on during the weekends."

"I have to stay in jail until then?" I'm incredulous.

"At least until then," says the policewoman. "That's when you'll be arraigned."

"Arraigned? What do you mean arraigned. But what about my brother?"

"I don't know anything about your brother," she says. "But that's the first chance you'll get to post bail. No exceptions."

She puts me in a cell with three other women. Two hefty blonds sit together. A dark haired girl huddles in a corner bawling her eyes out. Well, that's exactly what I feel like doing so I wander over.

"You okay?" I ask.

She waves me off choking and crying.

There's nothing I can do. Ordinarily I carry a handful of tissues for Jar out of habit. There aren't any in this orange suit.

The older blond stares at me. "What are you in for?" she asks.

"They made a mistake," I say. "I didn't do anything."

"Me too," she laughs. "None of us have done a thing. Right, Frankie?"

The other blond grins. "Right, Trudy."

Well, that makes me feel a whole lot better. I make no mention of the fact that Frankie is a guy's name. It wouldn't be polite.

"So we're all in the same boat? Does the county always make mistakes like this? Arresting innocent people?"

"Oh, all the time, sweetie," Trudy assures me.

I look over at the one crying. "Her, too?"

"Yeah," says Frankie. "Her, too."

"You're lucky," I say. "Orange looks good on the both of you, but not me. They shouldn't do this to people. It's lowering. Jail's bad enough without making you wear a color that doesn't suit you."

The two blonds look at each other and smirk. The brunette keeps on crying. After a while, it gets on my nerves.

"What's her name?" I ask Frankie.

"Misty," Trudy answers. She and Frankie both snicker.

"That's going to ruin your complexion you know, Misty," I say to her. "And make your eyes all wrinkled."

"My name isn't Misty!" she wails. "It's Sara! And I want to go home!"

She's not the only one. I sit myself down on a cot and think about what is going to happen to me and even more what is going to happen to Jar.

We've never been separated this long. Is he getting enough to eat? Is he safe, or is Lonnie taking him into taverns.

Each time a police person walks by, I shake the bars. "Hey! I got a brother to take care of and livestock to feed. Can I make just one more call? Please?"

Leo, I think. I should have called him first just like he asked me to. That does no good now. Like shutting a barn door after all the goats have busted loose.

"They won't give you the time of day. Might as well give up," Trudy holds her nails up and examines them. I start biting my own.

When the four of us are handed dry bologna sandwiches for dinner, I resign myself to spending a couple nights. I lie down on the hard cot and pull a scratchy wool blanket tight around me.

I remember I left the coop door open so the chickens could get out to forage. I feel bad about that as maybe cats or foxes will get them. And then I wonder if I closed all the windows in the trailer. If it rains everything on my desk will get wet. I didn't leave the trailer thinking I wouldn't ever be back. Did I turn off the stove? If I didn't, the trailer will get burned down. Thinking these gruesome thoughts doesn't make the time pass any easier. I toss and turn.

My biggest worry is Jar. How is he? Is Lonnie taking care of him all right? My head aches and my jaw is tight. I'm thinking maybe Uncle E was right about my worrying. That it hasn't done me a bit of good. I cogitate for hours and for the first time in my life can't come up with any bright side to my current situation. Those rose colored spectacles have turned into dark sunglasses. The weekend passes in a blur.

Eight a.m. on Monday morning a lady guard comes to take Sara away.

An hour later Trudy and Frankie are taken out.

"Good luck Sweetie." The two of them wriggle their fingers in a wave.

I try to smile but it just won't come out. Instead, I pace back and forth hoping I'll be next. After an hour, I set on the edge of my cot. I jump up every time a door opens. Finally, I stretch out and put my hands behind my head.

Another hour. Then another. My thoughts are not good ones. I'm in here because people think I'm a thief. I turn on my stomach. My brother Jar is taken away and Lonnie has the upper hand. I swallow down a lump in my throat. Deep inside I always believed I was a good person. Not necessarily smart, you have to go to college for that, but I knew enough about what was right and wrong. At least I thought I did. Now it seems as though I'm just like all the other Tyrees. I push my face into the pillow so nobody can see me cry. And then I guess I fall asleep.

The rattle of keys in the door gets me to pop right up. Maybe I'll be released.

It's a policewoman with lunch.

"What time is it?" I ask.

"Twelve forty-five," she says.

"How did Frankie and Trudy get out so fast and I'm still here?" I chew on a dry cheese sandwich.

"Their pimps paid the bail," she tells me.

"What about that girl named Sara?"

"Her parents came."

I have no pimps and no parents. She starts to leave and I grip the bars.

"Do you have to go? How long have you been a police woman?" I ask. She looks kindly. Like a grandmother.

"I'm a guard, not a police woman," she says kindly. "My name's Nadine."

"Is this your main job?" I ask.

"It's my only one," she says.

"You mean you only have one?" I say.

"Of course, just one." She stares again. "Why?"

I give a snort. "I hold down four jobs at least. Having only one would be a vacation. You should thank your lucky stars," I say.

I'm grateful Nadine stays there talking to me. It kills the time.

"Someone said you have a little brother who's disabled," she asks. "That must be hard."

"Not hard at all. But the county took him away. Said I was neglecting him, but that's a lie thought up by my cousin Lonnie," I say. "He's a sneak. And he's gotten himself in charge of my brother, which I am not one bit, happy about. That's why I have to get out of here."

Nadine pulls out pictures of her kids. She brags on them and I brag on Jar.

"He's real special," I tell her. "And he's a big help making whirligigs and taking care of the chickens."

Late that afternoon I'm taken out and introduced to a man by the name of Mr. Norman Dubois who says he's my court-appointed attorney. I'm relieved to note he has gray hair. Those who have gray hair are usually more experienced. After that, I'm officially charged with my crimes that I didn't do. But nobody wants to hear my side.

The two of us stand in front of Judge Donna Hudderbetter. Uncle E used to have to go in front of Donna for his DUI's. She's one of the Marysville Hudderbetters. Encumbered by both name and looks like all the Hudderbetter girls. But smart, as she went to college. That's how she ended up being a judge. I guess it's good to have smarts if you don't have looks. I have neither.

Judge Donna reads off charges of fraud and theft and a bunch of other things that I can't catch.

There's a lot of wrangling between Norman and another lawyer they call the prosecutor. The two of them object back and forth for a while like hens fighting over a slug. I hear the words *illegal search* and *probable cause* and *extenuating circumstances.* I'm pleased to note that, while the prosecutor kind of has the look of my hen Annie, Norman puts me in the mind of Cauliflower. A real ankle biter if you catch my drift. Ankle biters are good to have in your corner.

Judge Donna starts asking somebody or other about me being a flight risk.

"She's no flight risk." A large man wearing a suit stands up and says this. I stare real hard.

"Holy Moses! Is that you, Leo?" I blurt out.

Norman Dubois places a finger over his lips. "Shush," he tells me.

There's a person sitting next to Leo. It's Madeline. I press my lips together so I don't burst into tears.

Leo raises his hand. "Your honor, I'm a reputable business owner in Spring and Miss Moorehaven with me here is a character witness. Tammy Tyree is a long-time resident and employee. She also has family in the area. A brother who needs her care," Leo says.

"I second that," Madeline says and she stands up. "I can vouch for her. And if it's bail funds she needs, I have that here." She holds up her purse.

And my heart just gets full.

It looks like I got more than just Norman in my corner. Maybe things aren't so dark. There's a light at the end of my tunnel and it may not be a train coming to flatten me after all.

CHAPTER TWENTY-THREE

I'm released, which is the good news. The bad news is it's only temporary. Just until the trial. Leo had to go back to the café so Madeline gives me a ride home in her bookmobile van.

I'm quiet all the way back to Spring. Chewing on my lip and figuring out my options, if I have any. I pull my jacket tighter, but it doesn't make me feel any warmer.

Fighting with Lonnie has stirred up a real hornet's nest, that's for sure. Uncle E was one hundred percent right about it being impossible to stuff yellowjackets back in their nest after they're stirred up. I feel them buzzing around ready to sting me.

"What's going through that head of yours?" Madeline peers at me sideways. Her look is soft. Like she cares about what I have to say. Being with Madeline is like having a mother again. All this time I've been on my own. Even when Uncle E was alive I never thought I had anybody to depend on other than myself. Her concern warms me.

"Lonnie won't quit until he sees me in jail," I say slowly "I have to locate my brother before something bad happens to him. I suppose I have to take Dolly and start hunting for Lonnie in each and every tavern until I run him down. I hope he hasn't given Jar the habit of drinking. Jar sober is hard enough," I reflect.

Madeline shakes her head. "Going into bars might not be a good idea, Tammy," she says. "You're out on bail and I don't think they like it when you fraternize with criminal elements. Why don't you come along home with me and stay at my place? Then in the morning we can ask someone with authority to search?" Madeline asks. "Like Officer Smithers."

"I don't think Clarence will give me the time of day." I look over at Madeline consideringly. "But he might if you asked him." I say hopefully. "And thanks for the invite, but going back to the trailer and using Dolly is my only hope of finding Jar. I can't wait until morning."

"I'll call Officer Smithers as soon as I get home," she promises. "I'll tell him you're out of jail and that you need a hand. He'll listen to me."

"Thanks, Madeline," I say gratefully. When she gives my shoulder a pat the van veers only slightly.

It's near dusk when we enter Spring.

Madeline lets me out at the bottom of my driveway. Her bookmobile doesn't appreciate the challenge of potholes like Dolly does.

"You take heart, Tammy. Things will work out for you. I know they will," Madeline squeezes my hand. "You need to keep on being an optometrist like your Uncle." And she winks at me. Well, I can't help but get tears in my eyes at hearing that.

I stare hard at her tail lights as she drives off. Things certainly look black for me and Jar right this minute. Fact is, I know now I didn't appreciate being poor. What I'd give to go back a year with Uncle E alive and me just working my tail off. The sigh that comes out of my mouth could inflate a tire.

I turn around to face the long trudge up the hill. Our mailbox is leaning to the side like it's been hit. The inside of it is so full the door can't close. I pull everything out and cram it into my pockets making a bulge so big I look like Jar with his rocks.

Jar.

Where is he and what is he doing? Is he scared? Most probably.

When I get to the trailer, I'm thankful to see Dolly huddled in the side yard. She's muddy and forlorn. I give her a pat before I go inside. The trailer door is unlocked. The air inside is stale and cold.

"Hello?" I call out, but there's no answer. I walk from room to room. Lonnie isn't around, but there's evidence that he's been. Empty beer bottles are scattered. Pizza boxes are tossed on the floor. Cigarette butts are ground into dirty plates. I can't face any of this right now.

I feel filthy and not just from dirt. Like the collected bad thoughts from all the wrong doing I'm accused of, covering up my skin.

I head into the bathroom, peel off my clothes, and jump in the shower. The bar of soap barely lathers. There's no hot water but frigid clean is better than no clean at all. I'm still shivering as I pull on tee shirt and jeans. As I slip back into my jacket, the bills prick my side like they're reminding me of their presence.

I'm not going to stop and toot that horn. I have enough troubles for a full on orchestra.

The kitchen is dim. I flick on a light switch, but nothing happens. Electric company finally ran out of patience, I guess. Jar will have a tizzy fit in the dark. I better locate a flashlight. I search around in a drawer like a squirrel hunting for nuts. The batteries are all dead in the big ones, but I find a small one that still works.

I trek on out to the coop and check on the chickens. The gate hangs open and they're free in the yard. I'm relieved to see everybody safe and accounted for. They're foraging in the muddy grass, picking at slugs and seeds and anything else they can find. Annie strolls over and nibbles on my shoelace. I scoop her up and hold her close.

"I'm sorry if you gals got neglected. A lot has gone on," I whisper to the side of her head. "First off, Lonnie's got Jar. That's real worrisome. And then I got arrested. Maybe you heard about that, or maybe you didn't. I don't know whether the rumor mill of Spring gets up this far."

Annie doesn't look surprised, so, I guess she heard, or maybe chickens take things like being arrested in stride. They don't have control of their lives anymore than Jar or I. Things just happen to them like they happen to us.

"And I may go to prison and never ever see Disneyland or Harrison Hot Springs or Canada or anyplace other than jail or Spring my whole darn life," I add. "How about that?"

In answer, Annie does a long, low *brock* that stretches out for miles. It sounds like she cares. Either that or she's telling me she's never had any expectations of her own so she can't really sympathize. I set her down and she steps delicately to the feeder. There are only some moldy bits. I clean it out with my fingers then fill it full with the last of Jar's Fruit Loops. The chickens cluster around pecking hungrily.

"Don't get greedy," I chastise them. "Anyway, I'm not entirely sure this is good for you." I feel bad. They trust me to provide for them just like Jar does and I've failed them all.

I wipe a tear out of the corner of my eye.

Cauliflower comes out from inside the coop. As soon as she sees me, she goes straight for my ankles.

"Stop that," I say and push her aside with my toe.

She clucks with an attitude. Like she's missed having altercations with me.

"Trusting humans isn't what it's cracked up to be," I lecture all the chickens. "Fact is, trusting anyone too much can get you into trouble. It's important to have a low gullibility quotient, I guess."

Gullible.

I guess that describes me.

I think on Dr. Barinas. What's he doing now? What's he thinking? Is he laughing at me? Does he feel guilty for stringing me along? There's no chance for me to check my email until Two Spoons closes for the night. But is there any use?

I'd like to think of myself as hopeful but when does that turn into me just being a fool?

And Jar. What about him?

I rub my chest expecting to find a deep hole there. It's hard to relax and cool my heels waiting for Madeline to get in touch with Smithers. Maybe I can make some phone calls and try to track down Lonnie. In the meanwhile, I got to do something.

I march inside and pick up the phone. There's no dial tone. The service has finally been cut off. I tick items off on my fingers. No electricity. No phone.

Suddenly I can't stand it. How bad could it be if I did hit a couple bars? Who would know? I trot over to Dolly and shove in her key. *Rarrarrarr.* Sounds like nuts in a blender. There's a loud bang and smoke puffs out the hood. Well, that can't be good.

I open her up. Oil is splashed all over the engine and the smell of it tells me she's thrown a rod. Well, that's that. I let Dolly's hood drop and the noise echoes. She'll be out of action for a good long while, which means I'm out of action as well.

How fair is that?

I throw Dolly's keys as far as I can pitch them, which makes all the chickens run like crazy to what they think is food.

How low is it possible to go? How much trouble am I in?

I think back on my last conversation with Mr. Dubois, my attorney.

It was right after I got released and Leo had already left. Madeline and I had sat down in his office. He'd showed me Lonnie's statements, signed, sealed, and delivered. Madeline pursed her lips and did that tsk tsk thing to show her displeasure.

"What's Tammy going to do?" she'd asked.

"We can say her cousin put her up to it. Or she was set up. Tell the judge she's just gullible. That there was no intent to defraud."

I could tell my lawyer was looking for an angle. A loophole. He turned to me. "I really wish you hadn't answered the detective's questions." And then he brightened. "Are you sure they asked you about wanting a lawyer? Maybe they forgot to read you your rights?"

"I'm not a liar. Nobody put me up to anything!" I'd started to lose my temper. "And I wasn't set up. I didn't think I needed a lawyer!" I said.

He sighed. "Tammy we have to consider what this whole thing will look like to a jury," he said. "They aren't going to believe a person was that naive to think they were going to get money from Africa. They'll figure you were complicit."

"But if I told them they were missionaries? That they're my cousins from Spokane? Everybody knows about that!" I turned away not liking the way the lawyer was looking at me. Like I was a criminal. "Barinas told me I was worthy," I said stubbornly. "And it wasn't like I was just doing it for myself. I was doing it for Spring. I thought I was helping," I added weakly.

"Spokane isn't Africa. And they'll want proof." He'd answered patiently. "A jury isn't going to think anything but that you took this as an opportunity to take advantage. I hate to be blunt, but it's the truth."

The truth. What was the truth?

"I appreciate your opinion, Norman. Can I call you Norman or do I have to call you Mr. Dubois?"

"Norman is fine," he'd said.

"And in case you're interested, truly I wasn't running a scam or intending to defraud anybody. I guess to be accurate it was a scheme. There's a difference," I said stiffly.

"How so?" Norman asked.

"My Uncle E said a scheme is a deal that helps out your friends and family and a scam is when you're only trying to benefit yourself." Right as I said those words, I got to thinking that maybe it was time to stop believing everything Uncle E told me.

"Okay a scheme, if that makes you feel better," Norman said. "But the court will still consider it fraud." He looked at me straight on. "I'll do the best job I can for you, but you'd better be prepared for the worst," he said.

"But I'm not guilty," I'd said.

"Oh, Tammy," Norman had shaken his head. "Everyone's guilty of something."

Well, that was like a dash of cold water in my face.

I stand in my back yard all alone with the sun gone. I'm frigid to the bone.

It's dark. No bright side in sight.

Maybe this whole thing has been a test by Karma. To see if I truly was worthy. To see if I could make an honest decision. To see if I knew what was right, and what was wrong?

Is that what I'm guilty of? Hopefulness?

The sound of tires crunching on gravel and the flicker of headlights warn me of an approaching vehicle. I hear three short siren whoops. A police car pulls around Dolly and goes all the way behind the trailer next to the coop. It comes to a stop at my feet. It's Clarence.

My heart thumps with nerves. I swallow down my pride. Madeline must have gotten a hold of him and he decided to help.

"Hard to fit back here," I say trying to make a joke.

Smithers squeezes out of his car and I give him a weak smile. “You’re a sight for sore eyes,” I say. “I guess Madeline told you I have to go tavern hopping and find Lonnie and recover my brother. Dolly’s conked out. You’re in the nick of time.”

Smithers kicks through the chickens like a pile of leaves. They cackle in protest. His face is stony.

“I’m not helping you do nothing.” Smithers spits out. “I came here to give you a warning,” He points a V in front of his eyes. “I’m watching. One wrong step and your ass is going right smack back to jail,” he stabs the air with his finger. “Count on it.”

I take a step back. “Look Clarence,” I start to say.

“Officer Smithers to you.” He glares.

“Okay, then. Officer Smithers.” I clear my throat. “It’s not like they’re saying. I didn’t do nothing on purpose. And it isn’t like Lonnie says either. I never beat on Jar. It isn’t fair. Nobody’s being fair.”

“Well, boohoo to you, too,” Smithers sneers. “You want to hear fair? My Missus kicked me out. I’m at the county sleeping in a damn jail cell. She didn’t take to the idea that I borrowed from our retirement fund and handed it over to a Tyree.”

Before I can reply, there’s the sound of another car coming up my driveway.

“You expecting visitors?” Smithers hitches up his holster belt. “Or having a party with all the money you stole?”

"I don't have any stolen money." I protest. "And I'm expecting no one."

A car door slams. There's the sound of voices. One I don't recognize, the other I do.

"It's my no-good-lying-cousin Lonnie and I don't know who else," I whisper. Smithers car is well hid behind my trailer and I get an idea. "They can't tell anybody's back here," I say. "I'm getting him to admit the truth. And while I'm at it I'm appropriating my brother Jar from his custody."

"The truth?" Smithers' eyes narrow. "You mean the truth about you stealing? The truth about splitting up your proceeds? Maybe I'll arrest all of you together. Nab your whole gang at once."

"I don't have a gang," I say. "And will you listen up? I'm going to get him to admit his wrong doing. Hunker down, stay hid, and take notes."

Smither's leans against his car and folds his arms over his chest like he's prepared to be amused. "Okay then. I'm staying back here out of sight, but I guarantee I won't hear anything to change my mind about you or anything you done."

I leave Smithers and sneak around to the front. On the way, I spy a rake leaning against the side of the trailer. Good. A weapon. I grab it on the way.

I raise the rake up and step around the corner.

"None of you move!" I yell. "Or you'll get pronged."

Lonnie and his buddy stare at me in surprise. I look around for Jar but I don't see him.

"Well, well. Somebody got an out of jail free card." Lonnie narrows his eyes. "How'd that happen?"

"Bail," I say. "Where's Jar? Tell me or you'll get a whack up the side of the head." I wave the rake. The smell of alcohol is strong on their breath.

"Tsk. Tsk. Tammy. Bail will be revoked if witnesses say you've threatened people. They'll throw you in prison and toss away the key. You don't dare swing that rake," Lonnie says smoothly.

I slowly lower my arm, hating to admit he's right. "Why you doing this, Lonnie?" I ask. "What's our affairs to you?" I look around. "And where is Jar?"

"Safe as houses," Lonnie says, his eyes dart. "And as for why?" He cocks an eyebrow. "The little retard will be my ticket. He can get a good-sized check from the state each month. You were too proud to apply for it, but I'm not. I'll be on easy street." And he smiles again.

"So you lied about me beating Jar?" I say loudly hoping Smithers will hear.

Lonnie rolls his eyes. "Yeah, I lied! What of it?"

"Get off my property." I raise the rake. I'm thinking I can accidentally hit my cousin. Smithers has to have heard what Lonnie admitted.

"It isn't all your property," Lonnie says. "Half of it's Jar's. I plan to stay here legal with my poor little retarded cousin."

"Stop saying he's retarded." I spit out. "Where is he?"

"Well, here's the thing," Lonnie looks uneasy. "I need your help on that. He's sort of vamoosed."

"Vamoosed?"

"Taken off. High tailed it somewhere. Run away. Fact is, I came here to hunt for him. You're just in time to help."

"You lost him?" I lower the rake.

"In a manner of speaking," Lonnie says. "He ran away."

"Well, I'm not helping you do anything!" I say. The thought of my brother being on his own this whole time has me really worried.

There's a heavyset man standing next to Lonnie holding a can of beer. "Who are you?" I ask.

"Darrell," he salutes with his beer. "Nice to meet you."

"He's my business partner." Lonnie says.

Darrell strolls up to the trailer. He scans it and the woods behind and then nods. "You were right. This place is perfect, Lon. Quiet. Isolated."

"I told you," Lonnie said.

Darrell gives a chuckle. "The cops would never suspect a thing."

Lonnie's face darkens. "You can shut up, now." he says.

Darrell frowns. "I'm just saying I like your place."

"How do you figure it's his place? And what would the cops never suspect?" I say this last part real loud hoping Smithers is getting every word. It sounds to me like there's more wrong doing being planned.

"You forget," Lonnie smiles at me. "Soon you're gonna be locked up. It's how I told you, I'm gonna be guardian of Jar while you're in prison for fraud." Lonnie says confidently. "I'll be making all his financial decisions," he says. "And doing my deals on the side."

"What deals?" I ask.

"Just a place to store stuff before we re-sell it," Darrell says. He drains his beer in a single gulp.

Lonnie scowls. "Shut up, Darrell," he says.

"But you lied to those social workers." I say. "And the judge."

"Stop harping on that." Lonnie says. He sounds impatient. "Darrell you need to get busy and unload the stuff out of the car."

"What I need is another beer," he says. And he walks to the back seat of the Cutlass and pulls out a six pack.

Where the heck is Smithers? He should be hearing all this. What Lonnie said shows I didn't mistreat Jar. Somehow that's a lot more important to me than the thought that people believe I'm a thief. Or Lonnie's criminal deals.

"Clarence!" I call out again.

"Nobody's gonna hear you yell." Lonnie says. "And you'd best remember I'll be in charge of Jar when you're in jail. And if you don't want to see him beat up or institutionalized then you're gonna have to play by my rules."

Now that was a definite threat. Before I can react, Lonnie snatches my arm and twists. I drop the rake in surprise. It falls at my feet.

"Clarence!" I yell again. Smithers better be taking notes on everything that's happening. It ought to be clear Lonnie admitted he lied. That should count for something.

"The police are around back!" I say desperately.

"Yeah, right." Lonnie laughs.

"Clarence is there. Aren't you, Clarence?" I shout.

"What if he is?" Lonnie looks at Darrell and the two of them snicker. "One fat assed cop and a pip squeak of a girl? I'm real worried."

Darrell drains another beer.

"Lay off that," Lonnie says to Darrell. "You get stupid when you're drunk and we got things to do."

"You're gonna be." I retort. "Smithers! Come out here!" I yell.

"Nobody's coming to help you." Lonnie's laugh is like a rooster crowing.

There's an answering hen-crow from out back. *Cauliflower.* I hold my breath. Seconds later the white hen comes strutting around the corner. When she sees Lonnie, she halts. She's never much liked Lonnie. There's a glint in her eye and she gives a loud *ba-GOCK*! She comes closer. Examining him with one bright eye and her head cocked.

Lonnie smiles. "I do believe I got a hankering for a chicken dinner," he says and shoves me aside.

"Me too," Darrell says. Lonnie slowly reaches for Cauliflower's neck. The two men approach Cauliflower from either side.

The minute Lonnie's fingers touch her feathers she gives a screech that curls my toes.

Cauliflower lurches up into his face flapping those white wings of hers, and scratching with her talons like a poultry whirlwind. Lonnie stumbles back, screaming and covering his eyes. Then she goes for Darrell.

I leap into action. I may be getting myself into more trouble, but I got to do something. Overconfidence has always been my cousin Lonnie's downfall. I consider this as I let my knee fly into my cousin's groin for the second time in a month. He doubles up.

"I'm just defending my hen!" I shout and whack my cousin two thuds in the throat with the side of my hand.

"And protecting myself from being deflowered!" I say as I shove Darrell in the stomach with my booted foot. The combination of that plus his alcohol level flattens him. He's down for the count.

"And my property!"

Lonnie crawls for the safety of the car, but Cauliflower and I are having none of that. We cut him off at the pass. Cauliflower chases while I scoop up the rake and get to pounding.

"I'm feeling real threatened being only a girl and all," I yell as I slam my cousin on the head.

My crossways thud to Darrell's Adam's apple puts him right in line for one of my double toe-heel kicks. That sets him up for a game-ending displacement blow to the willywagger.

Cauliflower rears up flapping those wings and crowing victory. That hen and I are a team no doubt about it. I'd give her a high-five if she had fingers.

"We make a good team," I tell her.

Cauliflower casually pecks at the ground in agreement. At the sound of a roaring engine, she skitters away. Smithers' cop car zooms around from the back of the trailer where it was hidden. He slams on the brakes just before he crashes into the Cutlass, which is blocking my driveway.

"Hold it right there!" Smithers yells. His door flings open. He's got both hands jerking at his holster. "Hold it!" he says again, struggling with his gun.

"Well, it's about time!" I shout. "I could have been beaten up and killed no thanks to you. You heard what Lonnie said, didn't you? About lying? About trying to take advantage of Jar? And we've got to find my brother. He's somewhere lost. You've got to help me look for him."

"I heard that part." Smithers says. "But I'm not entirely convinced you're innocent. It may have been an act."

"An act? Planning crimes?" I'm exasperated. "How'd you come up with that?"

"I'm taking you in for questioning." Smithers lowers his gun. "We need to get to the bottom of this."

"Me?" My mouth drops open. "Taking me in? For what?"

"Why, for assaulting these men," Smithers says.

"But I was defending myself!"

"As I see it you may have been having a tussle with your criminal buddies here." Smithers insists. "I caught you red-handed!"

"I told you before I don't have a gang," I say. "And what did you catch us doing?"

"Like I said. Planning something."

Lonnie pulls himself upright next to the Cutlass and Darrell struggles to his knees. "I need a beer," he says.

"Stop right there." Smithers waves his gun.

"Officer we're cooperating," Lonnie says. His tone is oily. "It's her you need to worry about. See? She still has a rake."

Smithers moves his aim from me to Lonnie to Darrell.

"You should have cuffed them all when you had the chance," I say bitterly.

"He's right. It is you I have to worry about," Smithers says. "You're the ring leader. The one with the brains."

"I don't have brains," I protest. Smithers slaps a pair of cuffs on me. "I defuse you and the rest will fall like plums off a tree."

"They don't look like fruit to me," I say. Both men are standing there looking at each other and smirking.

"I'm going to need backup," Smithers mutters. "And I know just where to put you so you're out of action." He drags me around back to the workshop. Before I can protest, he tosses me inside and shuts the door. I hear the bar drawn across the latch.

Well, talk about major setbacks. I beat on the door with my cuffed hands.

"Hey!" I yell. "HEY, IT'S DARK IN HERE!"

"I got you now, Tammy Louise Tyree!" I hear Smithers' taunting voice on the other side. "You and your gang."

"There is no gang!" I shove the door with my shoulder. "CLARENCE!" I scream. But there's no answer.

I press my ear to the door and listen.

At first there's just talking. And then raised voices. Something about the Cutlass. Then there are sounds of a scuffle. Lonnie and his friend must have decided not to cooperate. My heart sinks. Two against one. That isn't good news for Smithers and it isn't real good news for me either. And being cuffed no less. Uncle's workshop is built like a brick outhouse. When the door's barred, it can't be kicked through.

I crane my ears listening. Trying to figure out what's what.

It's so dark my eyes can't even adjust and my ankles are going numb. I stretch out my legs and settle down for a long wait. There's a hard lump against my hip.

The flashlight. I fumble in my pocket and jerk it out. It drops onto my lap and I work it with both hands until I can turn it on. At least I have light. The black shape of me makes shadows on the ceiling.

There are more shouts outside but I can't make out who it is or what they're saying. A sharp pop that sounds like gunfire. The sound of glass breaking. Laughter. Another pop. And then another. It definitely is gunfire. I'm sweating now.

I hear footsteps outside the workshop. I brace myself. Is Lonnie planning to shoot me?

There's the creak of the wooden bar as it slides and a thud as it drops to the ground. I grip my fingers into a fist and lurch to my feet. I won't go down without a fight.

The door opens a crack and the first thing I see is a headlamp and then a flapping hand.

"Okey dokey." I hear a familiar voice whisper.

"Jar," I cry. "Oh, Jar! You are a sight for sore eyes." I try to hug him but it's hard with the cuffs.

"Org wallup," he says.

My brother's face is smeared with mud. He's got his camo pants below and Leo's leather jacket on top. Three flashlights dangle around his neck along with his lit headlamp. His has a backpack that bulges ominously.

"Am I glad to see you," I say. "What's going on out there?"

"Otter cup," he says.

"I guess I know Clarence is in trouble," I say. My brother likes to state the obvious.

"Bang banger," he says.

"Yeah, well, target practice using Smithers' car and gun probably wasn't the brightest idea that man Darrell's ever had," I say. "Why don't they skedaddle, I wonder. Why are they hanging around?"

"Sap fuzz," Jar says and feels around in his pocket. He brings up two sets of keys. I recognize Smithers' key ring by the large fuzzy dice attached to it. The other I guess is Lonnie's Cutlass.

"How'd you come by those?" I ask.

"Tiddle foot," Jar tells me.

"Well, that certainly explains it. Good on you," I say. I try to give my brother a high five. It's hard with the cuffs. "And I do agree it's dumb to leave ignition keys in a vehicle, but then folks are used to doing it. Can't break them of the habit I guess." I try to slide my hands out of the cuffs. "I need to get loose," I say.

"Ally jig," Jar agrees and hunts in Uncle E's toolbox. He holds up a hacksaw. His flashlights are swinging around making us flicker like we're under a strobe.

"Wait one second," I say. The thought of my brother sawing away at my hands in the dark gives me the willies, but it may be the only way to remove the cuffs. I prop my own flashlight on the workbench and raise my cuffs to see better.

Right away, Jar points and laughs. "Fodder!" he cries.

There on a string hanging down from the middle of my handcuffs is the key. I never even noticed.

"Well, it seems Clarence is too darn clever by half, keeping the keys right with his cuffs." With a bit of wrestling I extricate myself.

"Kiddie pitch," Jar takes the handcuffs and key and pops them into his pack back. I notice it's chock full of rocks.

"I'm sure you're right," I say. "Clarence would charge us for them if we lost them. And handcuffs are expensive."

"Hog trot," Jar says.

"Right you are," I say. "No sense hanging around."

The tough get going when the going gets tough.

And the two of us high tail it out the door.

CHAPTER TWENTY-FOUR

My brother leads the way.

The two of us duck under the barbed wire and head into a thick stand of trees.

"Hold up there, Jar." I hesitate under the cover of the forest and place my finger to my lips. "Shush," I say.

The two of us stand quiet. I strain to listen. I hear shouts, an occasional gunshot, and then cackling laughter. I need to know what's happening.

"Follow me," I whisper. The two of us skirt along the edge of the woods around to the front of the trailer. We hang back in the shadows.

The rear end of the Cutlass is facing us and its headlamps are fixated on Smithers' cop car. Smithers himself is on the ground propped up against his rear wheel. He doesn't look too good. His hat is squashed on his head and his holster is empty. His face is lit like he's under a spot light. There's blood smeared across one cheek.

My cousin has a cigarette dangling off his lip. He waves Smithers' gun in the air with one hand and take sips out of a liquor bottle with the other. I'm wishing real hard he forgets which hand is which.

"My turn." Darrell staggers toward Lonnie.

"No, mine," Lonnie says.

"Nothing doin'," Darrell slurs. He lunges for Lonnie's forearm but my cousin shoves him down hard. There's a thud as Darrell hits his head against a rock. He lies prone.

Good, I think. One down.

My cousin aims at Smithers holding the gun with both hands. It wavers side to side.

"Gorp," Jar whispers.

"Yep, Clarence sure is in a pickle," I whisper back.

The gun goes off and Smithers' hat flies into the air. I hear him moan.

"Lob rat," Jar says.

"You're right. We can't leave Clarence stuck like that." Jar is real conscientious that way. Always thinking of others. "But what can we do?"

Right as I say that, I hear the sound of a motorbike starting up and I'm cheered.

Leo. If he's heard the gunshots, he'll come up. But then, I don't want him in the line of Lonnie's fire.

I hear a loud click and then another. Lonnie shakes the gun. "Out of ammo," he mutters.

He grabs Smithers by the cheeks. "Where do you keep your ammo, Smithers?"

"I ain't telling." But Smithers' eyes travel to the back of his car.

"Just what I thought," Lonnie says.

My cousin pops the trunk lid and searches around inside.

He gives a little crow. "Found it!"

He fumbles with the gun.

"You stay here, Jar. I got to warn Leo." I push my brother down to the ground. "Play possum for real," I say.

I quickly speed down the driveway keeping out of sight. I meet Leo halfway down and wave my arms. He slows and stops. His face is grim.

"You okay?" he asks. "I heard shots."

"I'm fine, but Smithers is in trouble. It's Lonnie." Before I can say anything else, Leo swerves around and zooms past me.

"They have a gun!" I yell at his back. But I think from the loud bangs it's obvious. I hike back to retrieve Jar. But he's not where I left him.

Leo's motor cuts.

"Ouch!" I hear. Another ouch. And a flurry of curse words.

Thud. Double thud. Thud. I know that sound. My brother is no longer playing possum, instead he's heaving rocks to beat the band. Ripping them out of his backpack and hurling them at Darrell and Lonnie.

"Cap foot!" he yells. "Otter gob!"

"You tell 'em, Jar," I encourage my little brother. "Sometimes rock throwing is just what the doctor ordered," I say.

"Ack!" Jar goes. He doesn't like to be reminded of doctors.

Leo has a boot in the small of Lonnie's back and is pushing hard. He holds the firearm in his gloved fingers. "Check on Clarence," Leo says.

I go over and pat Smithers on the cheek. He doesn't respond. "Out like a light," I say.

"Leave him be for now, then." Leo says. "You got duct tape?"

"In the back end of Dolly," I tell him.

"Get it," Leo says.

"What about him?" I point to Darrell.

"He's not going anywhere."

Leo's right. Darrell is busy dodging Jar's rock volley. Tough to avoid rocks when you're drunk.

I quickly get the tape and then help Leo truss them all up like turkeys. Being a chef and waitress allows for talents like that, I guess.

I shake Clarence's shoulder. "Hey, Clarence, wake up." But Clarence just wobbles.

"We need to call for help," I say to Leo. "And get an ambulance for Clarence. He looks bad."

Leo bends over Smithers. "He's breathing and his color's okay."

"Drug gang. Assault. Under arrest," Smithers mumbles.

My brother peers at him. "Olive prick," he says. He scrounges in his backpack, pulls out the cuffs, and tosses them at Smithers' feet.

"Thanks Jar." I hang the cuffs back on Smithers' belt.

"Drug dealers, you say?" Leo says he rubs his chin. "That gives me an idea."

He goes to his bike and carefully lifts out his Wonderbread Bag. He stands there holding it shaking his head sadly.

"They aren't dealers," I say. "And neither am I." I pull Jar close to me. "I missed you, Bug," I say and give him a quick Dutch rub.

"Org wallop," he says.

"But if drugs are found," Leo says. "Plus the assault on Clarence. I'm just trying to figure out a way to keep that cousin of yours out of your hair for a few years."

"Well, I appreciate the effort but how exactly are you going to do that." I kiss the top of my brother's head.

Lonnie is cursing Leo. He struggles against the duct tape binding his arms and legs. Darrell is quiet and still. His eyes are watching Leo.

Leo lifts up his Wonderbread bag. "I just got a new harvest." He sighs. "It's a waste of good weed, but it's for a valiant cause. I've been thinking about cutting back anyway."

He moves from Darrell to Lonnie and stuffs several clear plastic bags of marijuana into each of their back pockets.

"It's not hard drugs but at least it will throw a spoke in their wheels," Leo says.

I watch him walk over to the Cutlass and toss a couple bags into the glove compartment. He leaves the door of it hanging open.

I go over to close it. "Let me help," I say.

"NO!" Leo says sharply. He holds up a gloved hand. "No, I don't want your prints on the car."

I go back to Jar. He's watching avidly.

"Don't you be getting ideas," I say.

Leo tosses a few more bags into the back seat of the Cutlass, then reaches down, and pops the lid. He walks around to where the trunk's yawning open and empties the last of his Wonderbread bag inside.

He freezes there and emits a long low whistle.

"Well, what have we here?" he says.

"You leave that alone! That's ours," Lonnie yells.

Jar and I go to look. The back of the Cutlass is chock full of boxes labeled DANGER EXPLOSIVES.

Leo smiles. He looks over at me. "I guess we know where the dynamite from the construction site disappeared to."

He looks over at Darrell "What were you planning on doing with this anyway?"

"Don't you say nothing," Lonnie shouts.

Darrell looks from Leo to Lonnie.

Leo walks over and plants his foot on the back of Lonnie. Lonnie gives a loud Oomph!

"I was asking Darrell," Leo says pleasantly. "Darrell?"

I see a calculating look in Darrell's eyes. "It's to catch fish," he says.

"Catch fish?" Leo looks puzzled.

"Yeah, you throw the sticks into the water and it explodes and you can scoop up the fish real easy. Lonnie had it all planned."

"He did, did he?" Leo rubs his chin and slowly smiles. "I just love it when a plan comes together."

Groans are coming from Smithers. "I need back up. Where am I?" He attempts to rise. I go to his side and touch his shoulder. "You're at my trailer. You got to relax a minute Clarence. We need to get you an ambulance."

"I don't feel well," Smithers says. "What happened?"

Leo walks over and kneels by Smithers. "You're a hero. You single handedly caught a couple dangerous criminals. They assaulted you. We need to call for help on your radio." Leo says. " Make it all legal. Get a warrant to search the Cutlass but then I guess with all the doors and trunk open you won't need that. I suspect they're terrorists. Probably have a plan for the dynamite. That fish story sounds fishy to me." And he gives a laugh. Leo stands up and studies Darrell. Lonnie is twisting his arms in an attempt to get loose. Darrell is still quiet.

"Yep, Clarence. I see a commendation in your future. You nabbed yourself a gang of terrorists," Leo says.

He bends down to Darrell. "You hearing all this? Officer Smithers found your stash and the explosives in your trunk. The gig's up for you both."

Leo dusts off his gloves. "Of course, they may have it wrong. For example, at first Clarence thought Tammy was involved. But we know that's not true, right?"

Leo reaches down and grabs Darrell by his cheeks. He makes him nod up and down.

"Right. I thought so."

Smithers blearily looks from Leo to the two men tied up on the ground. He furrows his brows. "I don't remember."

Leo remains next to Darrell chatting with him conversationally.

"Maybe you can find it in yourself to help Smithers out," Leo says.

Darrell looks puzzled.

"Here's the thing. More cops will be here soon. All these potential charges are worth a whole lot of prison time. Federal most likely."

Leo folds his arms.

"Fact is, I've heard people say around here that this cousin of Tammy's mouths off about blowing up post offices and bypasses and banks and I don't know what else." He stares at Darrell consideringly. "I'm sure you know that the government is real interested in home grown terrorists. And I'm sure you know that testifying against him would get you off."

"I think I heard him mention something," Darrell says slowly.

Lonnie is screeching like Jar now.

"I didn't say any of that," he spits out. "It's for fish."

"Oh, yeah. The fish. I think you ought to stick with that one, Lonnie," Leo says. "But you and I know the real story don't we, Darrell?" And he winks.

Lonnie sputters like butter in hot pan.

Leo pokes Darrell in the chest. "If I were you I'd spend the time waiting for the hoard of cops to descend by getting your story straight about Lonnie being a terrorist. Heck, you could even say you played along so you could help the cops nab him. If you turn state's evidence against Lonnie, I bet you wouldn't even serve a day. Fact is, they'd maybe even give you a reward. It'd be your word against his." Leo shrugs. "I'm sure you see the logic in that."

Leo moves away from Darrell and goes to Clarence.

"Hey, Buddy, lets get you into the car." He helps him into the front seat. "Looks like Lonnie made threats to Tammy not to mention attempting to murder you. Tammy and Jar were the ones who saved your butt," Leo says.

"They did?" Smithers looks at us blearily. Leo unhooks the mike off the dash and hands it to him.

The radio crackles.

"Officer down." Smithers says groggily. "I need some back-up in Spring. At the Tyree place. I got a terrorist."

Twenty minutes later, our driveway is full of the FBI the ATF and COP's and SWAT's and every kind of law enforcement abbreviations. Deputy and otherwise.

Smithers sits with his head in his hands.

"That man Lonnie Tyree assaulted me," he says. "And my car. He stole my gun."

"Officer I'd like to confess." Darrell says as a deputy lifts him to his feet. "It was Lonnie Tyree who was shooting. And I'm confessing that Lonnie made me sell drugs and tried to blow up a post office."

"He's lying!" Lonnie screams. "We was going to get fish with that dynamite."

"Oh, so you're admitting to stealing the dynamite?" The FBI agent says.

"Mind if we search the car?" Another officer says.

"You have the right to remain silent," a different officer tells him.

"Good job, Officer Smithers." And they shake his hand.

After picture taking and the bagging of evidence and measuring trajectories and avoiding Cauliflower running over to protest the disturbing of her sleep, the law packs Lonnie and Darrell up and they drive away. A tow truck comes later and hauls away the Cutlass.

"You sure you don't need to go to the hospital?" I ask Smithers.

"ACK!" Jar goes. He hates hearing the word hospital.

"Nope," Smithers says. "You need to come down to the station. I'll need you all to make statements. I began this, I'm going to finish it. Now what did I do?" He asks Leo.

"It's late and Jar needs to go to bed." I frown. "Can't it wait until tomorrow?" I don't want Smithers to remember anything and making up an excuse to put me back behind bars.

"We can go now," Leo says.

I scowl at Leo.

"We do what we got to do," Leo says. "Have patience." He brushes a wisp of hair off my forehead.

I get into Smithers' car. "Come on over here next to me, Jar." I pat the back seat.

"Ag wit," Jar says. He's always wanted to ride in a cop car. He hops up and climbs over my lap.

"Only problem is I still can't find my keys." Smithers pats his pockets.

"Give them up, Jar," I whisper.

My brother reluctantly hands them over. I quickly lean forward and drop them on the front seat.

"Hey, Clarence, your keys are right here. You must have mislaid them."

Smithers tries to slide behind the wheel, but he loses his balance.

"Tell you what," Leo says. "You get in back with Tammy and I'll drive," he offers.

When Leo starts Smithers' car, it sounds like Dolly on a particularly bad day. He revs it up and it knocks wildly.

"Sounds like they might have nicked something in your engine," Leo says. We lurch down the driveway.

Smithers and I are scrunched together on one side in the back. When we hit the highway Jar gets on his knees and hangs out the window sticking his tongue out in the breeze like a dog.

"EEEEEE!" he goes.

Leo is concentrating on driving. Each time he hits the accelerator there's a squealing noise. He has to go about twenty. This will take all night. I roll my eyes.

"I'm sure glad you came when you did," I say to Leo.

"It wasn't a stretch," Leo shrugs. "I heard the gunshots."

"EEEEE," Jar howls.

"Roll up that window and settle down, Jar Tyree." Smithers rubs his temple. "I've got a headache. Make him stop," he says to me.

"He's only bored," I say.

"Well, make him unbored," Smithers says.

"He needs entertaining. I don't have a book to read to him." I pull Jar next to me. The bills in my pocket crinkle. I pull them out. "But I may have something better," I say.

I look at the back of Leo's neck. Time to unburden myself.

"Listen up, Jar," I say. "You too, Leo and Clarence. I'm going to tell you all a story."

I take a deep breath. "*The Sad Sad Tale of the Tyree Financial Downfall.* It's a good one," I say. "A real cliffhanger."

I open up an envelope. It's from the utility company.

"Once upon a time," I start off. "There was an electricity bill. People for miles around yearned for communication from the PUD."

I deepen my voice. "*Dear resident.*" I say. "*Your electricity has been shut off due to non-payment.*" I pat my brother's leg. "How about that, Jar? We'll have to use kerosene and chop wood just like the pioneers. Won't it be fun to be a pioneer?"

"Ig bottom," Jar agrees. He snuggles next to me and sighs.

"*If you want to reinstate your service you must bring current your account.* Oh, no! Those Tyrees are in dire straits. What else can go wrong in their lives?" I say.

The next envelope I open is from the phone company.

"Poor Tammy and Jar. What are they going to do? All of a sudden they hear a ring."

"Ding!" Jar says softly. "Ding! Ding!" he goes. His eyes flutter. I know he's getting tired.

"Good for you, Jar," I say. And to Leo. "My brother likes interactive stories."

I see Leo glancing at me through the rear view mirror.

"What other disaster can befall the Tyrees? Listen here. It's from the phone company. *Due to non-payment, your account has been suspended and your telephone service is discontinued.* Hey, we can use cans and strings now, Jar. Won't that be fun?" I tell him.

He puts his fingers in his mouth and lolls his head to the side. "Atta way," he murmurs. His eyes slowly close.

I tear open a big fat envelope with my teeth so as not to disturb Jar. I lower my voice.

"This one must be a doozy," I say. "A real important communication."

I unfold it. "Uh oh," I say. "It's from the bank. We know what that means. This one has my own personal name on it. A real special letter just for me. *Dear Miss Tyree,*" I read. "*Valley Federal appreciates valuable customers like yourself. Please contact our Financial Assets Department for Investment Opportunities.*"

I unfold our statement. Jar is snoring next to me. His head is heavy on my arm.

"Well, isn't this fancy." I smooth the paper out. "An investment opportunity."

Leo whistles. "Well, I'll be," he says. "All you need for this fairy tale is a handsome prince riding in on a white horse," he says.

"Now, that'd be real nice." I smile thinking my prince rides a motorcycle. I clear my throat and read. "Debits. Previous Balance. Deposits."

It's right there that I stop dead. My mouth drops open.

"Bbbbbbalance," I stutter. "Bbbbalance."

"Tammy you okay?" Leo asks.

"Bbbalance," I try to say. It's stuck in my throat.

"Tammy?" Leo's voice comes from far away.

My tongue won't work. My heart gets to beating. Thud. Thud. Thud.

"Something's wrong with Tammy," Smithers says. "I think she's choking. Stop the car."

Leo hits the brakes. My forehead whacks against the back of the front seat.

The bank statement flies out of my hand and Smithers snatches it before it flies away.

He stares at it and his mouth opens and closes like a fish.

"Holy moly," he spits out. "Holy damn moly."

And he looks from me to Leo to the paper and back again. His eyes are bugging out.

"Holy damn it to Hell Moly. Tammy Louise Tyree has got five million bucks in the bank." He shakes his head like he can't believe what he's saying. "It says it right here. It's a bank statement so it can't be wrong. So it's true," he marvels. "It was true all along. The Tyrees are rich. Heck we're all rich!" And Smithers slaps me on the back so hard, I cough.

My heart gets to pounding. I'm in a dream.

Leo looks at us through the rear view mirror. "Are you sure?"

"I always believed in you. I always knew it was true," Smithers stammers.

My brother's weight is making my arm fall asleep. It tingles so I know I'm awake. This is all for real. I jiggle him and he snores.

I tug on my brother's ear. "Hey, Jar," I whisper. "Our money's finally come. We're rich. We can get anything we want. We're safe now." But he's fast asleep.

Jar conks out like this when he feels safe. And that's just when it hits me. *We're both safe.* After me being in jail, after Jar getting taken away, after being accused of scamming, and getting shot at by my no-good cousin Lonnie, we're finally safe.

After making our statements to the authorities, the police are kind enough to gives us a ride back to Spring. They drop Leo off at his Café and me and Jar get a ride all the way up to the front door of the trailer. The cops even lend us a couple of high powered flashlights until we get our power back on.

My brother is all tired out.

I lead him into his bedroom and tuck him in his bed.

"Goop kitten," he says sleepily.

My brother is right. I never did finish the story.

I lean over him. "There's only one possible ending," I whisper in his ear. "We all lived happily ever after. Each and every one of us."

I settle down on my brother's bed, gather him into my arms, and start in on rocking him. I rock, and I rock, and I kiss my brother's forehead, and I tell I him I love him and I keep on rocking.

And right then it hits me. Jar and I always had everything we needed. We were always rich. We were always safe.

We had each other.

EPILOGUE

It's the one year anniversary of Uncle E's passing. The early morning sun is peeking over the mountains. I sit on my back porch staring at the sky and bringing my uncle up to speed on what's occurred in Spring, just in case he hasn't had a chance to look down on us as often as he'd like. The air is crisp. A breeze freshens making the branches of the fir trees swing to and fro, like they're waving at me. I take that to mean Uncle E is nearby and listening.

"Uncle Edward you been gone twelve months now so I thought it was time you and me had a little chat," I say. "First off, I'm sure you'll notice I'm calling you by your given name. I decided enough was enough and it was time you got the respect you deserve."

I pause wishing I'd done it while Uncle E was alive. I swallow hard.

"You'll never believe the year we've had," I say. "That African letter everyone thought was me doing a scam ended up being true after all. All the criminal charges against me were dropped because everybody got paid back and then some. There was no taking away of Jar because Doctor Harms came back from vacation and took my side and I threatened to sue so those social workers backed right down."

I sit silent and listen.

There's amusement from Uncle Edward

"Oh, and Cousin Lonnie got in trouble again. He's behind bars. Walla Walla this time. He decided to take a plea on the terroristic charges and the theft of the dynamite. Seems even saying he was going to blow up salmon was a crime. He'll be locked up a good long while."

I try and organize my thoughts. What to tell and what to leave out.

"I know what people say behind my back. *Gullible*, they call me."

I feel my cheeks get hot telling Uncle Edward that.

"Embarrassing that is," I say. "As I see it, there's a fine line between being gullible and recognizing a potential opportunity. Oftentimes something becomes an opportunity in retrospect. If you make money, it's an investment. You lose money it's a scam," I muse. "You were the one who told me that."

Uncle Edward told me lots of things. I stare down at my hands remembering.

"It was Leo who saw the article by the investigative reporter. It was in an old Wall Street Journal someone left in a booth. Seems it was all a matter of PR. Business for Nigerian scammers was going to hell in a hand basket. It got so bad they all got together and resolved to fix up their bad reputations in order to increase profits. I guess their marks were getting wise. That's what they call their customers. *Marks.* Things were on a downwards spiral so they decided to switch gears, say they were from Botswana, and choose someone to pay out to," I say.

"And I was the one. They paid out to me. They said I was worthy," I say proudly. "And it isn't illegal if someone actually gives you a fortune like they promised."

I listen hard for the response from Uncle Edward and it comes right away.

"Of course, I thanked them. Fact is the very first thing I did was email Dr. Barinas to communicate my appreciation of his efforts on my behalf just like you taught me. I got a message right back saying the email I sent was undeliverable. Twice more I sent it and twice more I got it back. At first, I was disappointed, but then I had to conclude that maybe that's what solicitors do to break off a relationship. It meant his job with me was done and he was busy with other fish to fry. It made me hopeful that he truly was on the up and up. That he'd really had my best interests at heart all along. That we had made a connection meaning him and me were kind of like cousins. Fact is, I think of Barinas as family. I imagine him on holiday somewhere with his wife and kids. Wearing shorts and sipping a drink by a pool. You see it's a real caterpillar, as you'd say. Deep down inside? I didn't want Dr. Barinas to end up being a scammer. He's a doctor after all. I'd hate to think less of the man."

I can feel Uncle Edward understands my position.

A churning clatter comes from the workshop. I cover my ears and raise my voice.

"Jar?" I yell. "Pipe down! I'm trying to have a conversation here!" That rock tumbler of Jar's can sure make a racket. The bad thing is the constant noise. The good thing is it nipped all Jar's rock tossing in the bud.

"And I guess you know Jar's sixteen now," I remind Uncle E. "His birthday was last week. He's gotten the idea that he should be getting his license and driving Dolly. That's not gonna happen."

The idea of Jar driving gives me the heebie jeebies.

"Don't you worry, Uncle Edward," I say. "Jar carries on your whirligig business just fine and on the side he sells polished rocks to jewelry makers and collectors. Some days he makes twice as much money as I do. You'd be real proud of him."

I'm pretty proud of Jar myself.

"And he's gotten taller and thinner," I say. "He's really sprouted up. You'd hardly recognize him now. A full on teenager if you can believe that."

I think on it. My brother sure has blossomed. And he even uses some words everybody understands, not just me.

"But things weren't all rosy after we got the money," I tell Uncle Edward. "It was a regular mare's nest what with me having to return all your Social Security money I got after you died, which wasn't one bit fair because they kept on depositing it into our account. It was the government's fault, really, but they didn't see it that way. How was I supposed to know it was my job to notify them that you passed? They could have read about it in the paper. Was it fair I had to do their job for them?"

I shake my head remembering. "Fines, penalties, and taxes. Yep, you can't mess with Uncle Sam or else I'd probably be tossed back in jail. And, of course, my overdue bills. I had to have Norman, and a tax lawyer and a CPA guy to straighten it all out. There was your loan for the property to pay off and the lawyer helped put together a trust for Jar to keep him in Skittles and Fruit Loops, which is a huge relief."

I look around the yard and point to the coop. "See there, Uncle Edward? The chicken coop is all tricked out. I got a bunch more hens and redid the skylight on their roof. It's solid Plexiglas. Egg production has gone sky high. And I installed a washer and dryer in the bathroom. I never made it to Harrison Hot Springs, yet, but you shouldn't have everything you want all at once. It isn't good for you."

It's so companionable chatting like this.

"I sure miss you, Uncle Edward. I knew you'd be curious how it went about the money," I say. "I split it with everybody in Spring, even those who didn't help. Like the Nedermyers. They were the ones who tried to have me arrested for theft. Sue Ann wasted her share on a boob job. Like painting lipstick on a pig in my opinion. And her husband did some deal to make Shop and Save a container store but it went belly up bust. They got greedy, I guess."

I count on my fingers. "Peggy, Josephine, Walter, Clarence, they all got a piece of the action. Curtis used his to go to LA. And oh, my lord you'd never believe it! While he was there, he let himself out of the closet and got himself a rich partner named Jesse. The two of them are moving back here and buying the Bed and Breakfast from Josephine Munn. She's retiring. I guess LA isn't really what it's cracked up to be. Leo went to their wedding. He says they're as happy as a couple of same-sex clams. Or are clams already same-sex? I don't really know. I'm not a scientist."

I pause, wondering what else to tell Uncle Edward.

"Oh, yeah. Peggy added more washers and dryers like she planned and bought the old five and dime and turned it into a latte store. She sells muffins and donuts too. Oh, and you'll never in a million years guess. She went and married Walter Howard. The two of them share more than a parking lot now. Walter's got a brand new lawn and garden department at the back of his hardware store. People come from miles around to buy his home-made specialty potting soils and our Whirligigs. Walter's secret ingredient is our chicken crap. I keep mum about that so Nosy Parkers won't steal our idea."

It's then I have to stop and swallow hard. Not everything that happened was good.

"Madeline Moorehaven died three months ago. She just didn't wake up." I shade my eyes and swallow hard. "But then I suppose you know that already."

My throat constricts.

"The good part is she's up there with you, now," I say. "Are you two having fun dancing and carrying on? I hope so."

A drop of wet trickles down my cheek.

"Are you making it rain Uncle Edward? Can you do that?"

Another drop hits my cheek and I wipe it off. I guess he can.

"I suppose Madeline told you she built herself up quite a nest egg over the years dabbling in the stock market. That's how she afforded my bail when I got tossed in the slammer. She left most of her money to the library and the rest of it to the people of Spring. It was sure a surprise."

I scratch my head and consider.

"Leo Skinner opened a Harley restoration and repair business with his share. Built a pre-fab metal building and everything. He wouldn't take any money from my deal even though I offered. I guess he's more comfortable taking money from dead friends than living ones. He does a booming business on the side. That's what really keeps Spring going, if you want to know the truth. Those motorbike riders come into town with their wives, spend the night at the Bed and Breakfast, and eat their meals at the café. The guys all hang out with Leo talking about bikes. The brave ones take a survival class from Kev. The women buy lattes and get their hair done at Peggy's. After that, they buy flowers and plants at Walter's. When they're done, they fill their tanks at Annette's Gas & Go and head on back home. Yes sir, Spring has really sprung to life. That's a joke Uncle Edward. Get it? Spring sprung?"

I get the feeling Uncle Edward is slapping his knee and letting out a guffaw.

"Oh, and I almost forgot. You'd be pleased to know they're putting back Spring Hill. Every shovel full! The bypass is kaput. Those university people discovered it was the only place in the world home to some kind of endangered slug. Hell's Bells, all the slugs at my place are endangered whenever I get a hold of a box of salt. Of course, I never tell that to the university people. Anyway, they sued the state and now the government has to rebuild our hill. Serves them right. But there's the government for you. Half the things they do is a waste of money and the other half's unnecessary."

Now it's raining for real. I hope Uncle Edward doesn't have any pressing engagements. I'm still needing to talk to him. I hate the idea of letting him go.

"And did I tell you I got promoted? I replaced Curtis as manager of Two Spoons," I say. "Leo had to hire another part time waitress and an assistant chef. I don't like to brag, but I'm a topnotch manager. I treat everybody fair and square. I even use Curtis' old system of *meets, exceeds, and not meets expectations.* All my workers get *exceeds.*"

Jar comes out of the workshop. "Otter wot?" he asks.

"I'm talking to Uncle Edward," I tell him. "We're catching up."

"Okey Dokey," Jar looks around and flaps his hands.

"He's here right now listening. Tell him hello yourself," I say.

"EEEEE," Jar says and he scoops up a rock from the ground and pitches it up at the sky.

"Good for you, Jar. You remembered," I say approvingly.

There's the sound of a motorcycle engine thrumming in the distance. I hold my breath listening. *Leo.* There are some things I don't talk about. Not to Jar. Not even to Uncle Edward. I keep them to myself.

Leo and I been hanging together. Playing music behind Two Spoons, going on Sunday afternoon motorbike rides. Leo even named a soup after me. *Tammy's Sweetbread Gumbo.* Sounds dire, but it's real tasty. And he bought me my very own helmet for absolutely no reason. It wasn't my birthday, or Christmas, or anything. It's green and has *Tammy* written in cursive on the side.

Oh, and he quit smoking weed for me. Well, I think he did it for me, but as he explained it, being as it's legal now, it's just no fun. It goes against his anti-disestablishment credo. He tells me we're just friends and that I'm too young for him. But I'm thinking all that adds up to Leo liking me. And anyway, each year I'm getting older.

"I like an experienced man of the world, Jar," I say. "What's your take on the matter?" I ask. "You think Leo likes me?"

"Okey dokey." Jar shrugs.

"Well, I believe he does," I say.

My brother always agrees with me, except for when he doesn't.

He heads into the workshop to finish whatever he was doing.

"Well, Uncle Edward that about wraps it up." I say. I sit there for a moment. The silence is punctuated with brocks and croons as the chickens discuss their morning plans while eating.

"I guess you see that Annie's still around. She's stopped laying eggs and is missing part of her foot, but I'm not putting her in a stew pot. Nope. She's retired. Every night I put her in her very own straw filled box. She doesn't have to fight for a roost, no more. That hen has it good now." I pause. "But Cauliflower's gone. Got eaten by a fox. It pained me, that did. The hen was a trial, but she knew how to come up to scratch when were down to the wire. I buried what was left of her under a clump of forget-me-nots. Watch out for her up there," I warn. "She was always good at sneaking up on you."

A brown speckled banty stretches her neck and runs after a bug. Just as she catches it, one of the Rhode Island reds steals it, and then another steals it from her. Just like life, I guess.

And then I remember.

I shove my hand deep in my pocket and feel for the folded sheet of paper I stuck there the night before.

"Just one last thing," I say. "A business matter I need your advice on."

I pull the paper out and open it up. I don't need to read it again. I know what it says.

"I got an email here from Freetown, Sierra Leone. A Mr. Gabriel Abukabarr says he needs to get ten million dollars out of his country real quick. He writes that if I help him, I'll receive forty percent. I just have to arrange to have his check deposited into my account and at the same time wire him his portion. I'm wondering what I should do about it."

I hold my breath and listen. The breeze kicks up a notch and Uncle Edward's answer comes right on the tail of it.

I smile.

It makes perfect sense to me.

The End

READERS GUIDE FOR CUPIDITY

DISCUSSION QUESTIONS

- Did you feel sympathy for the main character? Why or why not? Which characters did you feel sympathy for? Do you feel the author intentionally made Tammy sympathetic or unsympathetic and why?

- What do you think the novel says about gullibility and being naïve? Is this an intrinsic part of Tammy or is it part of coming of age? Does everyone go through this stage?

- There is a fable about Stone Soup where a stranger and hungry villagers create a meal from nothing. Could this be a metaphor for Tammy as a catalyst for the success of the town of Spring? Do you think just the thought of riches made the townspeople motivated to change their circumstances?

- We hear of smart people falling for Nigerian Scam letters and losing their life's savings. What are your feelings when you hear about these stories? Are you sympathetic at all? Can you envision a person falling for this scam? Discuss what scams you have experienced.

- Tammy says there's no sense in wanting what she can't have. Why do you think she feels this way?

- What are your thoughts on Uncle E. Did your attitude about him remain the same through the entire novel? Why or why not?

- Many of the characters are stereotypical. This can be a literary strategy to make a point. Why do you think the author did this and what purpose did it serve?

- Why did it seem the more Tammy denied her inheritance the more people believed in it. Is this an important aspect of a con?

- In the ending of the novel, Tammy is faced with a decision. What do you think she will do? What do you think Uncle E advised? Does history repeat itself? Do people change and learn or do they constantly make the same mistakes?

AUTHOR QUESTION AND ANSWER

What was your motivation for writing this book?
Greed and avarice are interesting concepts. Scams and cons take advantage of the victim's instinctual trust. I wondered how it would play out in a small town if a person were taken in by one of those Nigerian Scam emails, and what would happen if it ended up being true. I also am fascinated by rural mores and culture.

Some of the characters appear to be unlikeable. Was this intentional? Why or why not?
I think it is interesting how we ridicule those who fall for a scam. We often are unsympathetic unless it's an elderly

person or someone whom we otherwise perceive as disadvantaged. The thing is we should scorn those who perpetrate the scam, not be shaking our head over who could be so stupid as to fall for it. All Tammy was doing was having hope that something good would finally happen to her. Is that a bad thing? The townspeople demonstrated their greediness to try and get a piece of Tammy's pie and then abandoned Tammy when the chips were down. Tammy demonstrated her loyalty by holding to her word when the money arrived. I was trying to create a morality tale with a narrator with a simplistic viewpoint.

Why choose a Nigerian Scam letter?

The idea of a con is compelling to me. Originally, this scam was called The Spanish Prisoner. There are instances of this dating back to the 1600's. They are ubiquitous. They come from everywhere and to everyone. You say the phrase Nigerian Scam Letter and immediately people know what you are talking about.

I wondered about those who instigate these cons. Most people I talk to say they'd never fall for it but there are other scams: those who take advantage of tourists, advertising scams, home repair scams etc., which have multiple victims. It intrigued me to think they all must be successful on some level or why would they continue to be sent.

Tammy's life appears to be a train hurtling towards a collision as soon as she decides to follow the instructions in her inheritance email. What made you choose to do this?

Tammy's life is most certainly a train wreck about to happen. Like driving past a car accident slowing and staring, human nature being what it is, the reader is incredulous and I hope skeptical but still unable to look away.

We humans have this curious desire to gloat over other's misfortune or when we hear of good fortune, feel a degree of avarice. I wanted to push the envelope and allow the reader to feel Tammy was getting what she asked for (both good and bad) and to experience those feelings of superiority that we certainly would not be taken in. But is this true? I wonder.

Why make Jar have mental challenges?
Even though I create a story in a world with a community of characters, I do not purposefully "make" a character any specific way. Jar arrived on Tammy's coat tails fully formed. Upon reflection it's a testament to Tammy's strong and family oriented nature to be there for her brother no matter if it's difficult for her. As it happens, Jar's situation creates tension and numerous pitfalls for Tammy. She has to work hard and make sure Jar is provided for.

Is it unrealistic for an author to think a reader will suspend disbelief that a scam like this would end up being true?
Possibly, but this is fiction after all. This is a milieu where we are coerced to believe in aliens and boy wizards. The legal ramifications of whether five-million dollars could magically show up in an individual's checking account

are part of that device. I think that rather than concern myself with what a reader would believe or feel realistic, I am entranced with creating this unrealistic "what if scenario" and seeing how it plays out on the written page.

Made in the USA
Middletown, DE
15 January 2018